DATE NIGHT WITH DEATH

A WELCOME TO MOONRIDGE NOVEL

AVERY ARUJO

A Note from the Author

Stories have the power to heal, but they can also stir up difficult emotions. This book explores themes that may be difficult or triggering for some readers. I've done my best to approach these topics with empathy and care, and I want you to feel safe as you move through the pages.

Please know that this story includes references to the following:

Attempted suicide
Death and grief
Mentions of domestic abuse
Mentions of abortion
Mentions of infidelity
Cancer (specifically a brain tumor)

The cancer storyline is deeply personal. My aunt lived with the same diagnosis featured in this book, and many aspects of the character's experience are drawn from what my family members went through. Writing it was emotional. Reading it might be, too.

If any of these topics feel too close to home, please take care of yourself however you need to, whether that means reading with caution or choosing to skip this book entirely. There's no wrong way to protect your peace.

Your well-being matters more than any story.

With love,
Avery

for Aunt P.
I miss your cackle

CHAPTER ONE

Mina

The booking software sits open on my laptop. Rows of empty slots stare at me like missin' teeth. Twelve rooms, and only three have been booked in the last two months. I tap my pen against the desk and wince as another headache blooms behind my right eye.

Outside my window, orange and yellow leaves skitter across the lawn like they're runnin' away from summer. October in Moonridge is one of my bread-and-butter months. I normally have guests booked three months in advance for the Haunted Fall Festival. This year? I can't pay people to stay here.

I snap the laptop shut and dig my thumbs into my eyes. The headaches have grown more frequent, almost unbearable. And I know what it means. Doctor Patterson didn't mince words when she showed me the MRI scans six weeks ago.

The grandfather clock in the hall hammers out six chimes. Its deep toll rattles the floorboards of this empty cage of a home. Halloween is a week out. By rights, these rooms should be packed with guests, all of them sippin' apple cider and leavin' crumbs of pumpkin bread on the rugs. Instead, it's just me and the dust bunnies, and even they don't want much to do with me.

I rise and stretch. My spine cracks like a dry branch. Too much time hunched over the laptop lookin' for money I don't have has me all dried up like a dead tree.

Six years ago, I poured every cent I had into this place. A fresh start, I thought. Away from all that troubled me in Scotland. And for the first few years it was exactly what I needed. Now I'm the proud owner of a three-story Victorian that's fallin' apart faster than I can patch it up.

She's not listening again.

The voice is soft and feminine. It floats on a draft across the room. I freeze. My heart stutters and I scan the parlor. No one else is here.

"Hello?"

Silence.

There I go talkin' at empty rooms again. It has to be the stress. The doctor said stress could make the symptoms worse.

Someone should tend to the flowers. They're dying. Like everything else around here.

The scent of wet roses drifts through the room and then vanishes.

The whispers started a few weeks back. Always at night. Always when I'm on my own. It happens every year, like clockwork, but usually the dead have the decency to wait until a day or two before Halloween. Not this year. They showed up about a month early, and they really have somethin' to say.

My phone pings. I pick it up and see it's another notification from the Trippa app. I swipe it open even though I know it's just lookin' for a way to make my mood worse.

Moonridge used to be charming, but after what happened with those werewolf attacks this summer, I wouldn't risk bringing children here. The B&B owner was nice enough, but one star for safety concerns.

One star. Brilliant.

I toss my phone onto the desk. My B&B did nothin' to encourage what happened, so why am I gettin' negative reviews? Hell, it wasn't even the wolves' fault. That witch Ravena was the one stirrin' the pot, and we stopped her. There's nothin' to worry about now. But try tellin' that to a tourist from New Jersey.

I check the clock again. Already six-fifteen, which means Lily and Jasper Brooks will be here any minute. I tuck a stray bit of red hair behind my ear and head toward the kitchen. I catch my reflection in the hall mirror and have to do a double-take. My appetite's been absolute shite lately and it shows. My cheekbones are sharp enough to cut glass and my eyes look far too big for my head. I pinch some color into my cheeks and yank my sweater straight. Not much else I can do about it now.

The kettle starts its screamin', pullin' me away from my reflection. I'll get Lily's chamomile ready and have Jasper's black coffee waitin', his doctor's orders be damned. Some battles just aren't worth the breath ya waste fightin' 'em.

I arrange homemade shortbread cookies on a blue ceramic plate. My hands tremble as I set out the teacups. Another new symptom to add to the pile. Doctor Patterson says it'll get worse before . . . well, before everythin' stops for good.

The doorbell chimes, and I plaster on my best hostess smile. Show time.

"Mina, my dear!" Lily Brooks throws her arms around me, her floral perfume a welcome reprieve from phantom flowers. At seventy-nine, she's still a beauty. And a relentless hugger. "Don't you look lovely!" Lily steps back, hands still on my shoulders.

"She needs to eat more." Jasper emerges from behind his wife. He leans heavily on his cane. "Too skinny."

If only he knew. Stage IV doesn't leave much room for appetite. Not for food or for the future I'd once had planned.

"Jasper!" Lily swats at him. "Don't be rude!"

I laugh and usher them inside, away from the bite of the autumn air. "It's so good to see ya both. Room two is all ready for ya, just how ya like it."

"With the view of the garden and the maple tree?" Jasper's bushy eyebrows climb toward his nonexistent hairline.

"With the view of the garden and maple tree," I confirm with a pat on his arm. "And I've put extra blankets in the chest. I know how ya like to sleep with the window cracked, even when it's cold enough to freeze the ears off a brass monkey."

Jasper grunts, but I see the corner of his mouth twitch. He's a grumpy old bastard, but he's got a heart in there somewhere. He and Lily spent their honeymoon here decades ago and they haven't missed a festival since. They're as reliable as the seasons, these two. Bickerin' one minute and finishin' each other's sentences the next. I guess sixty years of marriage'll do that to ya. I used to want that. That shared history. The comfort of someone knowin' exactly what ya need before ya even ask.

But that was before. No use gettin' sappy now. Dr. Patterson's diagnosis stole all those dreams with three words: glioblastoma multiforme. Inoperable. A death sentence wrapped in fancy words.

Lily takes my arm as we walk toward their room. "Are you doing okay, dear? How's business?"

I hesitate. Lyin' to Lily feels like a sin, but there's no reason to burden her with my problems. "Oh, ya know. It's been a bit quiet since the summer festival."

"Since those wolf boys lost their marbles?" Jasper asks from behind us. "You all have a reputation now. Must be bad for business. Should've seen the news coverage. We know better, but other tourists don't."

"It wasn't the wolves' fault." I feel the need to defend the pack. I was there, and I know what really happened. I know the mess Ravena made.

"Tell that to the tourism board." Jasper shakes his head. "Salem's probably loving this. Getting all your October business."

I sigh. "You're not wrong. Things have been rough. Honestly, I'd probably be sittin' here talkin' to the wallpaper right now if it weren't for the two a ya."

"I wish there were more we could do. You won't close down, will you?" Lily clutches my arm.

"That's the last thing I want to do, love." I pat her arm. "I'm hopeful things will turn around. I just had a last-minute bookin' last week that could help fix our reputation." I can't keep the excitement out of my voice. "The Real Vampire Wives of Obsidian Hills is filmin' their cast trip here. They'll be here for six nights."

And if this doesn't work, I'm out of options. Not the legacy I'd hoped to leave.

Lily's eyes widen. "The reality show? With the—" She mimes fangs with her fingers.

"The very one." I can't stop the grin from rearrangin' my face. "They've booked eight rooms for cast and crew. They arrive day after tomorrow. Can ya believe it?"

"Those trashy shows." Jasper wrinkles his nose.

"Those trashy shows might just save my B&B." I help them down the hall to their room. "Once people see Moonridge on TV, and see that we're not the mess the media made us out to be, business will bounce back. It has to."

Because, and what I don't say is, I don't have time for a backup plan.

The Vampire Wives reservation came by way of a desperate email from a location scout lookin' to house cast and crew. She'd heard about Moonridge's 'authentic New England haunted town vibe' and wanted to film a cast trip here. I'd said yes before I even finished readin' the email. I practically threw my details at them. Now, with only three rooms available, I feel a flicker of somethin' dangerously close to hope. I don't have a staff and I'm runnin' on fumes, but I'll find a way to make it work. My livelihood, or what's left of it, depends on it.

I head for the door to let them get settled, but Lily stops me. "Mina? Remember that first year we came after you bought the place? We were your first guests after you reopened. You were a nervous wreck."

I smile and lean against the doorframe. "Aye. I remember."

"You've come so far since then. Don't let a rough patch get you down."

I step into the hall, her words of encouragement like a supportive hand at my back. I take a breath and steady myself. The house doesn't feel so much like a tomb anymore. The clock ticks and the floorboards groan under the weight of real guests. This place will spring back to life yet, and that spot of hope warms up the parts of me that have been frozen solid for weeks.

I'm halfway through thumpin' the sofa cushions back into shape when the front door practically flies off its hinges and a wall of noise hits me.

"Knock knock, hermit!" Hazel's voice enters the room before she does. She steps inside and unwraps herself from her pink puffer jacket. "We've come to drag you back into society!"

Coco bounces in right behind her, grinnin' like she's won the lottery. La'Tasha brings up the rear. She hooks the door shut with the toe of her boot while she balances a massive fall bouquet.

My shoulders finally drop. These three are a colossal pain in the arse, but they're my pains. I never thought I'd find a group of people who'd actually notice if I went missin' for a day. Who'd call me up just to say hi and make sure I'm okay. They're the sisters I never asked for and definitely don't deserve. And I wouldn't trade them for nothin'.

"You lot are a sight for sore eyes," I say, huggin' them one by one. Coco's bulky, purple hand-knit sweater is soft against my cheek. La'Tasha's flowy green top smells faintly of sage and lavender. "Did I mention lately how fond I am of ya?"

"You have, but you can say it more, Mami." Coco plops down on the couch, her bright eyes full of mischief. "And since you're so fond of us, that means you have to join us at every festival event this year."

I let out a groan and sink into the chair next to her. "Aye, not this again."

"Yes, this again." La'Tasha nudges her glasses up on her nose. "You cannot keep hiding in this B&B. It's been three weeks since you joined us for a proper night out."

"I've been busy," I mumble. "Runnin' this place on my own isn't exactly easy work."

Why don't you tell them?

"But not networking is also bad for business," Hazel says. "We're not asking for every night, but you need to be seen. Blake and the other wolves have been asking about you. Blake misses your fresh scones."

You really should tell them.

What? That I'm not long for this world? That this might be the last Halloween festival I'll ever see? That every headache could be my brain givin' up? No. Not now.

I stand and slice the pumpkin bread I'd baked earlier and pour mugs of hot cider. The spicy-sweet aroma warms the room. "Well then, tell that great wolfy boyfriend of yours to get his hairy arse over here to see me. The man's got two good legs, hasn't he?" I hand out the mugs, savorin' the scent that reminds me of fall. "And besides, I do show my face. Someone has to pick up supplies for this place."

"Going to the market once a week doesn't count," Coco says through a mouth full of pumpkin bread.

"Look, we're worried about you." La'Tasha pulls a branch of burnt-orange maple leaves from the bouquet and arranges it carefully in the vase.

I open my mouth to protest, but she cuts me off, tuckin' a sprig of goldenrod into place.

"And before you say 'I'm fine,' just know we all recognize that as code for 'I'm drowning but too stubborn to ask for help.'"

She always gets to the point.

"That said," she adds a dusky sunflower to the vase, "we need help with the Spirits and S'mores booth on Thursday. Would you be willing? Two hours tops."

I sip my cider, stallin'. These women could guilt a saint into sinnin'. "Fine," I relent. "But no costume."

"Half costume," Hazel negotiates. "At least some cat ears or something."

"We'll see," I say, which is code for not bloody likely.

Coco perks up, changin' the subject. "Oh my God, you won't believe who's coming to town!" She wiggles in her seat like a kid at Christmas. "The Real Vampire Wives of Obsidian Hills!"

I laugh. "Aye. I know. They've gone and booked nearly every room I have."

La'Tasha's jaw hits the floor. "Wait, hold up. You're for real? The whole damn cast is crashing here? Under this roof?"

"Cast and crew and most likely, their egos, too," I confirm, unable to keep the pride from my voice. "Eight rooms for six nights."

"Oh my God, Mami! I think I'm gonna faint." Coco places her hand on her chest and breathes deep. It's like she's havin' a religious experience. "I. Cannot. Believe. This! I'm gonna breathe the same air as Vivienne St. James. She gives me life. And her fashion? Literally unmatched! Did you see the episode where she turned that pendejo to stone for a week just for breathing on her? She left him in the garden so the crows could poop on him. Iconic."

"That was staged," La'Tasha says with an eye roll. "But I get it. I love Vivienne, too, but Ayana is the real deal. She's my melanin sister. That woman is allegedly almost 300 years old and still slaying. If that's for real, I'm gonna need that skin care routine. And you know she has tea on important people in history. I'd kill for an hour with her."

Hazel shrugs. She leans against the counter, unimpressed. "Are we sure they're even legit vampires? Not just actors with expensive veneers?"

"Of course they're real!" Coco looks like Hazel just offended her soul.

"I'm leaning toward real," La'Tasha says.

Hazel shrugs. "Well, either way, this is a massive win for you. Exactly what you needed."

"Tell me about it," I say. "One more month like I've had, and I'd be turnin' off the electricity and eatin' nothin' but bread and water."

"We would not let that happen," La'Tasha says as she places the finished vase of flowers in the entryway.

And I believe her.

Hazel glances toward the window, her brows pinched. She tucks a curl behind her ear, her nervous tell.

"What's that stuck in your head?" I ask.

She sighs and runs a hand over her forehead. "The energy around town is really off. We spent most of the day reinforcing the barriers just to be safe. For some reason the veil feels thinner than normal this year."

La'Tasha nods and takes a seat at the table. "It's almost unsettling."

So it's not just me, then. I'm a hair's breadth from spillin' the truth about the whispers I've been hearin' in the walls, but I bite the words back. I don't need them worryin' about me when they've already got plenty on their plates.

"Do ya think it's connected to what happened with Ravena?"

"I don't know for sure." Hazel shrugs and shakes her head. "She stirred some shit up, no question. Blake's been patrolling near the abandoned mill, but he hasn't seen anything that seems off." She takes another sip of cider. "Still, her threats before we entombed her really rattled me. And I could have sworn I saw her standing under a tree in the park the other day."

"I think we all have a little PTSD after this summer," La'Tasha says, helpin' herself to a slice of pumpkin bread. "But I'd rather be paranoid than dead. And I don't want to risk her crazy ass getting loose and rampaging again. Especially with the festival. This town can't take another hit."

The veil cracks. She knows it cracks.

The voice comes from across the room. I look around, but none of them seem to have heard it.

"Exactly," Hazel nods. "Plus, I've got Penny Fisher testing my last damn nerve. She wants to learn and do all the magic. I'm like, girl, just because you can read a spell, doesn't mean you can do a spell. We have rules in place for a reason."

"Oh, the new librarian? I met her a couple of months ago. She seems sweet." I force myself to concentrate on the conversation. Push back the static crowdin' my thoughts.

"That's her," Hazel sighs. "She's got ability. I'll give her that. But it's all over the place. Her adoptive parents hated magic and never let her practice, and now that she's on her own, she feels she can just do anything she wants. She has no focus, no training. It's like giving a toddler a flamethrower."

"That bad?" I wince.

La'Tasha pours herself another round of cider. "Last week, she tried a basic light spell and nuked her eyebrows right off her face."

"Yikes."

Death will come to Moonridge.

The voice slithers into my ear. I nearly drop my mug.

Tell them to ask the witch about what sleeps below the library.

I set down my mug carefully and try to focus on Hazel's voice, but the whispered words keep comin'. It's a pile-up in my head. Too many voices at once.

The Mortician walks among you . . .

The Anchor wants her child . . .

Warn them!

"Mina?" Hazel's hand clamps onto my arm. "You're really pale right now. You good?"

I blink and use her touch as an anchor to stop the room from spinnin'. "Sorry, pet. Just tired. Been a hell of a day."

She studies me, eyes narrowed. She's far too perceptive.

"We should probably let you rest." La'Tasha begins to gather the empty dishes and takes them to the sink.

Though several hours have passed, I don't want them to go already. I don't want to be left alone with the voices.

"Promise you'll come to the 5K Festival kickoff on Tuesday?" Hazel asks as she puts on her coat.

"If the TV vampires are playin' nice and not breakin' wine glasses or raisin' hell, I'll try to make an appearance." It's the best lie I can manage.

We exchange hugs, and I usher 'em out. The house feels twice as big and three times as empty as soon as the door clicks shut. Then the phone rings, and I nearly hit the rafters. Who would call the landline at 9:00 PM? Either a scammer or a drunk lookin' for the pub, probably.

I should just let it ring and let the voicemail earn its keep, but, no. My hand betrays me. "Moonridge Bed and Breakfast."

There's a pause. Static crackles like a bad radio. Like someone is callin' from inside a wind tunnel. Then a voice, deep and strangely formal, cuts through the fuzz.

"Yes. Hello. My name is Dex Grimm. I'm looking for accommodations beginning tonight."

His voice. It's deep. Mysterious. The voice of someone used to not bein' told no. It makes my skin prickle.

"Oh! Well. You're in luck. I actually have a vacancy." I straighten my posture, even though he can't see me. "How long would ya be stayin'?"

"I'm uncertain of the duration. I'm a writer finishing a project that requires . . . solitude."

The way he says it feels like he's hidin' a body in the trunk. And who uses words like solitude anymore?

"A writer, eh? What's your flavor?"

Another pause. "Ghost stories primarily. I was told by an old friend that Moonridge would provide an inspiring atmosphere."

My gut says hang up now. My bank account is tellin' my gut to shut the hell up. There's somethin' oily about this man, but I'm bleedin' cash and need every penny I can make. And for some reason, his voice seems very familiar.

"We'd be glad to have ya, Mr. Grimm," I say, ignorin' the dragons in my gut. "I've got a quiet room on the third floor. It's on the east side of the house, very peaceful. When can we expect ya?"

"This evening," he answers cryptically. "Thank you, miss."

The line goes dead before I can ask for details. I stare at the receiver a moment before hangin' up.

Creepy bastard.

Death comes to Moonridge...

I shut out the ghostly voice. I don't need another reminder of the time bomb in my head.

I squeeze my eyes shut and push the whispers back along with the pressure buildin' behind my eyes. Keep busy. That's what I need to do. If this Grimm fella is showin' up tonight, I suppose I should get his room ready.

Room Ten is my favorite room in the house, tucked at the end of the east hall with bay windows that look out over the garden. The wallpaper is a posh damask that looks expensive when the light hits it just right. It's meant to give the room an air of elegance, but it's been so long since anyone's stayed in here, it's more of a dust collector. I've just started to wrestle fresh sheets onto the four-poster bed when the house starts its nonsense. A floorboard screeches down the hall. Then the slow, heavy grind of a door hinge.

I go stone still.

The air grows heavy, pressin' down on me like I'm underwater. Then come the footsteps from the floor above. Who the hell is in the attic? Every step sucks the warmth out of the room until I can see my own breath cloudin' the air.

"Hello?" I call out, my voice a pathetic croak.

No answer.

The temperature continues to plummet. It's like the entire

house decided to turn into an iceberg. I drop the pillowcase on the bed, and my hands begin to tremble again. I step into the hallway just as a sconce flickers. Once. Twice. A scent trails past, thick and sickly sweet, like old roses left to rot in a vase. But there haven't been flowers on this floor in months. Goosebumps scatter across my arms.

"Jasper? Lily?"

My footsteps thud against the hardwood as I make my way down to the second floor. I pause. Still quiet. Only thing I can hear is my bloody pulse hammerin' my eardrums. The silence feels out of place. The house is always makin' some kind of noise as old houses do. But this feels purposeful. It's like it needs to say somethin', but doesn't know how to say it.

A soft thump hits the back porch. I spin around so fast I nearly get tangled in my own limbs. The rotten flower smell hits me again. My heart hammers against my ribs as I scramble to the window at the end of the hall. My breath fogs the glass instantly. The porch below is empty, bathed in the silver beam of the motion light I installed last spring. The light flickers once.

"Pull yourself together, you daft woman," I mutter to myself. I force my breath to slow. "It's an old house. Old houses make noise."

I head back downstairs, determined to finish washin' up and not let my imagination get the better of me, but as I reach the foyer, the wind picks up outside, and the porch swing groans in protest. And then they come.

Three sharp, deliberate knocks on the front door.

I jump and a startled squeak escapes. I press a hand to my chest as I inch toward the peephole.

My breath catches.

A tall man stands on the porch, face half-swallowed by shadow. He holds a single bag in one hand, and in the other, somethin' that looks suspiciously like a cloak draped over a cane or walkin' stick. Is this the mysterious Dex Grimm? Certainly not.

It's been less than fifteen minutes since the phone call. I don't see a car, and I would have seen headlights had someone dropped him off. The train and bus stations are on the other side of town.

I hesitate, hand on the doorknob. My heart pounds in my chest. For one wild moment, I consider pretendin' I'm not home.

His eyes meet mine through the peephole. It's ridiculous, but I feel like he can see me.

"Hello? Is someone there? We just spoke on the phone."

That voice.

Deep. Familiar.

I take a breath to steady my nerves and open the door, one hand still braced on the frame, ready to slam it shut if I have to.

He stands perfectly still. Dark eyes that don't blink nearly enough. Medium-length black hair, stylishly cut. Pale skin that doesn't reflect moonlight so much as absorb it. Chiseled features. Hands folded over a sleek black cane topped with a silver skull.

He's like a work of art. Beautiful, the way carved statues are: cold, flawless, and a little bit off. Too perfect. Like a wax figure that got tired of the museum and walked out.

"Good evening," he says. Why is his voice so familiar? "I believe you were expecting me."

I swallow, suddenly aware of just how vulnerable I am in this big, mostly empty house.

Well. Not empty anymore.

CHAPTER TWO

Dex

She steps back and waves me inside. The threshold takes a moment to decide if it trusts me with its owner; it's like stepping through wax. This is a home with opinions. My scythe hums against my palm, restless.

The parlor light illuminates the woman's face, and I go still.

I know her.

My superiors told me they were sending me to retrieve a soul I'd failed to collect six years ago. I didn't expect they would deliver me directly to her doorstep.

Mina Cartwright. The woman I brought back because she said it wasn't her time.

But now it is. I see it lodged like a shadow deep in her brain.

"Mr. Grimm?" she asks, one hand gripping the door frame like she may slam it shut at any moment.

"Indeed." I keep my expression neutral. "Please. Call me Dex."

She nods. "I'm Mina. Ya got here fast."

"I was . . . nearby."

"Welcome to Moonridge Bed and Breakfast." She closes the door behind me and smiles. She obviously has no idea who I am. The last mortal I visited pressed herself against her hospital headboard whispering, "Please, not yet, not yet."

Mina looks different. The last time I saw her, river water streamed from her lungs as she fought to stay alive. She smells of cinnamon and baked goods. Love and joy. A little gaunt, but the vitality coming off her is almost aggressive. She's no longer someone whose hope has withered. But she lacks the usual scent of slow decay. Most mortals carry it. That faint sweetness of inevitable rot that clings to them from birth. Mina doesn't have it. She smells of birchwood and eucalyptus. Is it because I pulled her from death back into life?

"Ya travel light," she observes, eyeing my single bag and the gentleman's cane I carry. "Most guests arrive lookin' like they're movin' house permanently."

My cane is actually my scythe, compressed and veiled for mortal eyes. It hums against my palm. Something in this town has its attention.

"I find possessions burdensome," I reply. When you've watched civilizations rise and fall, you stop acquiring things. Though I do have a collection of interesting hourglasses back home. A professional indulgence.

She leads me through a foyer lined with mahogany furniture. The house begins to talk, something I've learned to filter, but the magic buzzing underneath is something else entirely. It's layered in a way that takes years to learn. Someone with immense power was here, and not long ago.

"This house has bones," I murmur, pausing near the sofa where the magical signature is strongest, "and they remember things."

"Pardon?" Mina turns, her red hair catching the light from a nearby lamp.

"Nothing of consequence." But it is consequential. Layers of complex magical residue cling to the air like incense. "Merely an observation about the Victorian architecture."

"Aye, good eye!" Her face lights up. "Late 1800s. The original owners were quite wealthy. They were drawn to Moonridge for its blend of humans and magical folk. Local legend says they were involved in some kind of secret society. Perhaps you can feature us in your book?"

Of course they were involved in a secret society. Humans and their desperate attempts to peek behind the curtain of mortality.

"Is somethin' wrong?" Mina studies my face.

"No," I lie. "Simply admiring the craftsmanship. You maintain the house beautifully."

She beams, and my chest lights up. She leads me up the stairs, and the pull of the magical signature fades slightly. We reach the third floor, and she turns left and then leads me down a long hallway.

"One of my favorites, this room," she says, pushing open a door marked with a brass number ten. "Lovely and quiet, with a proper view of the garden."

I almost laugh. Quiet. Like the dead observe quiet hours.

The room registers my presence the moment I cross the threshold. A hairline crack splits across the mirror's glass before I've placed my bag on the bed. If Mina notices, she doesn't let on.

"The bathroom is through there." She points. "Oh, and fair warnin' about the radiator. Makes a right racket sometimes, especially at night. Had it looked at twice, but the stubborn thing seems to have a mind of its own."

It clanks once in response.

"I'm sure it won't disturb me," I say, placing my bag on the four-poster bed. In reality, I rarely sleep at all. The dead are demanding company, and they don't observe mortal schedules.

"Well then." She hovers in the doorway, fingers working at the hem of her sleeves. My eyes fall to the small scars that litter the back of her hands. "If ya need anythin', my quarters are just down the hall from the kitchen," she continues. "There's also a phone in the hall with a direct line."

I nod, and she turns to leave. The magical signature hits me again. Stronger this time. It seems to cling to her.

"Mina?" Her name feels strange in my mouth. When was the last time I addressed a mortal by only their first name?

She turns back, eyebrows raised.

"This friend who was here earlier," I say, carefully choosing my words. "Are they a regular visitor?"

Her expression shifts, and her shoulders go stiff. "Friend?"

"I can sense . . ." I pause. How do you explain to a mortal that you can taste magic in the air? And this magic has a specific signature that I've met once before? "I have a sensitivity to atmosphere. Someone with unusual energy was here recently. Several someones, actually."

The wariness in her eyes deepens, but there's something else there, too. Recognition, perhaps?

"Just some friends from town." She picks at her nails. "We were plannin' for the Halloween Festival. Ya know how it is. Small town committees can get quite spirited."

Spirited indeed. These weren't casual festival planners. They were practitioners. Serious ones.

"Of course." I keep my expression neutral. "I've always appreciated the traditions of small towns."

She studies me for a long moment. Almost too long, to the point that I'm certain she sees right through my attempt at playing human.

"So, first time in Moonridge?" She leans against the door frame.

My grip tightens slightly on my cane. Does she remember me?

"No." The lie curdles on my tongue. "Your town came highly recommended for its atmosphere."

"Well, you've come at the perfect time for atmosphere." She shifts her weight. "The Halloween Festival starts soon. There'll be all your standard Halloween attractions with a special magical flair. The young witches are in charge this year, so it should be extra inventive. Rumor has it there'll be a haunted parade with spooky fireworks. Biggest event of the year, it is. The whole town goes absolutely mad for it."

"Celebrating death to keep it at bay," I murmur. "How quaint."

Her eyebrows lift, and she laughs instead of taking offense. "One way to look at it, I suppose. Most people just come for the candy and pumpkin beer."

She studies me like she's trying to figure me out. I won't tell her. Can't tell her.

"Will ya attend the festivities?" she finally asks.

"I hadn't planned on it. I'm just here for some solitude and to work on my book."

"Right, your ghost stories." She tilts her head. "Ya know, for someone who writes about ghosts, ya don't seem particularly spooked by them."

"Professional hazard."

She laughs again, and the air around me drops several degrees. "Well, if ya change your mind about the festival, let me know. I'm runnin' the S'mores booth on Thursday night. I make a mean ghost-shaped marshmallow."

"I'll consider it," I say, though the thought of navigating crowds of humans dressed as cartoonish versions of monsters and spirits holds little appeal.

A silence settles. She touches her collarbone as if checking for something that should be there. My eyes travel up her neck, then to the freckles that pepper her nose.

She glances around the room with a proprietor's eye. "The view from those windows is lovely durin' the day. You can see the whole garden, and the mountains beyond."

"I look forward to it."

She nods and offers one last smile. "Well, goodnight then."

I close the door and lean against it. The whispers start at once. The voices press in with intent.

She walks between . . .

I press my hand to the wall, extending my senses beyond

the room. That familiar magical signature is going to drive me mad. It's the taste of it. The way it subtly warps reality, bending it at the edges. I've felt this exact signature before. It tickles at memories from years ago when I relentlessly followed rules.

The whisper comes again, clearer now: *You're not wrong. The daughter is close.*

I freeze.

Bloodline magic. Someone here carries a power I've encountered before. My superiors didn't just send me to collect a soul.

Two quick knocks interrupt my thoughts.

I open the door to find Mina, arms full of folded linens, her hair pulled back. She's changed into a blue sweater frayed at the cuffs. "Sorry to bother ya," she says, fingers fidgeting against the towels. "I realized I hadn't provided the room with extra towels and pillows. Some guests fancy more than the standard bits and bobs." Humans and their need for comfort. Strange creatures. One pillow has always seemed sufficient to me. "The provided amenities are—" I'm supposed to be blending in. "I appreciate the gesture. The towels will come in handy."

She hands them over, and our fingers brush briefly. Warmth surges between us. Was that the reaper in me attaching to the soul I've been sent for?

Mina gasps, her eyes widening. The temperature fluctuates wildly, creating a pocket of swirling air between us that makes the curtains flutter.

"Static," she says quickly, pulling her hand back. She flexes her fingers as if she's lost feeling in them.

"Yes. Static."

"Glad to hear everythin' meets your expectations." She tucks a stray strand of hair behind her ear, exposing the line of her neck. "First impressions and all that. I want to make sure the room suits ya."

"It's perfect," I say, and mean it, though not for the reasons she might assume. The thin veil here will make my investigations easier, even if it does complicate everything else about this assignment.

"Great!" Her smile crinkles the corners of her eyes. "Have ya been to New England before? I know ya said this was your first time in Moonridge specifically, but there's something about ya, or maybe just your mannerisms. Ya seem very familiar. I feel like I know ya from somewhere."

My grip tightens on the door frame. Part of me wants to tell her that yes, we've met before. I saved her life. But then I'd also have to admit that I've come to collect her. And this time, I'm not allowed to save her.

"I've traveled," I say carefully. "Though I try to avoid staying anywhere too long. It makes writing difficult when you become too attached to a place."

"Are ya runnin' from somethin'?" she asks, then looks embarrassed. "Sorry. That was presumptuous."

If only she knew. The weight of every soul I've collected sits heavily on my shoulders. Heavier still is the knowledge I hold of her upcoming end date.

"Isn't everyone running from something?" I counter. "Or perhaps toward something they're not sure they want to find?"

"That's very philosophical for someone who just arrived in a small town to write ghost stories."

"Ghost stories are often the most philosophical tales of all. They force us to confront what we fear most and the unknown that comes after."

"And what do ya think comes after?" She studies my face.

"I think," I say slowly, "that death is not the ending most people fear it to be. It's simply . . . a transition. A doorway from one state of being to another."

She touches her collarbone. "That's a comfortin' way to think about it."

"Is it comfort you're seeking?"

She steps closer. "Sometimes I think we're all seekin' comfort.

Especially when things happen that don't make sense. When ya hear voices that shouldn't be there, or feel connections with people that have no logical explanation."

"What kind of voices?"

She blinks. "I'm sorry. I don't know why I said that. It's late."

"The voices. Do they happen often?"

She shrugs. "Since I moved here, sometimes I hear things. Whispers, mostly. My family always said I had an overactive imagination as a child, so I just assumed it was stress, or the old house settlin', or, well, anythin' but what it might actually be."

"And what do you think it might actually be?"

She looks directly into my eyes, and for a moment, I have the distinct feeling she knows exactly who I am. "I think some things exist whether we understand them or not. And maybe it doesn't matter whether they make sense. Maybe what matters is how we choose to respond to them."

What a peculiar answer.

"That's very brave," I say.

"Or daft as a brush," she counters with a shrug. "I've been told I have the intuition of a gnat."

The hallway light catches the scar on her chin. I look away. I was drawn to her once and it nearly destroyed me. I have a job to do.

"I really should let ya get some rest," she says finally.

"And I should let you return to whatever late-night tasks brought you upstairs with extra towels," I reply.

She laughs softly. "Caught me. I was actually restless and decided to do some bakin'. Nervous energy. The Vampire Wives arrive soon, and I want everythin' to be perfect."

"The Vampire Wives?"

"A reality TV show cast will be stayin' here during the festival. They're quite a force of nature from what I understand. Eight rooms full of drama and fangs and enough hair products to stock a salon." She grins. "It should be interestin'. Or completely mental."

A warning slides up my chest. Vampires tend to be sensitive to supernatural disturbances. If there are real supernatural forces at work in Moonridge, their presence could enhance things significantly.

"You don't seem worried about hosting them," I observe.

"Should I be? I don't think we see many vampires around here. Mostly witches and werewolves. Besides, I'm pretty sure they're just human actors playing characters for television. Although . . ." She pauses. "Some of the locals seem convinced they're actually vampires. Like, really convinced. It's become a bit of a runnin' joke in town."

"And what do you think?"

She shrugs. "I think people see what they want to see. Moonridge has a reputation for supernatural activity, so it's easy to let imagination run wild. We accept everyone here. We had some trouble this past summer, but normally everyone coexists just fine."

"Moonridge has a reputation?"

"Oh yes. Supposedly, we're very haunted. Thin veils between worlds, all that mystical stuff. The tourism board loves it, especially in October. It's one of the things that's kept me here." Something shifts in her expression. There and gone.

"Well," she hedges backward, "I really should let ya get settled. But if ya hear any strange noises tonight, don't worry. Old houses make all kinds of sounds."

"And if the house isn't the one making the noise?" I ask.

She meets my eyes steadily. "Then I'd keep that door firmly shut, if I were you."

She winks, then turns and walks away.

The supernatural activity swirls around me, lifting the tails of my shirt. The floorboards creak in a rhythmic pattern that sounds too much like a heartbeat. But it's the whispers I can't tune out.

The daughter was here . . .
The bloodline continues . . .
She carries the mark . . .

I step to the window and peer into the darkened garden. Moonlight spills across overgrown roses. A church bell tolls midnight. I count them silently.

In the mirror, my reflection wavers between human and the reaper who lives at my core. I place my cane against the dresser. It immediately begins to vibrate with agitation.

It remembers.

I *have* been here before. Not here at the B&B, but in Moonridge. Maybe Mina wasn't the council's only reason for sending me here. I get the sense this town holds another connection to someone or something that I need to put to rest.

The only question is whether I've come to bring peace, or open old wounds.

And for the first time in millennia, I don't know the answer.

THE REAL VAMPIRE WIVES OF OBSIDIAN HILLS

Episode 7: "Moonridge or Bust"

THE THEME SONG OF *THE REAL VAMPIRE WIVES OF OBSIDIAN HILLS* PLAYS

Ayana Bakari

My jewels are real, my fangs are sharp, and my patience is thin.

Vivienne St. James

Elegance never dies. And neither do I.

Caprice Le Vein

I may be dead but I still know how to accessorize.

Zara Dusk

My chakras are aligned and my crystals are charged. I'm living my best death.

Dahlia Devine

You can't bury the past. Trust me, I've tried.

FADE IN:

INT. DAHLIA'S MANSION - LIVING ROOM - DAY

The camera pans across an opulent living room with floor-to-ceiling windows. DAHLIA DEVINE sits perfectly poised on a white velvet sofa, her ice-blonde hair immaculate. VIVIENNE, CAPRICE, ZARA, and AYANA are arranged around the room on various chairs and couches, champagne flutes in hand.

DAHLIA: *(clasping her hands together)* Ladies, I've called you all here because I have the most wonderful announcement. This year, for our annual cast trip, we're going somewhere truly special.

CAPRICE: *(bouncing slightly in her seat)* Ooh! Are we going to Paris? I've been dying to see the catacombs again!

VIVIENNE: *(rolling her eyes)* Caprice, when did you visit the catacombs?

CAPRICE: Well I've been to Paris. Same thing, right?

CUT TO: TALKING HEAD

VIVIENNE: *(to camera, deadpan)* Sometimes I forget Caprice has only been undead for like, five minutes. The enthusiasm for everything is exhausting.

CUT BACK TO: LIVING ROOM

DAHLIA: Not Paris, darling. Somewhere much more atmospheric. We're going to Moonridge, Massachusetts.

Long pause. The women exchange glances.

AYANA: *(taking a sip of her wine)* Massachusetts? Honey, what's in Massachusetts besides bad accents and overpriced lobster?

DAHLIA: It's a charming little town known for its supernatural community. Very accepting of our kind. And they're having their annual Haunted Fall Festival that week.

ZARA: *(perking up)* Oh, that actually sounds amazing! The energy there must be incredible. I bet the ley lines are super active. Mortimer would love it, wouldn't you, baby? *(speaking to a small bat perched on her shoulder)*

VIVIENNE: *(sarcastically)* How lovely. A fall festival. Because nothing says "sophisticated vampire getaway" like apple cider and pumpkin carving.

CUT TO: TALKING HEAD

VIVIENNE: *(adjusting her designer jacket)* Look, I'm going through a divorce from a controlling, manipulative vampire lord. The last thing I need is to spend six days in some quaint New England town pretending to be charmed by leaf-peeping tourists. But . . . *(sighs)* the girls need this trip, and honestly, getting out of Obsidian Hills while Marcus is being a total bloodsucking dick might be exactly what I need.

CUT BACK TO: LIVING ROOM

CAPRICE: Wait, wait, wait. *(holding up her hand)* Are we talking about a *real* haunted festival? Like, with actual ghosts? Because I'm still trying to figure out this whole undead thing. Are ghosts jealous of us? I definitely can't handle ghost drama on top of vampire drama.

AYANA: *(chuckling)* Baby girl, you can barely handle life as it is.

CUT TO: TALKING HEAD

CAPRICE: *(pouting)* Everyone keeps treating me like I'm some newbie, but I've been a vampire for almost six months now! That's like . . . *(counting on her fingers)* . . .that's like thirty-six months in dog years! Wait, no . . .

CUT BACK TO: LIVING ROOM

DAHLIA: The festival runs for six days, and I've arranged for us to stay at a lovely bed and breakfast called Moonridge B&B. Very historic, very atmospheric.

ZARA: *(suddenly suspicious)* Wait, Dahlia, isn't that the same town where your mysterious husband we've never met supposedly has business interests?

Dahlia's perfect composure flickers for just a moment.

DAHLIA: *(smoothly)* I have no idea what you're talking about, darling.

CUT TO: TALKING HEAD

ZARA: *(rolling her eyes)* Okay, so Dahlia's husband is like this total mystery man. None of us has ever seen him, she almost never talks about him, and now suddenly she wants to take us to some random town in Massachusetts? Sus much? *(Mortimer squeaks in agreement)* See? Even Mortimer thinks it's weird.

CUT BACK TO: LIVING ROOM

AYANA: *(leaning back in her chair)* Well, I'm in. It's been too long since I've had front-row seats to some quality supernatural chaos. I could use a change.

VIVIENNE: *(standing up)* Fine. But I'm bringing my entire fall wardrobe, and if there's no decent spa in this town, I'm holding you personally responsible, Dahlia.

CAPRICE: *(jumping up excitedly)* This is going to be so fun! Do you think they'll have those cute little ghost tours? Oh! Maybe I'll finally figure out how to phase through walls!

CUT TO: TALKING HEAD

AYANA: *(grinning at camera)* Three hundred years of living, and these girls still manage to surprise me. A supernatural fall festival in small-town Massachusetts? *(raises her wine glass)* This is either going to be the most boring trip of my very long life, or somebody's about to catch some serious drama. Either way, I'm ready.

CUT BACK TO: LIVING ROOM

DAHLIA: *(standing gracefully)* Wonderful. We leave tomorrow evening. Pack accordingly, ladies. Moonridge is going to be unforgettable.

SMASH CUT TO TITLE CARD

The Real Vampire Wives of Obsidian Hills — "Next time on Vampire Wives . . ."

CHAPTER THREE

Mina

I squeeze the last drops of juice from the orange as the eggs sizzle. Movement flickers at the edge of my vision. For a heartbeat, I swear there's a child in a cowboy costume standin' there.

I turn, and he's gone.

"Someone there?"

I poke my head into the dining room. No one. Not this shite again. They kept me up all night with their whispers and now they're showin' up in my kitchen? Daft fuckers.

"Morning, dearie!" Lily's cheerful voice precedes her into the kitchen. She's all done up in a mint green cardigan with pearly buttons. "Something smells heavenly!"

I slide the spatula beneath the eggs, watchin' for that delicate line between runny and firm. Jasper likes his eggs "cooked proper," though what that means shifts with his mood.

"Good mornin'." I place the eggs on a plate and grab two scones from the rack. "Sleep well, then?"

"Like the dead," Jasper grumbles as he shuffles in behind his wife. "Until that blasted radiator started its midnight concert. Sounded like someone was having a heated argument with it."

"Jasper!" Lily gives him a gentle swat on the arm. "Be nice."

"What? I'm paying good money to stay here. I can complain about the radiator if I want to." But there's no real heat in his words. This is just our mornin' ritual. I love sparrin' with this old fart. He reminds me of my granddad, bless his soul.

I place their plates and a pot of coffee on their table. "The radiator's been actin' up all week. I've had it checked twice, but it seems to have developed quite the personality."

"Everything in this old house does," Jasper mutters, pokin' at his eggs with his fork. He takes a bite and makes a satisfied grunt. "Very good. Though Death himself couldn't make these scones any lighter." Jasper takes another bite, and nods with approval.

"They're perfect," Lily counters, slatherin' hers with a dollop of thick double cream.

I know they're perfect. I've been bakin' em since I was a kid. If only I could pay the bills with my scones. I could keep the B&B from becomin' a very expensive storage unit.

"Eggs are too runny," Jasper complains.

"Ignore him, Mina. He woke up on the wrong side of the bed."

"I've been waking up on the wrong side of the bed for eighty years," Jasper says through a mouth full of eggs.

Lily's eyes twinkle with mischief. "We met your other guest this morning. Quite the formal gentleman. Very polite, though a tad aloof."

My hand stills on the coffee pot. "Ya met Dex?"

"In the garden." Jasper points out the window. "Peculiar fellow. Just stared at the sunrise like it owed him money."

"He was perfectly lovely," Lily corrects. "Though I did think it odd that he was fully dressed at six in the morning. Three-piece suit and all. Who wears a suit to watch the sunrise?"

A suit? Is he plannin' to attend a bloody funeral? I pour coffee into their cups. "What did he say?"

"Not much," Jasper admits. "Wanted to know if anyone had ever been buried on the property."

Not buried yet, but I will be soon. "That's a strange question."

"That's what I thought," Lily says. "But he explained he was researching local folklore for his book. Writers ask odd questions, I suppose."

"So he seems a little off to ya?" I ask. I shouldn't be speakin' this way about my very sexy, and very weird, guest, but I'm desperate for a second opinion.

Lily stuffs part of the scone into her mouth.

"The man barely blinked the entire conversation." Jasper takes a sip of his coffee. "And when that crow landed near him, it didn't fly away. Just sat there staring at him like it was waiting for orders. So, yeah, I would say he seems off, but you may have different standards. You live in Moonridge, for hell's sake."

"Animals can sense things about people," Lily adds, ignorin' Jasper's jabs. "My grandmother always said so. Dogs know who to trust, cats know who's hiding something, and birds know things we don't."

Dex appears in the doorway, and I nearly drop the coffee pot.

"Good morning." He inclines his head toward the Brookses. "I hope I'm not intruding."

"Not at all!" Lily beams at him. "Mina was just telling us about your writing. Ghost stories, how exciting!"

Dex's eyes find mine, and my heart gives a double-knock on my chest again. They weren't kiddin' about the suit. Not bad, though. He cleans up right nice.

"I was hoping to join you for breakfast," he says to me. "If that's acceptable."

"Of course." Why is my voice so high pitched? "Coffee? Tea? I've got fresh scones."

"Tea would be appreciated. Earl Grey, if you have it."

I disappear into the kitchen and listen in on their conversation while preparin' a fresh cup of tea.

"Lovely morning," Lily says. "Perfect weather for the Halloween Festival. Are you planning to attend any of the events?"

"I hadn't given it much thought." Dex accepts the cup of tea I offer him and sits. "Though I understand there's quite a bit of local folklore associated with the festivities."

"Oh yes," Jasper jumps in, warmin' to his favorite subject. "This town's got more ghost stories than sense. Half the buildings claim to be haunted, and the other half are probably lying about not being haunted."

"Jasper doesn't believe in such things." Lily rolls her eyes. "Though he certainly enjoys the stories when it suits him."

"And what about you, Miss Cartwright?" Dex's dark eyes bore into me. "Do you believe in ghosts?"

Well, I bloody better. They're practically crawlin' out of my walls.

"I think," I say carefully, "that there are more things in this world than we understand. And maybe that's not such a bad thing."

Dex's expression shifts. "A diplomatic answer." He sets down his teacup.

"A Scottish answer," I correct. "We're raised to keep our options open when it comes to the supernatural. Ya never know what might be listenin'."

Lily claps her hands together. "How delightfully mysterious! Mina, you really should be the one to tell ghost stories at the festival. You'd be much better than the mayor. He tells the same stories every year. Where's the fun in that?"

The harsh ring of the landline interrupts our breakfast banter. I excuse myself and hurry to the old rotary phone in the hallway.

"Moonridge Bed and Breakfast, this is Mina speakin'."

"Mina." Hazel's voice sounds wrong. Something's happened. "Did you lose your phone again? I tried calling your cell."

I search my pockets. I honestly have no idea where my cell phone is. "Sorry. I must have turned the ringer off. What's up?"

She exhales. "I have some bad news."

I grip the receiver. "What's happened?"

"It's Mrs. Henderson." A pause. "She passed away this morning. At the library. Penny found her at the front desk."

Sweet Mrs. Henderson.

"How?" I manage.

"The paramedics think it was her heart. Penny found her sitting at the desk with a book open in front of her. Like she'd fallen asleep reading." Hazel's voice catches. "I'm heading to the library now to check on Penny. I can't imagine this is easy on her, and I don't want to risk her attempting a spell to cheer herself up. We all know how that would go."

"I'll come too," I say. "Let me do the washin' up after breakfast, and I'll be right there."

After hangin' up, I lean against the wall. Mrs. Henderson welcomed me from day one. She always had the best crochet patterns and knew exactly which book to recommend based on my mood.

I untie my apron as Dex appears in the doorway.

"Bad news?"

"The town librarian passed away this mornin'." I swallow a sob. "Mrs. Henderson. She was special."

Dex looks like he suddenly remembered he was supposed to be somewhere. "I'm sorry for your loss. Death is never easy, even when it comes naturally."

"Naturally?"

He lifts a shoulder. "At her age, I mean. I assume . . . she was older, yes? And it was, um . . . of natural causes? There's something peaceful about that."

That was the weirdest response I've ever heard. "Yes, it was of natural causes, and it sounds like it was peaceful."

"You're going to see friends?" he asks.

I nod. "I need to check on Penny, the assistant librarian. She found Mrs. Henderson this mornin'. I can't imagine how she must be feelin' right now."

"I'd like to accompany you, if I may," Dex says. "I'd like to see more of Moonridge. For my research."

Company would be nice.

"Right then," I decide. "Just let me tell the Brookses and grab some things."

I change into a black sweater and jeans. I throw together a plate of cookies, grab my jacket, and slip out the door, leavin' Jasper and Lily to argue over what their day might look like. Dex falls into step beside me. He moves like each step was choreographed, pausin' now and then to study the wrought-iron streetlamps with their ornate scrollwork.

"I can practically smell the memories," he murmurs, almost to himself.

Is he mad? "What do memories smell like?"

He considers this for a moment, his face serious. "Apples and woodsmoke. Leaves turning to soil. Things ending and beginning at once."

Better than my memories. "That's a lovely way to put it."

"Is it?" He sounds surprised. "I've never thought of it as beautiful before. More inevitable."

"Everythin's inevitable if ya think about it long enough," I say. "Doesn't mean it can't be beautiful too."

He's an odd bird. But at least I'm not gettin' a murdery vibe from him.

"You mentioned yesterday that you hear voices sometimes," he says suddenly. "Do they come more frequently during certain times of year?"

I cock my head. "Why do ya ask?"

"Research." He stops walkin' and tilts his head, left eyebrow raised. "The voices you mentioned. Do they whisper more clearly in spring or autumn?"

What a weird question. "October's always been the worst. Why would that matter?"

"Samhain approaches." His fingers tighten on his cane. "The world grows quiet. Death draws closer to the surface."

I stare at him. "Ya say that like ya know Death personally."

A hint of a smile flickers across his face. "I've studied these things extensively. When the year dies, barriers weaken. The dead find their voices."

I've got nothin'. I turn my attention to the cobblestone path.

"I wondered," he adds, "if your experiences tend to cluster around specific dates."

What can I say? The truth makes me sound mental, but I can't sit here starin' at him like I'm a mute.

"October's always been the worst," I admit. "Or the best, dependin' on how ya look at it. The voices are more persistent. Like they're tryin' harder to get through."

"And last night?"

I stop walkin' and stare at him. "How did ya know about last night?"

"You mentioned at breakfast that you barely slept. And you have the particular exhaustion that comes from fighting something you don't entirely understand."

Is he psychic or somethin'? "Yes. The voices were stronger than usual. Like they were tryin' to warn me."

"Perhaps they were."

I jerk my head in his direction. "Warn me about what?"

"Change," he says with a shrug. "In my experience, spirits become restless when significant changes are approaching. Deaths. Arrivals. Things that alter the fundamental balance of a place."

"That's either very reassurin' or completely terrifyin'."

"Often both," he agrees.

An ambulance rumbles out of the parking lot as we approach the library. Hazel's Jeep is parked outside next to the sheriff's cruiser. Is this what the B&B lot will look like when I finally kick it?

"That's Hazel's car," I tell Dex, pointin' to the maroon Jeep. "She's one of my closest friends and one of Moonridge's more powerful witches."

Dex's steps slow as we reach the library steps.

"Is somethin' wrong?" I ask.

He stares at the library with uncomfortable intensity. "The energy here is complex."

"Complex? How?"

The library door opens and Hazel rushes down the steps, her auburn hair tucked under a beanie. Her face opens up when she sees me.

"Mina, thank goddess you came." She wraps me into a tight hug. "Penny's holding up, but barely."

Over her shoulder, Dex hasn't moved. He studies her like she's a foreign object that just dropped onto his head.

I turn to introduce them. "Hazel Thornton, this is Dex Grimm. He's stayin' at the B&B."

Hazel extends her hand, but her smile appears painted on. "Nice to meet you."

Dex takes her hand, eyes never leavin' her face. "I know those eyes," he says quietly.

Hazel goes still and passes me a sideways glance. "You what now?"

"I'm sorry," Dex says. "You remind me of someone I knew long ago. A trick of the light, perhaps."

Hazel laughs. "Yeah. Eyeball twins. Super common."

He gives her a blank expression.

She looks at me then back at Dex. "But I get it. Everybody looks like somebody, amiright?"

I shift the cookie basket to my other arm. "How's Penny holdin' up?"

Hazel passes another glance at Dex and then back to me. "She's trying to stay strong, but she's devastated. Mrs. Henderson was more than a boss to her—she was like a grandmother figure. Come on, let's go in. She'll be glad to see you."

Dex hangs back slightly, his gaze still fixed on Hazel. Through the glass, I can see Penny movin' around inside. Hazel knocks, and Penny rushes over to unlock the door. Poor thing is a wreck. A coffee stain blooms on her white blouse, half-covered by a pink cardigan she's thrown over her shoulders.

"Oh, Mina," she says, her voice scratchy. "Thank you for coming."

I step forward and hug her. Her thin frame shakes with grief. The cookie basket dangles awkwardly from my elbow as I try to offer what comfort I can.

"I brought cookies," I say when she pulls back. "Double chocolate chunk. Mrs. Henderson's favorite."

Penny looks at me and then at Hazel. "Um, Mina. She's dead. She can't eat these."

Oh, Penny.

I clear my throat. "Yes, love. I know. I brought them for you. In honor of her."

Penny nods, expression blank. "Oh, well. Thank you. She always said you could cure anything with the right combination of chocolate and butter."

"I do my best."

She takes the basket and gestures for us to go inside. Mrs. Henderson's glasses still sit on the circulation desk next to a half-finished crossword puzzle, as if she might return any moment to pencil in another answer.

"This is Dex Grimm," I tell Penny as we settle near the desk. "He's a guest at the B&B. A writer."

Penny tucks a wisp of hair behind her ear and straightens her cardigan.

"A writer? How wonderful," she says, her voice suddenly lighter. "We have an excellent collection of local history and folklore, if you're interested in research. Do you do readings or signings? Maybe we could do a book event. It would be lovely to have you."

"Thank you," Dex replies with a smile. "Perhaps when circumstances are more appropriate."

He moves toward the far wall where a framed map of historical Moonridge hangs between two tall bookcases. His fingers trace the glass over certain markings along the town's perimeter.

"These symbols," he murmurs. "They're quite unusual."

Penny perks up. "Local legend says they're protection symbols the founders used to keep evil spirits away from the settlement."

Dex traces one of the symbols with his finger, and his eyebrows scrunch together. "Interesting."

"What?" Hazel asks, steppin' closer.

"Your founders weren't just trying to keep evil out." His voice drops to barely above a whisper. "They were trying to keep something in."

Penny laughs. "That's a disturbing thought. Keep what in?"

Dex's gaze shifts to Hazel, then back to the map. "Something they couldn't destroy."

Death comes for you.

Oh, bloody hell. They found me.

Hazel glances toward the back of the library with a frown. "Penny, is there anyone else in here?"

"No." She looks toward the back of the library. "Though Mrs. Henderson always said this place had a mind of its own. Doors opening and closing, books reshelving themselves. She called them her helper spirits."

"Helper spirits?" Dex's attention sharpens.

"Just a joke," Penny says with a wave of her hand. "Mrs. Henderson had a wonderful sense of humor about the town's supernatural reputation. She always said if there were ghosts in the library, at least they were literary ghosts with good taste in books."

He nods, eyebrows furrowed.

"Well," I say, tryin' to break the strange tension that's settled over us, "what can we do to help? With arrangements or the library or anythin'?"

"The board is sending someone to help me sort through Mrs.

Henderson's things," Penny says, acceptin' the subject change. "Her daughter will be here tomorrow to collect her personal effects. I just keep expecting her to walk through that door and tell me I've miscategorized something."

She sniffs, and Hazel places a hand on her arm. Dex's eyes trace her every move. I don't like it.

"Perhaps we should let ya get back to what ya need to do," I suggest. "But please, call if ya need anythin' at all."

Penny nods. "Thank you, Mina. For the cookies, for coming by. Mrs. Henderson always adored you."

I pat her arm. "She meant a lot to me too."

We step outside, and I take a deep breath of cool autumn air. I feel like I need a cookie and a nap.

"Your friend is quite powerful," Dex says suddenly.

I stop walkin'. "Powerful how?"

"She has a very strong presence. Old magic, well-trained."

How could he possibly know this?

"Hazel's a good person." I won't let him think otherwise. "Whatever ya think ya sensed about her, she's one of the best people I know."

"I'm sure she is," Dex replies. "That's not always enough to protect someone from their family's past, though."

"What's that supposed to mean?"

"Mina!" La'Tasha hurries toward us from the town square. Her buttery yellow swing coat billows in soft, wind-drawn arcs around her legs.

"I've been looking everywhere for you." She takes a breath. "I want to talk to you about tomorrow."

"Tomorrow?"

"The Vampire Wives!"

Oh, for fuck's sake. I've been so preoccupied, I've forgotten about my reality TV guests arrivin' tomorrow. "Oh god. I still have so much to do. The rooms aren't perfect, and I haven't planned anything special, and—"

"Girl, breathe." La'Tasha grabs my shoulders. "You'll be fine. They want authentic New England charm, and that's exactly what you provide." She smiles. "I mean, how hard can it be to babysit a bunch of dramatic vampires with cameras following them around?"

"Ya say that now."

"Would you be okay if I come over and meet with the production team tomorrow? I want to see if we can get them involved in some of the activities. Coco wants to come, too."

"Production team meeting, huh? Are ya sure you're not just tryin' to rub elbows with the celebrities?"

She chews her lip. "Okay, maybe partly that, but I do want to get them involved in as many activities as I can. It'd be great for publicity. I think it's a win-win for Moonridge and for the show."

"Yeah. Okay," I nod. "I'll likely need help."

"I'll see you then." She squeezes my arm. "This is going to be great. I need to get to the shop. See you tomorrow."

I wave and then glance at Dex, who's been listenin' to this exchange with interest. "Famous last words," I mutter. Because if there's one thing I've learned in Moonridge, it's that nothin' good ever starts with themed cocktails and fangs.

CHAPTER FOUR

Mina

The town square looks like Halloween threw up all over it. I steer Dex around a ladder before he walks into it, and the man stringin' fake bats above us doesn't even glance down.

"Is it always like this?" Dex asks.

"Only in October." I snag two cups of Mrs. Peterson's cider from a passing volunteer and hand him one. He looks at it like I just handed him a cup of acid. "Moonridge takes Halloween seriously. People come from all over New England."

He takes a drink of the cider, and his eyes widen. "That's quite enjoyable." He downs the rest of the glass without so much as a wince. I look at the steam risin' from my cup. I'd get a bloody third-degree burn on my esophagus if I tried that.

"What are they building?" Dex tosses his empty cup over his shoulder and nods at a half-assembled booth frame.

Is he some sort of animal?

"Everythin'," I say. "Give it two days, and ya won't recognize the place."

I turn back to pick up his cup. "And this." I hold it up so he can see it. "Goes here." I drop it into a trash bin. "I don't know what things are like where you're from, but we don't litter around here."

He looks at the trash bin and nods once, then takes off again, eyes grazin' the crowd. I pull him sideways before he steps into a trail of orange fairy lights someone's draggin' across the cobblestones. "A curious way to celebrate the thinning of the veil."

I blink at him. "The thinnin' of the what now?"

"There's Hazel." He points to where Hazel plants a kiss on the cheek of her werewolf boyfriend, Blake Carter. His brother, Calvin, sorts through a box of decorations next to them.

"Come meet Blake and Calvin." I guide us toward them. "They're good people. Occasionally a bit intense, but still good."

"The werewolves." Dex nods.

He catches my arm to stop me from trippin' over a pumpkin. "How did ya know?"

"They smell like wet earth and pine." He looks at me like I should know this. "And they stand like predators."

Weirdly specific. I sniff the air, but don't smell any of what he just said.

We approach the booth. The soft glow of Hazel's crystals dims the closer we get until they go completely dark.

Hazel freezes, hand above the amethyst. "That's weird." She crouches down and peers at the stack of rocks.

Blake's hammer stops mid-swing, and Calvin's head snaps up. Both go still. Alert.

"What's happening?" Hazel pulls her hands back from the crystals, which have lost their luster. She looks our way, and her eyes go directly to Dex. "Oh. Hey. Uh, Blake, Calvin. This is Dex, Mina's new guest at the B&B."

Blake sets down his hammer and approaches. I go in for a hug, ignorin' the faint scent of sweat and wolf musk. I brush a bit of sawdust off his shirt. "Ya look like you've been workin' hard as always. Smell it, too," I joke.

Blake locks eyes with Dex. His gaze narrows before he extends a hand. "Blake Carter."

Dex hesitates. Blake's nostrils flare, and his frown deepens at the slight.

"Blake and his brother run Carter Construction." I pat Blake on the shoulder. "Half of Moonridge has either been built or patched up by ya, right? Houses. Decks, the whole lot."

Calvin wanders over, his typical sunny smile stretched at the edges. He glances at Hazel's darkened crystals before comin' in for a hug of his own. He steps back and lifts his chin in Dex's direction. "I'm Calvin. Don't mind my brother. He gets twitchy around things he can't categorize."

"A wise approach." Dex's thumb traces the skull at the end of his walking stick. "In a world full of unexpected dangers."

Calvin's eyebrows climb. His eyes flick toward Hazel.

"So." I clap my hands. "How are the booths comin' along?"

"Good. I think." Hazel's eyes drift toward Dex again. That's three times now. "We're setting up half the booths today, and the rest tomorrow." She glances at her still-dark crystals. "Though it seems we're being plagued with a little weirdness."

"What kind of weirdness?" I ask.

"The crystals seem to have lost all their energy when you walked up. They're supposed to help pull positive energy toward the festival." She crouches down to examine them more closely. "Ya know, keep people engaged, and happy. Something's fucking with them."

Blake's eyes flick to Dex. "Something, or someone?"

I glance at Dex, who stands expressionless.

"Speakin' of the festival." I pull Hazel's attention away from the crystals. "Ya still need me at the S'mores station Thursday night, yes?"

"Wouldn't be the same without you." Hazel nudges me. "Though I still haven't given up on the cat ears."

"Cat ears?" The corner of Dex's mouth twitches.

"It's tradition." Hazel grins at my discomfort. "Everyone

who works a booth wears at least a partial costume. Mina has been fighting it since she moved here."

"I don't do costumes," I insist. "I always look like an idiot. And they're itchy."

"Says the woman who wore an inflatable sheep costume to La'Tasha's birthday party last year," Blake teases.

"That was different! And I was promised no one would ever mention it again." My cheeks heat up. "Besides, I lost a bet."

Calvin chuckles, though he stays focused on the darkened crystals. "The Spooky S'mores station won't be the same without some festive headgear at the very least."

"I'll consider it," I grumble, just to shut them up. "Anyway, we were just passin' through on our way back from the library. Thought we'd see how things were comin' along."

Blake's expression sobers. "We heard about Mrs. Henderson. Tough loss for the town."

I nod and fight back the lump risin' in my throat. I glance at Dex and find his eyes are stuck on the old church in the distance. I follow his gaze to the ravens circlin' the steeple. What's goin' on in that head?

"Shall we return to the B&B?" Dex glances down at me, his dark eyes unreadable. "Your other guests will be returning soon."

His fingers tap once against his cane, then still. Hazel's crystals pulse with weak light before goin' dark again.

"Yes," I say, surprised he remembered the Brookses' schedule. "They'll want tea, and I should start plannin' dinner. Oh, and do one more pass of all the rooms. I want everythin' perfect before the chaos starts."

"Chaos?" Calvin asks, perkin' up with interest.

"The Vampire Wives arrive tomorrow," I explain. "The reality show?"

Blake snorts. "That ridiculous show? Calvin loves it."

"Hey. I appreciate the fashion and the eccentric personalities," Calvin defends himself, not lookin' up from the string of lights he's tryin' to untangle. "And the chaos. Sometimes you need a little manufactured supernatural drama in your life."

"They've booked eight rooms," I continue. "It could really help turn things around for the B&B. Especially with the televised publicity."

Hazel hugs me goodbye. "I'll call you later," she whispers. "We need to talk about Mr. Sexy Weirdo Dude."

I smile and squeeze her arm.

We turn to leave, and Blake places a hand on my shoulder. "Be careful." His eyes are fixed on Dex's back. "Something's off about him. He doesn't smell right."

"What do ya mean?" I ask, voice low.

Blake frowns and shakes his head. "He doesn't smell like . . . anything. Everyone has a scent. Even other supernatural creatures have signatures we can read. He's just blank. Like he doesn't exist at all."

Gooseflesh prickles across my arms. "Maybe he just uses unscented soap," I joke.

Blake looks down at me with a raised eyebrow. "Wolf instincts are rarely wrong. Whatever he is, he's not what he seems. Just watch yourself, okay?"

I nod, pushin' back the unease that builds in my chest as I walk toward the edge of the square where Dex stands, eyes fixed firmly on me.

The walk back to the B&B feels longer than it should. I steal glances at Dex as he strolls beside me. He doesn't seem to be bothered by much of anythin' that just happened. He's hard to read, this one. The autumn sun catches in his dark hair, addin' subtle highlights of midnight blue, makin' my fingers twitch with the urge to touch, even as instinct warns me away.

"Your friend doesn't trust me," Dex says, breakin' the silence.

"Blake's protective," I reply. "He's like that with everyone."

"No," Dex counters, his cane clickin' against the pavement. "He's like that with potential threats. There's a difference."

I glance at him. "And are ya? A threat?"

He considers this longer than the question deserves. "I suppose that depends on one's perspective," he says finally.

Well, that's not ominous at all.

"Ya know," I say, "most people would just say 'no.'"

The corner of his mouth twitches. "I'm not most people."

No, he most certainly is not. Most people don't talk like they've stepped out of a Victorian novel. They have a personality that fits in with anyone born in the last fifty years.

As we approach the B&B, Dex stops and holds out a hand as if to brace me. "Something's wrong."

My arms begin to prickle. He's right. The dark-eyed Juncos, normally chatty this time of day, have gone quiet. And why are the curtains drawn in the parlor?

Dex places a hand against the front door. "It feels too still."

I unlock the door and push it open. The dim light of the foyer throws shadows on the walls that look like hungry fingers. I walk to the windows and yank back the curtains. The midday sun pours through. Better.

Dex holds up a hand. "Hear that?"

"I don't hear anythin'."

"Exactly." He moves to the sitting room. "The house isn't talking today."

He's right. Old houses have voices, and mine is particularly chatty, always complainin' about the weather or celebratin' when I bake somethin' delicious. But now it's silent. Holdin' its breath.

"Hello? Jasper? Lily?"

Nothin'. They're probably still in town.

"The fire's out." Dex nods toward the fireplace.

"How? I built it up before we left. It should have lasted half the day."

I remove my jacket, then move to the fireplace and touch the logs. Cold. As if they've been out for hours.

The grandfather clock stands frozen, its pendulum motionless. I wind it religiously every Sunday. My voice catches on the rise of panic. "Why did the clock stop?"

Dex runs his fingers along the clock's wooden frame. "Time behaves strangely sometimes. Especially in places where the boundaries grow thin."

"Okay, Shakespeare. What does that even mean?"

A soft thump from the kitchen interrupts us. It's followed by the unmistakable sound of a chair scrapin' against the floor.

I exhale. "That must be the Brookses. They probably came back through the garden door."

"Lily? Jasper? Is that you?" I call as I head toward the kitchen with Dex silently behind.

The kitchen door swings open under my touch, and every one of my senses short-circuits. Someone's at my kitchen table. Cardigan buttoned wrong. Silver hair. Glasses on a chain. For a moment, I think it's Lily, but then she looks right at me and— Mrs. Henderson. She looks exactly as she did the last time I saw her. Except now, her edges shimmer with a soft translucence that carries just enough wrongness to make my skin prickle.

"There you are," she says calmly. Her voice echoes like she's comin' at me in surround sound. "I've been waiting for you. Most inconsiderate of you to keep an old, dead lady waiting."

No.

I watched them haul her away in an ambulance less than two hours ago. She cannot be sittin' at my kitchen table givin' me the look she reserves for late lemon bar deliveries.

"Mrs. Henderson?" My voice cracks.

"Who else would it be, dear?" She adjusts her glasses with a gesture so familiar it makes my heart ache. "Though I imagine finding me here is somewhat alarming. Given that I dropped dead at the library this morning."

My phone slips from my fingers and hits with a heavy thud. This house doesn't have room for another ghost. The kitchen tilts. I reach a hand for the door frame and miss, fallin' against the counter.

"You're—" The scent of lilacs fills the air. Her signature scent amped up to a thousand.

"Dead?" Like it's perfectly normal. "Yes, I'm aware. Dreadful timing, honestly. Thanksgiving's next month, and I promised to bring the turkey. They'll starve without me."

The temperature drops so fast my breath fogs. Frost crawls up the kitchen windows.

I glance over at Dex, who stands with his hands in his pockets. My heart is about to beat the bloody hell out of my windpipe, and this one stands here like a dead woman at a kitchen table is an everyday occurrence. "You're not supposed to be here."

Mrs. Henderson lifts her chin. "And neither are you. Yet, here we are."

"What's happenin'?" It comes out all wheezy. "Why—how are you here?"

Mrs. Henderson's form flickers like a bad TV signal. "I don't know how I got here. But the library—it isn't safe. They've been looking for so long, and now they—" Her form flickers. "They're here. Penny—she can't—she isn't strong enough. And they have Fi—she's not dead. They took her, but she's not—"

"Who's not dead?" I demand.

Mrs. Henderson's form shifts until I can barely see her. "She'll end Moonridge. They're coming back—they won't be stopped." Another flicker. "The witches aren't ready. Warn them, Mina. They took her and now she's one of them and they're going to—"

"Took who?" I can barely breathe. What is she sayin'?

"I need to go home." Her voice thins. "I can't—I don't know which way. They'll find me here." She looks at Dex. "You can help me. Can't you?"

"They?" he asks.

Too much has happened at once over the last few weeks. My tumor. The voices. Then Dex's arrival, and the dead woman sittin' at my table like she came to play bridge. My knees buckle, and the floor rushes up to meet me. The last thing I see is—

CHAPTER FIVE

Dex

I gather Mina into my arms. Her ponytail falls across my sleeve, vibrant as fresh blood against the darkness of my suit. Flashes of that night in Edinburgh when I last held her like this invade my mind. Her lifeless body. The choice I made.

The house notices me the moment I step into the hall.

I've walked through enough old places to know the difference between memory and presence. This house assesses me the way a human would, something vast and unhurried settling its attention on me, and I have the distinct impression it doesn't much like what it finds.

Then Mina stirs in my arms, and the house makes its decision. The floor shifts, and I feel a tug at my leg as if something is pulling me down the hall, helping me get its owner to safety.

It pushes me to the left, and a door at the end of the hallway eases open with a pop and a creak. I edge it inward with the tip of my shoe. I maneuver my way around a dresser filled with knick-knacks. My eye lands on a long-dormant antique hourglass, all of the sand collected at the bottom.

I gently place her on the bed, nudging aside a one-eyed stuffed bear, its fur worn smooth by years of comfort.

She stirs, eyes fluttering awake. "What happened?"

She tries to sit up, and I place a hand on her shoulder. "You fainted. You've been pushing yourself too hard. Rest for a bit. I'll take care of things."

She drops her head back on the pillow, and I duck out before she can ask any more questions.

I nudge open the swinging kitchen door and see that Mrs. Henderson hasn't moved from her spot at the small tea table.

"You know what I am," I say, taking a seat across from her.

She nods, the movement making her entire form shimmer. "I can only assume. It's the only reason I can think of that would have led me here."

"But why here?" I ask. "You died this morning. You should have crossed over."

A frown ripples across her translucent face. "That's the problem. I remember dying. Quite peaceful, actually. Reading my favorite book. Then, darkness, a tunnel of sorts, just like they say, but halfway through . . ." She shudders, and for a moment, I can barely see an outline of her form. "Something pulled me back. It was quite painful. Like a hook in my center."

"Did no reaper appear to assist you with crossing over?"

She shakes her head. "I felt a presence, but it wasn't at all comforting. It felt dark and dangerous. Like I needed to stay away."

I lean forward, resting my elbows on the table. "And you came here? To Mina's B&B?"

"I didn't know where else to go. I couldn't return to the library. I kept bouncing away, like a tennis ball. So I started to walk. And then I felt a pull, saw a sparkling white light that everyone talks about, and I thought, 'Okay. I'm headed in the right direction.' It kept going and going, and the next thing I knew, I was here. I decided to stay a bit because it felt like something was waiting for me."

Mina clears her throat from the doorway.

I stand. "I told you to rest."

She throws up a hand. "First of all, you are in my house, and no one tells me what to do in my house. I can rest when I'm dead. But right now, someone needs to tell me what in blazes is goin' on."

She stumbles as she reaches for the tea kettle. I move to help her, and she brushes me away. "Mrs. Henderson is dead. I just came from mournin' her at the library. So why is she sittin' at my kitchen table? And why are ya talkin' to her about crossin' over?"

I consider my options. Lying would be easiest, but what's the point? She'll know the truth soon anyway.

Mrs. Henderson looks between us, her ghostly features pinched with worry. "Perhaps I should give you two a moment—"

"No," Mina says. She ignites the stove and drops the teakettle onto a burner. "No one's goin' anywhere until someone explains what's happenin'."

Her fierce will catches me off guard.

"Dex?" she prompts, her green eyes searching my face. "Who are ya really?"

I straighten my suit jacket, a habit formed over millennia of difficult conversations. "I am exactly who I said I was. Dex Grimm."

"And?" She crosses her arms.

Just say it.

"And I am also one of many known as Death." I deliver this simply, without drama. "A Reaper, if you prefer the colloquial term."

I glance up. Over her shoulder, a crow sits on the windowsill, black eyes peering curiously through the glass.

Her face goes pale. She stands and wraps her arms around herself. "The Grim Reaper." An exhale. "The collector of souls, are ya?"

Rather than answer, I tap my cane against the floor twice. It shivers in response, the glamour briefly wavering to reveal my scythe before settling back into disguise.

"Bloody hell." Mina drops into a chair at the table. Then she laughs, which was not at all what I was expecting, though I recognize it for what it is.

"Well, that explains a lot. The formal speech, the perfect skin, the . . ." her voice trails off, and she shakes her head.

The connection you feel?

"You're taking this rather well," I observe cautiously.

"Oh, trust me. I'm goin' to have a proper breakdown later." She stands and begins to pace. "But, right now, I'm goin' to make tea and try to glue my insides back together while I do my best to make sense of this, because very little of it does."

She moves to the stove, her back toward us.

"She always was practical in the face of the impossible," Mrs. Henderson says to me. "When she first arrived in Moonridge and discovered it was full of witches and werewolves, her main concern was whether she needed to stock special dietary options."

A smile tugs at my lips. "That sounds consistent with what I've observed."

Mina looks over her shoulder in our direction. "I can hear you two talkin' about me. Ghost or not, it's rude."

"Apologies," I say automatically. "Mrs. Henderson was explaining that she's experiencing unusual difficulty crossing over."

The kettle whistles, and Mina pours water into two mugs, her hands steady despite everything. She slides one across to me, and I catch the hesitation and the question that flits across her face. I take the mug and nod in thanks.

"So what does all of that mean?" she asks, settling back into her chair. "Is she stuck here?"

"Not necessarily." I wrap my hands around the mug, my perpetually cold hands absorbing its warmth. "I can guide her. But the fact that no other reaper came for her suggests something's disrupting the natural order in Moonridge."

Mrs. Henderson reaches for both of us. Her hand wraps

solidly around my forearm, but passes directly through Mina. "Maybe something's blocking the paths. I tried to leave earlier, but the further I got from this place, the more difficult it became. Like trying to walk through a snowdrift. And that darkness. It felt hungry."

I keep my expression neutral as I consider this. "The spaces between life and death should never feel predatory."

"You're sayin' someone could be messin' with the barrier between life and death?" Mina asks. "Why would anyone do that?"

"Power," Mrs. Henderson says, and I nod in agreement.

I take a few moments to explain the relation between death magic and life forces, and how it's unlikely but not impossible to manipulate.

Mina's expression hardens. "Ravena."

Before I can ask what she means, Mrs. Henderson rises from her chair. Her form snaps into place. "I'm sorry. I hate to interrupt, but I don't want to be stuck here, and I fear we've wasted too much time already."

I stand, setting my untouched tea aside. Mrs. Henderson's edges blur like smoke. "We can go. I can help you cross."

Mina touches my arm. "Wait. Can I say goodbye properly? I didn't get the chance earlier."

I nod, and Mrs. Henderson smiles, her form taking on a rosy hue. "Oh, my dear girl. Of course."

I step aside so they can embrace. Or attempt to. Mina's arms pass partially through. I step forward and place a hand on her shoulder, making myself the bridge between their souls. I'm not prepared for the flood of emotion that rolls over me.

I've witnessed human emotions for centuries. This is different. It moves through my entire body and floods my senses. Deep and unhurried. So *this* is love.

"I'll miss your lemon bars," Mrs. Henderson says, her voice thick with emotion.

"And I'll miss your book recommendations," Mina replies,

tears tracking down her cheeks. "Who's goin' to be my secret smut dealer now? You were always so kind to me. Thank you."

Mrs. Henderson releases Mina and then turns to me. "I'm ready now."

I catch my breath, steadying against the surge of emotion that just passed through me. I offer my arm, and she places her ghostly hand upon it. "I'll take her to the woods. Out of view. In case your other guests return."

Mina nods.

Mrs. Henderson is out the back door before I've finished speaking. I nod to Mina and then rush to catch up to her.

"There's something in the basement of the library," she says, as soon as we're out of the house. "I don't know what it is. But I've sensed it for weeks, kind of like the way you feel a draft before you find the open window. Someone has been trying to get to it. More than once."

I file this without responding.

"I think they know that I noticed." She glances back toward the house. "It was there this morning, and I think it's trying to find me. Whatever it is, it's afraid of what I know."

"And what, exactly, is that?"

Her fists swing at her sides as she glides deeper into the woods, like she thinks the extra momentum will get us there faster. "Only that something is there. This morning, I tried to open the basement door, and I felt fear like I've never felt before. Darkness swirled around me, and I lost my breath. My chest was on fire. I went back to my desk to sit a spell, and the next thing I knew, I was standing on the other side of the desk looking at myself."

So, something *is* there, and someone wants it. Worth investigating. Perhaps it has something to do with the other energy disruptions around town. What concerns me more is that another reaper never came for her. That is no accident.

I pause when we come to a small clearing where filtered light streams through the dense canopy overhead. I do a quick scan, searching for the presence that Mrs. Henderson sensed was following her. Nothing.

I sense the veil and tap my cane against the soft earth. It quivers, then begins to morph, lengthening in my hand until the full form of my scythe emerges without so much as a second thought.

Mrs. Henderson gasps. "It's beautiful. Not scary at all."

"It's not meant to be." I grip the familiar weight. "It's a key, not a weapon."

A sweeping overhead arc and then a downward swipe will part the veil—

But it doesn't.

I feel it as pressure against my bicep, a burning in my chest. The veil is there, I can sense it, thin as paper. But there's a hesitation. An extra layer I wasn't expecting.

I swipe again, and this time the veil rips. The portal opens. Crackles. Soft blue light bleeds through, followed by the scent of summer rain. I know what awaits her. Loved ones who've already passed. A chance at a new life.

I step aside so she can look into the portal. "Oh. I see them. My Edgar. My parents."

"It's time to join them."

She turns to me and takes my hand. "Thank you."

I give it a little squeeze. "You should know the impact you've had in this life. The kindness—the love—you've given to so many. You made lost people feel seen. You made people feel welcome. That's not nothing. Leave here knowing that you do so with an impact. May your next life be as fulfilling as this one."

And then she hugs me. For the first time in my eternal life, my eyes grow wet.

With one last, grateful smile, she steps into the light. Her form solidifies as age melts from her, leaving her young and radiant. She turns for one last smile just as the portal closes behind her with a gentle pop.

I stand motionless in the now silent clearing, staring at where the portal had been. My hands shake slightly as I lower the scythe. That almost drained me. Left me winded. Never have I had to fight to open a portal like that.

And what's even more concerning is how thin the veil feels in Moonridge. It's almost gossamer thin.

A twig snaps behind me. I turn my head to find Mina at the clearing's edge, tear tracks shining on her cheeks.

"You watched?" I ask.

"I'm sorry." Her voice is rough as rocks. "I know ya said to stay behind, but I couldn't. I wanted to see—Wanted to make sure she—Needed to know what it was like."

I should be angry. Mortals aren't meant to witness such things. But how can I be angry when I'll do this very thing with her in a matter of days if her chart is correct.

"Are you all right?" I ask.

She nods, wiping her eyes. "It was beautiful. I thought death would be scary, but that was . . . it was like watchin' someone go home."

"That's precisely what it is."

I return the scythe to my palm, and her eyes meet mine. I see the moment she places me. Not as a random guest, but as the reason she's standing here at all.

"Ya saved me." Her voice is rough. "Didn't ya? In Scotland? That's why ya feel familiar."

"Yes." I don't offer more than that.

She looks at me for a long moment. Then she holds up a hand and shakes her head.

Message received.

She turns back toward the house. I follow in silence, the only sounds the crunching of fallen leaves and twigs.

I know she knows. And we have, without discussing it, agreed to let that sit for now.

"Thank you," she finally says when the B&B comes into view.

"For helpin' her. That was kind."

I pause.

Kind.

No one has ever described my work that way before.

"It's my purpose," I hedge. "Nothing more."

"No." She stops walking and turns to face me, eyes wet with tears. "That was more than duty. And what ya did . . ." She swallows hard. "For me. Back then? Thank you. But I don't want to talk about it right now, and I don't want to talk about why you're really here. Just know . . . I'm not ready. Not now." Rivers flow down her cheeks.

I nod.

"We should return," I say stiffly. "Your other guests—"

I'm cut off by a sharp cry from the direction of the house. "What on earth have you done here?" The woman's voice echoes through the woods.

Mina stops and looks at me. "That's not Lily. Who the fuck is in my house?"

She wipes her cheeks and picks up her pace.

"Mina, wait," I say, porting forward to stand in front of her. "We don't know who or what is in there. Let me take the lead."

The scent hits me before we're through the door. Sulfur and bones. The particular cold of a soul that's arrived somewhere it shouldn't be.

I catch Mina's arm before she can move further into the foyer. A ghost in elaborate Victorian dress stands imperiously before the grandfather clock, shaking with indignation.

Mina shrugs me off. "Excuse me. Who the hell are ya and what are ya doin' in my house?"

"Your house? Yours?" the ghost asks. "I am Madeline Murphy, and this is *my* home. I demand to know what you've done to it."

Mina's shock gives way to irritation. "Excuse me? By the looks of ya, you haven't lived here in over a century. I've poured my heart and soul into preservin' this place!"

"You call this preservation?" Madeline waves dismissively at the cozy furnishings. "In my day, this was a music room. My Broadwood piano stood right there! And these curtains—cotton! Mine were silk damask imported from France!"

I step between them. Under normal circumstances, a ghost appearing is mildly inconvenient. What concerns me is Mina, already closer to the veil than she knows. If an agitated ghost—especially one who has been dead long enough to forget that she is—makes contact with someone in her condition, we're looking at possession risk, or at minimum an ectoplasm situation that will take hours to resolve, and questions I don't want to answer.

I turn to address the ghost. "Mrs. Murphy, may I ask why you've chosen to visit tonight?"

The ghost falters, confusion crossing her aristocratic features. "I . . . I was minding my own business when I suddenly felt pulled. And thank God it happened because being dead is dreadfully boring. I was so happy to finally be at home where I belong and then—Well, this monstrosity is most certainly not the home I expected to come back to."

I give Mina a look, silently begging her to let it go, when movement outside the window catches my eye. A figure in a Union Army uniform walks through the garden, calling a name I can't quite make out.

"There's another one." I point. "In your garden."

I follow Mina to the window. The front door swings open behind us, and I turn to see an elderly man in work clothes step through. A gardener from the early 1900s, by the looks of his attire.

"The boiler's acting up again, Mrs. Murphy," he announces, then stops, pointing at Mina and me. "You're not the Murphys."

"No, they're not," Madeline agrees crossly. "And you're not supposed to be here, Jenkins. You died of influenza in 1918."

"Did I?" The gardener looks down at his transparent hands. "Well, I reckon that would explain things."

My scythe pulses with heat against my palm as the energy vibration hits me, air thinning. The veil isn't just thin, it's rupturing. Mina's breath fogs, and frost spreads across the windows.

But what worries me the most is that Mina can see them all.

"Dex?" Her voice is remarkably steady. "What's happening?"

The house fills with ghosts, fragments of its past bubbling up through time. I move to the center of the foyer and plant my cane firmly on the floor. The disguised scythe responds with a pulse of power that makes the lights flicker.

"Enough." The word drops into the room like a boulder in a pond. The ghosts freeze mid-motion, turning their eyes to me. "You cannot be here."

The spirits exchange confused glances.

"But we were just drawn here," the maid says timidly. "They said we're supposed to be here."

"We followed the light like they said," the soldier agrees, looking directly at Mina. "We followed the beacon."

I feel the pieces clicking into place. It's not the house drawing them here. It's Mina.

I take a step forward, shoes squeaking against the polished hardwoods. "This house is no longer yours. Your time here ended long ago. This home is under my protection; return from where you came." I raise my cane slightly, letting it shimmer with power. Madeline places a hand to her throat and the others freeze, eyes on me.

"You're him," the soldier whispers. "The Reaper."

"I am." I hold my scythe in front of me. "Leave this house in peace."

I wave my scythe across the air once. The ghosts begin to fade, their forms thinning to pale outlines before disappearing. All that remains is a lingering chill and the faint scent of leather and freesia. The house exhales around us. A silent thank you for doing my job, but a thank you nonetheless.

Mina stands in the middle of the foyer, arms wrapped around

herself, her mouth a silent O. I take a step forward, ready to catch her should she faint again.

She looks at me. "That was . . ."

"Unusual," I finish. "And likely quite alarming. I wish I knew how to explain it."

She laughs breathlessly. "I was goin' to say 'amazin'.' Any way I could get me one of those ghost banishin' sticks?" She looks around the empty foyer. "Are they really gone?"

"I believe so. Let's hope they found their way on their own."

She moves to the parlor and melts onto the floral sofa. I follow, sitting in the armchair across from her.

"This has never happened before," she says. "Not since I've lived here."

I study her face. "Have you ever seen spirits before today? Before Mrs. Henderson? I know you said you've heard voices before, but—"

"Yes." She twists her cardigan sleeve between her fingers. "When I was little, I'd tell my mum about the lady in the garden who wore old-fashioned clothes. Or the man who sat in the corner of the kirk during church." Her voice drops. "Gran called it 'a gift.' She had it, too. But not my da. He thought it was evil. Said I'd bring the devil himself into the house if I didn't fix it."

"What happened?"

"I got sent to doctors, specialists. They said I was makin' it up. Probably to make Da feel better." A bitter smile crosses her face. "Eventually, I learned to pretend I didn't see them. And after a while, it just stopped. Like closin' a door and lockin' it."

"Until today," I observe.

She shrugs, then meets my gaze directly. "Death himself comes to town, and suddenly I'm seein' ghosts again."

I lean forward. "My presence may draw them to me, but typically, I only attract spirits who need help crossing over, not the ghosts of those long past. I have noticed that the veil between worlds is dangerously thin here, though."

She tilts her head and scrunches her brow. That likely wasn't the answer she was hoping for.

"The veil thins naturally this time of year, but not like this. This is something different." I pause. "I intend to stick around for a while and find out why. I have a feeling my superiors sent me here as more than just a ferryman."

"Superiors?" She raises an eyebrow. "Death has bosses?"

"Everyone answers to someone. I help maintain one small part of universal balance."

She leans forward. "And the balance is off in Moonridge?"

"From what I can tell. What happened tonight shouldn't be possible. Spirits don't simply wander through without guidance. Something pulled them here." I pause. "Or someone."

Her eyes widen. "*You* think *I* pulled them here?"

"I don't know. If you did, it wouldn't have been intentional, obviously. But the soldier called you a beacon. Mrs. Henderson was drawn to your B&B specifically. That's unusual."

She sinks back, her fingers tug at her bottom lip. "Brilliant. Now I'm the human ghost magnet."

I find myself smiling at her ability to find humor in this.

"Maybe you could assist me in understanding what's happening. Your connection to the human world could provide insight I might otherwise miss."

And maybe it will allow me to buy you more time.

"Me? Help Death solve a supernatural mystery?" She shakes her head. "That sounds like the premise of a really weird TV show."

"Reality is often stranger than fiction."

She considers this, then nods. "All right. I'm in. But we'll have to work around my schedule. I've got eight rooms of reality TV producers and vampires checkin' in tomorrow. I need to get movin'."

She stands, and I follow her. The lamplight catches the shadows under her eyes, and I can't help noticing the slight tremor in her hands as she pushes open the door to the dining room.

"Thank you, Mina."

She turns, catching the door before it can swing shut. "For what?"

"For not running away screaming when you learned what I am."

She smiles, and a tightness grips my chest again. "I'm Scottish. We don't run from the supernatural, we invite it in for tea and biscuits."

I proceed up the stairs and pause at the landing, listening to the out-of-tune humming coming from the kitchen. My hand tightens on the banister. She's so different from the empty woman who stood on that bridge that night. That woman had already taken inventory and found that there was nothing left. I could have let her ending come. Instead, I made a choice that was not mine to make, and the consequence of that choice is a happier version of her, wiping down her counters, planning for several tomorrows she knows she won't have.

Moonridge gave her what Scotland couldn't. Purpose. A found family that would burn the town down if someone tried to hurt her.

I gave her this. And now I have to take it away.

Back in my room, I sit on the edge of the bed. The doctors gave her a year. My presence has shortened that considerably, and she knows it. She isn't ready to go, and I want to honor that, but I can't. But what I *can* do is stall for as long as possible.

Outside my window, a raven settles on the roof. It cocks its head, studying me through the glass with one bright eye.

"Did they send you to watch over me, old friend?"

It doesn't respond, only stares. Waiting.

CHAPTER SIX

Mina

My alarm clock screeches, and I'm yanked from a fitful sleep filled with judgmental Victorian ghosts and Dex draggin' me to the afterlife. I want to just wrap the blanket over my head and stay here, but that's not an option.

I slam my hand on the snooze button and stare at the ceilin'. "Get your arse out of bed, woman, there's work to be done." What the fuck even is my life? I can't believe Death himself is in this house.

Which means it's already my time.

But it doesn't add up. The doctors said I had months at least. Maybe even a year or two. It can't be, can it? But it must be. Not like Death to just drop by and say hi and then leave you be.

The huff and clang of the radiator grounds me in the present. I can't think about all that right now. The Vampire Wives arrive today, and I have about a million things to do before they show up.

I drag myself to the shower, catchin' a glance of myself in the mirror. I look like I lost a fight with a hedge trimmer. Dark circles rim my eyes, and my red hair has that 'just survived a natural disaster' aesthetic. I splash cold water on my face and try to focus on the practical. Ghosts or no ghosts, I have a business to run.

I mentally tick through today's to-do list while washin' my hair. There's far too much to do, and somehow I still need to manage to make myself presentable for celebrities and their camera crew when they arrive at my doorstep.

I pause at the bottom of the stairs. The B&B is surprisingly still, the foyer empty, the stairway clear, no whispers risin' from anywhere, and no fashion-forward ghosts just waitin' to critique my choice of shoes. I cross the foyer to the sitting room and pull open the drapes.

"Hello, Madame Sunshine. Good to see ya." Leaves of orange, yellow, and brown chase each other across the driveway. Sunny. Peaceful. It looks to be one of those beautiful fall days we're known for. Is it too much to hope it stays this way?

I square the sofa cushions, then brush the front of my shirt flat as I head to the kitchen.

Thump.

My head whips toward the hall. I swear, if Madeline Murphy floats around the corner and has a go at me, I'll lose what's left of my mind. I step into the kitchen and crack every cupboard, even the oven, daring a ghost to lunge out at me.

Silence.

I press my palms flat on the counter and roll my neck until the tension eases up. I miss the days when I could afford a full staff and could make time to do yoga in the mornin'. A burst of pain flares behind my right eye.

"Not today. Not now." I fight back a wave of vertigo. If it's not the ghosts, it's the bloody brain parasite. I ain't got time for none of this shite.

I reach for the pancake mix and fire up the stove. I pull the eggs from the fridge, and my hand shakes so bad I drop the carton.

"Bloody hell." I sit on the floor and let myself have a right good cry. Five minutes. Ten. Then I wipe the tears and exhale.

"No time to feel sorry for yourself, woman."

I pull myself up. Dizziness mostly gone. Headache manageable.

"You can do this."

There are four good eggs left; I can get more later. It's only a crisis if I make it one. I grab a measurin' cup and get to work on the pancakes.

Jasper's telltale shuffle comes from down the hall. I wipe my eyes, then push open the kitchen door. "Good mornin', ya old coot."

"Morning," he grunts, headin' straight for the dining room and the coffee pot. "You look terrible."

"Thanks. Just what every woman wants to hear first thing in the mornin'." I return to the stove and flip the pancake, then give it a good smack with the back of the spatula like it was the one that insulted me.

"What?" He winces after takin' a sip of steamin' coffee. "I'm just saying you look tired. Someone needs to tell you your eyes have bags big enough for a week-long vacation."

I shrug. "Well, when you put it that way."

Lily steps into the dining room and smiles. I have to wrestle my own brain into place for a second. Nope. Not my gran.

"Jasper, it's too early to be harassing her." Lily stops at the doorway with her arms crossed. Somethin' about her posture makes me feel like I've been caught stealin' from a church. "You do look exhausted, dear. Trouble sleeping?"

I wobble my head and look away.

"Just pre-arrival jitters." I reach for two plates. "The Vampire Wives check in today."

"Oh, that's right!" She grabs the plate of pancakes and carries it to the table like she works here. Like she's family. "I've never met a vampire before."

"I told you. They're not real vampires, Lily," Jasper croaks. "It's just a TV show."

"Well, of course, they're real vampires. Why else would they call the show 'The Real Vampire Wives'?"

"For the same reason they call it 'reality' TV when there's nothing real about it."

I tune out their bickerin' and focus on servin' up breakfast. I can almost pretend yesterday never happened.

Then my phone rings. And rings again. And buzzes with three texts in rapid succession.

"Popular this morning," Jasper observes when I try to check my messages while jugglin' a serving platter.

Hazel. I swipe to read her message as I walk back to the kitchen.

Festival booth layout changed. You'll be near the stage. Also need supply list.

I start to type a response, and the phone buzzes again. My blood pressure goes up about ten points. The serving plates clatter into the sink.

"Everything all right?" Lily asks.

I pocket the phone. "Fine, just festival stuff." I slide bacon onto their plates and check the clock. Seven fifteen. The next batch of cinnamon rolls won't bake themselves.

I measure flour, leveling the cup with the back of a knife. My phone buzzes. Then again, and again.

"Christ." I check the screen. Coco wants to know whether Vivienne St. James would prefer a glitter protection charm or somethin' more subtle. How the bloody hell would I know?

I try to respond one-handed, and the flour bag tips over, sendin' a white cloud across the counter. I sneeze three times in quick succession.

"Bless you!" Lily calls from the dining room.

"Thanks," I call back while I try to salvage what I can of the flour situation.

I'm so distracted that I don't notice the time until the sharp smell of burnin' cinnamon and sugar hits my nose. I spin around to find the first batch of cinnamon rolls smokin' in the oven.

"No, no, no!" I yank open the oven door and wave away the

acrid cloud. The rolls are charred. Now they're just ashy little tragedies.

The smoke detector starts its shrill screamin' just as my phone rings again.

"Not bloody now!" I snap, grabbin' a dish towel to fan the smoke toward the window.

A creak from the hallway makes me freeze. The hairs on my arms stand up. It's the same sound I heard last night, right before the ghosts appeared. I wait, dish towel suspended mid-air, half-expectin' a ghost to pop out of the oven with a burnt cinnamon roll in its hand.

Nothin'.

"Is everything all right in there?" Jasper calls. "Smells like you're burning the place down. Do we need to evacuate? Call 9-1-1?"

"Just a small mishap!" I yell back, tossin' the ruined rolls into the trash. "Everythin's under control!"

The burnt pan clatters into the sink. My phone buzzes again, and I'm tempted to throw it in the trash.

I'm scrapin' burnt sugar from the pan when Dex floats in, his crisp black shirt huggin' muscular arms that have carried me twice now. And boy, do his jeans highlight and hug all the important bits. I don't even bother hidin' the fact that I'm checkin' out his assets. Is this what flirtin' with death looks like?

"Good morning," he says, voice smooth and formal.

"Mornin'," I manage, suddenly aware of my flour-streaked appearance and wild hair. "Sleep well? Or do you even sleep? Is that a thing Death does?"

"Occasionally," he replies. "You seem distressed."

"What gave it away? The smoke or the alarm accompanied by a general air of panic?"

His mouth twitches. "A combination of factors." He steps into the kitchen, and the temperature drops another few degrees. "Perhaps I could assist?"

I blink at him. "Ya want to help? Think you're ready for domestic chaos, do ya?"

"I will admit, I find myself curious about such activities." He says it like he's admittin' to a strange new fetish. "Your morning routine appears complex."

"Well." I look around at the half-finished disasters litterin' my kitchen. "If ya really want to help, ya could start a fresh batch of cinnamon roll dough while I deal with this mess."

I hand him the recipe card, and he studies it like he's about to be tested on it. I place flour, sugar, cinnamon, milk, eggs, and butter in front of him, then help him measure everythin' into the mixin' bowl.

"The texture should be smooth and stretchy. Let that mix for roughly five minutes. I'll be right back."

He stands over the mixer, hands on his hips, completely at the mercy of a five-minute timer. He's so committed, I could kiss him for it. "This process requires more attention than I anticipated."

My phone rings again, shatterin' the moment. I groan and answer, tuckin' it between my ear and shoulder while I scrub the pan.

"Mina! Did you get my texts about the booth layout?" Hazel's voice is far too chipper for this hour.

"Yes, and the ones about the supplies, and the costume, and the—" A crash from the back porch cuts me off. "Bloody hell. I need to call ya back."

I race to the back of the house. The screen door hangs sideways, ripped from its top hinges. A gust of wind must have caught it. Just perfect.

"Add it to the list." I readjust the door and lock it in place before the wind sends it twirlin' into town.

When I return to the kitchen, Dex studies the mixin' bowl. "The consistency appears adequate."

But then he tries to stick a finger in the bowl to test the dough.

"Careful!" I pull his hand back. "That thing will break your finger."

He holds his hand out in front of him and flexes his digits.

"Thanks for the help." I pat him on the back and grab my phone to call Blake.

"Blake Carter," he answers on the third ring.

"It's Mina. My back screen door just shit the bed. Any chance someone could swing by to fix it today?" I catch my reflection in the window and wipe a streak of flour off my cheek. "I've got the Vampire Wives checkin' in soon and—"

"I got you." A nail gun fires in the background. "I'll send Leo over as soon as he finishes up at the Anderson place. Probably within the hour."

I lean against the counter, one eye on Dex. "You're a lifesaver."

"No problem. How are things otherwise? Any more unusual visitors?"

Oh, so Hazel told him about the ghosts. Should've figured. Those two don't keep secrets from each other.

"Nope. It's fine." I glance at Dex, who sprinkles cinnamon and sugar over the rolled-out dough like it's an art project. "Just busy. Thanks for sendin' Leo."

I hang up and lean against the counter, takin' a moment to breathe. I watch Dex roll the dough. I know this man—or whatever he is—was sent here to collect me, yet here he stands helpin' me make cinnamon rolls instead. He's so patient and unhurried, like he has all the time in the world.

If only I did.

The lump in my throat rises. I press my fingers to the cool countertop and blink hard. I can't think about that right now.

A floorboard creaks in the empty hallway, and I freeze again.

"The spirits seem to be growing more active, even after my banishment," Dex observes, not lookin' up from his work.

"Should I be worried?" Because I'm not. When did I become at one with a potential poltergeist infestation?

"It seems harmless, but who can say?" He slices through the

dough, usin' his fingers to measure between each slice. "I still don't fully understand what draws them to you."

I bat my eyes at him. "My shinin' smile and winnin' personality, maybe?"

"No." His response comes too quickly, and I don't know if I should be offended.

"Would I be able to help them? The spirits, I mean?"

He shrugs. "That I don't know. My presence may play a role. I haven't ruled that out. But I have walked beside the dying for millennia and never witnessed this. It's the fact that you can interact with them that perplexes me."

Voices waft in through the parlor. I step into the hallway. Coco bursts in, followed by La'Tasha and her big bag of magic.

"Hazel said you're low-key stressed, so we're here to save the day!" Coco strikes a superhero pose. Her oversized lime-green sweater flaps like a cape. "Mira, la salvación has arrived!"

"Everything okay here?" La'Tasha asks, leanin' in for a hug.

"Barely. And would offerin' salvation just be a thin excuse for gettin' front-row seats to the Vampire Wives' arrival?"

La'Tasha at least has the decency to look embarrassed. "We really are here to help. The gawking is just a bonus."

"Uh-huh. Well, if you're serious about helpin', there are welcome baskets that need assemblin' in the dining room."

"On it!" Coco drifts to the window overlookin' the front garden instead. "The flowers look a little sad. Like, actually tragic. Mind if I perk them up?"

"If you think you can save them, be my guest."

She dances out the door in a blur of mismatched socks and chunky boots. I glance out in time to catch her revivin' an entire bed of marigolds.

"She's getting better at that." La'Tasha steps in beside me. "Last month she tried to revive Mrs. Peterson's pink roses and turned them all blue instead."

"As long as she doesn't turn my garden into somethin' from

a horror book, I'm grateful for the help." I grab my cleanin' supplies and move. La'Tasha falls into step behind me.

She peeks around the corner and eyes Dex. "Hazel mentioned you have a new guest. Is that him? She said he's a writer?"

"Yes. Dex Grimm. He writes ghost stories." I move away from the kitchen, hopin' she'll follow. She can't get near Dex. If anyone will be able to figure out who—or what—he is, it's her, and I'm not ready for those questions. Not yet.

"Ghost stories, huh?" Her voice lilts with curiosity. "Cute booty. Nice hair. I think you need to get you some of that."

She winks, and my face turns as red as my hair. "You are incorrigible." I busy myself by wipin' imaginary dust specks from the fireplace mantel.

It's not like I haven't noticed those long, muscular legs and that tight little butt. But are they even real? Isn't the Grim Reaper supposed to be a tall skeleton in a robe? Does he even have . . . parts?

La'Tasha's posture shifts suddenly. "Mina." Her voice has a suspicious edge. "What's going on in this house?"

I straighten. "Nothin', love. Same old restless house it's always been."

She closes her eyes. Her hand finds her chest like it's lookin' for somethin' to hold onto. Great. She's in the zone.

"No, there's something here that hasn't been before." She moves toward the kitchen. "It's like it's trying to suck all my joy straight out of my ass."

She pulls out a small bundle of herbs from her bag. "Mind if I do a quick cleanse? Just to clear out the bad shit before your celebrities arrive."

I hesitate. Last thing I need is for her to wake the ghosts and pull them back in. But maybe a cleanse would help keep them away?

"Sure, knock yourself out." I gesture vaguely at the space around us. "Just don't set off the smoke detectors. They're sensitive after this mornin's cinnamon roll massacre."

She lights a bundle of herbs and makes her way through the sitting room. I pretend to pull somethin' up on my laptop, keepin' one eye open for rogue ghosts. She disappears down the hallway that leads to the two first-floor guest rooms. No ghosts have jumped out to call her names, so I call that a win. She returns ten minutes later, still fully intact. But when she reaches the door to the basement, she staggers backward.

"What in the actual hell?" She rolls her amethyst pendant between her fingers. "There's something here that feels like concrete. It keeps pushing me away. What are you hiding down there?"

Oh, god. I don't have time for whatever ghost mob is tryin' to keep her out of the basement. "Why don't ya focus on the second-floor rooms? Where the wives will be stayin'. That's more important anyway."

She shakes her head. "We need to take care of whatever just tried to shove my ass out the door."

Before I can respond, Coco bounces back inside. "Garden's all glamoured up! Those flowers will stay perfect for at least a week now."

She glances at Dex over my shoulder and then leans in conspiratorially. "So, is that the mysterious writer guy? What's his deal? Is he single? Does he have a type, and is it maybe witches with top-tier magic and questionable fashion sense? Asking for a friend, obvio."

"He's not your type," I say firmly.

"¿Perdona? Excuse you! I do not discriminate based on looks, gender, race, or magical species. Everyone is my type, literal. I'm an equal opportunity flirt!"

"Trust me on this one." I catch La'Tasha's raised eyebrow as she walks by. "Plus, I'm older, so I get first dibs."

Coco pouts but quickly rebounds. "Fine, keep your sexy writer to yourself. Oh, but speaking of sexy—" she gestures dramatically at my flour-streaked jeans and faded T-shirt. "Ay, por favor . . . this is not it. We need to get you camera-ready, chica! The Vampire Wives will be here in two hours, and you cannot go on TV looking like a literal jump scare!"

La'Tasha's hand is at her throat, worryin' her amethyst pendant. "Coco's right about the makeover, but wrong about the timing. That clock stopped working. They'll be here in an hour."

"What?" I check my watch in panic. She's right. The stupid grandfather clock stopped workin' again.

La'Tasha tucks her bundle of herbs into her bag, but her eyes never leave the direction of the kitchen. "I don't think that cleanse did a damn thing."

The temperature in the foyer fluctuates briefly. The lights flicker in the hallway, and finally the sitting room. It feels like somethin' large just moved in.

La'Tasha grabs my arm. "Did you feel that?" Her frigid fingers pull goose bumps out of me.

"Oh that? That was . . . it was just—"

"Oye, chicas, we ain't got time for this mierda rara." Coco grabs my other arm. "Right now, Operation Hot Innkeeper needs to start! I'm thinking a mix of neon and earth tones."

Before I can protest, I find myself bein' marched down the hallway to my bedroom. La'Tasha and Coco flank me like style-obsessed kidnappers.

"I don't need a makeover," I argue as Coco flings open my closet. "I need to finish the welcome baskets and check the dining room setup and—"

La'Tasha guides me to the chair at the vanity. "Girl, please. We'll handle all that with a little magic. You're the face of this B&B, and you need to look the part when cameras are rolling." She points a makeup brush at Coco. "And no neon. It's not 1986."

I'm about to argue further when Coco lets out a triumphant "Aha!" and pulls out a silky blouse I'd forgotten I owned. It's emerald green. Delicate buttons. A splurge from two years ago that I've worn exactly once.

"This with your dark jeans. And these boots." She tosses the items onto my bed. "It's giving polished but low-key, you know? Like you literally didn't even try."

"And your hair needs to come down." La'Tasha pulls my elastic free. My red waves tumble loose around my shoulders. "Coco, can you do that wave-enhancing charm? The one you did for her during the summer solstice party?"

Coco wiggles her fingers eagerly. "On it."

Twenty minutes later, I barely recognize myself in the mirror. My hair falls in soft waves that somehow look effortlessly tousled rather than bed-head messy. My eyes are brighter. My skin glows. I look good. Like the real me. Maybe I should ask them if there's some sort of glamour pill they can give me so I can at least exit this world lookin' like a semblance of my old self.

"Magic?" I ask.

"Not a bit. You're already hot A.F. You just don't realize it." Coco winks. "The base was already there, I just fixed the vibe. Digo, look at the material!"

La'Tasha stands back, admirin' their handiwork. "Perfect. Now you'll look amazing when you're in the background of all our selfies with Vivienne St. James and Ayana Bakari."

"So that was your real agenda!" I point a finger at them. "I knew you two hussies were only here for the celebrities."

"No, mami, we love you." Coco perches on the edge of my bed, eyes bright with excitement. "We're just really excited to meet the ladies. Don't you know we have weekly watch parties at La'Tasha's house with Calvin and Leo?"

I laugh. "Leo joins in, too?"

"They were Leo's idea," La'Tasha says. "He's more obsessed than any of us."

"He's mad crushing on Vivienne. Oh, I can't wait to meet her. And Zara and Ayana and Caprice."

"Don't forget Dahlia. She'd never forgive you." La'Tasha

points an eyebrow pencil at her.

Coco smacks her hand to her forehead. "Ah! I always forget about her."

"What's Dahlia like?" I ask, tryin' to get a feel for the cast I know nothin' about. I did a little research, but Dahlia is the least mentioned in articles online.

"Oh, she's the mysterious one," Coco explains. "Always watching, always listening. She never starts the bochinche, but somehow she's always there when it drops. Like she has a radar for when someone's about to have a breakdown and she's just there for the tea and the vibes."

"Very observant," La'Tasha agrees. "And very skilled at deflection. She routes the drama away from her anytime someone calls her out for keeping too many secrets."

Why did she look at me when she said that?

"What about you, Mina?" Coco turns to me. "Who's your favorite?"

"I, uh, haven't really watched much of the show," I admit.

They both gasp in exaggerated horror.

"¿Cómo que you don't watch it? And you're about to host them?" Coco asks, her hands flyin' up in drama. "Literal, that's actually a crime."

"I've been a little busy runnin' a business." I check my watch again. "Speakin' of which, we've got about thirty minutes before they arrive, and I still haven't finished those welcome baskets."

"I told you, we've got it covered." La'Tasha stands. "You just focus on looking calm and collected when the cameras start rolling."

"Calm and collected. Right." Easy for her to say when she's not the one with a house full of ghosts, and a tumor the size of a golf ball invadin' her brain.

As we head to the parlor, La'Tasha pulls me aside, lowerin' her voice. "Things aren't right in this place. What aren't you telling me?" She studies my face when I don't answer. "Are you sure you're okay?"

I could tell her. About the tumor. About what Dex said about the veil. But it's too much to deal with right now. My guests will be here soon, and I need to be on point.

"Everything's fine," I lie. "Just pre-arrival nerves."

I know she's not convinced, but before she can press further, Coco calls from the kitchen.

"Oye, Mina! Where do you keep your ribbon for the welcome baskets?"

"Second drawer by the sink," I call back.

La'Tasha squeezes my arm. "We're here for you, babe. Whatever you need."

I pat her hand, then turn to go.

"And Mina? Whatever that energy is in the basement? Be careful."

I smile and shrug. "I'm sure it's all goin' to be fine. It's all manageable."

And then the front door begins openin' and closin' on its own.

Maybe not so manageable.

THE REAL VAMPIRE WIVES OF OBSIDIAN HILLS

Episode 8: "Welcome to Moonridge"
EXT. MOONRIDGE MAIN STREET - LATE MORNING
A black luxury SUV convoy cruises slowly down the quaint main street. Through the windows, we see locals stopping to stare and point. Some hold up phones to record.
INT. SUV #1 - CONTINUOUS
VIVIENNE sits in the passenger seat while CAPRICE and ZARA are in the back. CAPRICE waves enthusiastically through the tinted windows.
CAPRICE: *(waving)* Oh my God, they're all staring! Do you think they recognize us? I feel like a celebrity!
VIVIENNE: *(not looking up from her phone)* Caprice, you are on a reality show. Technically, you are a celebrity.
ZARA: *(looking out thoughtfully)* The energy here is incredible. I can feel it humming through the earth. Mortimer's getting all twitchy.
(Mortimer squeaks from his travel carrier)
CUT TO: TALKING HEAD
CAPRICE: *(gushing)* I've never been somewhere where people actually got excited to see us! Back in Obsidian Hills, everyone's so used to seeing us they couldn't care less when we make an appearance, but here? I feel like a rock star!
CUT BACK TO: SUV #2
DAHLIA sits elegantly in the passenger seat while AYANA lounges in the back.
AYANA: *(chuckling)* Look at these people. You'd think they'd never seen a vampire before.
DAHLIA: *(mysteriously)* Perhaps they haven't. Not like us, anyway.
AYANA: *(raising an eyebrow)* Dahlia, honey, you're being more cryptic than usual, and that's saying something.
CUT TO: TALKING HEAD
AYANA: *(to camera)* Now, I've been around for three centuries, and I can smell a setup from a mile away. Dahlia's got something brewing,

and it's bigger than just a cute fall festival trip. *(wipes the edges of her mouth)* But hey, I'm here for the entertainment.

CUT TO: EXT. MOONRIDGE BED & BREAKFAST

The SUVs pull up to a charming Victorian mansion with a sign reading "Moonridge Bed & Breakfast." The front porch is decorated with autumn wreaths and pumpkins.

INT. SUV #1 - CONTINUOUS

VIVIENNE: *(looking at the B&B)* Well, it's . . . quaint.

CAPRICE: *(practically bouncing)* It's so cute! It looks like a movie set! Do you think it's haunted? Please tell me it's haunted!

ZARA: *(closing her eyes and breathing deeply)* Oh wow. The spiritual energy here is off the charts. This place has serious history.

CUT TO: TALKING HEAD

VIVIENNE: *(adjusting her designer scarf)* Listen, I appreciate charming New England architecture as much as the next person, but I'm going through a divorce from a vampire lord. I need thread counts above 800 and room service that doesn't judge my 3 AM blood bag orders.

CUT TO: EXT. B&B FRONT PORCH - CONTINUOUS

The women emerge from the SUVs in full glamour - designer luggage, perfect hair, dramatic sunglasses. MINA CARTWRIGHT appears on the front porch, looking slightly overwhelmed but welcoming.

MINA: *(nervously cheerful)* Welcome to Moonridge Bed & Breakfast! You must be the . . . uh . . . the Vampire Wives?

FADE OUT.

END SCENE

CHAPTER SEVEN

Mina

The first sign the Vampire Wives have arrived isn't the matchin' black SUVs crawlin' up my drive. It's the silence. Coco and La'Tasha have been planted at the front window for twenty solid minutes, yappin' like they're bein' paid for it, and then they just stop, mid-sentence, the pair of them, eyes gone wide. Then Coco lets out a squeal that could crack glass.

"They're here!"

I smooth down my silk blouse and take one last look in the mirror. The girls were right. I look camera-ready. Like someone who should be in front of a camera instead of stuffed in a closet away from the public eye. I wipe a smudge of lipstick off the corner of my mouth, then turn and reach for the doorknob.

"Remember," I hiss to Coco and La'Tasha, "you're here to help, not fangirl."

"Of course," La'Tasha says, applyin' another layer of lip gloss.

Coco gives me a military salute. "Absolutely."

I take a deep breath and open the front door just as a harried-lookin' man with a headset and clipboard charges up the steps.

"Kevin Morse, production manager." He doesn't offer a hand

and barely looks me in the eye. "Where's your loading entrance for equipment? Are those steps secure enough for our gear? We'll need to set up lighting in the main areas."

"Nice to—" I begin, but he's already off and yappin' at some-one on his headset.

"First wave ready for entrance shots. Cue Vivienne."

The black SUV door swings open, and a slim leg emerges, endin' in a stiletto that probably costs more than my last five medical bills. The leg is followed by Vivienne St. James herself, risin' from the SUV like Amphitrite from the sea. That is, if Amphitrite wore a blood-red silk blouse and had jet-black hair that cascaded over one shoulder in perfect waves.

"This must be the charming B&B Dahlia wouldn't stop talking about." She glides toward me with unnatural grace. Her eyes are indeed violet—or maroon, dependin' on how the light hits them—and they seem to look through me rather than at me. "You must be the owner."

"Mina Cartwright." I extend my hand. Her grip is so cool and smooth it feels like touchin' marble. "Welcome to Moonridge."

"Quaint." Her eyes rake over the porch. "Very authentic."

I weigh whether or not to be insulted when the second SUV door thuds open. A tiny woman topped with a shock of bubble-gum-pink hair steps out. She hugs a bedazzled pet carrier to her chest like it's a holy relic. Is this Zara?

"Mortimer needs his special feeding room prepared!" She doesn't seem to be addressin' any one specific person. "He's very sensitive to new environments."

"You can't seriously expect us to accommodate your emo-tional support bat," snaps an Asian woman as she climbs out of the limo. She flips her waist-length black hair over her shoulder and removes a blocky pair of sunglasses that remind me of the wrap-around cataract glasses my gran used to wear.

"Back off, Caprice. You have no idea what he needs to per-form optimally as my familiar." Zara clutches the bat carrier to her chest.

"But I do have a say in your constant demands. They're annoying. We're always waiting on you and your stupid bat."

Does all of this really require a screamin' match in my driveway?

Kevin, the producer, subtly angles a camera toward the brewin' argument. "Perfect, ladies. Keep that tension going."

The front yard fills with people unloadin' equipment: cameras, lights, boom mics, cases of mysterious technical gear. Three more crew members rush past me into the house without so much as a nod.

"Wait, you can't just—" I protest, but they're already settin' up in my parlor.

An impossibly tall Black woman approaches. So tall, I have to tip my head back to find her face. Dark umber skin, green eyes that don't catch the light so much as produce it. She holds out her hand. I take it. "Ayana Bakari. Ignore the theatrics. It's all for the cameras." Her grip is firm, businesslike. "Any chance there's a bar? The travel always puts Caprice on edge. Give her some alcohol, and she'll stop complaining."

"I have wine in the dining room," I offer. "And a selection of spirits."

She smiles, revealin' perfect teeth and two very sharp canines. "How appropriate."

Those teeth looked real. But if they are real vampires, how are they able to walk in the sun? I'm so confused.

The last vampire to approach doesn't just look at the B&B, she maps it.

"Dahlia Devine," she says. Her voice has this expensive, polished edge that makes me feel like an uneducated peasant. "The house is gorgeous. Oh, and the energy here . . . interesting."

"Total garbage!" someone yells from the porch. I turn to see a cameraman gesturing wildly. "Bad angle. We need to run the arrivals again, from the top!"

"The hell we are," Vivienne snaps. "I've already done my entrance. I'm not getting back in that car."

I show them to the foyer and feel it immediately. That drop in temperature, sharp and certain as a door slammin' shut. The crew slows around me, heads turnin', tryin' to figure where it's comin' from. Dex is close. That's the answer and the problem.

"Is the AC on?" one of them asks. "The temperature just took a nosedive."

I open my mouth to tell a lie when a horn beeps. I open the door to see Leo's cherry-red convertible pulling into the side driveway. He hops out and grabs his toolbox from the backseat, then stumbles forward with a bright smile on his face, oblivious to the shitstorm he's about to walk into.

"Blake said you had a door emergency?"

"You're a lifesaver," I breathe. "The back screen door is—"

"Well, hello there."

I don't even have to turn around; the scent of expensive perfume with a hint of lilies tells me Vivienne has found us. Leo stares at her with the blank, glazed expression of a man who just saw a UFO swipe his dog from his backyard.

"And who might this be?" Vivienne asks. She poses even though there isn't a camera in sight. He drops his toolbox and holds out a hand. "Uh, Leo Morales. Yeah. Hi. Big fan." His olive skin goes a shade pinker. "I'm gonna fix a door."

"How fortunate for us." Vivienne's eyes travel down to his tool belt and back up, slow and deliberate. "I've always admired a man who knows how to fix things."

Leo makes a noise that sounds like a dyin' radiator. He gestures vaguely toward the kitchen, his boots scuffin' the wood as he tries to remember how to walk.

"It's the back door." I guide him away before he has a right heart attack.

He waits until we're three steps into the kitchen before he finds his voice. "Wow. I can't believe that was—"

"Vivienne St. James," I finish for him. "Try to keep your tongue off the floor, or you'll trip over it."

He drops his toolbox, and the scatterin' of tools across the kitchen floor almost rattles the already fragile bones out of my skin.

I walk back to the front of the house, and the parlor stops me cold. Lights on stands throw harsh shadows up the walls, cables snake across my antique rugs, and some man with a clipboard is shovin' my furniture around like it's nothin'. I spent weeks on this room. Weeks. He undid it in two minutes without so much as a word to me.

"Excuse me, ya can't just move things without askin'," I protest.

"We need to create a better frame for the confessional shots," he explains without lookin' up.

Deep breath. This is temporary. The money will keep the B&B afloat for months. I can survive a few days of chaos.

Or so I tell myself.

But then the temperature drops again, and a translucent woman drifts through the room, beaded dress shimmerin' in the camera lights. She pauses beside the cameraman. My heart lurches. Not now.

The spirit looks up at me, head tilted. "Such interesting contraptions," she says in a voice like a curious child. "Whatever are they for?"

"Modern photography," I say out the side of my mouth. I really hope I don't look like I'm talkin' to myself. "Very borin'. Why don't ya go visit the garden instead?"

"The cell signal is garbage! What's the Wi-Fi?" one of the tech crew yells.

I keep one eye on the stray ghost while I hand him a card with the password printed on it.

"The lighting in this bathroom is homicidal!" Caprice's shriek pins me to the floor.

Homicidal? The woman hasn't even unpacked her toiletry bag, and she's already got opinions about the bulb wattage. I drag a breath through my nose and count to three, which is two more than normal when I'm this rattled.

I start toward the stairs when Zara's pink hair tumbles over the railin'. She scrunches her face. "I really wanted a room that faces the west so I can watch the sunset."

Two complaints. Nine seconds. And this isn't likely to happen because Vivienne has the west-facin' room. I suppose I could tell Caprice to ask her if they can switch and give them something else to fight about on camera.

The 1920s ghost claps her hands to her chest. "Oh, houseguests! How delightful. I haven't had proper company in ages."

"No!" But she's already floatin' toward the stairs. Fuckin' hell. Now is not the time for a ghost to pop in. I wonder whether homelessness has got any decent upsides I've been overlookin'. I know I need the money, but these women might cost me my sanity.

"Mina." Dex has appeared beside me without a sound. "You appear overwhelmed."

"What gave it away?" I gesture wildly at the chaos. "The vampire diva squad? The film crew dismantlin' my parlor? Or the 1920s ghost who just went upstairs to 'welcome' our guests?"

He raises an eyebrow and gazes toward the staircase. "Oh. Yes. Margot Ashford. She died in the influenza epidemic of 1920. We had a long conversation this morning."

"Can you—?"

"I'll handle it." But instead of immediately dashin' up the stairs, he picks up a suitcase that's been abandoned in the foyer and carries it with him.

A clipboard-clutchin' crew member steps in front of Dex. "Hey, what are you—"

Dex pivots around him without breakin' stride. "Helping Ms. Cartwright with the luggage. The sooner they're settled, the sooner filming can proceed."

I move to follow when the same tech guy from earlier approaches. "Hey, can you help us find the Wi-Fi password? No one seems to know where it is."

Oh, bloody hell. I keep my eyes from rollin' out of my skull and make my face do what it's supposed to do. "It's on the card in your hand." He looks at it like he's never seen it before, even though he's been carryin' it around for the last five minutes. "And we've also placed little blue cards in each room. Check the nightstands."

I turn, and Jasper is there, pinched frown coverin' his face.

"The cold spot is back. How am I supposed to nap when I'm shivering so bad my false teeth nearly fall out?"

"Oh, Jasper. I'm sorry. Let me see if I can get someone—"

"I'll take a look." Dex is already down the stairs, his gaze fixed on a point just above Jasper's head. "Probably just a drafty window frame."

Jasper lets out a sharp, dry laugh. "Drafts don't make the air ripple, kid."

Poor things. The thought of him and Lily catchin' pneumonia in this drafty old place tightens my chest, and the hollow clack-drag, clack-drag of his cane through the silence doesn't help. Dex draws nearer. His voice thins to somethin' I feel more than hear. "Likely another ghost," he says.

I lean back against the banister and let out a long, slow exhale. "How many more?"

Dex shakes his head. "That is what concerns me. I don't know. I still haven't decided if they're drawn to you or to me."

La'Tasha overhears the last part. "What do you mean? Did you say ghosts? Why are they drawn to you?"

Dex hesitates. I can practically see him weighin' how much to reveal. "I'm sensitive to supernatural phenomena," he says carefully. "It's what drew me to writing ghost stories, but I've found the more I've tapped into it, the more I attract spirits."

"Interesting." She dips an eyebrow and studies him.

But I have to hand it to the man. For someone who deals mainly with the dead, he has a knack for charmin' humans. He's like an air traffic controller. He says one quiet word to Kevin, and the shoutin' stops, and the next thing ya know, the wives have disappeared into their rooms without a peep.

And every time a camera lens swings toward a flickerin' shadow or a door driftin' shut on its own, Dex is there like a shield between the ghosts and the film crew, diffusin' the weirdness before it ends up broadcast to the entire country.

Vivienne calls for Leo again—somethin' about the 'atmospheric pressure' in her suite—and I catch a tiny, sharp tug at the corner of Dex's mouth as he studies them. It's the first time he's looked like a person and not a bodyguard.

"Somethin' funny?" I ask.

"Mortal courtship is . . . educational." He doesn't take his eyes off them.

"Educational?"

"I'm just noticing the patterns." His voice drops an octave. "You humans spend so much energy talking around the one thing you actually want."

"It's not always easy to say," I shrug. "The fear of rejection is too great, I suppose. Even for pretty people."

"Interesting." His eyes lock onto mine. "I guess I know the feeling."

My heart stutter-steps, but before I can ask what he means, a high-pitched scream of genuine terror echoes from upstairs.

La'Tasha snaps her head in the direction of the sound. "That sounded like Caprice."

We take the stairs fast, Dex first, me laggin' behind. Caprice is against the wall outside her room, pointin' at the door. Cripes. She spotted one of them. Which means everyone in the world will know if the cameras roll before we can choke this.

"There's a woman in my bathroom!" she gasps. "A dead woman! In a flapper dress! She asked if I needed help with my 'rouge'! What the hell is rouge?"

Behind her, through the open bathroom door, I catch a glimpse of Margot Ashford havin' a go at applyin' lipstick in the mirror.

"I thought ya handled that," I mutter to Dex.

"She's stubborn," he admits grimly.

The cameraman who followed us upstairs raises his camera, but Dex smoothly steps into his line of sight.

"Perhaps we should give Ms. Le Vein some space," he suggests. "Stress can trigger hallucinations."

"Hallucinations?" Caprice sputters. "I know what I saw!"

"Of course you do," Dex soothes. "Old houses can play tricks on tired minds. Why don't you rest while we investigate?"

Dex gets the cameraman movin', one hand on the guy's shoulder, voice low and easy, steerin' him toward the far end of the hall. The rest of the crew follows without bein' told. I take the gap and step into Caprice's room.

"Ya can't be here," I tell the ghost. "Not with cameras around."

Margot turns from the mirror, lookin' hurt. "But she seems so lonely, dear. All that paint on her face, and still she's not happy. I thought I might help. She looks like she could use a friend. I heard those other catty women saying nasty things about her."

"That's just what they do. And I appreciate your attempt at kindness, but ya need to go. Now."

"Oh, very well," Margot sighs dramatically. "Modern women are so difficult to understand. In my day, we were better with our words."

She fades slow, like she's givin' me a chance to change my mind. I don't. But I watch until the last bead disappears. At least she meant well. I exit the bathroom to find Dex waitin' in the hallway.

"Resolved?" he asks.

"For now. But how many more ghosts are goin' to show up? At this rate, the entire house'll be full of 'em by midnight."

"That," Dex says, "is exactly what I'm afraid of."

By mid-afternoon, my left eye's gone rogue, twitchin' every few seconds like it's tryin' to send a distress signal. My feet are murderin' me. I've told Caprice twice now that witches can't just manifest bigger mirrors, but at least Zara's bat has imported mineral water. I don't even want to know why. I duck into the pantry. I need thirty seconds where nobody's talkin' at me. The door clicks shut. I lean against the shelves, eyes closed. Just breathe. In through the—

The pantry door swings open.

"There you are!" Hazel looks far too put-together for the supernatural circus my life has become. "I've been texting you for an hour."

"Sorry." I gesture vaguely at the madness beyond the pantry. "I needed a minute where I didn't have to console needy reality TV vampires and helpless men with cameras who can't seem to follow directions or find things that are sittin' right in front of them."

"Typical men." Hazel glances over her shoulder for pryin' eyes, then slips into the pantry, shieldin' us from the chaos outside. She fishes a small blue bottle from her bag. "Drink this."

I eye the bottle suspiciously. "What is it?"

"Calming potion. Exactly what you need to chill your tits. By the looks of things, you need it. I added extra chamomile and a touch of valerian. You can thank me later."

"I don't need a potion. I need a time machine." But I take the bottle anyway and uncork it with a sigh. The liquid tastes like honey and lavender, with an undertone of somethin' earthy. Warmth spreads from my throat to my chest, then outward to my limbs. It's like the full body calm after a really good joint but without the skunk smell.

"Better?" Hazel asks.

I nod, surprised to find that my shoulders have dropped about three inches from their position near my ears. "Thanks."

"Look, I know you're stressed out. You're trying to deal with ghosts and all this chaos, without any staff. You need help," she says quietly.

I lean my head on the shelf behind me. "Yeah. Not exactly how I planned to spend my October, but here we are."

She lowers her voice. "Look, I gotta be honest. Things around town are whacked. Blake and I have been reinforcing the barriers, but they don't want to hold. It's like something wants in. Or out. I'm not sure which is worse."

A fire poker makes its way up my throat.

"And there's something else," Hazel continues, her voice droppin' again. "That man, Dex. He's not okay, Mina. Something's wrong with him."

My heart becomes a fist, clenching and barely releasing. "What do ya mean?"

"I can't put my finger on it. But when I touched his hand . . ." She shakes her head. "I felt very cold, but also very empty. Like standing at the edge of a big-ass black hole."

I keep my expression carefully neutral, though my pulse quickens. "He's just a writer, Hazel."

"No writer carries that kind of energy. And what's even weirder is that it felt familiar. It's been driving me crazy because I don't know where I could have felt that before. Or why."

I search for an explanation just as the pantry door opens again to reveal La'Tasha and Coco.

"Emergency witch meeting in the pantry?" Coco squeezes in beside us. "Cool."

Hazel keeps her eyes trained on me. "We're discussing the current situation."

"And my imminent nervous breakdown," I add.

La'Tasha folds her arms, joinin' us in the cramped space. "We've been talking. You can't handle all this alone, Mina. Not the dramatic vampires, and definitely not whatever is happening with the energy in this house."

"I've got it under control," I lie automatically.

All three women give me identical looks of disbelief.

"Right, then. I'm drownin', and I want to pull my hair out. Happy?"

"We want to help," Coco says. "For real this time, not just as an excuse to hang with the Vampire Wives."

"Coco," Hazel warns.

"Right, sorry. Focus." Coco straightens. "We were just thinking we can split shifts here. Help with the guests, take messages, run errands, provide entertainment. Oh! A talent show! What do you think mine—"

"Girl, chill." La'Tasha interrupts. "Nobody wants a talent show. We're going to work. The two of us can alternate mornings at the apothecary so one of us is always here while the other is at the store helping Hazel."

"I totally support this. And Blake's agreed to put Leo on call for any maintenance issues," Hazel finishes. "Just because you had to let your staff go to keep the lights on doesn't mean you have to do this alone."

I blink hard.

"I can't ask ya to do that," I protest weakly.

"You didn't ask. We offered." Her tone doesn't leave room for argument. "Besides, if the supernatural situation gets worse, you'll need magical backup."

Through the pantry door, we hear Vivienne's distinctive laugh, followed by what sounds like Leo's deeper chuckle. Coco wiggles her eyebrows. "And speaking of backup, looks like our resident goofy, awkward werewolf handyman is hitting it off with the vampire star."

La'Tasha rolls her eyes. "He's going to have masturbation material for years."

Coco shakes her head. "Not going to end well."

"Actually," Hazel says thoughtfully, "don't discourage it. We could use all the supernatural species cooperation we can get."

I take another deep breath. "Okay. I accept your help. All of it. But I'm payin' ya for your time."

"No money." Coco grins. "But unlimited access to your baking? Now we're talking."

"Deal." I push open the pantry door, ready to face the chaos again. This time with backup.

By nightfall, a strange sort of order's replaced the chaos. The Vampire Wives have retreated to their rooms to "prepare for confessionals," which apparently involves elaborate costume changes and ritual cocktails. The dining room belongs to the producers tonight. Laptops spread across two separate tables, footage runnin' on their screens while they talk over each other and eat. Papa Lupin's pizza boxes are stacked by the door. Any taller and the stack'll need a room of its own. I'll let it go. The money they're payin' me matters more than the mess.

The rest of the bottom floor's empty. Quiet. I make myself a cup of tea, standin' at the window while the last of the sunset turns the sky pink and purple. My heart rate drops a few hundred points.

I wrap my hands around the warm mug. A week ago, my biggest worry was bookin' enough rooms to make it through the winter. Now I'm fightin' off ghosts and managin' vampire celebrities. It's as if the script of my life was rewritten by a toddler.

"What in blazes am I doin'?" I whisper into my tea.

"A great job," comes a voice from the doorway.

I turn to find Dex. He watches me with dark eyes that almost unsettle me. He's wearin' a gray sweater now, not the black shirt from before. It's a small change, but it works against me. He looks like a very sexy man. Or man-like thing. And that's a problem for a dyin' and slightly horny me.

"How do ya do that?" I ask. "Appear without makin' any sound?"

"Practice." He moves in beside me. But there's tension in his movements now. "You seem troubled."

I sigh and gesture toward the chaos beyond the kitchen. "Reality TV crews. Vampire divas. Ghosts photobombin' cameras. And my best friend thinks you're hidin' somethin' significant."

His eyes close. "What did Ms. Thornton have to say?"

"That your 'energy signature' feels both familiar and dangerous. That touchin' your hand was like standin' at the edge of a black hole." My eyes stay glued to his face, but his expression is as nonexistent as his scent.

He rubs the back of his head. "You know why she feels that. Some people are more sensitive to otherworldly presences. Her reaction isn't entirely unexpected. You know what I am. She's likely not far behind."

"But why do ya act so strongly toward her? I noticed it yesterday at the library. She feels it, too."

He lifts a shoulder. "Some people have connections that cannot always be explained."

"That's not a proper answer."

"It's the only answer I can give you right now."

I don't know what any of this means, and he's not goin' to tell me. That much is already clear. He changes the subject, and I let him, because what else am I goin' to do?

"I'm concerned about something," he says. "And it's not just the increasing number of spirits. I've noticed fractures."

"Fractures?"

"In the barrier between worlds. Small tears that shouldn't exist." His jaw works like he's chewin' out what to say next. "The veil is dangerously weak, and it's not a natural shift. Something caused this. I'd bet it started long before I got here, which means the surge in ghost activity isn't just because of me. Something or someone else is involved."

The weight of my bones seems to triple. "What kind of somethin'?"

"I'm not sure yet. But whatever it is, it's old. Ancient. The magic is strong and doesn't feel like Moonridge's usual energy."

He meets my eyes.

"There's more." He takes my hand. He sighs like he's about to drop news I'm not goin' to like.

I brush his hand away and stand quickly. "I know what you're about to say. You've come to collect me. That's why you're here." My voice cracks. "But, please, Dex. I can't go now. The doctors said I have time—"

"No." he stands and places a hand on my shoulder. "I mean— yes, I do have to collect you eventually. But not this minute. That's not why I wanted to talk to you, even though we do need to have that conversation at some point."

I bury my face in my hands. Damn it. I can't deal with this right now.

He gently turns me toward him and wraps me in his arms. "Isn't this what humans do when they need comfort?"

Tension evaporates. I didn't know how badly I needed this. The closeness. The calm.

"What I was going to tell you," he says after a moment, "I was out in the garden. Listening to the whispers of the ghosts. They kept repeating your name. Over and over."

"But why?" I murmur against his chest.

"That day on the bridge. You had already crossed over. Your spirit asked for more time." His voice drops to barely a whisper. "So I gave it to you."

I squeeze my eyes shut. I don't want to think about that day. I was so lost then. So done with life. I'm not that person anymore.

"My suspicion," he continues, voice quieter now, "is that when you crossed over, even briefly, something changed. You brought something back with you. A thread, maybe. Some sort of connection. A bridge between worlds." He pauses. "I don't know how deep that connection goes, but I fear it's strengthening."

"You're sayin' I'm some kind of conduit?"

"Maybe? Look, none of this makes sense to me, but something is going on. The veil is much thinner than it should be, and the ghosts are migrating here in droves. If the veil gets any thinner . . . I'm afraid of what might happen."

I step away from him and go to the back porch. Air. That's what I need, air and a minute to let this land somewhere it won't split me open. I drop into the rockin' chair, and it starts doin' its thing, back and forth, back and forth, and the woodsmoke from somewhere down the block curls over the fence.

Dex leans against the porch and studies the backyard. "I'm worried that something evil has made its way to Moonridge. These fractures I'm sensing, they're not random. They form a pattern. It seems like someone is systematically weakening specific points in the veil."

"For what, though?"

"That I don't know."

I think of Mrs. Henderson findin' her way to my kitchen, of the Victorian ghosts who felt so at home here. What if it's not random? What if my near-death experience really did make me a conduit to the dead?

An owl calls. Shadows shift at the tree line.

"Mina." Dex offers me his hand. "We should go inside."

The shadows gather and thicken into unnatural shapes. Intentional. They don't approach. Don't retreat.

Testing the boundaries.

How long before they break through?

CHAPTER EIGHT

Dex

Pacing is a human habit, not something I do. Yet, here I am, wearing a path in the rug in front of my bed while the space seems to shrink around me.

The house hums, a constant nagging at my sternum. It knows just as well as I do that something isn't right. I place a hand against the window. "I know. I feel it, too."

I scan the garden below. Souls hungry enough to strip bones stalk the darkness at the edge of the forest line, waiting like wolves that haven't fed in far too long. And they're getting bolder.

The scythe vibrates within the cane. A shuffling. My head snaps toward the door. The energy expenditure is low but traceable, not entirely human. I open the door and step into the hallway.

Empty.

The old house creaks and settles around me, but beneath those familiar noises is a low rattling I can't quite place. I track it down the stairs, toward the ground floor, scythe straining against my palm like a dog pulling on a leash.

Someone stands frozen in the middle of the parlor, backlit by the moonlight pouring in through the large bay window. A crew member. The young man with the shaved head and piercings who was hauling camera equipment earlier, straining under barked orders and vampire wife demands. His body faces the wall, head lolling on his shoulders, dressed in only a T-shirt and boxer shorts. Everything reads as alive, except his energy radiates extreme cold, and frost patterns cling to his bare arms.

"Sir," I say quietly, not wanting to startle him.

No response.

The space above his head shimmers, and his head jerks back. His left arm and leg both lift, and he slowly pivots to face me on his right foot. Whatever that is above him is controlling him like a puppet. I place my hand on his wrist and push his arm down. The moment we touch, a rattled whisper fills my head. "The anchor is ready."

Images flood my mind. Moonlight glinting off blood-red water. A sigil burned deep into human flesh. Something rising from the dead.

I snap my hand back. No. Is it? I release my scythe and swipe it above the young man's head, snapping the strings that tether him. His head lolls forward and then snaps back, great, heaving breaths wracking his body as his soul snaps back into place. His eyes land on me, then the window, and then down at his feet. "How did I get down here?"

"I think you were sleepwalking." It's better than the truth. "You should return to your room."

I place a hand on his shoulder, sending warmth through him. He nods, his gaze drifting past me to the stairs. "Yeah. Sorry."

He shuffles away, and I track the familiar weight of his soul all the way to the third floor.

The soft clink of a spoon draws me toward the kitchen. Mina. I recognize her restlessness. She should be sleeping.

I enter the kitchen and find her standing at the counter, her back to me, red hair loose around her shoulders. She wears an oversized sweater and plaid pajama pants, her feet bare against the cold tile.

"Couldn't sleep?" I ask.

She startles, hand snapping to her chest. She spins to face me. "Christ almighty! Make some noise when you move, would ya?" She wags a finger at me. "That's it. I'm gettin' ya a belt with bells. You're like a cat, ya are."

"My apologies." I step fully into the kitchen. "I heard someone wandering around down here."

"That was probably me." She turns back to her tea, adding honey with unsteady hands.

I shake my head. "No. It was one of the crew members. Sleepwalking."

"Well, at least it wasn't another bloody ghost." She gestures toward the teapot. "Want some?"

I nod. Warmth is something I absorb rather than generate. This is one of the few ways it comes freely. "Please."

The scent of chamomile and honey arrives ahead of the cup she slides toward me.

"So." She leans against the counter. "Why are you awake at one in the mornin'? Wait. Do you even sleep?"

"Occasionally, I'll rest. When I choose to." I cradle the warm cup between my palms, the heat spreading through my hands and up my arms. "Tonight, however, there's too much activity."

"You're tellin' me." She shakes her head. "It's like someone stuck an electric probe up me arse and won't turn it off. I'm a jittery mess."

Her energy says otherwise. It reads like a sputtering candle trying to hold on, and she's been running at this frequency for days.

"Yes. The spiritual energy is unusually high."

"More ghosts comin'?"

"Possibly." I don't tell her about who I think was here. Not until I know for sure. "You should try to rest."

She laughs, a short, sharp sound. "Yeah, that's not happenin'. Every time I close my eyes, I feel like someone's watchin' me.

And not in a comfortin' guardian angel kind a way. More in a 'some ghost might bust through and kick my arse' way."

Her perception teases a laugh from me. I take a sip of tea.

"So what do we do?" she asks. "I don't think I can keep on like this. My nerves are shot."

Before I can answer, the sound of something shattering followed by a large thud cuts through our conversation. A scream follows. Mina is already moving, the teacup clattering against the table as we both turn toward the stairs.

I'm faster, my cane barely touching the floor as I take the steps two at a time, following the commotion to the east side of the house. The air grows colder with each step. Familiar. Something on the other side knows I've arrived.

"Which room?" Mina gasps behind me.

Another scream answers her question. The sound comes from the third door on the right. Caprice Le Vein's room. The light flickering beneath the door confirms what I already know. Something is in there with her.

I push the door open without knocking, and my breath clouds in front of my face. The room holds the texture of something dark—more than a ghost—that clawed its way from another realm. Caprice stands in the center of it, dark hair disheveled, silk pajamas askew, and I suspect she has no idea how close this deity came to harming her. Shards of glass, the remains of the ceiling light fixture, litter the floor around her. But that's not what has caused her panic.

Her phone lies on the bed, or what's left of it. The device has split open. The screen shattered, components melted and fused together as if it were pulled from a furnace. The tang of burnt electrical wiring reaches me through wisps of smoke rolling off the carcass.

"My followers!" Caprice gestures wildly at the still-smoldering phone. "I was live! Twenty thousand people were watching! And then it just—it just—exploded in my hand!" Her palm is angry red, covered in burn marks that seem to be healing themselves. Not severe, but definitely visible.

"Are ya hurt anywhere else?" Mina pushes past me, already in caretaker mode. "Let me see your hand."

But Caprice jerks away, still having a full meltdown. "Don't touch me! This is your fault! Your crappy old house and its faulty wiring could have killed me. Again."

The argument continues, but something more concerning than burnt fingers or broken glass pulls at my attention. The mist near the ceiling coils and shifts, tendrils reaching toward the women, then retreating, not at random, but in response, reading them. It has the same signature as what was controlling the young man downstairs.

I step into the center of the room, placing myself beneath the mist where the veil presses paper-light against the back of my hand.

Caprice looks at me, then up at the ceiling, eyes focusing on the invisible entity hovering above us.

"What is happening to my room?" she demands. "Is that smoke? Is there a fire?"

My cane is in the air before she finishes her question. "Power surge," I say. I direct a pulse upward through the scythe, dispersing the mist. "Old houses sometimes have electrical issues."

"The circuit probably overloaded," Mina adds. "Too many devices chargin' at once."

"But my phone—"

"We'll replace it," Mina promises. "First thing tomorrow."

Her reaction is curious to me. Are humans, or whatever Caprice is, attached to their electronics the way I'm attached to my scythe? Is it like her lifeforce? An extension of her? Her eyes keep darting to the ceiling where the mist is already reforming, but at least she's stopped wailing about her phone and her followers.

"You should sleep in another room tonight," I suggest.

After much drama and negotiation, we relocate Caprice to

the only other available room on this floor. She's still muttering about the light fixture as I hold the door open and wait for her to gather her theatrics long enough to walk through it. I close the door, blocking out the mist that continues to spread across the ceiling. The seal I placed is already fraying at the edges, and I don't know how long we have before whatever that was breaks through again.

"What was that misty thing hoverin' above the bed?" Mina whispers once we're alone in the hallway.

"Spiritual energy," I lie. "Probably from too many spirits trying to get through at once."

"So if we don't let the fuckers loose, they're just goin' to run around makin' all the electronics explode? Bloody brilliant."

I guide her down the stairs. "The B&B is becoming a spiritual lightning rod. This isn't just about ghosts anymore."

She stops at the bottom of the stairs, and her eyes meet mine. "Then what is it about?"

I shake my head. "I have my suspicions, but I can't say for sure. I think I'll explore Moonridge tonight. Map the extent of the damage to the veil."

"Now? In the middle of the night?"

"It's easier to map spiritual inconsistencies while humans sleep." I hesitate, then add, "Speaking of, you should try to rest."

She almost smiles. "Right. Like that's happenin' anytime soon."

We walk together to the front door and out onto the wrap-around porch.

She touches my arm when I start to leave. "Be careful."

The statement catches me off guard. In all my countless years, no one has ever said that to me.

I cover her hand with mine and offer a small smile. "I will."

***

The night sounds of rustling leaves settle around me as I walk Main Street alone. I tap my cane against the sidewalk, listening to the echo. It bounces back about a second later than it should. Everything I've found tonight is slightly off-center by just a breath. Not enough to be noticeable to the human eye, but enough to concern me.

I followed the breaks in the veil to Skipper Lake, Moonstone Circle, Amethyst Beach, and finally the falls. Nearly every corner of Moonridge glows with unnatural energy.

I stop at the corner of Elm and Main and press my cane into the ground. The town square feels heavy, the air thick. The fountain at its center bubbles with ordinary water, but the space above it ripples with the same distortion of reality that keeps popping up.

Another weak point.

The old church looms ahead, the graveyard beside it pulsing with faint red light. A shadow glides between the graves and across the ground like spilled oil, pausing at each grave marker before moving on. Searching. Hunting.

I stand very still, pulling myself slightly out of sync with the physical world, making myself undetectable. The shadow passes within feet of me. It reeks of sulfur and loam.

A scout.

Immense dread floods my body. The presence of this paranormal rodent only confirms my fears.

I follow it toward the public library, where it disappears into the bushes. A flicker of light behind frosted windows catches my eye. Who's inside the library at this hour?

I pull myself out of the physical plane once again and drift up the steps and then through the solid door. Penny Fisher hunches over a table surrounded by open books and scattered papers. Three candles form a triangle around a small crystal that glows red. Her lips move in whispered words as her fingers trace symbols in the air. Her attempts are clumsy but powerful.

Amateur magic playing with something she doesn't understand.

Enveloped in shadows, I move to the other side of the room as Penny draws a symbol on the table with chalk. Her hand shakes, smudging the lines. She curses under her breath, wipes it away, and starts again. The crystal before her pulses brighter with each attempt, responding to her frustration.

"Pull it together, Penny." She places both hands on the table and inhales. "You can do this."

I drift upward and study the books spread around her. Most are standard library texts on local history and folklore, but one immediately catches my attention. Leather cover soaked in the blood of the sacrificed, pages yellowed with age.

The Lost Testament of Holloway. The grimoire of the Concord Thirteen.

How did it get here? When the Concord was defeated in the early 1800s, the Bureau of Others collected this book and bound it with every type of binding spell they knew. It was locked away in a tomb where no one would ever find it. Even without a recharge, the binding spells should have held it for another hundred years. Maybe more.

Penny turns a page, revealing symbols that flash like warning signs.

Concord sigils.

Her eyes scan the pages with the casual interest of someone studying a basic recipe. She leans forward, her finger tracing a spiral pattern I recognize all too well. The Mark of Hollowing.

The same sigil I saw in my vision from the sleepwalking crew member.

Her untrained magic pulses outward with each word she sounds out. The crystal before her absorbs her energy, redirecting it into the patterns on the page.

Winds rush through the room, turning books and other small objects into projectiles. The candles die, plunging us into darkness save for the red-orange hue of the pulsing crystal.

Penny gasps, pushing back from the table.

The crystal fractures. An oily tendril snakes out of it, thickening as it rises. Faces push through the surface one after another, mouths torn open.

And then the shape stops morphing, settling on a single face that I haven't seen in centuries. Penny stands frozen, eyes wide with fear, as the oily face focuses on her, mouth stretched into a too-wide yawn.

I move without thinking. The disguised scythe crackles with energy as I sweep it in a short arc between Penny and the energy curling toward her.

Reality splits, just for a breath. The wisp recoils as if burned, its smoky tendrils curling back on themselves, face dissolving. With another flick of my cane, I open a tiny fissure in space, a doorway back to the void from which it came. The wisp struggles briefly, eyes focusing on me before it's sucked away.

The room drops into darkness, and Penny whips around. "Hello?" she calls, her voice shaking. "Is someone there?"

I remain motionless, cloaked in my non-human form, letting the shadows wrap around me. She squints into the dark, then fumbles for her phone, turning on its flashlight. The beam sweeps across the room, missing me by inches as I step further into the shadows. She gathers her books with trembling hands, stuffing them into her bag.

All except the grimoire. That she handles with reverence, wrapping it carefully in cloth before placing it in a locked drawer beneath the circulation desk.

I wait until she's gone before approaching the desk. My hand slips through the wood, turning the lock. I draw out the book, peeling back its cloth covering, and stare down at its ominous form.

I open the cover, and it hums with restrained energy, the symbols crawling across the yellowed paper like insects. I find the page Penny had been studying, focusing on the sigil that fills the page. A spiral ringed by thirteen marks arranged like a wheel. A trigger for the Hollowing.

I flip through more pages, skimming text I haven't seen in centuries. The ritual described requires thirteen members to complete it. It also requires an anchor. Someone who holds the combined power of the other members of the Concord Thirteen and leads the entire thing.

And most crucially, it requires a key. A human with unusual spiritual sensitivity. A human who's touched, but never made it to, the other side.

Someone like Mina.

I close the book, my hands trembling with fear. Not for myself, but for her.

They're going to do it here. In Moonridge.

Is Penny involved?

Her magic seemed too messy. Too hurried. I doubt she knew what she was doing. But someone made sure she found this book, and someone encouraged her—either directly or indirectly—to do this spell tonight.

I place my palm flat on the wrapped bundle and whisper words that bind and seal. The cloth grows warm beneath my hand, then cool again as the spell takes hold.

After returning the Testament to its drawer, I step back into the night. The stars have shifted, and the first hints of sunrise will soon begin to tease the tops of distant mountains.

I need to get back to Mina.

If I'm correct, and this is the Hollowing, they need thirteen binding points, one for each Concord member to exploit. The thirteen points would form a wheel around Moonridge, which would explain the unusually high paranormal activity. I just don't know how far along they are. How many bindings have already been activated? How many fractures are now quietly bleeding through the veil?

I reach the B&B as the grandfather clock chimes five times.

The house stands dark and quiet, but I can feel the energy building around it like a pressure cooker.

Inside, I find Mina in the sitting room, curled on the sofa in front of the fire. She's wrapped in a blanket, cradling a fresh cup of tea, staring out the window at the darkness beyond.

"You're back," she says without looking at me. "Find anythin' interestin'?"

"You've not slept? In the four hours since I've been gone?" I study the stubborn set of her jaw, the shadows beneath her eyes.

"I was waitin' for ya," she says. "And by the looks of it, ya found somethin'."

"Yes," I say simply. "And we need to talk."

She turns to face me and pats the spot next to her on the sofa. "Okay. Let's talk."

I set my cane against the wall and take a seat next to her. "We both know why I'm here."

She nods, swallowing hard. "Because this fuckin' tumor in my brain is goin' to kill me. And you're here to pick me up and drop me off wherever I'm supposed to go next."

I shrug and offer a small, sad smile. "Yes. I need to be honest with you. When I saved you that day—when I brought you back—I broke protocol. I didn't know there'd be a time limit on how much longer you could stay. I wish I could change that, but I can't."

A tear slips down her cheek. She doesn't wipe it away.

"But the good news is, I don't cause death. I don't decide when it happens. I'm just here to make sure you cross safely when it does. My orders weren't to kill you; that's not what reapers do. They were simply to collect the soul I saved."

She lets out a shaky breath. "So I'm not goin' to croak tonight?"

"No," I say. "Not tonight. For now, you're fine. But while I was out snooping around, I learned something disturbing. Someone's trying to tear down the veil between life and death for good. And I'm fairly certain they plan to use you to do it."

She huffs out a laugh. "Well, why not make the hag who runs the B&B the key to a ghost invasion?"

"I know this is a lot." I place a hand on her knee, and warmth spreads through me. "But it's serious. I worry that the Concord Thirteen are involved, and even more worried that I don't know how far along they are in their preparation."

"The who and what now?"

I take a deep breath. "They are an ancient cult. For centuries, they have sought to permanently tear down the barrier between life and death. They call it the Hollowing."

She shudders. "That sounds fun."

"It would allow entities from the void to enter this reality freely. Not just ghosts. Things that feed on living souls."

She places her teacup on the end table and curls her leg up under her. "And ya think they're here? In Moonridge?"

I meet her eyes. "Yes. I have reason to believe that they are."

For a long moment, the only sounds are the ticking clock and the crackling of the fire.

Then she looks at me. "Well then, I suppose we'd better stop the bastards."

A slow smile pulls at the corner of my mouth. "I suppose we should."

CHAPTER NINE

Mina

Cold water fills my lungs, and red hair floats like seaweed around my face. Moonlight filters through the river's surface, makin' shadows crawl across the silty bottom. But I'm not alone.

Hands reach for me from the darkness, the skin gone the gray-white of old candle wax, fingers brushin' my ankles, my wrists. I scream, but only bubbles escape my lips. The hands tighten, guidin' me down toward a dark spiral burned into the riverbed, deeper and deeper, the silt churnin' as the light overhead shrinks to a bruised smear. The spiral erupts into flames, and the river grows dark and red and—

I jolt awake and gasp for air, my sheets twisted around my legs like ivy. My breath puffs in front of my face. The bedroom is cold enough to freeze the tits off a polar bear.

"That bloody radiator." I crawl out of bed and check the thermostat, and notice the windows are frosted over. Lines appear, like a child tracin' the outline of a spiral, no, a sigil. The same one I saw in my dream.

I grab my sweatshirt and step out of my room, the wooden floor icy against my bare feet. I tiptoe down the hall toward the small alcove at the end of the hall, where the antique rockin' chair sits.

It moves.

Back and forth, back and forth, in a gentle, steady rhythm.

"What the fuck do ya want from me? Huh?" My voice cracks in the darkness.

The rockin' slows, then stops completely.

I should turn around. Go back to bed. Or at least make myself presentable, but my feet carry me toward the kitchen, where the warm heart of the house usually beats.

The first thing I notice is that the cabinets are all open, their doors wide like hungry mouths. The drawers have been emptied, silverware scattered across the floor. My hand shakes as I reach for a spoon. It's ice-cold, like it's been sittin' in a freezer.

"Havin' a laugh are ya?" I slam cabinet doors and shove drawers closed. "Ya fuckers are about to be on my last damned nerve." My hands won't stop shakin'. Footsteps sound on the back porch. Too early for guests to be up. The door creaks open, and my heart punches me in the throat.

But then I hear the distinctive tap of Dex's cane on the hardwood. He appears in the kitchen doorway, and everythin' feels safe again.

"You're awake," he says, surprised.

"Couldn't sleep." I focus on pourin' coffee into a filter. "Thought I'd get a head start on breakfast prep."

"You've slept less than an hour."

I glance at the clock. He's right. 6:47.

"Where were you?" I deflect as I grab a carton of eggs.

"Walking in the garden." He steps fully into the kitchen and leans his cane against the counter. "My head is full of too many thoughts."

"What kind of thoughts need walkin' off so early in the mornin'?" I push.

"The kind that involves preventing apocalyptic tears in

reality." His formal mask slips. He's really concerned. "And how to protect you from a blood-hungry group of nasty individuals who want to end the world as we know it."

A shudder passes across my shoulders. "Don't remind me."

I crack eggs into a bowl and whisk them, as if beatin' em hard enough will make all my troubles go away. The thought that I might help end the world makes my stomach clench.

An hour slips by in silence, both of us lost in thought as he helps me prepare breakfast. Who knew that havin' the very man who's here to take me away after I die would be so comfortin'? At least we make a good team.

Upstairs, footsteps creak on the stairs, soft at first, then louder, announcin' the start of another chaotic day. The Vampire Wives are upstairs, complainin' about the water temperature and thread count. I roll my eyes at Dex just as Dahlia enters the kitchen. She's dressed simply in linen pants and a cream blouse. Her ice-blue eyes appear both tired and laser-focused.

"Good morning," she says, her voice low and melodic. "I hope I'm not disturbing you."

"Not at all." I wipe flour from my hands. "You're up early."

"I don't sleep well in new places." She glides closer with eerie grace. "I wanted to let you know I won't be joining the others in town today."

"Oh? Are you feelin' all right?"

"Too much sun yesterday." Her hand touches her throat delicately. "I'm more sensitive than the others."

More sensitive to what exactly?

"I can bring ya some tea, if you'd like."

"Just privacy, please." Her smile seems forced. "I'd like to rest until this evening's taping. I need to be on point for the séance."

"Of course. I'll make sure no one disturbs you."

"Thank you, Mina." She turns to leave, then pauses. "This house . . . it has such interesting energy. It feels like it's listening. Waiting for something. Don't you agree?"

Before I can reply, she's gone.

"That was odd," Dex says quietly.

I yank open the refrigerator. "Yeah. Very random."

Dahlia's presence clings like smoke long after she's gone. I shake it off as the dining room fills with the familiar sounds of Jasper and Lily bickerin' over what time they should leave for the festival kick-off.

I've served them their breakfast and am halfway through brewin' a fresh pot of coffee when it happens.

"Good Lord Almighty!" Jasper's voice cracks with fear.

Dex and I rush to the dining room to find Jasper and Lily frozen at their table, both starin' wide-eyed at the window. I follow their gaze, and my heart hits my tonsils.

A woman, obviously dead, stands outside. She wears a torn and tattered hospital gown and wrist restraints. One of the old asylum patients by the looks of her. She presses one ghostly hand against the glass, eyes aglow with faint blue light as she peers inside.

"What in heaven's name is that?" Lily whispers.

My thoughts spin. "Oh, that's probably someone from town," I say with an awkward laugh. "Today's the Haunted Harvest 5K Fun Run. Everyone dresses up in costumes, remember? The festival kick-off event?"

"At eight-thirty in the morning?" Jasper squints suspiciously.

"They're very committed. They take this stuff seriously." I move to the window and wave at the ghost, who looks confused before dissolvin' to mist. "See? Just headin' to the race."

Lily doesn't look convinced, but Jasper seems to accept my half-assed excuse. "Well, that's a relief. Lily, maybe we should head into town. Get a good spot for the race."

I gather their plates and watch them leave. As soon as they're gone, I turn to Dex, whose face has gone several shades paler than usual.

"That was close," I sigh.

He nods and then steps outside, I assume to chase off other wayward spirits. I begin wipin' down the table, catchin' glimpses of him while he explores the garden and then the perimeter of the wraparound porch. Thorough, that one.

"I didn't see any others," he says as he steps back inside. "But it worries me that Lily and Jasper were able to see the ghost. Humans typically can't see them at this stage." He follows me back into the dining room.

My hands tremble as I place fresh napkins on all the tables.

Dex places a hand on my shoulder. "I know this is a lot."

I nod, unable to speak.

He places a finger under my chin and lifts my face so I meet his eyes.

"Are you okay?"

We're so close now I can feel his breath on my lips. His forehead nearly touches mine as he leans in. My heart pounds so hard I'm sure he can hear it.

His lips are inches from mine.

A faint discoloration on the wall above the mirror catches my attention. I step closer and squint. It's the same spiral pattern I saw earlier, burned subtly into the wallpaper like a watermark.

"Dex." I point at the wall. "Look."

He follows my finger, and his expression hardens. "When did this appear?"

"I don't know. I just noticed it." I reach out to touch the spiral, and the moment my skin makes contact, the room tilts sideways. For a split second, I'm underwater again, lookin' up at a faint light, while hands try to pull me under.

Hands grab my shoulders, and I'm sucked out of the vision to find myself gaspin' for air in Dex's steady arms.

"Are you okay?"

I nod, still tryin' to teach my lungs how to breathe.

"Don't touch it again," he says urgently.

"What is it?"

He doesn't speak. Just looks at me and then back at the sigil.

"Dex? What's wrong?"

"That's a reflection of a binding sigil. It's active."

I stare at the spiral, my heart beatin' the hell out of my ribs. "A what?"

"A binding sigil. They are marks that bind a Concord member to the mortal realm so they can complete their ritual."

"But how did it get inside my house? Have they been in my home?" The thought terrifies me.

"It may not be inside, but it's definitely somewhere on the property." His jaw tightens with anger.

They've invaded my property. Activated a binding.

Ghosts I can handle. Whispers in the dark, fine. But this? This is too much. Too invasive.

I slam my palms against the table, the sharp sound cracks through the air.

Dex startles. "Are you okay?"

I draw a breath, steadyin' myself. "Why are these bastards after me? I'm no one."

Dex's expression shifts. He steps closer and cups my face in both hands.

"I won't let them get to you. Okay?"

"Why can't they just let me be? Let me live out my days in peace? I've got enough shite on my plate. But if they want a fight, I'll give 'em one."

He places a hand on my shoulder. "You're quite incredible, you know that?"

I huff, the edge of a smile tuggin' at my mouth. "Just a stubborn old Scottish hag with no patience for magical bullshit."

His eyes hold mine. "No. You're brave. Fierce. I've never met anyone like you."

This time, when he leans in, there's no interruption.

His lips touch mine softly, but he holds me like he's afraid I might disappear. The kiss is gentle, reverent. It's been so long since I've experienced this. My body craves it. When we part, I'm breathless and want more.

"We should probably focus on preventin' the apocalypse," I whisper against his lips.

"Probably," he agrees, but neither of us moves away.

"But I'd really like to do that again."

He leans in for one more kiss. "We can pick this back up later. I need to find that binding and dismantle it."

He reaches for his walking stick propped against the wall. "Then I need to—"

He freezes, liftin' the cane to his face.

"What is it?"

"This isn't mine," he says slowly. "It's Jasper's."

My stomach sinks. "Do I dare ask?"

Dex's jaw tightens. Every possible disaster flickers across his face.

"With the right sequence of taps, my scythe could open a portal to the other side. And if enough spirits get through . . ."

He doesn't finish. He doesn't have to.

"So we've got a cranky old codger wanderin' about with a portable ghost faucet," I say. "And he's takin' it right into the middle of town durin' the festival kickoff."

Dex nods grimly. "We need to go. Now."

***

Runners already crowd the starting line when we get there, and the PA is so loud I feel it vibratin' in my lungs.

"Do ya see him?" I nearly collide with a stroller, then step around a young father consolin' a toddler screamin' over a dropped candied apple.

"Not yet." Dex's eyes narrow as he surveys the crowd. "We should split up. Cover more ground."

"Absolutely not. I can't get stuck battlin' ghosts or murdery cult members when I don't have a magical cane to help me out."

The hint of a smile touches his lips. "Fair point."

We shove our way through the crowd as the race announcer calls runners to their positions. Near the east side of the square, I notice Hazel and Coco signin' up the last of the runners at the registration table.

"Mina!" Coco calls, bouncin' in her teddy bear costume. "Are you running today? I didn't know you ran. Here's the sign-in sheet and—"

"Have you seen Jasper? The older gentleman stayin' at my B&B? Glasses, wispy hair?" I realize I just described half the men in Moonridge over the age of 73.

"The grumpy older dude?" Hazel asks. Her eyes flick toward Dex. "He was by the coffee stand about ten minutes ago."

We head that way just as the starting pistol fires. Runners surge forward in a wave of colorful costumes. The crowd cheers, and that's when I realize just how royally fucked we are. About half the runners fade in and out of view. Others stop in the middle of the road, and human runners pass right through them.

"Dex," I whisper, grabbin' his arm. "Do ya see this?"

His jaw tightens. "Unfortunately, yes."

A woman in a high-collared dress runs three steps, then drops to the ground, takin' down three human runners with her.

"Someone's goin' to get really hurt," I say.

"We need to find Jasper before—"

A crash interrupts him. About fifty feet away, Calvin Carter flies backward, landin' hard on the pavement. He sits up and removes an earbud, eyes fixed on a young man in 1950s attire—slicked-back blond hair, high-waisted jeans, white T-shirt with rolled sleeves. He looks as startled as Calvin.

"Are ya okay, love?" I ask, helpin' Calvin to his feet. I try not to stare at the guy. There's somethin' off about him. He just stands there, smilin'. Too still, too calm. And then I notice the shimmer at the edges, like the air folds around him.

He's not alive. He's a ghost.

But not like the others. He looks almost . . . solid.

"Yeah, just . . ." Calvin brushes off his T-shirt and readjusts the fake wolf tail hangin' off the back of his shorts.

"I like your shirt," the young ghost says.

Calvin blushes and looks down at the 'I like 'em hairy' shirt he wears. "I just threw something together this morning. It's a joke. I'm a werewolf, and, well . . ." he awkwardly gestures at the shirt and his fake tail.

Shit. Calvin can see this one. And hear him, too.

"I'm Everett."

He reaches out a hand, and Calvin takes it, then shivers. The young man's hand shimmers, but manages to latch on. I look at Dex, who stares at the young man with interest.

Runners shove past us with annoyed mumbles and shouts of "Get out of the road."

"We should get out of the way." Dex steps between Calvin and the young man. "Your knee is bleeding."

We walk Calvin to the side of the road, and when I look back, the young man has disappeared.

Calvin cranes his neck. "Where did that guy go? Everett? Did you see him? Do you know who he is? Cute, huh?"

My heart skips. "Yeah. Cute. Not sure where he went. Look, we need to find someone. Will ya be alright? Hazel and Coco are at the tent if ya need a bandage for your knee."

Calvin waves me off, searchin' the sea of faces for his ghost. "I'll be fine. It'll heal itself in a few minutes. Go ahead."

I take Dex's arm, and he leads me out of the crowd. We turn the corner, and I notice Lily clutchin' a race mug near the cider stand, eyes wide. She's clearly rattled.

"Lily!" I call out. "Where's Jasper?"

"He went to ask about the race route, and then he just wandered off. I can't find him. Can you help me?" She grips my arm.

I pat her hand. "Which way did he go?"

She points toward the center of the square, and that's when we see him.

Jasper stands alone at the edge of the park, Dex's cane raised in the air like a conductor's baton. His eyes have a faraway look, unfocused and dreamy. The air around him cracks with energy, and ghostly figures pop in and out of visibility around him.

"Oh my god," I whisper.

"What? What's wrong?" Lily clutches my arm.

"It's fine," I say, eyes stuck to Jasper as Dex moves toward him. "You wait right here. I'll be right back."

I rush toward them, heart poundin'.

"Mr. Brooks." Dex places his hand over Jasper's on the cane. "I believe you have my walking stick."

Jasper's eyelids flutter. His head tilts upward. "Oh. Mr. Grimm. I thought this felt too heavy to be mine. Pardon me."

"Nothing to apologize for," Dex says gently.

Jasper lowers the cane, lookin' around at the shimmerin' air around him. "These kids," he gestures at three spectral children dancin' in front of us, "they seem lost."

"Yes, they are." Dex carefully extracts his disguised scythe from Jasper's grip and replaces it with his own cane. The moment it leaves his hand, the spectral figures begin to fade. The little girl holds on longest, her sad eyes fixed on Jasper until, at last, she dissolves too.

The cane pulses once with faint blue light when it returns to Dex's hand, then goes dormant.

"I'm sorry," Jasper mumbles, lookin' confused and suddenly very old. "I was in such a hurry this morning, I must have—"

"It's all right." Dex pats him on the shoulder. "Simple mistake. No harm done."

But the tight line of his jaw says otherwise.

"So how bad is it?" I finally ask once Lily and Jasper have left. "On a scale of 'oops, I dropped my cookie' to 'everybody's goin' to die in a fiery hell'?"

Dex stops pacing. "Much worse than a dropped cookie, but not quite the fiery hellscape."

"Brilliant." I step away from him, watchin' the last of the contestants turn down Main Street. "I should have paid closer attention. I saw him leavin' for the race, I should have noticed—"

"This wasn't your fault. I shouldn't have left my scythe unattended. Besides, the veil was already dangerously thin. What happened today simply accelerated the process by a day or two."

"Can we do anything about them?"

"Manage them as best we can. The natural thinning that occurs at Samhain will make chaos more likely." He resumes his pacing. "More will come through with each passing hour."

I think about tonight's festival event, about half the town gatherin' in one place as ghosts run rampant. "This is going to be absolute shite, isn't it?"

"Very likely." He turns to face me.

I move closer to him, close enough to see the flecks of silver in his dark eyes. "What's the plan, sergeant?"

"You do what you need to do with the wives at the B&B, and I will monitor spiritual activity here at the festival. I need to see if I can try to identify Concord members."

I shiver at the thought of them walkin' around undetected, and then the knot in my stomach tightens. There's to be a live tapin' of a seance tonight at the B&B. With all of the ghosts runnin' free, are we about to light a match in a room full of gas?

THE REAL VAMPIRE WIVES OF OBSIDIAN HILLS

Episode 9: "Festival Frights and Delights"
FADE IN:
EXT. MOONRIDGE TOWN SQUARE - DAY

The town square is decorated with orange and black streamers, hay bales, and carved pumpkins. Festival booths line the streets. Carnival music plays in the distance. The VAMPIRE WIVES walk through the crowd wearing designer sunglasses and autumn fashion that's far too glamorous for a small-town festival.

CAPRICE: *(bouncing excitedly)* This is so cute! Look at all the little decorations! Oh my God, is that a real haunted hayride?

VIVIENNE: *(adjusting her designer scarf)* It's . . . charming. In a very Norman Rockwell meets Tim Burton sort of way.

AYANA: Honey, I've been to many a harvest festival. This is adorable, but back in the day we had actual demon summoning ceremonies. If you weren't careful your ass would be possessed before you made it to the food court. Now that was entertainment.

Suddenly, a TRANSLUCENT GHOST walks directly through a FESTIVAL WORKER carrying a stack of pumpkins. The worker stumbles, looking confused.

AYANA: *(bursting into laughter)* Oh! Did you all see that? Look at all these spirits just roaming around like they own the place!

CUT TO: TALKING HEAD

AYANA: *(grinning at camera)* So apparently Moonridge has a bit of a ghost problem. The living folks can't see them, but honey, I've got three centuries of supernatural sight, and this place is crawling with spirits having the time of their afterlives. These humans don't know what's about to hit 'em and I am here for it.

CUT BACK TO: TOWN SQUARE

A YOUNG FAN approaches nervously

FAN #1: *(starstruck)* Oh my God! You're the Vampire Wives! Can I get a selfie?

ZARA: *(in full star mode)* Of course, darling!

CUT TO: TALKING HEAD

CAPRICE: *(beaming)* The fans here are so sweet! Though I did notice some of them seem really cold. Maybe they need better jackets? I should start a jacket drive! Yes! I'll call it "Caprice Cares About Cold People!" *(pauses to write that down)*

CUT TO: FESTIVAL STAGE AREA

The wives approach a small stage where the RACE ANNOUNCER is speaking into a microphone

ANNOUNCER: Welcome to Moonridge's annual Haunted 5K! Runners, please line up at the starting line!

Dozens of runners in costumes gather. Several GHOSTS are also mingling among the crowd, completely invisible to the humans

VIVIENNE: A 5K race? How . . . athletic.

AYANA: *(watching a ghost trip a runner during warm-ups)* Girl, there are gonna be some busted butts today!

ZARA: *(looking around with concern)* The spiritual energy here is incredibly active.

VIVIENNE: *(deadpan)* Watching humans run for recreational purposes is fascinating from an anthropological standpoint. But, seriously. What's the point of running if you don't have to?

CUT TO: RACE START

The STARTING PISTOL fires. Runners take off, but chaos immediately ensues

RUNNER #1: *(stumbling)* Something just grabbed my ankle!

RUNNER #2: *(spinning around)* What's that smell? Did someone poop their pants?

RUNNER #3: *(stopping completely)* I swear I just saw a floating head!

Several runners trip and fall. One runner's pants fall down.

AYANA is doubled over with laughter

CAPRICE: *(confused)* Why is everyone falling down?

CUT TO: TALKING HEAD

ZARA: *(looking concerned)* I tried to tell some of the runners that there were spirits interfering with the race, but they just thought I was being "quirky reality TV vampire girl." Sometimes being honest about supernatural activity really doesn't pay off.

AYANA: *(still chuckling)* Three hundred years old, and I will never not laugh when people trip and fall. *(chuckles)* This is definitely going in my top ten most amusing mortal events.

FADE OUT.

END SCENE

CHAPTER TEN

Dex

This morning's kiss changes everything. It consumes my thoughts. And that's dangerous for someone like me. This is not who I'm supposed to be. I'm not supposed to feel love, or even attraction toward mortals—not anyone. But for her, I do.

And that could cost me everything.

Cool Earth welcomes me as I kneel beside fading marigolds. I take a wilted one in my hand. It's completed its cycle and will soon return to the earth. That's how existence should work. Grow, live, thrive, and move on when it's time.

Yet here I am, looking for ways to break the cycle, contemplating chaos, for Mina and for myself.

The thought of guiding her across tears me in two. The thought of being there to help her from this realm to the next is comforting, but the thought of knowing she'll be gone forever is almost too much to bear. She deserves more time. I'd gladly leave here today and never see her again if it meant I could leave knowing she'd have several more fulfilling years of life ahead of her.

I stand and roam the garden, lost in my thoughts, when ice prickles at my fingertips. Frost creeps across the surface of my cane, creating intricate ice crystals. The disguised scythe pulls me forward, the tug intensifying as I approach a patch of earth near the stone birdbath.

I drop and dig my fingers into the soil. Three inches down, they brush against something hard and smooth. I unearth a small clay disk, roughly the size of my palm. Ancient symbols spiral across the surface, and right at the center, the spiral with thirteen dots.

"Clever." I carefully lift the artifact. "Hidden where nature's energy masks its signature."

At my touch, the disk pulses with dark energy, sending electrical sparks through the air. Plants around me wilt and blacken. This is worse than I feared. A binding artifact, already activated, drawing power from Moonridge itself to weaken the veil.

How did I miss it, so close to the house?

I press the disk between my palms and murmur words meant to weaken the binding. The sigil resists but eventually fades, retreating into the stone until the disk no longer pulses against my palm. The pressure in the air eases, tension unraveling. I kneel and bury the neutralized artifact where I found it. Better to leave no trace, no sign it was ever disturbed. Maybe that way, they won't reactivate it.

My hands shake as I brush dirt from my palms. This just proves they've been on her property, leaving unwanted gifts right under her nose. That thought chills me more than I want to admit.

I have to stop them.

Back in the house, I find Mina at the small kitchen table, eyes distant, lost in thought. She looks stunning in black slacks and a plum-colored silk blouse. Her red hair falls in waves over her shoulders and looks almost electric against the dark fabric of her top.

She turns and smiles when she sees me, but the smile fades when she notices the look on my face.

"Why do ya look like ya just found a dead rat in your shoe?"

I sit in the chair next to her. "I found something in your garden."

She runs a hand across her forehead. "What now?"

"A binding artifact. Concord-made." I rest my cane against the counter. "Buried near the birdbath."

"In my garden?" Her voice spikes.

"Yes. I believe that's what caused the mark on the wall."

She sighs and drags a hand through her hair. "So some bastard's been skulkin' about my property, encouragin' the world-endin' ritual? What do we do now? How do I find out who it is?"

The slow, deliberate groan of old hinges cuts her off. We both turn. At the far end of the hallway, a door stands open that wasn't before. It slams shut on its own.

She startles. "Are the ghosts here already? The seance hasn't even started yet."

"I think it was just the house sending a warning," I say, helping her up. "I believe it wants to help."

"You're sayin' my house is alive?"

"No. Just aware. Not alive as you understand it, but not entirely inanimate either."

The lights flicker. A whisper echoes through the walls.

Mina shivers. "I've always felt like it had a personality. Sometimes I swear it's tryin' to tell me off."

A cabinet creaks open. The lights flicker again.

"It's looking out for you. As best it can," I assure her.

"The Vampire Wives are plannin' a séance tonight," Mina says, washing her hands. "It's part of what I agreed to. I thought it would be harmless, but now . . ."

She catches the look on my face and goes quiet.

"Honestly? I don't think it's a good idea," I warn. "The veil is already dangerously thin, and after what happened this morning, even playacting could have consequences."

"How am I supposed to stop it? It was part of the contract I signed."

Before I can answer, the front door bursts open. Coco strides in wearing what appears to be a fortune-teller costume, complete with jingling bracelets and a crystal-embedded headband. La'Tasha follows close behind, dressed in linen pants and a stylish wool coat.

"Reinforcements have arrived!" Coco announces, striking a pose. "We heard there's a séance tonight, and we're here to provide magical backup."

La'Tasha gives her a look. "What she means is, we're here to make sure nothing goes tits-up during the filming. I don't trust the wonky energy I've been picking up around here."

"Oye! And we brought protection charms," Coco adds, holding up a handful of small cloth pouches. "Estos bad boys will keep the muertos from making trouble for the vampire ladies."

Mina shoots me a questioning glance. I nod slightly. Their help, while chaotic, might be valuable. They can provide stability while I patrol the festival.

"Perfect timin'," Mina tells them. "We just found out that my house is a bloody supernatural magnet, and there's an evil cult tryin' to use it to end the world."

Coco grins. "Halloween in Moonridge, amiright? So, what's the plan?"

"The plan is, you two watch over Mina and keep the spirits at bay. I have some business I need to attend to around town. I don't know how long I'll be gone."

"You got it, jefe." Coco salutes me before following Mina and La'Tasha into the parlor.

The old grandfather clock sends eight notes reverberating through the floorboards. I slip on my coat and take up my walking stick.

A soft voice drifts from the hallway near the ground-floor guest rooms. I follow the sound, my footsteps silent against the hardwood. The mumbling grows clearer as I near the corner that leads to the Brookses' room.

"I've missed you so much. It's been so long since I've seen you, Frances."

Lily stands alone at the end of the hall, her back to me. She's dressed in a nightgown and robe, her white hair loose around her shoulders. She faces the wall as if speaking to someone.

But no one is there.

Her voice cracks. "I always hoped I'd see you again someday. And, look, here you are."

The air shimmers where she stares. Recognition prickles my skin.

"But what are you doing here?" Lily whispers.

Two voices fill the room at once, one high and forced, the other low and ominous, neither human. "I'm here waiting for you, Lily. I miss you. Help me cross back."

The Mortician. A corrupted Reaper turned Concord servant who chose the path of stealing souls rather than ushering them safely to their final resting place.

I move in, sliding between Lily and the shimmering air. "Mrs. Brooks," I say firmly, "step back, please."

The shimmer intensifies, condensing into a vague human shape. A woman's features form within it. Kindly eyes, a gentle smile.

"Lily, don't go," the apparition pleads. "I'm here for you. Help me."

"Stop this." My voice echoes with bass, making the windows rattle. "You have no right to be here."

The false Frances flickers, and beneath the perfectly coiffed hair is a face of tattered flesh that barely clings to a cracked skull.

I raise my hand, summoning my power. "You are not welcome in this house. Leave now."

The apparition hisses, abandoning its disguise. The skeletal face emerges fully now, empty sockets fixed on me with pure contempt.

"Brother." The word drips with acid. "Your love for humanity is so disappointing."

"I am not your brother. And this woman is under my protection."

The Mortician laughs. "Of course she is." Its form begins to dissipate. "We'll speak again soon."

With a final flicker, the entity vanishes.

Lily sways next to me, eyes still unfocused, hand on her heart like she's checking for a beat. "Oh. Oh, dear. I was . . ." She looks around, bewildered. "I was going back to my room and then . . . I don't remember."

I take her arm, steadying her. "You were sleepwalking, Mrs. Brooks. Let me help you back to your room."

"Oh. Yes." She allows me to guide her down the hall. "I was dreaming about Frances. My sister."

"Yes, just a dream." I offer her my arm and walk her to her room, keeping my voice at the same low, careful pitch I'd use with something I didn't want to startle. "Where is Mr. Brooks?"

"Playing cards with that nice camera fellow. He said he'd be in later." She looks up at me, her eyes clearing slightly. "You're very kind, Mr. Grimm. Thank you."

I nod and close the door. I walk back to the corner, searching for any Concord residue. Using the Mortician? That's bold.

Or calculated.

***

Main Street is electric with festival energy. Jack-o'-lanterns leer from every porch and storefront, their carved grins in direct juxtaposition to the danger that lurks. Children dart between booths dressed as ghosts and goblins, their fake blood and painted-on scars a direct insult to the dead who walk among them. A couple walks by, sharing kisses and cotton candy, she in a witch's hat and he in a tattered black robe carrying a plastic scythe.

I've a right to be insulted.

"Enjoying the festival?"

The voice startles me. I turn to see Hazel standing behind me, arms crossed, wolf brothers flanking her.

"It's very gothic," I reply, turning to face them fully. "You've done an excellent job with the decorations."

"Thanks, we worked overtime this year," Calvin says. He at least tries to smile. He's not as brooding as his younger brother, I'll give him that.

Blake stands with his hands in his pockets, stance wide, nostrils slightly flared. Testing my scent, no doubt. I let him search.

"I hear you're helping Mina with her ghost problem," Hazel says, her tone carefully neutral. "How's that going?"

"It's progressing." I match her neutrality. "The situation is more complex than we initially thought."

"That's interesting." She steps closer. "Since you're so good at paranormal activity, maybe you could explain to me why the town's protective barriers keep degrading faster than we can fix them."

"Almost like someone's deliberately sabotaging them," Blake growls.

I sigh. I get it. I arrived in town, and things got worse. I know how that reads. If I were them, I'd suspect me, too.

"I assure you, I'm not here to cause problems." I keep my voice steady. "We share the same concerns."

"Do we?" Hazel's eyes narrow further. "Because every time I'm near you, it feels like standing next to an open grave. There's something not right about your energy. And if you do anything to hurt Mina, you're going to have a coven of witches up your ass and a pack of werewolves chewing on your balls."

I turn my attention to the crowd. I could tell them what I am. Maybe then I could get them on my side, and we could work together to stop what's brewing. But Mina made me promise not to tell. They'd have questions as to why I'm here, and Mina isn't ready for them to know the truth. Not yet.

"Mr. Grimm?" Calvin's voice pulls me back to the present. "You okay?"

"My apologies." I blink, refocusing. "Just . . . considering our situation."

"While you're considering," Blake says, stepping forward, "maybe explain why you've been skulking around town at night, taking notes at all our historical sites. I saw you the other night while I was out patrolling."

"Just research for my book." The lie slides out easily.

Hazel studies me, her head tilted slightly.

I step around them. "If you'll excuse me, I need to continue my research."

They don't try to stop me as I walk away, but I feel their eyes tracking my departure.

I don't bother looking back as I follow the heat points to the white church that sits at the end of Willow Lane. Fresh paint gleams on the clapboard siding, and the brass bell catches the evening moonlight. To any casual observer, St. Mary's looks like every small-town church should.

But the energy's off here.

I walk the grounds slowly, my cane lightly tapping the brick path, sensing the pain that radiates from the space around me. This ground remembers fire. It remembers screams when the Thornbridge Cathedral burned to ash seventy years ago in this exact spot.

The air grows dense as I approach the rear of the church, near where the original altar would have stood. It thickens like walking through smoke that isn't there. Like breathing through wet cloth. My skin prickles when I pick up several different energy signatures. The fire wasn't an accident.

I make my way around to the side yard, where a small garden has been planted as a memorial. In the center is a small plaque that reads:

In Memory of Those Lost in the Fire of 1955.

I follow the energy I've been tracing to a row of bushes where the pull is strongest. I brush away mulch and dirt with the tip of my cane until it scrapes against something about five inches deep. I dig back the dirt to reveal a spiral cut deep into a rock. I trace it with my cane, and the hidden scythe glows faint blue. The symbol lights up. Ancient. Way older than either church.

Another Concord binding point carved centuries ago. The sigil pulses with active power, dark energy flowing. This is what caused the first fire. And it's still active.

I reach out, holding my hand above the sigil. Power rushes up to meet me, cold and hungry.

"Admiring our work, brother?"

The voice slithers from the shadows behind the memorial. I rise slowly, turning to face the speaker.

The Mortician materializes fully now, no longer hiding behind a stolen face. Tattered robes hang from his skeletal frame. Where my face appears human, his is grotesquely misshapen, bone gleaming through torn flesh, and empty sockets where eyes should be.

"I am not your brother," I tell him, my voice echoing in the empty churchyard. "You forfeited that bond when you joined the Concord."

"Such righteousness." The Mortician drifts closer, his form occasionally fragmenting like static. "Yet here you are, playing at humanity. Forming attachments. Breaking protocols."

I tighten my grip on my scythe. "What does the Concord want with Moonridge?"

He drags a skeletal finger through the dark energy that rises from the sigil. When he looks up, his lipless mouth stretches in a ghastly smile. "Death's tyranny is almost worse than the vile humans that are allowed to walk this earth unchecked. It's time for a new sense of balance."

"Meaning?"

"It's our time."

Before I can react, his bony fingers dart out and press against my forehead. My vision goes white, and I'm no longer at the church—

An overturned SUV. Shadowy figures removing a woman from the wreckage.

Her body dragged into a circle of black candles.

"The anchor is here," the voices chant.

—The vision ends as abruptly as it began. I stagger backward, my scythe the only thing keeping me upright. The Mortician lowers his hand, a deep, hollow laugh fills the space between us.

A red SUV crumpled in a ditch near Skipper Lake. That memory comes first. Overturned like a toy abandoned mid-play. Wheels spinning. Engine still ticking.

I'd focused on the male in the driver's seat first because he had already passed. The woman held on. But when I returned, she was missing, only a tattered and blood-soaked blue scarf left dangling from the broken mirror.

Then a soft, broken sound from the back seat. The child was alive. Stuck in her car seat, pressed between twisted metal and shattered glass. Her life force flickered. Reaper protocol demanded I wait, collect her after her final breath.

I took human form, reached into the wreckage, and pulled her free. I rushed her to the hospital. When the nurse turned to ask questions, I was already gone.

"You could have stopped this decades ago if you'd waited. But I got to Fiona first," he boasts. "The Thornton blood we needed to complete our thirteen."

That was Hazel I saved. I altered her path. Just as I did with Mina in Scotland. Two lives pulled back from the edge when I should have followed protocol.

Two paradoxes.

"But the anchor is ours now. I feel like I should thank you."

His form begins to dissolve into mist. "You're too late, brother. On Samhain, your precious Mina will help tear the veil for us."

I lunge forward, swinging my scythe through his dissipating form. The blade passes through empty air, leaving only a whisper behind.

"You can't save her."

And with that, he's gone.

I move through the night faster than I should, barely maintaining my physical form in my haste. I need to find the other binding points, and I need to find a way to inactivate them. This is partly my fault. If I'd stayed with Fiona all those years ago and ushered her across, they never would have taken her.

And now her daughter is at risk. Mina, too. Along with countless others.

All because I failed.

And yes, I know I could fix this tonight. I could usher Mina across without stalling further. Save her soul, stop the Concord.

But my heart. My heart says no.

CHAPTER ELEVEN

Mina

My reflection is all wrong. I tuck back a strand of hair, but the me in the mirror waits a tick before mimickin' the movement. I blink. It blinks a second later. I move closer until my nose almost touches the mirror.

"I don't know if you're real, or if you're just a side effect of the bloody nugget in my brain, but I'm at my wits' end with the fuckery. Ya hear me?"

She winks, and I flip her the bird.

I take a deep breath and smooth the purple blouse Coco insisted I wear for the séance tonight. I'd much rather be in a sweatshirt and pajama bottoms, but I have to be camera-ready tonight.

The me in the mirror completely disappears, and Hazel stands in her place. Then my gran. And then my ma.

I stumble backward. The back of my knees hit the edge of the bathtub, and I barely catch myself before fallin' in.

"Stop this," I whisper.

My reflection morphs into me again and tilts its head. Its lips move, formin' words too soft to hear. I lean closer, drawn by a terrible need to understand.

"What do ya want?" My voice trembles.

The reflection's mouth moves again. *You are the key. Come play with us.*

The key. The same word Dex used when explainin' the Concord's plans for me.

The air in the cramped room suddenly feels like it's thick as exhaust, and I can't catch my breath. The mirror's surface ripples, and my reflection fades. For a split second, I see not my face but a spiral of darkness with thirteen points of light arranged in a spiral.

Then everythin' snaps back to normal. Just me, pale and wide-eyed, starin' at my own terrified face.

I back toward the door, unwillin' to turn away from the mirror until I have to. I step into the hallway, and cool air fills my lungs.

Shadows stretch too far, curl at the edges. The floor vibrates as I make my way down the hall, and the walls pulse in my peripheral vision, expandin' and contractin' like lungs. When I focus directly on them, they appear normal, but the moment I look away, they move again.

Fabric rustles behind me. I whip around, expectin' to see Coco or one of the vampire wives. Instead, a woman in a black mourning dress stands there. Her face partially obscured by a heavy veil.

"Who are you? What do you want?"

She doesn't answer. Instead, she glides through me.

My organs shift like they're bein' rearranged by frozen fingers. I gasp, and double over as she emerges from my back and continues down the hall without acknowledgin' that she literally just passed right through me. My lungs won't work properly. My heart stutters in my chest.

I reach for the wall to steady myself, but my hand presses against the floral wallpaper and sinks in up to my wrist. I jerk back with a strangled cry. I test it again, but this time it's just solid wood and plaster beneath vintage wallpaper.

"What in blazes is happenin' around here?" I whisper.

The house groans, sound vibratin' through the floorboards. Down the hall, a door opens and closes on its own. The rockin' chair in the corner of the room begins to move as if pushed. Pictures tilt on the walls, straighten, then tilt the other way.

I press my back to the now-solid wall, steadyin' my thoughts. "What are ya tryin' to tell me?"

I'm answered with laughter and conversation from the parlor, a stark contrast to the flickerin' shadows and heavy air that's followed me from my room. I push off the wall and take a deep breath as I continue down the hall. Dex will be back soon. La'Tasha and Coco are here to watch over me. I'll be fine.

I follow the sharp click of designer heels on hardwood toward the parlor, where controlled chaos and fabricated drama are well underway.

Caprice storms into the room, one hand pressed dramatically to her forehead, the other clutched against a silk robe closed over designer pajamas. The cameras swivel to capture her performance.

"My ex-husband is haunting me!" Caprice announces. She pauses, makin' sure the camera has her good side. "I heard him calling my name from the closet. He said that my haircut makes me look like a disgruntled harpy in a cheap Halloween wig!"

Zara sighs and puts down her phone. She flips her bubblegum pink hair over her shoulder. "But isn't he, like, always haunting you? Probably because of that binding spell you made the witch do when we were in New Orleans a few weeks ago. Isn't it basically asking him to haunt you?"

"I said I wanted him with me in spirit, Zara, not that I wanted him to hide in my closet and hurl insults at me. Do you know how humiliating this is?"

La'Tasha and Coco flank me on either side, completely entranced with what plays out in front of them.

Zara shrugs. "You get what you ask for."

Dahlia glides down the stairs, lookin' perfectly composed

as always. "What are you complaining about now?"

"Don't even start on me. This is your fault." Caprice shoves a finger in Dahlia's face. "You're the one who suggested I do the binding spell. And you're the one who planned this entire trip, and I fully believe that you pre-planned everything that's happened to me just to make me miserable."

Vivienne and Ayana emerge from the dining room, wineglasses in hand, followin' the drama.

Dahlia looks around the room. "Are the rest of you miserable? Do you think I brought you here just to humiliate and inconvenience you?"

Zara shakes her head.

"Girl, what are you complaining about now?" Ayana asks. "It's always something with you."

I hover at the edge of the room, watchin' cameras move around the group to capture every eye roll and dramatic hair flip. This is much better than bein' haunted.

Caprice's eyes fill with tears. "I have a right to voice my displeasure. I'm being verbally assaulted by my dead ex-husband, my phone blew up in my face, and my glam person refuses to come to this place because she swears it's haunted. I'm being attacked, and I look like shit."

Ayana crosses her arms and tilts her head. "And how is this different from any other day?"

Kevin gives a thumbs-up from behind the main camera.

Caprice gasps, hand flyin' to her chest. "How dare you!"

"Three, two, one . . . and break," Kevin calls. "Great stuff, ladies. We'll pick up with reaction shots in five."

The Vampire Wives immediately drop their hostile postures, fallin' into casual conversation. Vivienne's eyes drift toward me, her gaze sharp. She excuses herself from the group and crosses to where I stand.

"You look a little pale, Mina." Her eyes scan my face. "Are you okay? Did all of Caprice's drama make you sick?" She winks.

"Nothin' to worry about." I try to smile, but my mind is still on the reflection in my bathroom.

"You sure? You can trust me." She coaxes me off to the side, out of earshot of the others. "I've been around for over a century." She lowers her voice. "You learn to recognize the look of someone who's going through some shit. What's going on?"

Before I can answer, Coco and La'Tasha appear beside us, practically vibratin' with excitement.

"Diantre! You look really pretty," Coco says to Vivienne with a smile that could blind the sun. "This is like one of your best outfits yet, literal."

"Thanks, hon. I designed it myself," Vivienne says with a wink. "It will be part of my fall line. It's inspired by Bram Stoker."

"Wow," Coco says. "I don't know who that is."

La'Tasha scoots Coco aside. "Okay, I gotta ask. Is it true you dated him?"

"God, no. He was thirty years older than me. I did meet him, though. A year or two before he died."

"What did you talk about?" Coco presses.

"Not a lot. Though I had only been a vampire for a few years by then, and I remember telling him that I wish his book had been more accurate." Vivienne rolls her eyes. "He got so many details wrong."

"Like what? I need the tea, girl." La'Tasha leans against the wall, ready to eat up the details.

"The reflection nonsense, for starters." She gestures toward the mirror above the mantel. "How else would I know if my eyeliner's even?"

They laugh while I process what she just said. "You're really quick with that."

"What do you mean?" Vivienne asks.

"The whole Bram Stoker story and the reflection bit," I say. "But, I guess ya have to be quick when people ask ya these things if ya need to convince them you're real vampires."

The entire room goes silent. Then Ayana bursts out laughin'.

I glance around. Every wife stares at me. Then, as if on cue, they all bare their fangs. Five sets of blood-red eyes lock onto me like dogs on raw meat.

"Bloody hell." I take a step back. "You're actually real vampires."

Vivienne retracts her fangs, and her eyes shift back to their normal maroon color. "Very much so. The drama is enhanced for ratings, but that's the only thing manufactured."

She glances at my neck with a smile that's probably meant to be a tease, but it sends chills down my spine.

"I'm so glad you're real," La'Tasha laughs. "I always assumed, but there are rumors."

"I knew it." Coco shoves a finger at me. "So, what's it like living for centuries? You, like, must know everything."

"Not quite, but I have lived through a lot and have witnessed a lot of change. Mostly good, but then some, not so much," Vivienne says, droppin' onto a chair. "When I was human, I lived in a time when a woman's job was to get married and serve a man. Now, all these years later, that's the last thing I want. I don't serve anybody."

"Amen to that," La'Tasha says. "I'd rather die than spend my life serving a stank-ass man."

I wince. I agree with her for the most part. Just without the dead bit.

"Were you afraid?" I ask. "When you were dyin', I mean."

"Terrified." Vivienne strokes the long black braid draped over her shoulder. "Dying definitely changed me. Not in some existential, 'I've seen the sins of my old ways, and I vow to do better,' way. At first, I felt like I'd be better off dead. I didn't want to hunt and kill. It took me a while to settle into it. When all is said and done, the person you were before ends up being a small piece of who you are after."

"Was it worth it?" I ask softly.

She tilts her head and places her hand over mine. "Yes. I can honestly say that now. I couldn't always. Still, everything comes with a price."

Coco plops down on the sofa next to me. "So, like, how can you walk around in daylight? I thought vampires burned in the sun."

"Gotta love modern chemistry." Vivienne frames her face with her hands. "Special sunscreen."

"What did you do before that?" I ask.

"Spent a lot of time in rainy places and prayed for cloudy days. Or just stay inside a lot." She grins. "Very limiting."

I excuse myself and walk toward the kitchen to brew myself a cup of tea. All this talk of death and rebirth is gettin' to me. Do I wish I had Vivienne's life? Would I want that over the life I've been dealt?

I'm startled out of my thoughts when a hand drops on my shoulder. I turn, half-expectin' a ghost, but it's just Dahlia.

"Sorry, love," I say. "Ya frightened me."

"No apologies needed." She smiles and pulls her shawl tight over her shoulders. "You look like something's bothering you. I noticed it earlier. Is everything okay?"

Well, can't hide anythin' from vampires then, can I?

"Ay, I'm fine. Thanks for askin'. It's just been a rough few weeks. Runnin' a B&B by yourself catches up with ya after a while, if ya know what I mean. Tea?" I ask, hopin' to change the subject.

"Only if you have A negative."

My face blanches, and she smirks. "Sorry. Vampire humor."

I add a teaspoon of honey to my cup. "So, ya really do drink blood then?"

She nods. "Yes, that part is true. We can eat other things, but we do need blood to keep up our strength."

I sip from my cup to keep my reaction from spreadin' across my face. "Do ya have to . . . kill people?"

"Killing?" Dahlia wrinkles her nose. "No, hon. That's very

last century."

"Then how—?"

"Willing donors." She examines her nails. "And there's even synthetic blood now. It's especially popular for our vampire vegan crew."

"I guess they can make anythin' these days now, can't they?"

"Surprisingly tasty."

A high-pitched shriek cuts through the house. Dahlia and I rush to the foyer and collide with a panicked Zara, pink hair wild around her face.

"I can't find Mortimer!" she cries. "I've looked everywhere!" Her breath comes in short gasps. "What if he flew outside? What if a hawk got him?"

"Oh, hon. I'm sure he's fine. We'll find him," Vivienne assures her, takin' her by the shoulders.

I nod and set down my tea. "Where did ya last see him, love?"

Zara sniffles and dabs at her mascara-streaked cheeks with a monogrammed handkerchief. "After lunch. I gave him his organic blueberries and left him napping in his carrier while I did my facial routine."

"And the carrier was in your room?" Vivienne asks.

"On the dresser by the window. He likes the afternoon sun." Her bottom lip trembles. "What if he flew outside and got lost?"

My B&B transforms into organized chaos within minutes. Vivienne coordinates the search like a general, while Caprice complains that her dead husband's ghost is more important than Zara's bat. Kevin looks like he's won the lottery, sendin' one cameraman with each party. I get that genuine distress likely makes for excellent television, but this feels wrong. Or is this one of their orchestrated storylines? Will we find Mortimer happily loungin' in a dark corner while snackin' on strawberries and then move on?

"I'll take the east wing," Vivienne says, her heels clickin' on the hardwood as I lead Zara up the stairs.

"And I'll do a summoning spell in case he's lost and needs guidance," Coco adds as she pulls small pouches of herbs from La'Tasha's bottomless bag.

Zara and I head to her room first, a camera operator trailin' us. The room looks like a cosmetics counter exploded. Bottles of serums and creams cover every surface, three different suitcases open on the floor.

"That was where I left him." She points to an empty jewel-encrusted carrier on the dresser.

I check under the bed and inside the closet. No sign of a bat, but the room hums with an odd type of energy that makes my stomach boil.

"Does Mortimer usually wander off?" I ask, checkin' behind the curtains.

"Never! He's very well-trained." Zara opens her bathroom door, callin', "Mortimer? Sweetie? Mommy has treats!"

We move methodically through the rest of the second floor, openin' doors, checkin' cupboards. In every room, I notice that same, heavy energy.

"Is your house always this electric?" Zara rubs her arms as we step into the guest bathroom at the end of the hall.

"No," I admit. "It's just the—"

"Oh!" Zara gasps and points toward the bathtub.

I follow her gaze. A small, dark shape lies motionless on the white porcelain. Zara rushes forward, the camera operator scramblin' to capture her reaction.

"Mortimer!" she cries, reachin' for the tiny creature. "What happened to you?"

One of the bat's wings is spread wrong, the other folded back on itself.

Her face crumples as she reaches for him. "Something's wrong."

I step closer and peer at the tiny creature cradled in her palms. No visible wounds. No signs of trauma. His eyes are open but glazed, wings a dull gray instead of the shiny black when he was alive. I've seen this before in a nature documentary. The way spiders leave their prey drained from the inside, external appearance mostly intact.

"Oh, love, I'm so sorry," I say, placin' my hand on Zara's shoulder. Her body trembles beneath my touch.

"What happened to him?" she asks, lookin' to me like I might have the answer. "He was fine a few hours ago. He's not been sick, and he's only a few months old."

I look at my tiny reflection in his beady, lifeless eyes and shake my head. "I don't know, love." Though I have a terrible suspicion.

The camera operator steps closer, zoomin' in on the dead bat. "This is gold," he mutters. "The network is going to love this."

Zara's head snaps up. Her eyes flash red, and her fangs extend. "Turn that off! This isn't to be broadcast!"

The operator steps back, face white. He holds up a hand. "I'm sorry, Zara. Kevin said—Look, I'm just doing my job."

"Not this," she hisses, cradlin' Mortimer protectively. "Let me grieve in peace. Please."

I gently guide her away from the cameras, toward her room. "We'll find somethin' to put him in, pet. I'm so sorry."

I walk her to her room, and I swear the wallpaper ripples as if the ocean moves beneath it. I need Dex. And we need to do somethin' about these hungry ghosts.

Now.

CHAPTER TWELVE

Mina

The production team has transformed my parlor into a séance chamber, and if I weren't preoccupied with thoughts of ghosts and demon cults, I might be impressed. A round table draped in dark velvet sits in the center of the room, and black candles line the antique sideboard. Cameras ring the space like mechanical sentinels. Lights covered with black paper create just enough illumination to film while maintainin' the proper ambiance for a televised séance.

The crew bustles around the entire first floor, ignoring the fact that one of the cast members' pets just died under mysterious circumstances. The show must go on, apparently.

"I think we should postpone," Ayana says. Her eyes survey the room like she's waitin' for somethin', or someone, to crawl out of the TV. "The energy feels unstable."

Kevin refuses with a sharp head shake. "Not possible. We have a schedule to maintain. The producers in LA are expecting all the raw footage for episode six no later than noon tomorrow. Episode six specifically calls for a séance."

I glance toward the corner where Zara sits hunched in a wingback chair. Coco kneels beside her, one hand on Zara's knee, the other holdin' a crystal that pulses with soft blue light.

"It's okay to grieve, mija," Coco says gently. "He was your familiar. You had a special bond."

"He was such a good boy," Zara whispers, tears leavin' fresh trails through her makeup.

Coco nods and pats her on the shoulder.

"I don't think I can do this tonight," Zara continues, lookin' up at Kevin. "I can't pretend to contact spirits when I just lost my friend."

"I'm sorry, but you're contractually obligated," Kevin reminds her. "My hands are tied. My job depends on this, and you know that if you don't have me for a showrunner, then you're going to get Kristy."

The entire room groans. What did this Kristy do to these people?

"We can dedicate the episode to him," Kevin promises. "He'll be here in spirit, and we'll include what just happened—respectfully, of course—as part of the narrative."

Zara looks ready to argue, but Vivienne steps forward. "We'll honor Mortimer during the séance. Include him in our communication with the other side. Like Kevin said, he'll be here in spirit."

I watch this exchange with increased unease. They're talkin' about the séance like it's just a TV segment, not an actual attempt to communicate with the dead. I can only pray that it stays that simple.

"Maybe we should—" I start, but Caprice interrupts.

"Can we just get on with it?" She examines her manicure with boredom. "Some of us have pre-scheduled lives on OnlyVamps."

"Fine." Zara straightens her shoulders. "I'll do it for Mortimer."

"Good." Kevin smiles. "Like I said, we'll add a dedication card."

The crew springs back into action, creatin' the perfect ambiance for what I can only hope won't turn into a complete supernatural disaster. No one comments on how the flames of the black candles burn blue instead of orange, or how they lean toward the center of the table regardless of air currents. I tell myself it's the tumor and I'm just imaginin' it.

"Places, everyone!" Kevin finally calls, checkin' his watch.

The Vampire Wives take their assigned seats around the table. I glance at the clock and smooth my shirt just as a massive pain shoots through my right eye. I close my eyes and press my fingers against the bridge of my nose. I look up, and La'Tasha catches my eye, and mouths, *Are you okay?*

I give her a tight nod and force a smile.

My eyes scan the table before us. Dahlia rolls her neck, almost as if she's slippin' into character. Unlike the others, she seems perfectly calm, almost expectant. She looks up and catches me watchin' her, and smiles.

"You can stand closer." Dahlia gestures to a spot near the table. "Your presence might strengthen the connection."

She turns and beckons La'Tasha and Coco to come closer, too. I know they're eager to be on TV, but I have a bad feelin' about all of this. I look at Coco and shake my head.

"We'll just observe from here," I say. "Don't want to interfere with your process."

Dahlia's eyes narrow slightly, but Kevin nods approvingly. "Good idea. Let the talent handle the séance while you watch. You can provide color commentary if you'd like. You will be on camera, so reactions will be expected."

I position myself near the doorway where I can see everythin' while maintainin' some distance. La'Tasha moves to stand beside me, her protective instincts clearly activated.

I lean toward her. "This is a terrible idea."

"What is?" Coco appears beside me, makin' me jump. "Sorry! Didn't mean to sneak up on you."

"The séance," I say, keepin' my voice low. "With everythin'

that's happenin'. We shouldn't be invitin' more spirits in."

Coco squeezes my arm. "That's why La'Tasha and I are here. We've got protection spells ready. And we've put silence spells down the hall so that Lily and Jasper won't be disturbed. It'll be okay. Serious."

She says it with such confidence, I almost believe her.

Almost.

But she doesn't know about the Concord. Or that hundreds of ghosts seem to have taken up residence in my B&B.

I place a hand on her shoulder. "Just stay close, okay?"

"Promise." She links her pinky with mine. "Witch's honor."

"Everyone ready?" Kevin directs. "I know this is all pretend and will be filled with special effects, but we have to really sell it. Remember, we want authentic reactions. Keep it visual."

From my position, I watch the candle flames flicker wildly, then steady, their light bendin' slightly in my direction. No one else seems to notice.

"Cameras ready," Kevin says. "Sound check?"

"Levels good," a tech replies.

"Dahlia, you'll lead as discussed. Ladies, follow her cues and treat all of this like it's real. Remember. We have to sell this. Ratings matter."

I take a deep breath, ignorin' the fact that I can see the reflections of at least twenty people in the mirror above the fireplace, and none of them are the reflections of anyone in this room.

"Rolling in three, two, one . . ." Kevin points, and the red lights on the cameras illuminate.

Dahlia adopts a solemn expression, her voice droppin' to a hypnotic tone. "Tonight, we gather in this historic house, where the veil between worlds grows thin. We seek contact with those who have passed beyond."

The candles flare brighter. The mirror no longer reflects the room at all, just swirlin' darkness punctuated by pinpricks of light like distant stars. At least the ghosts are gone.

"Join hands," Dahlia instructs the other wives, "and close your eyes. Open your minds to the energies around us."

I lean against the wall as the Vampire Wives link hands around the table. But even as an observer, I feel the pull. The air thickens, cracklin' with energy that makes my skin crawl. Behind my eyes, even with them open and focused on the séance, I begin to see things. Fragments of visions. Water. Darkness. Cloaked figures, blood fallin' from the sky, and a spiral pattern burnin' just above the table. Another blast of pain fills my skull, and I wince.

Not now.

Whispers hit me from every direction. The door between worlds has started to open, and even from where I stand, it feels like I'm the one turnin' the key.

The candles flicker as Dahlia's voice drops to that TV-ready spooky tone. I press my back against the wall, but an invisible hook tugs from behind my navel, pullin' me forward.

"We call upon the spirits of Moonridge," Dahlia intones, her fingers linked with Caprice and Ayana on either side. "Those who have passed beyond the veil, we invite you to communicate with us."

Kevin gives her a thumbs-up from behind the main camera. Another cameraman walks in a circle around the table, likely gettin' a close-up of each of the women's faces. Zara wipes away a tear.

"In memory of those we've lost," Vivienne interrupts, noddin' toward Zara, "we open our hearts and minds."

Dahlia looks at Vivienne, back straight. Her face is a mask of serene focus, but her eyes lock with Vivienne's. An uncomfortable beat passes between them, loud enough to shift the energy.

La'Tasha catches my eye from across the room, her forehead creased with worry. Beside her, Coco shifts nervously from foot to foot, her protective crystals clutched in one hand.

The first candle flares, its flame stretchin' upward before it snaps back to normal. Either it was real, or a special effect placed by one of the crew. No draft caused that. Every window is closed.

"If there are any spirits present," Dahlia says, her voice growin' deeper with each word, "give us a sign of your presence."

Cold slams into the room, and the mirror cracks as flecks of ice trace a line down the center. The production crew exchanges glances.

"Is this part of the setup?" Kevin whispers to his assistant.

"No." He shakes his head. "I could never rig something like that. And the cooling system isn't even on."

Dahlia's eyes close, her head tilts back slightly. When she speaks again, her voice deepens with an underlyin' echo, as if two voices speak at once.

"We seek the Collector," she says.

Ayana's mouth falls open. Her eyes dart between the other wives.

Dahlia inhales and then continues. "Ancient one, keeper of wayward souls, we offer you passage as you seek the missing one."

The candles shift to electric blue, flames standin' perfectly still. A burst of pain fills my skull and then leaves as quickly as it came.

"Cut!" Kevin's voice shakes. "Let's reset the—"

Mics shriek with feedback, and static fills the screen of both monitors. The boom operator yanks off his headphones, cryin' out.

Dahlia's spine arches backward, her neck extendin' at an unnatural angle. Bones crack and pop, the sounds of vertebrae shiftin' beyond their limits. Her neck extends, but it's not quite strong enough to hold her head. It keeps floppin' side to side and then back. Her arms bend at odd angles, but her hands remain locked with Ayana and Caprice. They try to pull away but can't break the grip.

"My God," La'Tasha whispers. "Coco, where's my bag?"

Coco is frozen in place. "What's happening to her?"

Dahlia's head snaps up, and she no longer has eyes. Skin has grown over her eye sockets, and her mouth has tripled in size.

Dark lines erupt across her skin, then branch outward toward her temple and the corners of her mouth.

"Holy shit." Kevin scurries away from his malfunctionin' camera. "How is she—"

Her head rotates toward him. Her mouth opens wide, revealin' pointed, gray teeth that look like rows of needles.

"The Collector does not perform tricks," says a voice that can't possibly be Dahlia's. It's layered, like multiple voices speak in unison. Her head bends all the way back, and the entire house seems to bounce.

A cameraman drops his equipment with a crash. "What the hell is happening?"

I'm frozen in place, unable to move away from the wall, but the force that tugged at me earlier has sunk its hooks into my soul.

Come closer.

Ayana tries to yank her hand free from Dahlia's. "Bitch, you best let go of me!" she commands. "This isn't funny, Dahlia!"

"Dahlia is merely a vessel." The voice ripples through the air. "A door willingly opened."

Caprice sobs openly now. "Please, someone help us!"

Vivienne alone remains calm, her ancient eyes narrowed. Is she controllin' this? Did she and Dahlia plan the entire thing?

Finally, she says, "You're one of the Concord."

How does she know about the Concord?

The thing wearin' Dahlia's body smiles, exposin' rows of dagger-like teeth. "The vampire remembers us. As you should."

The grandfather clock in the hall strikes nine. Then keeps goin'. Ten. Eleven. Twelve. Fifteen.

The production crew has abandoned their cameras. Kevin creeps toward the front door, eyes still trained on Dahlia.

Dahlia's body rises several inches above her chair, her spine still bent at that unnatural angle, her head twisted to survey the room. The dark veins have spread across every visible inch of her skin now.

La'Tasha strikes first. Her fingers cut through the frigid air, leavin' blue traces that glow like someone drawin' patterns with light. Her hands move quickly as she chants. I try to push away from the wall, to help somehow, but my body won't respond. I'm stuck, pinned like a butterfly in a display case, while the thing inside Dahlia watches with those terrible pale eyes.

La'Tasha begins to chant under her breath, and the glowin' sigils she's drawn expand outward to form a dome of bright, shimmerin' blue light around the séance table.

Coco pulls crystals from what seems like every pocket of her fortune-teller costume. She arranges them in a hasty circle on the floor, each stone aglow with internal light as she places them strategically around the table. Beams of light shoot upward from the crystals, they connect with La'Tasha's spell, creatin' a visible cage around the possessed Dahlia and the other Vampire Wives.

The thing pauses, head crooked on Dahlia's shoulders. The levitatin' objects slow. The candles, though still blue, flicker instead of rage.

Then Dahlia's distorted mouth stretches into a mockery of a smile. "Your petty spells cannot sever what has been at work for centuries."

She releases Ayana and Caprice, then raises one hand. The barrier visibly weakens. The blue light dims, then flickers. Cracks appear across the magical dome.

Caprice jerks to her feet. "I'm getting out of here!"

She lunges toward the door. But she stops mid-step, frozen like someone hit pause.

"No one leaves," the Collector says simply.

Caprice's body slowly, unwillingly returns to her chair like some kind of marionette. She collapses, mascara tracin' dark rivers down her cheeks. "Please," she whimpers. "I don't want to die again."

The Collector, or whatever speaks through Dahlia, laughs, a terrible sound that seems to come from every corner of the room.

A picture frame crashes to the floor. Glass shatters.

Vivienne sits with her hands folded in her lap, eyes narrowed as she studies Dahlia. She's the only person in the room who looks completely unbothered.

"The Concord was destroyed centuries ago," she says, voice steady. "The Bureau of Others hunted you to extinction."

The Collector's attention shifts to her. "Ah. The vampire knows our history. How useful." It tilts Dahlia's head at an unnatural angle. "We have rebuilt. And now the wheel turns."

Once again, cracks spider across La'Tasha's barrier.

"Switch to banishment!" La'Tasha calls.

Coco nods, rearrangin' her crystals into a new pattern, and their magical barrier changes from blue to deep purple, contractin' around Dahlia's possessed form.

Dahlia throws her hand toward La'Tasha.

She flies backward as if someone picked her up and threw her like one of those bad wrestlin' shows. Blood trickles from her nose.

Coco doesn't give up. "We need to try something else! Maybe if we—"

"Enough," the Collector says, and Coco's voice cuts off mid-sentence.

She clutches at her throat, eyes wide with panic. No sound emerges, though her mouth moves. Her face turns blue.

I break free of whatever had me pinned to the wall and drag myself forward. "Get your bloody hands off of them," I yell.

The thing inside Dahlia smiles at me. "Or what?"

Sometimes the dumbest idea is your only option. If this thing wants me as a key, if it's already connected to me somehow, maybe I can use that connection against it. I've seen enough horror movies to know this is probably suicide, but I won't let La'Tasha and Coco suffer.

Three steps and I'm at the edge of the séance table. Dahlia extends one hand toward me, fingers bent at unnatural angles.

She points to the center of the table. "Take your place at the center of the wheel."

Instead, I lunge forward and grab her outstretched hand. A visible blue-white current crackles between our bodies. My muscles lock, and my spine goes rigid. My teeth clamp together so hard I'm afraid they'll shatter.

Someone screams. Maybe it's me. I can't tell anymore because somehow I'm both in my body and bein' pulled into darkness. Red energy engulfs both Dahlia and me. It swirls. Pulses. Through the pain, I sense the Collector's surprise. It wanted me to surrender, to become a passive conduit. It didn't expect me to fight.

But I did. And I'll continue to.

My consciousness rips free from my body and plunges into a stream of images. Moonlight. Twelve hooded figures, faces hidden. Blood drips from their palms. A red-headed woman stands at the center of their circle, beggin' them to let her go. She cries for her daughter.

"The anchor is here," they chant in unison. "The anchor is ours."

The vision shifts to the old church, then Skipper Lake. At each location, robed figures perform blood rituals, carvin' symbols into stone.

My physical body feels distant now, like a coat I've left hangin' on a hook. I push deeper and come face-to-face with The Collector's true form. A vast, shapeless thing with too many mouths pressed into an eyeless skull with skin that's too tight. I see its connection to the other Concord members through twelve strings that radiate outward from its torso.

And I see what it doesn't want me to see.

"You need me to come willingly." The realization shoots through the center of me. "You can force Dahlia because she's just a vessel. But me? You need me to be your key. I have to choose. You can't force me."

Rage pushes against me, and I feel like I'm about to implode.

"You will choose us! The wheel is nearly complete."

I'm shoved back into my parlor. Dahlia's body convulses, and the red energy between us fluctuates wildly.

La'Tasha and Coco watch wide-eyed, unsure what to do next. I will them to leave me be. I don't want them to get hurt. Dahlia's mouth stretches impossibly wide as the Collector screams in frustration. The sound rattles windows.

"I saw ya," I rasp, my voice barely audible over the entity's rage. "I know what ya are. I know what ya want." I tighten my grip on Dahlia's twisted hand. "And I will never join ya."

Pictures crash from the walls. The blue candle flames stretch upward, turnin' from electric blue to deep violet.

With the last of my strength, I force myself deeper into our connection, lookin' for the string that will force the Collector out of Dahlia.

Pain tears through my head. I look directly into that terrible, eyeless face and think one final command:

Get. Out.

The bond between us snaps like a cord pulled too tight.

Red-gold energy blasts outward, knockin' everyone back a step.

Dahlia's body jerks once more, then goes limp, hoverin' momentarily before droppin' back into her chair. But a dark, smoke-like figure with hollow eyes and too many limbs lingers above her. It writhes and twists, its form unstable now that it's been forced from its host.

For a moment, it hovers there, empty eye sockets fixed on me. Then it lets out a shriek that makes everyone clutch their heads in pain.

The room falls silent, broken only by our ragged breaths. One by one, the candle flames shrink to steady yellow, then flicker out, plungin' the space into semi-darkness. Only the production lights remain, castin' long, distorted shadows across the walls.

Dahlia slumps forward onto the table. "What—" she whispers, her voice raw and delicate. "What happened?"

No one answers immediately. The production crew remains pressed against the walls, too shocked to move.

Somehow, I'm still standin', but my mind feels scraped raw. Tremors wrack my frame. My legs shake.

"It's gone," I manage to say. "For now."

Vivienne moves to Dahlia's side and checks her pulse. "She'll need rest. And protection." She looks my way. "So will you."

I try to nod, but daggers of pain shoot through my skull. The room tilts sideways. My knees hit the floor, then my palms. I try to push myself back up, but my arms fold beneath me.

"Mina!" multiple voices cry out.

Hands reach for me. La'Tasha says somethin'. There's a strong grip on my shoulders. Fingers graze my forehead.

Voices fade in and out. I fight to stay conscious just a little longer. I need to tell them what I saw. About the binding sites. About the Concord.

But my body has reached its limit, and the dark wins.

CHAPTER THIRTEEN

Dex

I stand at the edge of Skipper Lake, watching water curl upward against gravity. Below the surface, near the center, a crimson light pulses. The energy is particularly strong here, but Moonstone Circle had been worse. All fourteen ancient stones thrummed with power, the earth itself breathing beneath my feet. When I touched the center stone, vibrations traveled through my bones, so strong that they would have killed a human if they'd touched it.

At Hollow Glen Asylum, oily liquid had coated the basement's walls in spiral patterns. Thirteen coils surrounding a central eye. The substance burned through my glove on contact.

I need to get back to Mina, but when I enter Moonridge proper, the library draws me like a lodestone. Should I leave it? I could, but what if it's another binding point that needs to be inactivated?

I move in that direction, and I've just turned a corner when I spot Penny Fisher huddling on the library steps, head bent over a book. Her blue stocking hat is pulled low, brunette braids resting on her shoulders. She pushes her glasses up on her nose, and the streetlight above her flickers, casting her in sickly yellow light. She mutters to herself, completely absorbed in whatever she's reading. She doesn't see the shadows crawling around her. Are they naturally drawn to her, or has she summoned them?

And what is she doing out here at this hour?

I move closer and tap my cane against the bottom step. She jumps, and the heavy tome tumbles from her lap, landing with a dull thud.

"Jesus!" Her hand flies to her chest. "Mr. Grimm? What are you doing out here?"

"I could ask you the same question." I retrieve her fallen book, an ancient text on protective spells, its pages yellow and brittle with age. "The library closed hours ago."

She takes the book with a sheepish smile, tucking a loose strand of hair behind her ear. "I just live a couple of streets over. I wasn't ready to go home yet. It's too quiet there. Too empty." She glances around, suddenly aware of the emptiness surrounding us.

I drop beside her on the step, allowing my cane to rest across my knees. The scythe within it pulses gently, responding to Penny's aura.

"It's cold out," I observe. "Why didn't you at least stay inside?"

Her shoulders slump. "I stayed late to finish up a few things I've fallen behind on since Mrs. Henderson passed. I still haven't hired someone to take my old position, so I'm doing the work of two people, and it's a lot. I just needed a minute before I head home." She sighs and pulls mittens from her coat pocket. "I could use magic to get things done, but Hazel caught me using it without her permission this morning and banned me. She put a tracking spell on the library to alert her of any unsanctioned spellwork. I don't understand why she hates me so much."

"Why do you think she hates you?"

"I honestly don't know. I've asked for mentoring, and she refused. And then she went and hired Coco, and now she says she has to focus on mentoring her and has even less time between Virtus Suprema duties and running her shop." She gestures toward Blue Moon Apothecary, visible down the street. "I want to be useful. I want to be like them."

Her words echo in the empty street.

"I know how to do basic magic, but I wasn't raised like them," she continues, words tumbling out faster now. "My adoptive parents didn't believe in magic. Didn't want me using it. So I hid it. Pretended I was normal. And now . . ." She taps the book. "Now I'm trying to study and memorize every spell I can so that when Hazel is finally willing to mentor me, she can see that I know my stuff. Maybe even more than her."

She grips the book until her knuckles whiten. Her jaw clenches.

"Did you ever think that maybe you're trying too hard?" The way she looks at me makes me think I must have struck a nerve. "You said yourself that you can already do magic. Maybe you just need to trust yourself."

She looks up, skeptical. "Is that supposed to make me feel better?"

"We're all born with some sort of potential. Some discover it early. Some later." I place a hand on the book in her lap. "You likely already know everything you need to know. And I know you and Hazel haven't been seeing eye to eye, but maybe if you try a different approach . . ."

She shrugs, some of the tension leaving her shoulders. For a moment, we sit in comfortable silence, two outsiders finding unexpected common ground.

A low, wet growl shatters our peace. The sound carries a hollow quality, an entity forced into a form it was never meant to wear, and obviously not from this world.

Penny freezes. "What was that?"

I turn toward the alley beside the Blue Moon Apothecary. Shadows approach, rising and falling, disappearing behind bushes.

"Get behind me," I say, standing and stepping in front of her. "Now."

Another deep, hungry growl emanates from the darkness.

The thing emerges like a living nightmare. Bone and sinew held together by rusted wire and rotting leather. Its skull hangs at an impossible angle, connected by metal pins. Pale fire burns in empty sockets, casting sickly light on the library's brick walls.

The Graveborn straightens to seven feet of pinned-together horror and fixes its burning eyes on me.

Penny's fingers dig into my sleeve. "What is that thing?"

I recognize the symbol branded into its forehead. A spiral with three interlocking rings slashed with a jagged line. The Mortician's mark.

The creature takes a step forward. Air distorts around it, causing the light from the streetlights to bend away.

My scythe vibrates, sensing my intent. I will it to show its true form, but the transformation is sluggish. Wrong. When it finally emerges, the blade shimmers, translucent at the edges.

The monster tilts its head, studying us. I know without a doubt that it was sent for me.

It shifts, and suddenly it's ten feet away and then directly before me, bone-fingers slashing toward my face. I raise my scythe to block. The blade connects with its arm, but the beast doesn't flinch.

It snaps its jaws, forcing me back. My feet slide on damp grass as I struggle for balance.

Penny mumbles behind me, and I turn in her direction. A tiny spark appears at her fingertips, then sputters out.

The distraction costs me. The beast slashes across my side, bone-fingers tearing through my coat, piercing skin. I gasp, nearly dropping my scythe. Black ichor seeps from the wound, followed by blood.

But I'm not human. I don't bleed.

The immense amount of pain that tears through my abdomen is so foreign. So wrong. I've never felt pain like this before. I can't breathe. Is this what death feels like? I touch the wound and then bring my hand to my face as if to prove to myself that it's real. I'm injured.

"Mr. Grimm!" Penny's voice sounds distant.

I swing around, whipping my scythe in a wide arc, trying to create space between me and the creature. The blade passes through the Graveborn's midsection, a blow that normally would have cleaved it in two. Instead, my weapon flickers, its edge barely affecting it.

The monster makes a sound between laugh and growl as it grabs my scythe with both hands. Ice crystals spread along the handle. I refuse to let go despite the numbing burn.

"Flames rise, embers glow!" Penny chants again, voice stronger. A larger spark appears, hovering for three seconds before dissolving. "Why won't it work?"

The creature wrenches my scythe aside, pulling me off balance. White-hot pain slashes through my wound. I collapse to the ground. I reach for my scythe, but the Graveborn's foot stomps down on my wrist.

"Please!" Penny screams, tears streaming down her face. "Please help us!"

The Graveborn looms over me, jaw snapping inches from my face. Hot, fetid breath smelling of rotten meat and sulfur fills my nose. It could easily rip me limb from limb.

My heartbeat echoes in my ears. If I die, where will I go? What will become of Mina?

A deafening crack cuts through the night, followed by a primal howl. A familiar voice calls from a few feet to my right. Hazel.

The beast's head snaps up just as a blur of motion slams into it from the side. Bones crunch. The Graveborn goes flying across the library lawn.

Blake Carter stands in its place, caught between human and wolf, amber eyes glowing. The transformation isn't complete, but the power rolling off him is all wolf.

"Get up," he growls, voice deeper than usual. "Can't hold it off forever."

My limbs refuse to cooperate. My vision swims.

Hazel appears beside Blake, hands wreathed in blue fire.

"What is that?" she demands, eyes fixed on the monster as it rights itself, joints clicking.

"Graveborn," I barely manage. "Concord creation."

"I don't know what that means, but okay," she says, eyes trained on the Graveborn.

Penny rushes to my side, hands shaking as she helps me sit up. "I tried a spell to stop it. I promise. But it wouldn't work."

"You screamed for help." I lean on her shoulder, hand clamped to my bloody side. Where is all this blood coming from? "That was enough."

The creature assesses the new threats, its burning eyes flickering between Blake and Hazel. It charges, and Blake's half-transformed body launches at the beast's legs, powerful jaws clamping around one crooked knee. It swipes, catching him across the shoulder hard enough to send him rolling.

"The forehead." Every syllable costs me.

Hazel nods, eyes narrowing on the sigil. The blue flames around her hands flare, then erupt from her palms, wrapping around the creature's forearm like a rope. The stench of scorched flesh hits the back of my throat. Penny gags.

"Blake, now!" Hazel shouts, using her hold to yank the creature off-balance.

Blake doesn't hesitate. He lunges at the Graveborn's back. They slam into the ground with enough force to crack the pavement. The creature thrashes in his grip, but Blake digs in, claws sinking into its spine.

"I can't hold it!" Blake's whole frame shudders against the creature's weight.

Hazel steps forward, hands extended, witchfire flaring around her fingers. "Keep its head still."

Blake adjusts his grip, forcing the creature's skull against the ground. The Graveborn's jaw snaps, teeth clacking as it tries to twist free.

Hazel drops to one knee beside its head. The Mortician's mark pulses with sickly light, feeding its animation.

"Let's send you back to the shithole you came from." She presses her palm directly against the sigil.

The creature goes rigid, back arching. The flames in its eye sockets flare, dim, then flare brighter again. A high-pitched wail emerges from its jaw as it begins to break down.

Blake leaps clear as cracks appear across the creature's body, glowing with blue light. The cracks spread, widening, until it disintegrates into crystalline black particles that float downward, covering the ground in that familiar oily sheen.

"What just happened?" Penny's voice trembles beside me.

I attempt an answer, but consciousness slips. I slump against her, the wound pulsing, spilling blood and ichor down my pants.

"Dex?" Hazel rushes to my side. She steps back when she sees the blood. "Oh, you're hurt. Oh, no. It's bad."

Blake approaches, eyes still glowing amber. "That's not all blood."

"No," I barely manage.

Hazel examines the wound without touching it. "The damage goes deep. It's corrupted."

I nod. "That thing was designed specifically to take me out."

Her eyes widen. "I knew it. You're not human."

"No." No point denying it now. "And if the Concord can do this to me, imagine what they can do to any of you."

Blake lifts me as if I weigh nothing, careful to avoid the wound. "We need to get him back to the B&B. Now."

The streets pass around me in pieces. A lamppost. A sliver of moonlight. Blake's shoulder under my arm, and the pain in my side just sharp enough to keep me from passing out.

The B&B's front door swings open of its own accord as we approach. Inside, the air feels thick enough to chew, pressing against my skin like unseen hands.

Blake carries me across the threshold, and the house reacts. Floorboards creak in recognition. The walls pulse with a steady rhythm, expanding and contracting like the chest of an enormous beast. But it isn't welcoming me.

It's warning me.

Something happened here tonight.

"Blake? What's happened?" Mina appears. She looks like she's been through hell, but her face grows even more pale when she sees me. "Dex!"

She rushes forward, stumbling as the floor ripples beneath her feet. Behind her, shadows stretch and curl along walls, forming shapes that almost resemble reaching hands before dissolving.

"Put him on the couch," Mina directs, already moving pillows to create space. Her hands tremble, but her voice remains steady.

Blake gently lowers me onto the sofa. The movement sends a fire through my entire torso that takes my breath away. Never have I felt anything like this, and never do I want to again. Dark ichor mixed with blood soaks through the fabric of my shirt, dripping onto the floor.

Mina reaches for me, then pulls back when she sees the blood and darkness seeping from the wound. "What happened? Can't ya heal yourself?"

I shake my head. "It's some sort of poison. My power won't respond."

Hazel's fingers hover above the tear in my clothing, not quite touching. Heat radiates from her fingertips.

"What did this?" Mina asks.

"Concord," I say. "They sent something to kill me."

"But you're Death," Mina whispers, a tear slipping down her cheek. "How can they kill Death?"

Hazel's eyes grow wide. She looks at me and then at Mina.

"Uh, I need to stabilize you. This won't heal you, but I think I can stop it from spreading." She closes her eyes and begins to chant under her breath.

"You're getting really good at this," La'Tasha says. "Almost better than me with your bad healing self."

"Hold him still," she instructs Blake, who places his hands on my shoulders. "This will hurt."

Her glowing hands press against my wound. Fire explodes along my ribs, tearing through muscle. It goes deep, touching the core of what I am. I arch against Blake's grip as pain rips through me.

I grit my teeth and push through. Eventually, the pain recedes to a dull ache. Hazel lifts her hands, revealing the wound. It's still open, but the edges look cauterized, no longer draining the life out of me.

"That's the best I can do," she says, voice ragged with exhaustion.

I nod my thanks, not trusting my voice. The pain is there, but more manageable now.

"Will someone please explain what's happenin'?" Mina's voice rises. Her hands shake at her sides. "What attacked ya? Why can't ya heal yourself?"

I push myself to sitting, ignoring Hazel's protests. "The Concord sent a Graveborn to eliminate me. It nearly succeeded."

"Graveborn?" Blake asks. "Is that what those things are called?"

I nod. "It's a constructed undead."

"But why?" Penny asks from the door. She hovers at the periphery like she's afraid she doesn't belong.

"The Mortician sent it to remove me from the equation."

"Mortician?"

I wince against the pain. "A former Reaper who joined the Concord—"

"Another Reaper?" Hazel's eyebrows shoot up. "There's more than one of you?"

"I'm one of many. We serve—"

"They're trying to kill ya so they can get to me," Mina interrupts.

I nod. "It appears that way."

Silence stretches between us. If Death himself can be wounded, what hope do the rest of them have?

Blake shifts uncomfortably. "So, if you're a reaper, why are you here? And who is the Concord? What do they want with Mina?"

Before I can answer, a low rumble shakes the house. The walls stretch and distort like melting wax, then snap back into place. The air pressure changes.

Then Mina's eyes roll back, irises barely visible. Her body goes rigid for a heartbeat before she collapses, hitting the hardwood floor with a sickening thud. Convulsions wrack her frame, her limbs jerking in violent, uncontrolled spasms.

"Mina!" Coco screams, dropping to her knees beside her friend.

La'Tasha grabs cushions from the couch, trying to position them around Mina's head to protect her from the hard floor. "It's a seizure. Don't try to hold her down!"

Hazel fumbles for her phone, hands shaking as she dials. "We need an ambulance! Now!"

The convulsions continue. I count the seconds the way I've counted them at ten thousand bedsides, and I've never once wanted the number to stop climbing the way I want it to now.

Then, as suddenly as it began, Mina goes completely still. Her breathing shallow and rapid. But she's alive.

For now.

"The ambulance is coming," Hazel says, kneeling beside Mina's motionless form. "They said to keep her on her side."

We all stare down at her still figure, the reality of her mortality crashing over me, bringing with it the reminder of why I was sent here in the first place.

THE REAL VAMPIRE WIVES OF OBSIDIAN HILLS

Episode 10: "Spirits and Secrets"
FADE IN:
INT. B&B PARLOUR - NIGHT
The room is in disarray. Candles are knocked over, chairs are scattered, and there's an overturned Ouija board on the table. The women sit around looking shell-shocked.
CAPRICE: *(voice shaking)* What the hell just happened? I thought séances were supposed to be fun! Like, talking to dead relatives and getting lottery numbers!
VIVIENNE: *(calmly straightening her hair)* That wasn't a séance, darling. That was a hostile takeover.
CUT TO: TALKING HEAD
AYANA: *(to camera, completely deadpan)* So let me get this straight. We came to small-town Massachusetts for apple cider and pumpkin spice lattes, and instead we got *The Exorcist: Bed & Breakfast Edition*. *(takes a sip of wine)* This is why I stick to wine. Spirits in bottles are much more predictable than spirits from beyond the veil. Okay?
CUT BACK TO: DINING ROOM
DAHLIA: *(sitting perfectly composed despite her ragged appearance)* I'm fine, really. Just a little . . . spiritual indigestion.
VIVIENNE: *(studying Dahlia suspiciously)* You were possessed by what felt like a very old, very angry entity. Most people would be at least slightly traumatized.
ZARA: *(through tears)* Poor Mortimer! He was trying to warn us! The spirits killed him because he was protecting us!
CUT TO: TALKING HEAD
ZARA: *(mascara running, clutching a box we assume contains Mortimer's remains)* Mortimer wasn't just my emotional support bat, he was my familiar! He could sense dark energy, and he was going crazy all day trying to tell me something was wrong. *(voice breaking)* And now he's gone because I didn't listen!

CUT BACK TO: DINING ROOM

CAPRICE: *(hyperventilating)* This is not what I signed up for! I can barely handle being a vampire, and now there are angry ghosts? What if they come back? What if they possess *me*? I don't even know how to handle my own supernatural abilities, let alone someone else's!

AYANA: *(to Caprice)* Baby girl, breathe. The spirits are gone. For now.

CUT TO: TALKING HEAD

VIVIENNE: *(to camera, ice-cold)* Listen, I've dealt with the Concord before. They're not your garden-variety spirits. They're ancient, powerful, and they don't just show up for amateur hour séances. Someone at that table knew exactly how to call them. *(adjusts her jewelry)*

CUT BACK TO: DINING ROOM

AYANA: *(standing up)* All right ladies, I don't know about y'all, but I need something stronger than champagne after watching my friend get possessed and our hostess start floating three feet off the ground.

MINA: *(entering the room, looking pale and shaken)* I'm so sorry, everyone. I don't know what happened. I've lived in this house for years and—

CAPRICE: *(jumping up)* Oh my God, Mina! Are you okay? You were like, fully possessed! Your eyes went all white and you started speaking Latin!

MINA: *(confused)* Latin? I don't speak Latin.

CUT TO: TALKING HEAD

AYANA: *(shaking her head)* Three hundred years on this earth, and I'm still learning new ways supernatural situations can go sideways. Dead bats, possessed innkeepers, floating furniture . . . *(shakes her head)* That scared the hell out of me, but I must admit, this is the most entertaining thing that's happened to me in decades.

CUT BACK TO: DINING ROOM

ZARA: *(standing up shakily)* I need to bury Mortimer properly. He deserves a ceremony with crystals and sage and . . .

DAHLIA: *(interrupting smoothly)* Perhaps we should all retire for the evening. It's been a very eventful night.

VIVIENNE: *(not moving)* That's one way to put it.

AYANA: *(to Dahlia)* You seem awfully calm for someone who just had a demon in her. Girl, your head was rolling around like your neck gave up.

DAHLIA: *(pats her hair)* I've always been good at compartmentalizing.

CUT TO: TALKING HEAD

CAPRICE: *(still visibly shaken)* I came on this trip because I thought it would be fun and maybe help me figure out my vampire powers. Instead, I've learned that there are things way scarier than not being able to turn into a bat. *(voice getting higher)* What if those spirits come back? What if they possess me next time? I don't even have a familiar to warn me!

CUT BACK TO: DINING ROOM

VIVIENNE: *(standing and smoothing her dress)* Well, I don't know about the rest of you, but I'm going to my room to call production. This is out of control.

CAPRICE: *(also heading for the stairs)* And I'm going to call my lawyer. This is ridiculous.

AYANA: *(chuckling)* Honey, I don't think the Concord accepts restraining orders.

The women begin to disperse, each looking shaken in their own way. DAHLIA remains seated, staring at the overturned candles with an unreadable expression.

FADE OUT.

END SCENE

CHAPTER FOURTEEN

Mina

A shrill, rhythmic beep drills into my skull. I pry my eyes open. A plastic tube rests beneath my nose. I blink rapidly. Dusty rose colored walls. A TV mounted in the corner. A tube snakes from my arm to bags of clear liquid that hang from a metal pole.

Hospital. I'm in a hospital.

"Mina? Oh, thank God." Hazel's face swims into view, eyes puffy and rimmed with red. "She's awake!"

More faces blur into focus. Blake, his usual stoic expression cracked with worry. And Dex, standin' slightly apart from the others, lookin' like absolute hell.

"What happened?" My voice comes out as a croak. My throat feels like sandpaper.

"You had a seizure." Hazel grabs a plastic cup from the bedside table and pours me a glass of water. Her hands shake. "At the B&B. You collapsed."

The water soothes my throat, but it does nothin' for the poundin' in my head. Memories surface slowly. The séance. Dex bleedin' out on my couch.

"How long was I out?" I ask.

"Almost twelve hours." Blake steps closer. "The ambulance brought you in last night. It's a little after noon now."

"Ambulance?" I attempt to sit up, but my body weighs as much as waterlogged sandbags. Hazel helps me adjust the bed, so I'm more upright. The movement sets my head to spinnin'.

Hazel's face crumples. "Why didn't you tell me? We're supposed to be friends. Do you not trust me?"

I flinch back against the pillows, her words like slaps. I narrow my eyes at Dex. "Ya told them, didn't ya?"

"I had to." Dex's voice sounds weak, and it's lost its formal edge. "The paramedics needed to know about your diagnosis. Your medical history."

Now that I can see him properly, I realize how bad he looks. Dark circles ring his eyes. His skin has a grayish tinge, and he leans heavily on his cane.

"You look terrible," I tell him.

A ghost of a smile touches his lips. "You should talk."

"Don't joke." Hazel whirls on him. "This isn't funny. None of this is funny." She turns back to me, eyes shiny. "How long have you known?"

Before I can answer, the door opens. My oncologist, Dr. Patterson, steps inside.

"Mina. Good to see you're awake." She steps to the foot of the bed. "How are you feeling? That was a pretty bad seizure."

"Fuzzy-headed," I tell her, "but I've felt worse."

She nods and gives me a small smile. "I've reviewed your scans."

Blake straightens and crosses his arms. Hazel's grip tightens on my hand.

I straighten in the bed. "Just tell me. I'm okay with them bein' here. I need them to know. It's bad, isn't it?"

Dex remains perfectly still, his eyes locked on my face.

"Yes. I'm afraid it is." She flicks the screen on her tablet. "The tumor has grown significantly faster than we expected. I've never seen anything like it, to be honest. The seizure was due to increased pressure in your brain."

No surprise since my head has literally felt like my brain has grown three sizes in the last two days.

"So what now?" Hazel asks.

Dr. Patterson hesitates. "As Mina already knows, the location of the tumor makes it inoperable. We could try radiation to potentially shrink it temporarily, but I need to be clear—this wouldn't be curative."

I already know this. When she first told me two months ago, I was a wreck. Not today. Because I know my time is up. Death only comes knocking when it's time.

I meet Dex's gaze, and he offers a sad smile. I wonder if it's easier for him when the person knows what's comin'. When they have time to prepare. To say goodbye.

"What's the timeline?" Blake asks, his voice rough.

The doctor's eyes flicker to me, then back to her tablet. She clearly doesn't want to say this in front of me.

"It's okay," I tell her. "We need to know."

She sighs. "Based on the current growth rate and your symptoms . . . not long. If you're lucky, a couple of months. Perhaps less."

Hazel makes a choked sound beside me. Blake puts a hand on her shoulder to comfort her.

My guess is I likely have days. Otherwise, why would Dex have been sent now?

"I'd like to adjust your steroids to reduce the swelling," Dr. Patterson continues. "And anti-seizure drugs will prevent—"

"What about my guests? The B&B?" I interrupt. "Will this affect my ability to work?"

Dr. Patterson blinks, confused. "I'm sorry, Mina, but—"

"There's so much to be done," I say quickly.

"We'll help." Hazel places a hand on my arm. She smiles through unshed tears.

The doctor nods and then continues. "I'll have the nurse

come in to go over your medication schedule. Try to rest. Avoid stress." Her eyes sweep over my visitors. "And perhaps try to keep your emotions in check. This is a lot for Mina to process. She needs to remain calm right now."

Calm. Right.

She leaves without another word, the door clickin' shut behind her. The silence of the room is broken only by the steady beep of machines.

"Mina—" Hazel starts.

I raise my hand to cut her off. "Don't. Please. I can't handle pity right now."

She bites her lip, anguish spillin' over. Seein' her pain makes this real in ways the doctor's words didn't.

My eyes drift over to Dex. Wounded and weakened from tryin' to protect me. The irony isn't lost on me. Death fightin' to keep me alive. At least for now.

Hazel's grief transforms into steel-hard determination. She whirls on Dex.

"This is your fault!" She jabs a finger at him. "This is why you're in Moonridge, isn't it? You came for her!"

Dex doesn't flinch. He stands motionless, shoulders squared. He accepts every word like a man who's weathered storms far worse.

"You knew she was dying and you didn't do anything!" Hazel continues, her voice risin'. "You could have helped her! What good is being some powerful being if you can't save one person?"

"Hazel—" Blake reaches for her arm.

She shakes him off. "No! Don't defend him! He's been here for days while Mina's been dying. Playing house, pretending to care, when all along he was just—just waiting to collect her!"

Her voice cracks on the words, and my throat constricts. This. This is why I kept quiet. I didn't want to watch them hurt for me.

"It doesn't work that way," Dex says quietly. "I don't choose who lives or dies."

"Then what good are you?" Hazel's voice cracks. "What's the point of you?"

Dex winces, but not from her words. He shifts, and I can see the effort it takes for him to remain standin'. The wound at his side is clearly causin' him pain.

"This is much deeper than you realize. The Concord attacked me precisely because I interfered," he says, each word measured. "They weakened me because I've been trying to protect her."

"Well, you failed!" Hazel's magic flares, sendin' a gust of wind through the room that rattles the blinds and knocks a plastic cup off the bedside table. "She's dying, and you've not done anything to stop it from happening!"

"Hazel, please," Blake tries again. "This isn't helping."

"Don't tell me to calm down! Mina is dying!" She rounds on Blake now, her grief searchin' for new targets. "Did you know? Did everyone know except me?"

"No one knew." I straighten against the pillows.

Hazel doesn't seem to hear me. She turns back to Dex. "Fix this! You have to fix this!"

"I can't." Dex winces; the admission clearly pains him more than his wound. "All I can do is collect. I'm not allowed to save."

I respect him for not tellin' them the truth. That he's already saved me once, and he's only here now because he's been forced to fix that mistake.

"I've known about the tumor for almost two months," I say to Hazel, redirectin' her attention away from Dex.

She turns to face me, mouth slightly open.

"What?"

"I was diagnosed a few weeks after all the Ravena business. It's inoperable." The words are heavy on my tongue. "I didn't tell ya because I couldn't . . . I couldn't make it real by sayin' it out loud."

Maybe I should have done this weeks ago. It sure feels better havin' it all out in the open now.

Hazel sinks onto the edge of my bed, shoulders slumped. "You've been carrying the weight of this for two months?"

I nod. "I thought I had more time. The doctors initially said I might have a year. Maybe a little more. I was goin' to tell ya after the festival. After the B&B was back on its feet."

"Oh, Mina." Her voice breaks on my name.

"Dex didn't tell anyone my secret until he had to," I continue. "He showed up at the B&B because that's his job. He comes for people who are . . . who are about to die." The words stick in my throat, but I force them out. "He didn't cause this. He's just the collector."

"But he's Death," Hazel whispers, lookin' back at Dex like she hopes he'll hand her a different answer. "Actual Death."

"One aspect of it, yes." Dex grimaces as he shifts his weight. "It's like I said before. My job is to guide souls, not claim them. I don't cause death. I help with the transition."

"Then why are you still here?" Blake asks. "If you can't save her . . ." He stops. The realization dawns on him, and his eyes fill with tears. He turns away.

"Look, my time is obviously limited." I refuse to break down. We have to focus on the larger issues at hand. "Ya both need to know that somethin' huge is happenin' in Moonridge. We suspect that an ancient cult plans to use me to tear open the veil between worlds. Dex has been tryin' to stop them."

"And failing," Dex adds quietly. "And now my wound prevents me from accessing my full powers. The Concord planned this well."

Hazel stares down at her hands, expression unreadable. Blake stands at the foot of the bed, mouth scrunched, unable to form words.

"How do we stop them?" Hazel finally asks.

"I have some ideas," Dex says. "But I'm going to need help."

Blake nods. He wipes his nose. "Whatever you need. The wolves will help however we can."

"Yes." Hazel takes my hand. "Whatever we can do. The witches—all of us—are here. I'll call in The Regency if I need to."

"I'm sorry I didn't tell ya," I say to Hazel, squeezin' her hand. "I thought I was protectin' ya."

She squeezes my fingers so hard it hurts. "That's not your job. Your job is to let us be there for you."

"I know. I'm sorry."

Blake moves to stand behind Hazel, placin' a hand on her shoulder. Anchorin' her when she needs it most.

"So what now?" he asks.

I peel back the IV tape with clumsy fingers, wincin' as it pulls at my skin. It needs to go. All of it needs to go. These devices aren't savin' me, they're measurin' my decline, and I have things to do, and all of this beepin' is about to drive me mad.

"Mina, what are you doing?" Hazel grabs my arm.

I brush her away, grit my teeth, and slide the IV needle out of my vein. A drop of blood wells up at the site, bright red against my pale skin. I press a tissue against it.

"Have you lost your mind?" Blake steps forward, but doesn't try to stop me.

I pull the nasal cannula from my face next. The moment I remove the pulse oximeter from my finger, a high-pitched, insistent beep fills the room.

"They're going to think you're coding," Hazel says. She glances nervously at the door.

"Good." I swing my legs over the side of the bed, the thin hospital gown barely coverin' my thighs. My head swims with the movement, but I push through. "Someone hand me my clothes."

A nurse blows through the door and stops in her tracks. Her eyes go to the monitors, then to me, then back to the monitors like she's tryin' to figure out which one of us is lyin'.

"Ms. Cartwright, what are you doing?" The nurse, Shannon, accordin' to her name tag, hurries to silence the alarms. "You need to lie back down."

I close my eyes against the dizziness and sigh. "I'm leavin'."

The nurse stares at me like I've just announced I'm plannin' to sprout wings and fly home. "I strongly advise against that. You've had a major seizure. You need monitoring and medication."

"For what?" I meet her gaze. "To buy me a few more weeks in a hospital bed while my brain rots from the inside out?"

Shannon's expression shifts. She takes a deep breath and folds her hands in front of her. "Ms. Cartwright—"

"Mina," I correct her. "My name is Mina. And I'm signin' myself out."

"You can't—"

"I can, actually." I fight back against the dizziness that threatens to topple me. "I have the right to refuse treatment."

Shannon looks helplessly at my friends. "Can someone talk some sense into her?"

No one says a word. Even Hazel stays quiet.

"I need my clothes," I repeat. "Where are they?"

"In the closet," Blake says. He nods toward a narrow door by the bathroom.

Hazel hesitates, then moves to open it for me. She pulls out my neatly folded jeans and sweater.

Dr. Patterson appears in the doorway, summoned by the commotion. "What's going on here?"

"Ms. Cartwright is attempting to leave against medical advice," Shannon explains.

"I'm not attemptin'." I curl my toes against the cold floor. "I'm doin' it."

Dr. Patterson steps fully into the room, tablet clutched to her chest like a shield. "Mina, I understand this is upsetting news, but leaving now is extremely dangerous. You need medication to prevent another seizure. We need to monitor—"

"Monitor what, exactly?" I ask. "The tumor that's killin' me? The one ya just told me will end my life in a couple of months or less, no matter what ya do?"

She at least has the decency to look uncomfortable. "But if you stay here, we can make you comfortable. Manage your symptoms."

"I don't want comfortable." I plant my hands on the edge of the bed to steady myself. "I want to live whatever time I have left on my own terms, in my own home."

"And what terms are those?" Dr. Patterson asks.

I take a deep breath. "I have a bed and breakfast to run. I have guests dependin' on me." I glance at Dex, still perched silently in the corner. "And I have personal matters to attend to. I intend to spend whatever time I have left livin'. Not wastin' away in a fuckin' hospital bed."

Dr. Patterson looks down at her shoes, then back at me. "Mina," she says gently, "I don't think you understand the severity—"

"I understand perfectly." I wobble slightly, and Hazel reaches out to steady me. "I have a tumor sittin' pretty in the middle of my brain, and it's goin' to kill me, but I'll be damned if I spend my last days rottin' away in this bed."

Blake moves to my side, his warm hand takin' me by the elbow. I'm grateful for the support, even though I hate that I need it.

"I'll sign whatever forms ya need," I tell Dr. Patterson. "Releasin' you from liability. Acknowledgin' I'm an idiot. Whatever paperwork makes ya feel better about lettin' me walk out of here."

"That's not what this is about," she protests. "You have terminal cancer. You just had a severe seizure. You could have one again at any time. I'm trying to look out for your well-being."

I laugh, a short, sharp cackle. "My well-bein' went out the window the moment my brain decided to malfunction on me. Now it's just about me takin' control of what little time I have left."

Dr. Patterson sighs, her shoulders droppin' slightly. "I'll have the forms prepared. But I strongly advise against this."

"Noted," I say. "And I know you're only doin' what ya think

is best for me, but right now, what's best for me is bein' at home with my friends." I look around at all of their faces. "With my family."

She nods, then leaves to get the paperwork, Shannon trails behind her with a last concerned glance over her shoulder.

Hazel approaches with my clothes. "Are you sure about this?"

"I've never been more sure of anythin'." I take the bundle from her. "Help me get dressed?"

She nods.

"Turn around," I tell Blake and Dex. "Unless ya want a titty show. I'm past the point of bein' modest."

Blake turns red and quickly turns his back. Dex follows suit more slowly, his eyes holdin' mine for a long moment before he turns away.

It's harder than I expected. My limbs feel like they're made of lead, and my fingers fumble with buttons and zippers. Hazel helps me without comment, steadyin' me when I sway.

"You know this is crazy, right?" she whispers as she helps pull my sweater over my head. "Leaving the hospital to fight some supernatural cult when you can barely stand?"

"Probably." I manage a smile. "But dyin' in a hospital bed, while the world ends seems crazier. Besides, I'll be much easier to claim by the Concord if I'm laid up in hospital."

By the time I'm dressed, I'm exhausted. Who knew that coverin' your bits took so much effort? But I'm standin', and I'm dressed, and I'm makin' my own choices.

Blake turns back around once I'm decent. "What's the plan?"

"Get back to the B&B," I say. "Figure out what the Concord is plannin' next. Find a way to stop them."

"And how exactly do we do that?" Hazel asks.

I look at Dex, who's turned to face us again. "That's where our resident reaper comes in. He's familiar with them. Right, Dex?"

He nods slowly. "We need to find and neutralize as many of the thirteen binding points as we can. Without them, the Concord can't complete the Hollowing."

"I still don't fully understand who this Concord group is. And what's a Hollowing?" Blake asks.

I fix my hair as best I can while Dex fills them in on what we know—and what we suspect—so far.

"But why Mina?" Hazel asks. "I still don't understand how she plays into all of this."

"What I've determined is they need her as their key," Dex says with a sigh. "Her connection to both life and death makes her the perfect conduit." He swallows hard. "Her tumor may increase her usefulness. We just have to make sure . . ."

He trails off. I turn to him, eyebrow raised. "Make sure of what?"

He sighs. "That if you . . . pass . . . before we stop them, that I usher you as quickly as possible so they can't get to your soul. If they can get to you, they'll use you even after you're . . ."

"Dead," I finish. "These bloody bastards are tenacious, aren't they?"

The room falls silent as we all absorb this. It's strategic. And a potential disaster if I, or what's left of me, falls into the wrong hands.

I look at all of their faces. My allies in the massive shit-show that my life has become.

"Well," I say, forcin' a smile and a little bravado into my voice, "I always wanted to go out with a bang, but this is a bit much, don't ya think?"

No one laughs.

A knock at the door announces Shannon's return with a handful of forms. I sign them without readin' them, my signature shaky but legible.

"Your personal effects," she says, handin' me a plastic bag that contains my phone, wallet, and watch. "And Dr. Patterson prescribed these." She offers a paper bag of medication. "Anti-seizure meds and steroids for the swelling. Instructions are inside."

"Thank you," I say. I know I'm a right pain in the arse, and she doesn't have to be this nice to me.

"You'll need to leave in a wheelchair," she continues. "Hospital policy. We can't be faced with a lawsuit if you fall and hurt yourself on the way out."

I want to argue that I can walk out on my own two feet, but the truth is, I'm not sure I can make it that far. Pride isn't worth fallin' flat on my face in the hospital corridor.

Wheelchair it is.

CHAPTER FIFTEEN

Dex

Light streams through the windows of the foyer, and for a moment, I can almost pretend that we're returning home from a pleasant outing. But, that's not reality. I'm wounded. Mina's dying. And we have no idea how to stop the Concord.

Coco, La'Tasha, Leo, and Vivienne sit around the kitchen table sipping on drinks and nibbling cookies, unaware that their world is about to shatter. They look up when we enter, conversation dying mid-sentence.

"You're back!" Coco jumps up, then freezes, her smile faltering as she takes in Mina's appearance.

Mina steadies herself against the door frame. She's been silent since we left the hospital. Determined. Stubborn. I've collected billions of souls across time, and I've rarely seen such tenacity in the face of certain death.

She takes a deep breath. "Right, so, I'm glad you're here. I need to let ya know that I have a brain tumor. It's aggressive. Doctor says a couple months at best, but . . ." No sugarcoating.

"Que?" Coco's coffee cup clatters against its saucer. It sloshes over the rim, staining the white tablecloth. She moves toward Mina. "No. No, no, no. Don't say that."

La'Tasha's hand flies to her mouth, eyes wide.

Hazel helps Mina to a chair, her hand hovering protectively at Mina's elbow. Blake stands behind them, arms crossed, jaw tight.

Vivienne reaches across the table and takes Mina's hand, her touch gentle despite her long, dangerous-looking nails. "How long have you known?" she asks.

"Two months," Mina admits. "I kept it to myself. Didn't want to worry anyone."

La'Tasha wipes a tear from her face. "That's why you've been so exhausted. And keeping to yourself . . ."

Mina nods. "The seizure was because the tumor is growin' faster than they expected."

I hover apart from the group. My cane scrapes against the floor, and six pairs of eyes turn to me. The mysterious guest haunting corners.

I meet Mina's gaze and give her a slight nod.

"Dex . . ." she starts, but suddenly chokes up. "Um, Dex can . . ." She waves a hand, prompting me to fill in.

"Mina is dying," I say. "And I was sent to retrieve her. It's my job."

"Your job?" Leo's brow creases. "I thought you were a writer."

"Not exactly." I tap my cane against the floor, and my scythe flickers into existence. Dull, but there.

"He's Death," Hazel says, matter-of-fact. "Like, the actual Grim Reaper."

Silence.

Then Leo barks out a laugh that lands somewhere between a cough and disbelief. "Come on."

Blake shifts beside him. "No. She's not joking."

"I'm *a* reaper," I clarify. "Not *the* reaper. There are many of us."

I notice the lightbulb flick on behind La'Tasha's eyes. "*That's* why your energy's off."

"And why they tried to take you out," Coco adds, catching up. "You're protecting Mina."

"Trying to protect her." The words stick in my throat. "Not succeeding."

Vivienne still hasn't let go of Mina's hand. "Can you help her?" she asks. "Stop the tumor?"

"I wish I had a loophole to offer. But death doesn't work that way," I say softly, locking eyes with Mina. "Even for me."

The truth settles like fog in the warm kitchen.

"I can't stop what's coming for her," I finish. "I can only be there when it does."

"So what, we just give up?" Anguish spills across Coco's face. "Let her die?"

"No." Mina's voice cuts through the despair. "We accept it. There's nothin' we can do about this, pet. It's inoperable."

"And there's also the Concord we have to deal with," Blake adds.

Leo blinks, glancing from face to face like he's missed a step in the conversation. "Wait—what's the Concord?" he asks. "Is that a person? A place? What are we talking about?"

Blake places a protective hand on the back of Mina's chair. "This crazy-ass, apocalyptic, supernatural group. They're planning something big. And they need Mina to do it. We have to protect her from them."

"That's why they targeted Dex," Hazel adds. "To weaken him. To get him out of the way. So they can use her."

"And it worked." Heat pricks at my neck as the shame burns through me. "The wound refuses to heal. My powers are . . . limited. I don't know what's happening to me. I do know that I can't do this alone."

"Tell them what we're up against." Mina beckons to me to step closer.

I straighten, shifting against the ache in my ribs. Then, once again, I tell the story. Who the Concord is. What they've done. What they want.

"They need thirteen binding points to tear open the veil

between worlds," I finish. "And Mina is their key."

"Why her specifically?" Leo asks.

"Because her connection to both life and death makes her the perfect conduit." I glance down at Mina, her fingers twitching slightly in her lap. "They intend to offer her immortality in exchange for her cooperation."

"So just refuse," Leo says, like it's that simple.

Vivienne lets out a sharp breath, then leans back in her chair, arms crossed. "I've dealt with them before. It doesn't work like that. Even if you say no, they'll twist your will, or bypass it entirely. Dead or alive, they take what they want."

"They'll hijack her soul," I add. "Tether it to their own power. But only if they get to her before I can usher her to the other side."

Mina reaches for me, and I step forward without hesitation, wrapping my fingers gently around hers.

"If we can't stop the ritual," she says, voice steady but low, "then my only option is to die—which is goin' to happen soon anyway. And for Dex to usher my soul across before they get to it."

Hazel's breath catches. She looks like she wants to argue, but can't find the words. Tears glisten at the corners of her eyes. "That's why we have to stop the ritual," she says fiercely. "So we can keep her here with us. As long as we can."

La'Tasha sets her teacup down with a soft clink. Her eyes never leave Mina's face, locked in a kind of quiet analysis. She rises and walks over to Mina's chair.

"Your energy's been off since the séance," she says, voice low. "May I check something?"

Mina nods, too drained to question it. "Go ahead."

La'Tasha lifts her hands to either side of Mina's head, fingers splayed like she's cradling a glass figure. Her fingertips begin to glow. A soft indigo light pulses from her hands, steady and calm.

Magic has a scent, though most humans never notice. La'Tasha's smells earthy and alive. It's a combination of fresh rain on loam, with a hint of spice. It spills into the kitchen like steam from an open teacup, curling into every corner. Even I feel it. My skin prickles, every hair on my arms rising. Her power is immense.

Her eyes close in concentration. The light spreads from her fingertips, creating a faint halo around Mina's head. It pulses in rhythm with Mina's heartbeat, a rhythm I can hear as clearly as if my ear were pressed against her chest.

Unnatural quiet fills the kitchen. Even the old house holds its breath. Hazel and Blake exchange worried glances while Coco watches, transfixed. Only Vivienne remains perfectly still, her eyes missing nothing.

La'Tasha's brow furrows. The indigo light flickers, then flares brighter. Her breathing quickens, becoming shallow and strained, then she pulls back with a sharp intake of breath, breaking contact. The light vanishes.

"There's something attached to the tumor," La'Tasha says, her voice shaking. "The energy is almost parasitic."

Mina's face pales further. "What do you mean, 'attached'?"

"It's not natural," La'Tasha explains, rubbing her fingertips together like they're numb. "I sensed the tumor, but it's not entirely human if that makes sense. There's an energy wrapped around it that feels paranormal." She looks directly at Mina, concern etched in every line of her face. "When was the last time you had a scan to measure the growth?"

Mina shrugs. "Ten or so days ago. And it hadn't grown since my initial diagnosis."

"So something attached itself since then," Leo says.

"But what?" Coco asks.

Mina's eyes widen. Her face pales further. "The séance. When I connected with the Collector." She turns to me. "When I touched Dahlia, something got inside of my head. It showed me things. Do you think it stayed behind?"

I nod. "Perhaps the entity used the connection to plant something."

"But how?" Coco asks, voice higher with fear.

La'Tasha nods. "Psychic parasites. They're more powerful when they attach to existing conditions. Remember the trickster ghoul from this past summer?"

Hazel steps forward, her eyes bright with sudden hope. "If this thing is attached to the tumor but isn't the tumor itself, does that mean we can save her? Just remove whatever latched onto her?"

All eyes turn to La'Tasha. She hesitates, twisting her rings nervously.

"I don't know," she admits. "It's using the tumor, but I don't know why. I've never messed with parasitic magic before. I can do some research, but . . ."

The pieces click into place. "It's not exactly feeding off of the tumor so much as it is contributing to it," I say. "It's priming Mina's energy. Creating the perfect conditions for the ritual."

I've seen this before. Those who practice dark magic have been known to plant seeds of corruption in those they want to control. And I think I know exactly who might be responsible.

Mina's hands tremble slightly as she grips the edge of the kitchen table. The slight shake betrays her fear, but her voice remains steady when she speaks. "So the bloody bastards not only made themselves at home in my house, but also inside my head."

Blake pushes away from the counter, already bristling with energy. "So what do we do?" he asks, voice tight, jaw clenched like he's holding back a growl. "Tell me what needs to happen. We'll handle it."

Mina lifts her chin. "We fight. Not for me—I'm already on borrowed time. But for everyone else. For Moonridge."

"The first priority has to be to weaken the binding points," I say. "And we can't let them near her soul. The Mortician is skilled at hijacking them. It's happened before. One of us must always be with Mina, no matter what."

"Will you even be able to help her cross in your current state?" Vivienne asks.

"I have no doubt that when the time comes, Dex will do

what he came here to do. He'll make sure I cross over properly. So they can't get to me." Mina takes my hand in hers. So much trust. I can't fail her.

The silence that follows feels heavy enough to crack the foundations of the house. No one wants to acknowledge the truth of her words. No one wants to accept that we're not trying to save Mina anymore, we're trying to ensure her death doesn't destroy everything else.

"So, our best option is to target them directly while keeping Mina safe," I say, pulling us back on track. "Some of us need to work to destroy the bindings. Without the bindings, they can't siphon the power. The fewer bindings in play, the weaker they are, and we can stop the ritual from happening."

La'Tasha nods, recovering her composure. "Since there's no medical magic that can stop cancer, I'll do some research and see if there's anything I can do to interrupt the parasite and slow the growth. Try to buy us more time."

Mina smiles and mouths, *Thank you.*

"So what exactly are these binding points?" Blake asks.

"Each point siphons energy from the natural world. From ley lines." I tap my cane against the floor for emphasis.

Coco hugs herself, shivering despite the kitchen's warmth. "But how?"

"Each Concord member links to one of twelve binding points, siphoning energy through their connection. That energy funnels into an anchor positioned at the thirteenth point—the heart of the ritual. When the human acting as the key is delivered to the anchor through the blood ritual, the veil rips. And then all hell breaks loose. Trust me when I say that what will come through is a darkness that should never touch your world."

Blake straightens suddenly, exchanging a look with Hazel. Recognition dawns on his face.

"This feels a little too familiar," he says, crossing his arms. "Didn't we just deal with energy points that Ravena set up? We destroyed those. Were those binding points?"

"I can't say for sure, but I believe she was helping to set the stage for this," I confirm. "Testing Moonridge's defenses. Weakening what she could to let the Concord in."

"She was working with them?" Leo asks, brow furrowed.

"I'm not familiar with her," I admit. "My guess is she was likely either a new recruit or a lackey. They've been operating for centuries, replacing members as needed."

"Damn. And we thought *she* was a pain in the ass," Blake says, voice tight with disbelief.

"She was, but her friends are even worse," Mina deadpans.

The group shifts, unconsciously forming a loose circle in the kitchen. I find myself included in their formation, no longer standing apart as I have since arriving in Moonridge. Their acceptance should mean nothing to me, yet the simple act of being included feels strangely significant.

Mina looks at each face, at everyone willing to fight for her, and smiles. The afternoon light catches in her red hair, turning it to copper and gold. Even as she's dying, she radiates a quiet, stubborn kind of beauty. A life force that refuses to dim.

"I'll continue searching for the binding points," I announce. "Even weakened, I can sense them. Disrupt them."

"You can barely stand," Hazel points out, her tone gentle but firm. "We'll help."

Leo nods without hesitation. "Count me in. I'm good at fucking things up."

"I'm pretty good at tracking binding points," Blake adds. "And this time I can do it in my own body."

Hazel nudges him in the ribs, and Mina laughs.

Vivienne, who has been quietly observing until now, surprises everyone by speaking up. "Count me in. Just let me know what I can do. I've grown surprisingly attached to this quaint little town." Her red lips curve in a smile that doesn't quite hide her fangs. "And I have some unfinished business with the Concord."

"You know what this means, right?" Mina asks Vivienne. "We're talking about fighting an organization that's been around for centuries."

Vivienne shrugs elegantly. "I've been around for over a century myself. I know this group. They're evil. And they don't scare me."

In my long existence, I've seen countless human attempts to defy fate. Most fail. Some succeed only to make the situation worse.

But this group pulses with different energy. Perhaps it's because they're not fighting to save themselves. They're fighting for Mina, knowing they can't save her from death but determined to save her from a fate that's even worse.

"Back to the binding points," I say, bringing focus back to our task. "I've found four so far—Skipper Lake, the Moonstone Circle, the church, and Hollow Glen Asylum."

"I saw some of them," Mina chimes in. "Last night. When I touched Dahlia during the séance. You might want to check the caves that lead to the mines beneath the mill."

"Shocker. Exactly where we entombed Ravena," Blake says. "I guess it's time to pay that evil ho a visit."

One by one, they call out potential locations, their knowledge of Moonridge's hidden places impressing even me. They know this town, its secrets, its wounds, its power spots.

Mina listens to each suggestion, mentally mapping her town. "We need a base of operations," she says finally. "Somewhere to coordinate and track our progress."

"Here," Leo suggests. "The B&B. It's central."

Mina shakes her head. "Too compromised. They've already placed sigils here, and there's a binding point on the property. They've been in and out without us knowin'."

"Why not the apothecary?" Blake offers. "It's probably the most protected spot in town."

Hazel nods. "Why does it feel like we just did this?"

"Because we did." Coco shrugs. "I'll dig out the maps again."

"Then it's settled," Mina says with a nod. "You lot go find the points. I have guests to check on."

"Let me do that," La'Tasha says.

"I'm not dead yet," Mina says. "Let me live, would ya?"

La'Tasha places a hand on Mina's shoulder and looks her dead in the eye. "I'm helping. You just got out of the hospital."

"Fine, then. Help me up."

La'Tasha helps her to her feet and pulls her into a hug.

Hazel grabs her jacket. "I need to get to the festival. This afternoon's events are about to start, and I'm late."

Afternoon light streams through the kitchen windows as everyone sets out on their individual missions. For the first time since last night, I feel hope.

A dangerous emotion for one such as me. But perhaps, in this moment, a necessary one.

CHAPTER SIXTEEN

Mina

The Moonridge Halloween Festival is supposed to be fun. And it probably would be if I hadn't been possessed and then had a major seizure less than twenty-four hours ago. I know I should have stayed home, but I couldn't. I need to help however I can.

We decided to check out the festival after Coco suggested it might be a point of interest. He suspected the concentration of emotion could make it a perfect anchor for the Concord's magic. I insisted on comin' despite everyone's objections. If I'm goin' to die anyway, I'm not spendin' my last days hidin' out at the B&B. If I'm goin' to stay laid up in bed, I could have just stayed in hospital.

The doctors said to avoid stress. Right. On a normal day, that would be easy, but not so much when ghosts are poppin' up like bloody dandelions.

"You okay?" Hazel appears at my elbow, pirate costume flutterin' in the October breeze.

"Peachy." I paste on a smile. I don't bother to mention that each heartbeat drives spikes through my skull. "Just takin' in the sights."

And what sights they are. Jack-o'-lanterns leer from booths and tables, their carved faces glowin' with flickerin' light while children dart between games and food stalls, fingers sticky with candy.

I look up in time to catch a translucent elderly man in a suit from the Early Republic era lookin' longingly at the pies laid out for the pie contest. A few feet away, two little girls in pinafores play hopscotch in the middle of the walkway, fadin' in and out like bad TV reception.

"There are more of them." I point, and Hazel follows my gaze. "At least a dozen visible right now."

Hazel's fingers twist anxiously. "Can you hear them, too? Wait, do ghosts even talk?"

The whispers come before I can answer her question. Faint at first, then louder, more insistent.

the veil weakens

the anchor walks the falls

she's coming

they're coming

My knees buckle. Hazel grabs my arm as dizziness crashes over me, threatenin' to bring me down.

"What is it?" Her fingers dig into my sleeve. "Mina?"

The voices grow louder, pressin' against my skull from the inside. I close my eyes, tryin' to block them out, but that only makes them more insistent.

the daughter has power

the wheel turns, the door opens

I open my eyes and the world looks different, like I'm watchin' a 3D movie without the glasses. The colors are muted, and the humans around me seem slightly transparent, while the ghosts appear more solid and vibrant than before.

"You shouldn't have come here today. You should be resting. We need to get you back home," Hazel says, but her voice sounds far away.

I let her lead me toward a park bench. "Not yet. I just need to rest a bit, love. Like I told the doctor, I don't want to just lie in bed and waste away."

Her eyes fill with tears, and she pats my leg. "I know."

Damn it, now I'm gonna cry. I look away in time to see a ghostly little boy crouched behind a group of teenagers who are about to bob for apples. A young woman counts down to three, and the young men all fold over their barrels and put their faces in the water. But then the ghost boy presses both hands to one of the boys' backs, holdin' him under. The teen struggles, water sloshin' over the edge of his barrel. His friends laugh, but the boy continues to struggle.

"Stop that!" I stand and stumble toward them when the ghost boy notices me. He immediately releases the teen, who flips up, water runnin' down his face. He gasps for air.

"Did you see that?" I clutch Hazel's arm.

"See what?"

"The ghost boy. He tried to drown that young man."

Hazel's face pales. "That's not possible. Ghosts shouldn't be able to manipulate physical objects."

"Tell that to the kid who almost died." She follows my finger to the teen who is now towelin' off his head. He holds one finger to a nostril and spurts water and a big, yellow booger out of his nostril.

"We need to find Dex," I say through gritted teeth. "They're gettin' dangerous."

Hazel nods. She offers her arm to me, and we start toward the other side of the park, but we've not gone but three steps when I see it. A shadow moves between booths. Not a ghost. This is different. It has no definite shape, only the suggestion of movement, like a patch of soul-suckin' darkness, flowin' against the crowd.

And it's headed straight for us.

"We've got company." I gesture toward the approachin' shadow.

Hazel follows my gaze, and this time, she sees it too.

"What is that?"

"I'm guessin' it's Concord-related," I speculate. "Spyin' on me, probably. Checkin' me out."

The shadow pauses. It ripples, stretches, then retreats into the crowd.

"It's just scouting," Hazel says, though she doesn't sound convinced. "Come on, we need to find the others and let them know."

We move toward the festival entrance, and I glance back. Several ghosts watch me now, all of their faces solemn and expectant. The whispers rise again, a single phrase repeated over and over.

The daughter and the key. Together.

Whose daughter?

Before I can process the ghostly chorus, Penny bursts through the crowd like she's bein' chased. Her ponytail loose, glasses askew. She clutches an old book like it might escape.

"I brought this book," Penny gasps, out of breath. "Mr. Grimm said it might be the one that might be causing this, and I need to give it to you so you can get rid of it before it causes more damage."

She thrusts the tome toward Hazel.

"What is that?" Hazel doesn't touch it, but leans in for a closer look. The book's leather cover is worn at the edges, the color of dried blood. Strange symbols that seem to shift are etched into the surface. My headache spikes.

"'The Lost Testament of Holloway," Hazel reads from the cover in a whisper. "Is this the Concord bible Dex told us about? Where did you find this?"

Penny adjusts her glasses, fingers tremblin'. "In the library archives. In a box of donated books."

She doesn't meet our eyes when she says this, which tells me there's more.

"You did something with it, didn't you?" Hazel's voice turns sharp.

Penny looks as though she's about to deny it, but knows better. "I tried a few spells. They looked simple enough." Her words tumble out faster now. "Just little things—a summoning spell, a tracking spell, a divination spell—the instructions were so clear, and I've been trying so hard to practice easy spells, and they seemed so straightforward."

The symbols on the book's cover seem to pulse now. One of them reminds me of the mark I saw on the wall at my B&B.

"I had no idea what it really was," Penny continues, voice crackin'. "I'm sorry if I made things worse, I thought maybe I'd finally found magic I could actually do that wouldn't hurt anything, and that maybe you'd be impressed enough to finally—"

"You performed spells from a book you couldn't even read properly?" Hazel's jaw clenches.

"I could read it just fine." Penny straightens her spine. "The spells were in English. They read like beginner spells."

"That's the trap!" Hazel snaps, loud enough that nearby festival-goers glance our way. She lowers her voice. "Manipulative texts adapt to the reader. They show you what you want to see—"

"Wait," I interrupt as Penny's face crumples. "Hazel, she was manipulated. The Concord set a trap."

Hazel takes a breath, swallowin' her anger. "Yes. I'm sorry, Penny. It's been a rough few days. I'm on edge." She pulls gloves from her pocket—soft leather embroidered with tiny symbols—and slips them on. "Let me see it."

Penny hands over the book with relief. Hazel holds it carefully and runs her gloved fingers over the cover while chantin' words that make the symbols freeze.

"It's definitely ancient," she confirms. "An activation grimoire. It's been enchanted to entice the weak-willed."

"Like me," Penny says miserably.

"Like anyone who wants something badly enough." Hazel sighs and looks at her like she's about to tell her off again, but then, surprisingly, chooses a different approach. "Magic is seductive, Penny."

I watch their exchange, keepin' an eye on the ghosts who have moved in to watch.

Hazel carefully places the book in her bag. "You did the right thing bringing this to me. I'll lock it up until we can get rid of it safely. The important thing is we have the book now," Hazel says as she pats her bag. "One less thing to worry about with everything else that's going on."

I stumble, and Penny grabs me by the elbow, helpin' me back to the bench. "Are you okay?"

"Just need to rest. Dealin' with some health problems, and some other . . . things."

Penny places a gentle hand on my shoulder. "Anything I can do to help?"

Before I can answer, I spot Dex movin' through the crowd, his tall figure unmistakable even at a distance. He walks stiffly, favorin' his injured side, and right behind him is Blake, who takes in the festival with predatory alertness. Sheriff Harlow approaches them, his face drawn with worry. He speaks urgently to Blake, who points in our direction.

"Looks like the sheriff's havin' a rough day too," I say.

Penny glances over her shoulder. "The whole town is. People are reporting seeing weird things. I've seen more ghosts today than I have since I moved to Moonridge six months ago."

"You can see the ghosts, too?" Hazel asks.

"Well, yeah. Can't you? I thought everyone could. There are four just right over there."

I glance around and see an elderly man in a leisure suit laughin' at a woman whose dog's leash got tangled around her legs. And near the face-paintin' booth, three children dressed in Edwardian clothes watch the human children with wistful expressions.

Before I can speak to Penny about what else she's seen, Sheriff Harlow approaches. He looks like he's aged five years since I last saw him. His uniform is rumpled, and dark half-moons hang under his eyes. This is a man at the end of his rope. He's typically Mr. Calm-and-Collected, but today he looks ready to either give up or punch somethin'.

"Hazel." He nods curtly. His eyes flicker over Penny and me, but he's clearly here for a business chat, not simple pleasantries. "Do you have a minute?"

He glances at Penny and me and then tilts his head to the right, away from us, and they step toward the cotton candy stall. Far enough away that he thinks they won't be overheard, but close enough that I can hear most of their conversation since the sheriff isn't exactly good at keepin' his voice down.

"We've got problems," he says, scrubbin' a hand down his face. "Big ones."

"Yeah, I've heard," Hazel replies. "But we always get weird things happening around this time of year. You know that."

"No, you don't understand." He leans in closer. "I've got singing pumpkins keeping people up at night and three separate reports of levitating door mats. Don't even get me started on the number of people who have called in claiming that they woke up to find dead relatives hanging out in their houses."

"How many, exactly?" Hazel asks, crossin' her arms.

"Three. Which is three too many."

"Only three?" I mutter to Penny. From where I am, I can count at least a dozen ghosts millin' around, all of which are technically someone's dead relative in some way or another.

"My deputies are losing their minds," the sheriff continues. "Rogers swears he gave directions to a little girl who disappeared into thin air. Chen refuses to go near the fortune-teller's tent after he saw what he claims was his dead grandmother."

I glance toward the tent. Sure enough, an elderly Asian woman in traditional dress stands outside, watchin' the crowds with a serene expression.

"We're completely unprepared for this," Sheriff Harlow admits. "People are starting to panic."

Hazel's shoulders straighten. "Have there been any physical injuries?"

He shakes his head. "Not yet. Just sightings, and the things I mentioned earlier, but people are scared. I want to get ahead of this before someone loses their mind and does something stupid."

"We'll look into it. Why don't you try putting down a protective perimeter?" Hazel suggests.

"And how would I do that? I can't do magic," the sheriff points out.

"You don't need any special power for that. Just pour salt lines around the entire festival grounds."

"Salt lines?" He looks skeptical. He pulls a small notebook out of his jacket pocket and jots down a few notes.

"And place iron stakes at the cardinal points: north, south, east, west. I'd suggest putting them at the edges of the city limits and then another set around the park just to help repel the worst of it."

"Iron stakes." He looks at her with a raised eyebrow. He sighs and then writes it down. "We might have some rebar at the station."

"That'll work. And most importantly, we need to do our best to keep people calm." Hazel meets his gaze directly. "No mass announcements about ghosts. Frame everything as festival special effects gone wrong. A huge spike of emotion—especially fear—could make things worse."

His mouth twists. "Salt, iron, and keep everybody calm. Got it."

I suddenly notice that the ghosts tend to cluster around certain areas: the cryin' child near the balloons, the couple that argues by the caramel apple stand. Hazel's right.

"—and we need to temporarily close the haunted corn maze," Hazel says. "Something doesn't feel right about that area."

The sheriff nods and puts the notebook back in his pocket. "Look, I don't pretend to understand all this ghosty stuff. But I've seen enough today to know we're out of our depth."

"You're doing all the right things," Hazel assures him. "We'll manage the rest."

He glances at me. He must notice my pale face and the way I'm slumped on the bench because he says, "Ms. Cartwright, you don't look well. Should you even be out here?"

"Probably not," I admit. "But where else would I be when the world's goin' sideways?"

He nods and shrugs, unsure what to make of my statement. "Get some rest," he says gruffly, then turns back to Hazel. "I'll get started with the salt lines."

He walks away, already barkin' orders into his radio about road salt and perimeters.

"He's in over his head," I say when Hazel rejoins us.

"We all are." She sits beside me. The heavy book in her bag clunks against the edge of the bench. "But at least he's willing to listen."

Penny points toward the carousel. "Look at that couple fighting. Is it just me, or is there something weird around them?"

We follow her pointed finger. The air ripples and distorts around the couple. Three ghosts hover nearby, growin' more solid by the second.

"Like I said, the spirits respond to emotion," Hazel explains. "The Concord must have known. The festival is the perfect emotional battery. Hundreds of people experiencing joy, fear, excitement, all in one place. And it's more likely to pull in even more paranormal energy because of the time of year."

I haul myself to standin', ignorin' Hazel's protest. "We need to check the other emotional hotspots. Anywhere feelings run high."

"You need to rest," Hazel insists.

"I'll rest when I'm dead," I retort, then wince. "Sorry. Gallows humor."

We move, and I notice another ripple in the crowd, that same shadowy presence from earlier. It moves with purpose, slidin' between festival-goers who shiver as it passes.

"It's back," I murmur to Hazel. "The shadow."

She follows my gaze but shakes her head. "I don't see anything."

That's new. She saw it earlier. Which means either my tumor is causin' hallucinations, or the thing is hidin' from everyone but me now.

The shadow waits near a group of children waitin' in line for cotton candy, then shifts direction, and disappears.

"It's gone now."

Hazel pulls her phone out of her pocket. "It's Blake. I'm going to take this."

"I don't even know what I'm doing here. I'm useless at this," Penny says as Hazel steps away from the crowd. "Completely, totally useless. All of you are working together to stop whatever is happening, and what am I doing? Making things worse with books I shouldn't have touched. Things probably wouldn't even be this bad if I'd just left the book alone."

She's not wrong, but I can understand her frustration, and especially her feelin' like an outsider. How many times have I felt the same way since my diagnosis? Useless. Helpless. Watchin' from the sidelines as others fight battles for me.

"Knowledge is power." I place a hand on her arm. "Especially now. Maybe you can't do magic, but we could use your research skills, your organization. And ya did the right thing bringin' that book to Hazel."

Penny shakes her head. "La'Tasha tried to teach me a simple protection spell last month. I couldn't even make the candle flicker. It whooshed into this huge fireball and burned my eyebrows off." She gestures to her penciled-on brows.

"Magic isn't everythin'," I insist, though I'm probably the wrong person to be givin' this pep talk.

"It is in Moonridge," Penny says miserably. "It's what makes someone valuable here."

Before I can respond, her phone chirps.

"Oh, gosh—I've got to get back to the library. I didn't realize how long I've been gone."

I call out a quick goodbye just as a familiar voice cuts through the crowd.

"Hey! Mina!"

I turn to see Calvin. He weaves toward us, his face lit with relief.

Behind him, barely visible to my ghost-sensitive eyes, a shadow spreads across the ground like a ghostly stain. Is it trackin' his movements?

He barrels through the crowd and wraps me in a bear hug that lifts my feet clean off the ground. The sudden pressure makes my head spin, but I don't complain. His embrace is warm and solid in a world that feels increasingly unstable. When he sets me down, I see his eyes are damp with unshed tears, though his smile could power the entire festival.

"I'm so sorry I wasn't there when you got home from the hospital," he says. His strong hands grip my shoulders like he's afraid I might disappear. "Blake told me everything. Why didn't you call me?"

I pat his arm, tryin' not to wince at his tight grip. "You were busy. And it's not like there's anythin' you could do."

He shakes his head fiercely. "That's not the point. I should've been there."

"Where were you, anyway?" Hazel asks.

His face transforms, worry lines smoothin' into a bashful grin. "I was on a date, actually."

"A date?" I raise my eyebrows, grateful for this slice of normalcy. "Well, well. Who's the lucky fella?"

The tips of his ears turn pink when he blushes. Behind him, the shadow I noticed earlier seems to pause and hovers just at the edge of my vision. Watchin'. I force myself to focus on Calvin instead.

"His name's Everett," Calvin says. He sighs and shifts his feet like an excited kid. "I met him during the 5K the other day. Literally crashed into him. You were there."

I nod. I know exactly who he means.

"He felt terrible about it," Calvin continues, face all lit up. "Apologized for an entire mile while we walked it off. We ended up getting coffee after."

"That's lovely." Unease works its way up the back of my neck. "What's he like?"

Calvin blushes. "He's amazing. Seriously. He's got this great retro style, and he has the sweetest smile. I don't know, he just . . . he somehow makes me feel like I'm the only person in the room."

The description and the way Calvin is already so obviously head over arse for this man sends my stomach to my toes, but I keep my expression neutral. "Sounds wonderful. What does he do?"

"He's a mechanic. Works on classic cars mostly." He runs a hand over his beard, still smilin'. "We've got so much in common. We both love running, both love dogs, but don't have time for one. Lucky for him, I can shift into a huge one."

He laughs, the sound pure and joyful, and my heart cracks a little because, honestly, when was the last time I saw Calvin this happy?

"That's . . . nice," I manage.

How do I tell him that I think this guy might not be alive?

"He knows a lot about Moonridge's history," Calvin continues. "Knows all the old stories, the founding families. Really fascinating stuff."

I have a feelin' Everett doesn't just know local history. He probably experienced it first hand.

"I can't wait for you to meet him," Calvin says. "I think you'll really like him. He's got a dry sense of humor, like you. And he asked about you specifically. Said he'd heard wonderful things about the local B&B owner."

"He asked about me?" The words come out sharper than intended.

Calvin nods enthusiastically. "Yeah, when I was telling him about my friends. I mentioned you run the old mansion, and he said he's always loved historic properties. He wants to meet all of you."

My hands tremble slightly. A mechanic from the 1950s, deeply familiar with Moonridge history, specifically askin' about me and my B&B right when the Concord needs their key? This can't be a coincidence.

"Calvin," I start, then stop. How do ya tell someone that their first real connection in years might not be what it seems? I have no doubt that the happiness he feels will only lead to heartache once Halloween has come and gone.

If we all survive.

"What?" He notices my expression and his brow furrows. "You look worried. Is everything okay?"

I glance at Hazel, who watches our conversation with concern.

"Just thinkin' it would be nice to meet him," I lie. "When are ya seein' him again?"

"Tonight, actually. We're meeting at the gazebo at eight, right after the costume contest ends. I'm nervous. It's been so long since I've felt this way about someone."

Eight o'clock. At the gazebo. I make a mental note.

"Actually," Calvin says as he pulls out his phone, "I think I have a picture. We took a selfie yesterday."

He scrolls through his photos, brow furrowed. "That's weird. It's not showing up. Must not have saved properly." He shrugs it off, but my stomach clenches.

"Maybe the lighting was bad," Hazel suggests weakly.

But I know it's more than that. Much more.

Across the festival grounds, near the ring toss game, I notice a figure in perfectly pressed 1950s clothes movin' through the crowd. Even at this distance, I can see the careful style of his hair, the vintage cut of his jacket.

Everett. And he's watchin' us.

When our eyes meet across the festival, he smiles. He raises one hand in a small wave.

Calvin follows my gaze, and his face lights up. "There he is!" He waves back enthusiastically.

Everett smiles and winks at Calvin, then steps behind a booth and vanishes.

"Isn't he handsome?" Calvin turns back to me with shinin' eyes.

I stare at the spot where Everett disappeared, a thousand different scenarios runnin' through my head.

Calvin suddenly sobers. "But enough about me. How are you doing? Blake said it's . . . it's bad."

The simple question nearly breaks me. How am I doin'? I'm dyin'. I'm seein' ghosts. I'm watchin' my friend fall for a man who is already dead, and I don't have the heart to tell him.

"I'm okay," I lie. "Takin' it one day at a time."

Calvin's not fooled. "We're going to fight this, Mina. All of us. Whatever it takes."

I smile, not trustin' my voice.

"Blake said you're working on some kind of plan?" Calvin glances at Hazel, then back to me.

"We're trying to disrupt the Concord's binding points," Hazel explains. She keeps her voice low. "We need to totally ruin their ritual before they can use Mina as their anchor. I have La'Tasha and Coco doing some research. From what she's sent me, they're ancient and very bad news. Total assholes, but like, in a major way."

Calvin's jaw sets. "Tell me what to smash. I'm good at smashing things."

A laugh escapes me, sharp and unexpected. "We're still figurin' that out. But we'll let ya know, love."

The shadow hoverin' behind Calvin is still there. It stretches toward us, then retreats, like it's testin' boundaries.

Or listenin' to our conversation.

And then I see Everett again, standin' at the edge of the food court.

A cold wind sweeps through the festival grounds causin' the decorative lights to flicker, and for a brief moment, the veil parts enough that I see dozens of ghosts. Hundreds even. Then the moment passes, and they fade back to the translucent forms only I can see.

"Did you feel that?" Hazel pulls her jacket tight.

"Just the wind picking up," Calvin says. "It's supposed to get colder tonight."

But it's not the wind and it's not a cold front.

"We need to go," I say, suddenly panicked. "See how the others are comin' along."

As if to punctuate my words, the carousel across the festival grounds starts to turn on its own. The melody warps, notes stretch, and wail out of tune. People startle and then laugh. They probably think it's just part of the festival special effects.

They have no idea what's really comin'. None of 'em.

CHAPTER SEVENTEEN

Dex

The crisp autumn air feels thinner today, like the entire atmosphere has been tugged too tight. The clock is ticking. We have to find these binding sites.

I head toward the library. My cane taps an unsteady rhythm against the cobblestones, my usual smooth gait made awkward by my recent wound. It still causes me a great deal of pain, which is unsettling. I'm not supposed to feel pain. Teenagers cut across my path, laughing as they make their way toward the carousel. Three ghosts drift behind them. All recent deaths, judging by their clothing. No surprise, really. The newly deceased often follow the living, pulled by memory more than nefarious intention.

Under normal circumstances, I would stop and guide the dead to their final destination. Help them understand what's happened. But not this afternoon. I need to save my energy for Mina's crossing. She's the only one who matters at the moment. The others will find their way eventually.

Halfway down Main Street, a familiar pair catches my eye. Lily and Jasper Brooks stand outside Timeless Treasures, admiring vintage lanterns in the window. Jasper leans forward and squints through his glasses at a particular lantern. Lily says something that makes him chuckle, her hand resting lightly on his arm. The air ripples behind them.

A woman in a Victorian-style mourning dress, her face partially obscured by a black veil, materializes near the shop entrance. She wrings her hands, her form more solid than any spirit should be outside a haunting. Unlike the other aimless spirits wandering the streets, this ghost has purpose. Intent.

"Thomas?" She wrings her hands, scanning the street. "Thomas, where have you gone?"

Neither Lily nor Jasper reacts. Not yet. As the ghost drifts closer to the shop window, my skin begins to prickle with the fear of what she might do.

Jasper steps away from Lily, moving closer to the window for a better look at the lantern.

"I'm going inside to ask about the price." He turns toward the shop door.

And finds himself face-to-face with the weeping woman.

Jasper freezes. His eyes widen behind thick glasses. His mouth opens, but no sound emerges.

"Thomas?" The ghost reaches for him with translucent hands. "Thomas, you promised you'd come back for me. Why did you leave me?"

"Who—" Jasper manages.

Lily steps toward him, eyebrows pinched. "Jasper? What is it?"

He doesn't answer. Or can't answer. His face drains of color as the ghost stalks toward him, her hands now inches from his face.

"You promised." Her voice rises with desperation. "Thomas, you promised!"

Jasper stumbles backward, away from the apparition. His cane catches on an uneven cobblestone. He loses his balance, arms windmilling helplessly as he falls.

I move, but I'm too far away.

He hits the ground with a sickening crack, his head bouncing against the cobblestones. His glasses fly off, skittering across the sidewalk.

"Someone help! Please!" Lily drops to her knees beside him, hands grasping his jacket as she leans over his still form.

The ghost vanishes.

I push through gathering onlookers, ignoring the stabbing pain in my side. Luckily, my job requires me to remain calm in an emergency. I tap into my authoritative voice as I nudge my way past a gawking family of four. "Step aside, please. I have medical training."

A lie, but I've observed enough illness and death and what causes each to know the basics. And even though it's not my main objective, I do know how to preserve a life when it's allowed, and by the looks of Jasper's life force, it is not yet time to transfer him to the other side.

I kneel beside him and take his wrist between my fingers. His pulse is present but slow and irregular. A trickle of blood seeps from his right ear.

"Give him some space," I instruct those who press too close.

Behind me, I hear a phone being dialed, then a voice explaining the emergency.

Lily's frail hand grabs my forearm. "Will he be all right?"

"The paramedics will be here soon," I deflect. "Try to stay calm for him."

Jasper's eyelids flutter. A soft groan escapes his lips.

I place a hand on his shoulder. "Stay still, Mr. Brooks. Help is coming."

Sirens wail as the ambulance pulls up. Paramedics take over, asking questions, applying a cervical collar. I step back, giving them space to work.

"Are you his wife?" one of the paramedics asks Lily.

She nods, still clutching my arm.

I pat her hand. "I'll tell Mina. We'll check in on you later, okay?"

She closes her eyes briefly. "Thank you."

They lift Jasper into the ambulance, and I help Lily in after him. The doors close with a solid thunk, and the siren wails once more as they pull away.

I stand alone on the sidewalk, watching until the ambulance disappears around a corner. The crowd disperses, and I turn my attention to the spot where the ghost appeared. Energy still lingers there, a cold spot in the autumn air. I raise a finger and draw a symbol to create a barrier against the dead. Given my condition, it's not as strong as it could be, but enough to discourage other spirits from manifesting here.

I retrieve my cane and continue down Main Street.

***

An hour after informing Mina about Jasper's accident, I finally make my way to the library. The normally quiet building hums with unusual energy. Magical energy. Judging by the discordant vibrations in the air, someone is trying to cast a spell, and they're doing it wrong.

When I enter, Penny stands on a stepladder by the main entrance, one hand braced against the door frame, the other tracing symbols that glow with a dull green light before fading into the wood. She balances an ancient tome on the top step as she sounds out words in a language she clearly doesn't understand.

"—ad spiri . . . tus mal . . . ig . . . nos excip . . . iendos? hunc locum custodi . . ." She stumbles over the pronunciation, her forehead creased with concentration.

I step closer, trying to piece together the broken Latin phrase. It sounds as though she's attempting to cast a basic warding spell, but the pronunciation isn't right.

"Penny," I call softly, not wanting to startle her mid-casting.

She glances down. Her eyes widen briefly before her expression hardens. "I know what I'm doing."

The defensive edge in her voice tells me otherwise. Her fingers tremble slightly as she attempts to trace a protective sigil that should form a barrier across the entryway, but her lines waver, breaking the pattern.

"That's not quite—"

"I have to do this," she interrupts, turning back to the door frame. "After the Concord book incident, I need to fix things. I have to keep them out of the library. Prove I'm not completely useless."

"Maybe this is the wrong approach. Come down and let's talk it through," I encourage.

Penny takes a deep breath and continues the incantation, her voice growing stronger with false confidence. "Ad spiritus malignos excipiendos."

I stiffen. She's inadvertently reversed the phrase. She just welcomed evil instead of banishing it.

"Wait." I step forward, raising my hand.

Too late. She completes the inverted phrase with a final flourish. The symbol flares bright blue, then inverts into a sickly green. As expected, she reversed the ward.

Books on nearby shelves rattle in their places as the air crackles with misaligned energy.

A stocky man in a pinstriped suit, features hard and pock-marked, suddenly appears, landing on his butt with a loud thunk. He pops up, hovering two feet off the floor, eyes taking in his surroundings.

"What the hell's goin' on?" the poltergeist asks, bewildered. He zeroes in on Penny. "You? You're the one yanked me outta there?"

Penny's face drains of color. "I—I didn't mean—"

The spirit advances, his frustration growing more evident with each step. "I've been waitin' for years, but I'm not supposed to be here. Not a library. I don't even read." He knocks several books off a shelf. "Where's my bar? I got customers waitin', and my boys are bringin' in a shipment of that good Canadian whiskey."

I raise my cane, but my scythe refuses to manifest. I duck as he sends a computer monitor flying. A patron sitting nearby drops her book, mouth open in shock. Another backs away slowly.

The ghost turns, noticing his audience. A cruel smile spreads across his scarred face. "Well, well. Looks like I got me a new establishment with new customers. But if I gotta work here, I need to make it more conducive to my needs."

He strides to the nearest bookshelf and swipes his arm across it. Books crash to the floor with solid thuds.

"Stop!" Penny scrambles down the ladder, book of spells clutched to her chest. "You can't—I didn't mean to—"

"Lady, I been stuck in that in-between hellhole for over ninety years," the ghost snaps, knocking over a display of new releases. "Ninety years of nothin'. No booze. No action. No nothin'."

A woman screams. A man drops his laptop, backing toward the exit.

The library doors burst open. Hazel and La'Tasha rush in, immediately assessing the situation before springing into action.

"Containment first." Hazel moves, and La'Tasha drops to one knee, charcoal already in hand, drawing a wide circle in quick, precise strokes.

The ghost catches on. "Oh no, you don't!" he snarls, lunging for her.

I step between them. "Sir," I say, gripping my cane with both hands, "that's quite enough."

He swings. His fist slices through my shoulder in a wave of icy fire. He doesn't land a full hit, but it's enough to hurt.

Hazel begins chanting, her hands weaving complex patterns in the air. Crackling blue magic pulses at her fingertips and stretches toward the circle La'Tasha just completed.

"Penny," Hazel calls over her shoulder. "All I can do is try to hold him off. You created this, you need to speak the reversal."

Penny fumbles with the grimoire, tears of frustration welling in her eyes. "I can't—I don't—"

"You can." I try again to block the ghost's path. "Find the page. Read exactly what's there. No improvisation."

The poltergeist grows more agitated, pacing like a caged animal. Books fly from shelves. Card catalog drawers eject and then fly into the air, spewing cards as they go.

"Hurry," La'Tasha urges. Her circle glows faintly, pulsing with contained power.

Penny finds the page, takes a deep breath, and begins reading. Her voice shakes at first. She stumbles over the first phrase, then corrects herself. The air around her shimmers as raw magical energy responds to her call. But it's far more energy than the simple spell should generate, and I notice Hazel and La'Tasha exchange confused glances.

The ghost freezes mid-stride. "What's happening?" He looks down at his hands. They've started to glow with the same pale blue light as the circle. "What are you doin' to me?"

"Sending you home," Hazel says. She nods at Penny, and together they direct their energy toward La'Tasha's circle.

The ghost claws at the air. His feet drag as if through thick mud. "No! What are you doing to me?"

La'Tasha tosses a handful of white powder at the circle, and it erupts in a blue fire that hovers above the floor. The ghost howls as he's sucked inside, feet first, until only his head and shoulders are visible.

Penny's voice grows stronger as the reversal spell gathers momentum. Darts of blue energy shoot from her hands, and Hazel's eyes widen in surprise. With a final cry, the ghost explodes into particles of light that spiral upward, then vanish. The circle dims, then fades completely. Papers drift from the ceiling to the floor around us, and a rogue reference card comes to rest on my shoe.

"That," Hazel says into the quiet, "was not supposed to happen."

"I'm sorry. Again." Penny snaps to and closes the book of

spells with shaking hands. "Please don't yell at me. I promise, I was just trying to help, and I know I messed up."

"Not that," La'Tasha interrupts, studying the residual energy that still sparks from Penny. "The amount of power you just channeled. That shouldn't be possible with your training level."

Penny blinks in confusion. "Huh?"

Hazel approaches, examining the fading magical residue. "You didn't just banish him. You pushed him completely across and into his final realm. How did you do that?"

"I just read the words," Penny says, bewildered.

"With enough raw power to fuel three witches," La'Tasha adds.

How does one hold that much power yet not know her own strength?

The library settles into an uneasy quiet around us. The last of the patrons have fled, leaving only the staff clustered near the circulation desk, staring at the mess around them.

I move to the reference section and reach for a book, one of the few to survive the ghost's outburst. It's a slim volume on Moonridge's ley line patterns, the very book I'd initially come in for. I place it on the table behind me, and the book falls open to a map from 1892, ley lines inked so fine they look like capillaries.

"Come with me," Hazel says, gesturing to Penny. They cross in front of me and stop beside the oversized dictionary resting on its wooden stand. A tall bookshelf blocks most of the view. The spot isn't exactly hidden, but it offers just enough privacy to allow me to listen in unnoticed. I keep my eyes on the map.

"That spell—" Hazel begins without preamble.

"I know. I shouldn't have done it. I was trying to set things right, and I messed up the wording—" Penny stares at the floor.

"That's not what I'm saying." Hazel leans against the dictionary stand. "The energy you emitted was way more powerful than La'Tasha, or I could have conjured together. We sensed it from three blocks away, which is why we came running."

Penny looks up, confusion replacing shame. "I don't under-stand."

"Neither do I. At least not completely." Hazel's voice softens. "You have power, Penny. Untrained, unfocused, but substantial. That sort of power can be dangerous."

"I know. I know," Penny says. "I shouldn't do magic without proper training. I just . . ."

I turn a page, feigning interest in a diagram of convergent energy points while keeping my ears tuned to their conversation.

"Moonridge is filled with all kinds of out-of-control energy. It's easy for things to go shit sideways around you. You understand that, right?" A beat. "But . . . with the proper training, that type of power can be very beneficial. Especially now." Hazel continues, her voice gentler. "We're facing serious threats. People's lives are at risk. We need you."

I glance up in time to see Penny's expression shift between disbelief and fragile hope. "Are you saying my powers might actually be good?"

"I'm saying we need someone like you." Hazel holds up a hand when Penny starts to bounce with excitement. "A trained you. I mean it when I say you have to follow our lead and work within our parameters. Okay?"

Penny nods excitedly.

"I think with the right focus, you just might be able to undo the damage you caused after using the Hollowing grimoire. Your power is something else."

"Really? You're not just saying that?" Penny challenges.

"When have you ever known me to be nice for no reason?" Hazel's eyebrows rise. "I'm just being practical. Both La'Tasha and I recognize that you have abilities our coven could use."

The word hangs in the air between them. Coven. Not just assistance or training, but belonging.

I flip to another page, this one showing the original town lay-out with thirteen structures arranged in a pattern that resembles the Concord's binding sigil. That's most definitely not coincidence. The town's founders knew all about magical architecture. Were they involved with the Concord? I slip the book inside my coat. This will come in handy later.

La'Tasha approaches the pair, having finished cleaning the charcoal markings from the floor. She carries a small velvet ribbon in deep purple. Without ceremony, she holds it out to Penny.

"A sisterhood bracelet," she explains. "We all wear them. It connects us. Protects us."

Penny doesn't take it immediately. "I don't understand what's happening."

"We're inviting you to join our coven." La'Tasha takes Penny's wrist and ties the ribbon around it. "To learn with us. Work with us."

Penny gasps, eyes wide. "I don't . . . What? I mean . . . Yes. Okay."

"Coco will be thrilled to no longer be the baby witch in our crew," La'Tasha adds with a warm smile.

I watch as Penny studies the bracelet. "What if I can't control it? My power? What if I make things worse?"

"Then we'll be there to help fix it," Hazel says. "That's what a coven does. No more learning magic on your own. We work and learn together. We don't do rogue here."

"We start with basics," La'Tasha explains. "Grounding techniques, energy sensing, and then build from there. Even if it's stuff you already know. You have to start with a proper understanding of the basics in order to build a strong foundation."

Penny wraps her hand around the bracelet, studying it closely, her expression shifting from uncertainty to cautious hope. Not confident yet, but no longer drowning in self-doubt.

"When do we start?" she asks, her voice filled with hope.

"We already have." La'Tasha gestures to the mess around them. "You whopped that ghost's ass good."

The three of them laugh, and I gather my cane. It's been a

long twenty-four hours, and I need to rest. I also need to make sure Mina is okay.

Wait. If we're all here . . .

"Who's with Mina?" I glance at Hazel, heart lurching as the question leaves my mouth.

"Calvin walked her home. She needed a nap. I asked him to sit with her until one of us could get back to the B&B," Hazel says. She lays a hand on my arm. "She's okay, Dex. Calvin won't let anything happen to her."

I nod, breathing deep, then continue on my way, stepping out of the library and into the fading afternoon.

***

Amber light bleeds across the garden in Mina's backyard as the sun sinks behind distant pines. I sit on the weathered bench, my cane propped beside me, watching the marigolds bob in the cool autumn breeze. From here, the festival lights have begun to twinkle in the distance. Cheerful. Oblivious.

Soft footsteps approach from behind. I don't need to turn to know who it is. She has a curious blend of vitality and fragility, and her presence registers differently than that of other humans.

Mina appears at the edge of my vision, her red hair catching the last golden rays of sunlight. She looks tired. Dark circles shadow her eyes, but her back remains straight, chin lifted. Defiant to the end.

She says nothing as she sits beside me on the bench, close enough that our shoulders nearly touch. For several minutes, we sit together in the growing twilight. No words. No explanations needed. Just shared understanding of what approaches.

"How are you feeling?" I finally ask, breaking the silence.

"Surprisingly well, seein' as how I was possessed by a bloody Concord bastard and then had a seizure less than twenty-four hours ago. That nap did me a world of good."

"And you've taken your medication?"

"Yes, father." She nudges me in the side. "Calvin made me take it before I took my nap."

I place my arm across the back of the bench, and she leans into me. "How's Jasper? It was quite the fall."

She sighs. "He's hangin' in there, but Lily has decided to have him transferred back to Vermont so they can be closer to their home and to their children. It's goin' to be a long recovery. They'll be safer there."

The temperature drops as the sun disappears completely behind the tree line. Streaks of purple and deep blue are left in its wake. A screech owl trills somewhere in the woods, its high, trembling call threading through the dark.

"I'm pretty sure Calvin's datin' a ghost," Mina says out of the blue. "Did I tell ya that? He has no idea."

The absurdity of it hangs between us for a moment before Mina's shoulders begin to shake. At first, I think she's crying, then a sound escapes her that is loud and heavy and unmistakably laughter.

"It's not funny," she gasps, wiping her eyes. "It's terrible. Also . . . I mean, of all the disasters . . ."

I find myself smiling in response. "Perhaps not the meet-cute he envisioned."

This sets her off again, laughter spilling out until it borders on hysteria. Then, as quickly as it began, the laughter transforms into tears of grief that contort her face and steal her breath.

"I'm sorry," she manages, struggling to compose herself. "I don't know why I'm—"

"You're dealing with a lot," I say. "Your world is unraveling."

She hiccups, a sound caught between sob and laugh. "If ya say so."

The sky darkens further, stars appearing one by one overhead. The festival lights now form a constellation of their own, promising fun and normalcy.

Mina wipes her face with her sleeve, then goes rigid beside me. Her body freezes, hand stopping halfway to her face.

"What is it?" I ask, instantly alert.

"A pullin' sensation . . ." She tilts her head. "It's hard to explain. Like gravity. A weight pullin' downward, but it's heavy."

I cover her trembling hand with my own. Her fingers are cold despite the mild evening. She closes her eyes, concentrating. "It feels like it's comin' from beneath the town itself."

The energy in the ground beneath us pulses stronger. I can feel it even through my weakened senses.

"It's stirring."

Mina's eyes open, wide and frightened in the dim light. "I can feel it now. It's impatient. Like it's been waitin' for a very long time."

"It has." I don't let go of her hand. "The Concord has spent centuries trying to do this. They're getting stronger. Smarter."

We sit in silence as stars multiply overhead, distant and indifferent. The temperature continues to drop, but neither of us moves to leave. Mina's head eventually comes to rest against my shoulder, and I instinctively rest my cheek against her head. I know I should keep my distance. Maintain professional detachment. That's my role.

But I'm already too far gone with this one.

In this moment, on this bench, with her warmth pressed against my side, I allow myself to experience the desperate sweetness of now. The value of connection.

I wrap an arm around her and pull her closer, feeling the weight of what waits beneath Moonridge.

CHAPTER EIGHTEEN

Mina

I wake to the weight of Dex's arm across my waist, his skin warm against my bare stomach. Mornin' light spills through my bedroom curtains, paintin' golden stripes across rumpled sheets. I press back against him, and his arm tightens around my waist as last night rushes back to me in fragments.

His hands in my hair. My whispered confession that I didn't want to die without knowin' what it was like to be with him, and the way his eyes went from hesitant to dark with hunger as I pulled him toward my bed.

I turn to face him. His eyes are closed, features relaxed. Dark hair falls across his forehead, makin' him look almost human. Almost.

"You're staring," he murmurs without openin' his eyes.

"Makin' sure you're really here." I trace a finger along his jawline, the slight scratch of stubble prickly beneath my touch.

His eyes open, gray as storm clouds and just as deep. "I'm still here."

"Does that happen often? You and . . . humans?"

"No." His face softens, and then somethin' like guilt fills his eyes. "This is new territory."

I prop myself up on my elbow and look down at him. "Did I take Death's virginity?"

His mouth quirks up. "Something like that."

"Well fuck me," I say.

"Again?" He smiles and winks.

"Maybe later." I lean in and steal a quick kiss. No mornin' breath. I guess that's another perk of shaggin' a non-human. "I have to check on my guests, and I need to call and check on Jasper."

His fingers brush my temple. "How are you feeling?"

"Better today." And I am. The constant throbbin' in my head has dulled to a manageable ache. "Maybe you're good medicine. I might need to keep ya around for a while."

"Or a bad influence." His thumb traces my bottom lip.

"Too late for regrets now." I kiss him before slippin' from beneath the covers. "Besides, the world's endin' anyway. May as well break a few rules on my way out. Guess what, world? I've literally been fucked by Death."

The floorboards feel cool as I grab my robe from the hook behind the door. I catch Dex watchin' me. His gaze travels the length of my body with an intensity that makes heat rush to my cheeks.

"Stop lookin' at me like that." I blush and wrap the robe around myself.

"Like what?"

"Like you're memorizin' me."

His expression goes distant. "Perhaps I am."

We stare at each other a moment.

"What's wrong?" I finally ask.

"Just . . ." he sighs. "You. I wish I could help you."

"Nope." I turn toward the door. "We can't waste time cryin' about shite we can't fix."

The light mood evaporates as reality presses in again. One night of stolen pleasure hasn't changed our fundamental situation.

"I'll make coffee." I turn toward the door and ignore the sad look on his face. His sorrow does nothin' to make me feel better. I mean, it has to be bad if even Death is sad for ya.

The hallway stretches before me, and for a solid beat, it appears to be growin' in length. I pause, and close my eyes, breath catchin' in my throat.

When I open my eyes, they're everywhere.

A woman in an old-fashioned nurse's outfit stands by the window at the end of the hall, and an elderly man in a nightshirt paces in circles, mutterin' numbers under his breath.

And there are at least a dozen more of them.

I press myself against the wall and make my way to the kitchen.

"The key is awake." The nurse turns suddenly.

Every translucent head turns in my direction.

They move toward me in eerie unison like they're drawn to me and can't stop themselves. I clutch my temples as a whisper skims the edge of my consciousness. They're not quite words. Just phrases repeated in different echoing tones, just beyond comprehension. They poke at my skull like cold fingers, probing, searching as the words become clearer.

Mina Mina Mina

Let us in Let us in Let us in

"Stop!" But the ghosts keep comin'. A little boy reaches for the hem of my robe with ghostly fingers. I force myself to move, pushin' past them.

LetUsInLetUsInLetUsIn

I rush out of the hall and through the doorway into the kitchen.

I freeze.

A boy, no more than eight years old, stands before the counter. His clothes are soaked, water drips onto the floor, but leaves no puddles. His face is bluish-pale, lips tinged with death. The boy turns, his eyes fixed on mine. Tears stream down his translucent cheeks.

"What do you want?" My voice shakes despite my efforts to remain calm.

"She said you'd open the door." His voice bubbles as if he speaks from under water. "It's time. Let us in."

The walls begin to pulse again, stronger this time. The whisper grows louder.

Minaminamina

Pain builds in my skull until I think it might split open. I turn and flee back down the hallway, past more ghosts, back to my bedroom, where I slam the door shut and press my back against it.

Dex shoots upright in bed. "What is it?"

"Ghosts." I gasp for breath. "Everywhere. They're lookin' for me."

He's beside me in an instant, wrappin' me in his arms. "How many?"

"Dozens." Terror claws at my throat. "They called me 'the key'. One of 'em said I'm to let them in."

"Samhain isn't until tomorrow." His jaw tightens.

For a moment, all I hear is my own ragged breath. Then it comes again. That same insistent voice, no longer a whisper but a clear, familiar sound that seems to vibrate through the floorboards beneath my feet.

Mina. Bring them home.

My knees buckle as I finally recognize the voice.

It's mine.

***

I turn the key with a soft click that echoes down the empty hall. Lily and Jasper's room feels hollow and sad when I push open the door, as if the space itself knows its occupants are leavin' and might never come back. The ghosts seem to have abandoned this particular corner of the house, takin' with them the cold spots and whispers that have become my constant companions for the last three hours. I flip on the light switch and set to work gatherin' their belongings.

The suitcase sits open on the luggage rack, half-packed with Jasper's medication bottles and toiletries. I move to the dresser where trousers and sweaters are neatly folded, Jasper's smellin' faintly of pipe tobacco and Lily's of gardenia.

I find the pipe on the nightstand, a beautiful piece, worn smooth by decades of gentle use. I wrap it carefully in a clean handkerchief before placin' it with his sweaters. Next, I collect Lily's book of crossword puzzles, the pages dog-eared and pencil-marked.

My hands shake as I fold their clothes. I have to pause and steady myself against the dresser as grief takes over. They've become like grandparents to me. They've carved out a place in my heart with their gentle bickerin', and I'll never see them again after today.

I sigh and wipe the tears from my eyes. It's right that they're leavin'. I'd never forgive myself if somethin' worse happened to either of them because of their connection to me. They won't be safe here.

I work methodically, gatherin' the small souvenirs they've collected around town, packin' the little gifts Lily bought for their grandchildren at the festival. On the windowsill, a snow globe of Moonridge rests quietly, the miniature town frozen in perpetual calm, white flakes driftin' through a gentle, endless storm. For a moment, I can almost see how Moonridge used to be: quiet, normal, a place where the most supernatural thing was maybe a friendly ghost or two. If only Moonridge could be guaranteed that kind of perpetual peace. I set it carefully in the suitcase and close the lid, zippin' it shut.

An hour later, Dex and I pull into the hospital lot. He insisted on drivin' me, just in case I had another seizure. Honestly, we might've been safer if I'd had a seizure behind the wheel because Dex and vehicles are a terrible combination.

A white van with **Mountain Medical Transport** painted in neat blue letters on the side idles near the entrance. I spot Lily immediately. She wears her baby blue pea coat and has her purse clutched firmly in both hands, eyes scannin' the lot.

"Perfect timing," she says as I approach. She smiles, but it's strained around the edges. "They're bringing Jasper down now."

Dex wheels the suitcases over to where we stand. He wishes Lily well and then leaves us to say our goodbyes.

"I got everythin' packed up, and I even stuck a couple of scones and a few cookies in a bag for the drive," I tell her.

"Oh, bless you." Exhaustion colors her face. "You always take such good care of us, dear. And you know how much Jasper loves your scones."

The hospital doors slide open with a mechanical hiss, and two attendants in crisp uniforms wheel Jasper out on a gurney. He looks alert and ready to tell someone off at the first inconvenience, though his face is still pinched with pain.

"Ya nearly gave me a heart attack, ya old coot," I tease. "What am I gonna do with ya?"

"Can't nobody keep me down," he says with a weak smile. "I'm too tough for that. Good thing I hit my head. Nothing in there to mess up."

I laugh and do my best to fight back the tears. I love this old fart. "Ya take good care, okay?" I bend over and kiss him on the forehead.

"I'll be just fine. Don't you worry about me." He pats me on the arm, and the transport team transfers him carefully to the van's specialized stretcher.

When everythin' is settled and the paperwork completed, Lily turns to me and smiles. "Mina, I can't thank you enough. You've done so much for us over the years."

"Always a pleasure, truly." I mean it more than she knows.

In a town overrun with ancient powers stirrin' beneath our feet, Lily and Jasper's simple love has been a reminder of what's worth protectin'.

She hugs me, her arms tight around me. "You always give us a place to feel young again," she whispers against my ear. "Even if only for a few days."

My throat tightens. "Ya know you're welcome back anytime."

She pulls away, her eyes bright with unshed tears. "Jasper's going to be just fine. We'll be back next year. Same room, same time. We'll see you then."

I force a smile and swallow the lump in my throat. Except I won't be here. This is goodbye. But I can't tell her that because I don't want to upset her.

Lily steps back and takes my hand in hers. She gives it a firm squeeze. "And Mina? Don't wait too long to choose what you want. Time doesn't give second chances, and we never know how much of it we have left."

The unexpected advice catches me off guard. Especially since my time has almost literally come to an end. "What?"

Lily looks past me toward where Dex waits.

"He cares for you," Lily says softly. "More than he understands himself, I'd wager. And you for him. I know love when I see it."

My face burns. I look down at my shoes, unable to meet her gaze. "It's complicated."

"Love always is." She pats my hand with gentle authority. "But that doesn't mean it isn't worth choosing. Sometimes the complicated things are the most worthwhile."

A transport worker calls Lily's name. She turns, and he gestures toward the van where Jasper is settled inside, comfortable and secure for the journey. She gives my hand one final squeeze.

"Take care of yourself, dear," she whispers. "And remember—choose what makes you happy, even if it doesn't make sense."

I watch as she climbs inside the van and the attendant closes the door behind her. I wipe a tear from my eye as the van pulls out of the lot, takin' Lily and Jasper away from Moonridge.

I turn slowly. My eyes find Dex still waitin' next to my SUV. He stands perfectly still, a dark silhouette against the afternoon light, his face unreadable at this distance.

Lily's words echo in my mind: *Don't wait too long to choose what you want.*

I already know what I want. I want to live and I want Dex to be human and I want to be with him.

But none of that is possible.

Whatever exists between us has never been simple. It began the moment he saved my life six years ago, and it's only deepened since. What we share is raw and real and unbearably bittersweet, because in all my life, no man has ever made me feel so seen, so safe, or so deeply cared for. The only comfort I have is knowin' that when the time comes, his will be the last face I see before I step into whatever comes next.

And I can only hope it's not the fiery depths of hell.

The whispers in my head grow louder, almost drownin' out my own thoughts. It sounds like it's comin' from beneath my feet, risin' up through the concrete like voices from a buried well. My name pulses through the sound, called by a chorus of entities.

She comes tomorrow.

The door opens tomorrow.

Yes. Tomorrow. All Hallows' Eve.

The day I die.

I close my eyes, tryin' to drown out the noise. My fingers tremble uncontrollably, and I shove them into my pockets to hide the weakness. When I open my eyes again, Dex is by my side, ready to catch me if I fall.

He doesn't speak. Doesn't ask questions. Just places his arm around my shoulder and guides me back to the car.

CHAPTER NINETEEN

Dex

I push my way through the organized chaos of the festival. A group of teenagers pushes past me, cutting between the merry-go-round and the ring-toss game, costumes flapping in the crisp October breeze, while their parents call after them to watch where they're going and keep an eye on their siblings.

The celebration feels alive, energy palpable from both the living and the dead. I've watched variations of these celebrations across centuries. Romans honoring their dead. Celts lighting bonfires to ward off spirits. Strange that this small-town festival in the northeastern United States might be the last the world will ever see if the Concord succeeds.

I spot Mina across the square, clipboard in hand, cat ears firmly clamped to her head, as she takes orders for s'mores while the town mayor recites ghost stories to a captive audience beside her booth. Even from this distance, I can see how she struggles to focus and the careful way she holds herself upright.

Images from last night flash through my mind. Her soft skin against mine. The surprising warmth of her as she wrapped herself around me, and the way she whispered my name as pleasure coursed through her. Reaper rules were broken, and there will undoubtedly be consequences. And yet, I don't regret a single moment. I finally tasted the carnal joys of humanity, and it was the most beautiful thing I've ever experienced.

Now I'm left with the lingering question I can't seem to answer: how am I supposed to say goodbye to her? For centuries, I've guided souls away from death and into the next life, but this one . . . this soul might be the one that finally breaks me.

And if it does? What then? Do I give up this life of ushering the dead for a chance to be human? It's possible. But what is the point of becoming human if Mina isn't here to share that life with me?

I turn my attention to the north entrance, where Hazel, La'Tasha, Coco, and Penny work to reinforce the protective wards. Hazel turns to La'Tasha, asking for guidance, almost as if she doesn't trust her own judgment. La'Tasha takes the clipboard from Hazel and points to something. Hazel nods and then points to the opposite side of the park. She turns, catches my eye, and waves. I nod and raise a hand. Why wasn't it her that the elders sent me back for? Why Mina? I have no ill intent toward Hazel; in fact, I've grown fond of her now that she knows we're on the same side, but if I had to choose between her and Mina . . . well, my choice is obvious.

An electronic squelch pulls me from my thoughts, and I turn toward the stage where the costume contest will be held later. Vivienne and Caprice test the mics while several fans stand to the side, snapping covert pictures of their favorite vampire wives. The two of them are tonight's honorary hosts. Vivienne's idea. Being on the stage will give her a better vantage point so she can watch for Concord energy. The other vampire wives mill about, greeting fans and taking selfies.

Caprice fluffs her dark bangs, pouting at her reflection in a compact mirror. "Should I go with blood-red lips or keep the burgundy for the first segment?"

"Burgundy," Vivienne answers without looking. "We're going

for subtle horror, darling, not cheap thrills."

A thin shimmer in the air catches my eye. The distortion ripples outward from center stage.

I straighten, grip tightening on my cane as I move closer. The tear spreads like a crack through glass.

A young boy, six or seven years old, dressed as a train conductor, complete with striped overalls, red bandana, and a small cap perched on brown curls, makes his way up the steps to the stage. He waves to his mother.

"Mom! Look at—"

His mouth stays open around the unfinished sentence. His arms drop to his sides. The shimmering distortion I noticed seconds ago hovers above him, tendrils of white smoke snaking down and over his rigid body. When he speaks again, the voice is deeper. Rough. Like someone who's smoked too many cigarettes and doesn't properly hydrate.

"The coupling failed just past Miller's Creek." The boy's eyes remain fixed on something only he can see. "I pulled the brake even though Rogers told me to leave it be. Said we could make it."

The boy's mother takes two small steps toward the stage. "Braedon? Honey, what are you doing?"

The boy shakes his head. "It was five a.m. on October 17, 1907."

The crowd's energy is a low, confused hum at my back. Someone asks if this is part of the festival entertainment.

"Braedon, come on. Come down from there." His mother's voice rises with panic.

The boy's head swivels toward her. "I can't rest until you know what happened that night."

Every jack-o'-lantern on the stage opens its mouth at the same time, amplifying the dead man's voice across the park. "So many people died."

The crowd startles, and a group of teenagers laughs.

"This is so fake," one of them yells.

"Lame."

"Please," the possessed boy raises his arms. "You have to listen. They're all dead. Sixteen people. Because of me."

The teens continue to heckle. One of them throws an apple onto the stage.

The boy's head tips back, and a deep, dark voice erupts from his throat. "Listen to me."

The pumpkins explode simultaneously, sending chunks of orange flesh and seeds spraying across the crowd. The glass lanterns hanging from the stage rafters shatter, raining sharp fragments on screaming spectators.

People push against each other in their rush to escape. Through the chaos, the boy remains rigid on stage.

I push through the panicked crowd, willing my scythe to please cooperate. This boy's life depends on it. I reach the stage just as Braedon's body begins to jerk and twitch, no longer under his control. I plant my feet and raise my scythe, using it to trace a containment sigil in the air above the child. Silver light trails from the skull, forming a complex pattern that hovers between us.

"What's that man doing?" A voice whispers in the hushed crowd.

"It's part of the show," another answers.

The sigil pulses once, then encircles the possessed child, providing a protective boundary to draw the spirit out.

"Conductor Hargrove?" I step closer. "You died in the Miller's Creek bridge collapse."

Braedon's head snaps toward me, confusion flickering across his childish features.

"You know me?" The spirit's voice wavers through the child's mouth.

"Yes." I move a step closer. "I was there that night. It was tragic, and I'd like to set your soul at ease, but I need you to leave this young man. He is not yours to claim."

"But they've forgotten," the conductor protests through the child's mouth. "The memorial plaque was removed. The tracks have been paved over. No one remembers!"

"I remember." I step closer, my scythe held steady. "I know the pain it caused. I guided all souls who perished. And I remember that you refused to come."

Confusion distorts the boy's face. "I couldn't leave. Not with their blood on my hands. I didn't deserve peace."

"It wasn't your fault." I lower my voice, speaking only to the ghost. "The bridge inspection reports were falsified."

The ghost cocks the head of the young boy's body. "But why . . . who would do that?"

I place a hand on his shoulder and meet him eye to eye. "The structure was compromised months before your train arrived. You tried to stop the train. Don't you remember? None of what happened that night was your fault."

The boy tilts his head. "How can you know that?"

"Because it is my purpose." I stand and hold out a hand, palm up. "It's time to rest, Conductor. Let me show you the way back. You've suffered long enough."

Braedon's body shudders violently. The ghost fights against my pull, clinging to this world through sheer force of guilt. Sweat breaks out across my forehead as I channel more power through the sigil, drawing on weakened energy. I can only hope for Mina's sake that this doesn't drain the last of my power.

"The passengers," the conductor whispers. "Did they suffer?"

"No," I lie. "It was swift. And they've been at peace for over a century. Only you remain trapped."

Around us, the containment sigil pulses brighter. I raise my scythe and bring it down in a swift, practiced arc, not touching the boy, but slicing through the spiritual tether that binds the conductor's spirit to the boy's vessel.

Braedon's eyes scrunch and his mouth opens in a silent scream, as blue light pours out. It coalesces into the transparent form of a middle-aged man in a conductor's uniform, his face lined with a century of grief. Our eyes meet for one moment of perfect understanding before he gives a slight nod and dissipates into particles of light that spiral upward, then vanish.

The child collapses. I drop to one knee, catching him before he hits the stage. His eyelids flutter as consciousness returns.

"Braedon!" His mother scrambles onto the stage, face white with terror. "What did you do to him?"

"He'll be fine," I tell her, helping her gather the boy into her arms. "Just a fainting spell from the excitement."

Her eyes dart to my scythe, which has already transformed back into an innocuous walking cane.

Parents surge forward, voices demanding answers. Mass panic in three . . . two . . .

"What incredible special effects!" Vivienne's voice cuts through the chaos, pitched to carry. She claps her hands as she strides to center stage, looking directly into the sea of recording phones. "This is exactly why we chose Moonridge for our Halloween special! A round of applause for Hazel Thornton and her coven: La'Tasha Morehouse and Coco Montoya. Special effects and witch magic together really have elevated this year's festivities, don't you think?"

She stands tall in her designer boots, not a hair out of place. A consummate performer stepping into the spotlight.

"The pyrotechnics were a bit more intense than rehearsed," she continues smoothly, flashing a camera-ready smile. "Our sincerest apologies for any alarm. The special effects team got carried away with the pumpkin and lantern explosions! I can't wait for you to see what they have planned next."

Caprice rushes forward, playing her part flawlessly. She dabs at nonexistent tears with a silk handkerchief. "It's just so real! Bravo to the entire team! I was genuinely terrified!" She fans herself dramatically. "The possessed child actor. Simply brilliant! So authentic!"

From the edge of the stage, Zara clutches her chest and sinks to her knees in an elegant faint that pulls attention away from the still-disoriented boy and his confused mother.

"Is she okay?" A young woman points to Zara's crumpled form.

"Just overcome with the excitement," Ayana assures the crowd. "Zara's always been a little on the dramatic side. She'll be fine."

Vivienne and Ayana work the crowd, touching shoulders and smiling. Each person they speak to seems to relax, nodding in agreement with their explanation of what just happened. I should feel relieved that another crisis has been averted. Instead, my stomach clenches when I notice the tar-like shadow beneath the stone fountain at the square's center.

Another Concord shade.

I take a step toward the fountain, and the shade expands, stretching like detached shadows across the cobblestones. It pulses once before vanishing between cracks in the stonework. Gone to report what it found, no doubt.

I search the growing crowd for Hazel. She stands near the bobbing-for-apples station, her face drawn and pale as she confers with the sheriff. I make my way over to her, the cobblestones somehow feeling far too uneven beneath my feet, like they've moved farther apart in the last hour.

"We need to talk." I keep my voice low, nodding respectfully to the sheriff. "Now."

Hazel reads the urgency in my face. "Sheriff, if you'll excuse me?"

He nods, distracted by a deputy calling from across the square. "Just keep those special effects under control," he says before walking away.

I guide Hazel toward a quiet corner behind the gazebo. "The Concord sent a shade. They're watching. How many bindings were you able to weaken today?"

"We found eight. That should have been enough to weaken them, right?"

"Unless they reinstated them. I have a feeling someone is

following us and knows exactly what we're doing. It's like they're six steps ahead of us."

Dark circles shadow her eyes, and her shoulders sag. The constant battle is draining her. "I don't know what else to do. See those lanterns?" She points out several lanterns strategically placed around the park. "We've hidden protective sigils inside each one. Twelve hours ago, they were strong enough to repel minor spirits. Now they barely register."

La'Tasha approaches, her face scrunched with worry. "There you are. I've been looking for you."

"What's happened?" Hazel straightens.

"I was near the cider stand," La'Tasha explains, "and I saw something like a double exposure on a photograph." She rubs her arms as if chilled. "For just a second, I saw this same festival, but wrong. The sky was red, and everyone was screaming."

"Timeline bleed," I confirm, the words heavy on my tongue. "The barriers between realities are weakening, and you saw what will happen if we don't stop them."

"Does that mean we've already lost? If she saw the future . . ." Hazel's face goes white.

"That was their planned future," I explain. "They've been planning this for years, and their endgame is to completely rip the veil between realities. What La'Tasha saw was a glimpse of their success."

La'Tasha pulls her jacket tighter around her. "So all our efforts to strengthen the wards have been useless."

"No. Every bit of work hasn't been for nothing. Like I said, you saw their success, but that doesn't mean they've won. We can still stop them," I counter. "You can't give up. We have to save Mina. That's all we have to do. Make sure they don't gain access to her."

Hazel nods, slowly at first, and then seems to make up her mind. "Yeah. We will. I don't know how, but we will."

"Like Dex said," La'Tasha says, "we just have to keep them

away from Mina."

"Which means we have to be willing to let her go," I say. Hazel opens her mouth to protest, and I hold up a hand. "I know. I don't want her to die any more than either of you." La'Tasha winces. "But she doesn't have much time left, and we have to be willing to let her go. It won't just save humanity. It will also protect her soul."

Silence stretches between us, and then La'Tasha nods. "You're right. As much as I hate this, we have to do what's best for her, whether she lives or dies; we can't let them gain access to her."

"I need to find Mina," I say finally. "I need to get her home so she can rest. Keep searching. See what you can find, and if I can safely get away tonight to assist, I will."

Hazel touches my arm and nods. La'Tasha mentions checking the perimeter one more time as they walk away.

I find Mina at the festival's candle memorial wall, a place where people light votives for lost loved ones. She stands alone before dozens of flickering flames, adding a small candle to the collection. Her movements are careful, deliberate, as she cups her hand around the new flame to protect it from the evening breeze.

I approach, not wanting to intrude on what feels like a private moment. She senses me anyway, turning as I draw near.

"Who's that for?" I ask, nodding toward the candle she's just lit.

"Me." A small, sad smile touches her lips. "Seemed like I should get one in while I still can."

The simple honesty of it steals my breath, and I have to look away. I reach for her hand, needing to feel her warmth against my skin. Her fingers intertwine with mine, and I never want to let them go.

She places a hand on my chest. "We haven't stopped them, have we?"

I don't insult her with false hope. "No."

She nods, accepting this with the same quiet dignity she's

shown since she first realized who I was and why I am here. "I know. The voice in my head isn't whisperin' anymore. I can hear it loud and clear."

"What is it saying?"

"That it's time to come home." She looks up at me, green eyes reflecting the candlelight. "Whatever that means."

I brush my fingers against her cheek, silently vowing to do whatever I can to shield her from what lies ahead in the next twenty-four hours.

"I need to go home and think," she says, her voice wavering slightly. "I'm tired."

Vivienne approaches, her timing impeccable as always.

"I'll walk with you," she offers to Mina. "I can have one of the other wives cover emcee duties for the costume contest. We'll make it a girls' night."

I'm grateful for her intervention. The shade's appearance means the Concord will be actively hunting now. Mina shouldn't be alone.

"We won't sleep," I tell Mina, gesturing to where Hazel and La'Tasha have been joined by Penny and Coco. "The witches and I will work overnight to stop this."

"I know ya will." She manages a smile, but it's not a convincing one.

I bend down, pressing my lips to hers in a kiss that feels too brief, too insufficient for everything I want to convey. Her hand tightens around my waist for a moment before she pulls away.

"See ya in the mornin'," she says.

"I'll be back as soon as I can."

She stands on her tiptoes and gives me one more soft kiss. "I'd love it if ya could," she whispers. "I'd like to spend my last night with ya."

I don't speak. I can't.

Her last night.

And there's nothing I can do about it.

CHAPTER TWENTY

Mina

The walk home feels like wadin' through mud, and each step costs more energy than I have. Vivienne keeps pace beside me, her heels click-clackin' against the cobblestones with perfect rhythm, designer outfit unwrinkled. Must be nice, bein' undead. No exhaustion. No expiration date loomin' just hours away. Hers has already come and gone. She probably looks better dead than I've ever looked alive. I'd hate her for it if I didn't like her so much.

"You're quiet." Vivienne's gaze slides sideways to assess me.

"Just knackered." I fish my keys from my pocket as we reach the front door.

The hinges creak as I push it open. The air presses against my skin like cold fingers. My shoulders grow tense. The energy in the house feels even more wrong, which is sayin' somethin' these days.

Vivienne feels it too. Her steps slow as we cross into the foyer.

"It's a party in here tonight." Her voice drops to a whisper.

The hallway lights flicker as we step inside, a pulse like a failin' heartbeat. Shadows stretch across the walls and bend at impossible angles. One reaches toward us then snaps back when the light steadies momentarily.

I sigh and hang my coat on the rack by the door. "Just another day at the club."

Vivienne heads toward the stairs. "I need to make a call. Can we talk after?"

"Absolutely," I say, though I'm not sure I'll still be conscious by then. I'm bone tired.

My bedroom feels like a refuge the moment I close the door. I kick off my shoes and strip away the day, changin' into an oversized T-shirt that swallows me whole. The mirror above my dresser shows a woman I barely recognize. Dark circles sit like bruises beneath eyes that seem too big for my face, cheeks hollow, skin pale.

I'm brushin' my teeth when the knock comes, three precise taps against my door.

"Just a sec." I spit minty foam into the sink and wipe my mouth.

Vivienne stands in the hallway. She's changed out of her festival outfit into black silk pajamas. She's washed her face, and without makeup, she looks younger and more vulnerable.

"May I come in?" she asks.

"Sure." I step aside, wavin' her in. "What's up?"

She settles into the armchair by the window, her posture perfect. "I didn't want you to be alone. How are you holding up?"

"Aye, well, ya know . . ." I force a laugh that sounds more like a dyin' donkey than a frail human. "Just dealin' with the fact that we still haven't found a way to stop those Concord bastards, which means tomorrow's likely goin' to be my last day alive."

She sighs and leans forward. "I'm sorry."

"Aye, well." I shrug, pickin' at a loose thread on my comforter with my free hand. "We all die sometime, right? Just turns out my sometime is now."

She moves to sit next to me on my bed.

Tears fill my eyes. "I'd hoped if we could stop the Concord, release whatever spirit is attached to me, maybe I'd get some time back. A few more weeks. Maybe months."

Vivienne takes my hand.

"Now I'm realizin' that's not goin' to happen." I wipe my face. "I have to go to sleep tonight knowin' it's the last time I'll sleep in this bed, and tomorrow will be the last time I get to see my friends." I breathe deep, fightin' back the tears. "This time tomorrow I'll be a corpse."

"Hey! Being a corpse isn't so bad," she offers. A hint of a smile plays at her lips.

"Says the corpse who is still kickin' about." I sit back against the headboard and wrap my arms around my knees. "Ya died, but ya got to stick around. I don't have that luxury. I have to leave my friends." My voice drops to a whisper. "And Dex."

Her eyebrow arches. "Ah, so it's like that with Death, is it? I saw that kiss tonight."

Heat floods my cheeks. A laugh escapes me. "We, um. Last night we . . ."

Her eyes grow wide, and her mouth drops open. "No!"

I nod, unable to stop the smile.

"You had sex with the Grim Reaper?" Vivienne scoots up on the bed and leans forward, all girl-talk excitement. "I had no idea that was even possible! How was it?"

Laughter bubbles up unexpectedly. "Good, actually." My voice drops to a conspiratorial whisper. "Really good."

"Details!" Her eyes gleam with mischief. "Is he . . . well-equipped?"

"Vivienne!" I toss a pillow at her.

"What? I'm 147 years old and in the midst of divorcing a man who is only well-endowed in ego. Let me live vicariously."

We both dissolve into laughter. Evidently, discussin' Dex's bedroom skills is enough to lift my spirits, at least temporarily.

"Thank you," I say once the giggles fade. "I needed that."

"Laughter in the face of darkness," she says with a small

smile. "It's how we survive."

But the lightness doesn't last. It slips away, quiet and quick, and the weight returns heavier than before.

"I don't want to die," I whisper. The words claw their way out of my throat without an invitation. "For the first time in my life, everythin' feels right. Like I'm exactly where I was always meant to be. I honestly feel . . ." I falter, the word thick on my tongue. "Loved."

Vivienne reaches across the space between us and grabs my hand. "I know."

We sit in silence for a long moment, listenin' to the B&B creak and settle around us.

"Maybe we can buy you a little more of it. Time, that is," Vivienne says finally. "Maybe we can understand what's attached itself to you. Perhaps even dislodge it."

I look up. Hope flutters weakly in my chest. "How?"

She purses her lips and takes a beat. "We need to talk to it directly. Find out what it wants." She pauses again. "We could likely access it the same way it attached itself to you."

"Another séance?" I can't believe she'd even suggest that after what happened last time. "Ya want to invite whatever's attached to me to come out and play?" My laugh sounds brittle. "Isn't that like tyin' a slab of meat 'round my neck and then pokin' a bear with a stick?"

Vivienne shakes her head. "No. We're not inviting it. Interrogating it. Learning what it is, what it wants." She leans forward, her eyes intense. "Knowledge is power, Mina. If we understand what's latched onto you, we might be able to dislodge it."

Floorboards creak overhead.

"And if we dislodge it?" Hope flutters dangerously in my chest.

"Then the Concord loses some of its power." Vivienne's voice drops lower. "Their ritual requires thirteen binding points, thirteen members including an anchor, and their key positioned at the convergence point. Break one link in that chain . . ."

"And the whole thing falls apart," I finish.

"It won't stop your tumor," she says. "But it might buy you more time. And it would definitely stop the Hollowing from happening tomorrow night."

I twist my fingers in my lap, weighin' desperate hope against common sense. The séance could work. Or it could speed up whatever's happenin' to me. Or worse. I could be possessed again, and this time I may not break free.

But what choice do I have? Worst case, my time is already up. But best case? I could buy more time. At least this way I'm doin' somethin'. Fightin' back.

"Okay," I say finally. "Let's do it."

Vivienne nods once, all business now. "We'll use the parlor. It has the strongest energetic resonance in the house, and it's where it all happened the other night. We'll revisit the scene of the crime."

We make our way through the darkness, doin' our best to ignore the ghostly eyes that stare us down from the shadows. The parlor stands empty and dark. Moonlight spills through the bay windows, leavin' silver rectangles on the hardwood floor. The grandfather clock in the corner reads 11:22. We have at least an hour before the other wives and the crew return from the midnight ghost parade.

"Close the doors," she instructs. She kneels to draw a perfect chalk circle in the center of the room.

I push the heavy doors shut, the wood warm beneath my palms. When I turn back, Vivienne has covered the mirror above the mantel with black cloth.

"Mirrors are thinner spots in reality," she explains briefly.

She arranges seven candles around the circle, then places a spirit board at its center. This isn't some cheap toy store version. Dark wood, polished smooth, with symbols that I don't recognize carved along the edges.

"Where did ya get that?" I ask. A chill runs down my spine.

"I've had it for decades." She sets a small triangular wooden object beside it. "I worked as a genuine medium before I became my current fabulous self."

I trace a finger over the board. This isn't a basic cardboard version you'd find in a cheap magic shop. This is legit. I don't bother askin' why she made it a point to bring this with her on the trip.

"This is my baby." She runs a finger over the smooth maple wood that's been polished to a nearly glass finish. She taps a jewel encrusted in the teardrop-shaped planchette. "This ruby was my mother's. I like to think she's with me whenever I use this."

My hands shake. "Vivienne, I don't know if I can—"

"It's okay." She places a gentle hand on my arm. "You're stronger than you think. I've watched you since I arrived. Most humans would have broken under the strain you've carried."

I know she probably meant it as a compliment, but it almost lands like a threat.

"We don't have to do this if you don't feel ready." She pauses, eyes studyin' me. "But it's the only way I know how to get the answers we need."

I hesitate. Do I really want to go through all of what I went through last night again? But what choice do I have, really? And I can trust her. Can't I?

I sit opposite her, and she places the spirit board between us. As I settle in, the house seems to exhale around us. Vivienne reaches into her bag and withdraws an ornate silver dagger, its handle encrusted with what appear to be diamonds and sapphires. She grasps the blade and drags it along her palm.

"Vampire blood enhances the protective circle," she explains as the thick liquid drips onto the chalk line. "It should help keep anything bad from getting in."

But can it protect against the thing that's already in me?

The moment her blood touches the circle, the chalk begins to glow with faint blue light. Vivienne begins to chant in a language I've never heard, syllables runnin' into each other until it sounds like one really long word. Her voice drops into a hypnotic cadence that makes my eyelids heavy.

"Place your hands on the board," she instructs. "Lightly. Just your fingertips."

I hesitate, my hands hoverin' above the polished wood. "What exactly are we askin' it?"

"What it wants. Why it chose you." Vivienne's eyes lock with mine. "Are you ready?"

No, I'm not ready. But I'm out of options and out of time, so here we are.

My fingers tremble. The moment my skin touches the wood, bright lights explode behind my eyes. My head snaps backward. I can't move. Can't scream.

I'm vaguely aware of Vivienne's voice, distant through the roar in my ears. My vision whites out as pain rips through me like I'm being torn apart at a cellular level.

Vivienne grabs my shoulders. She shouts, but I can't make out the words. I can't move. The pain in my head tightens and the candles flare into pillars, so high I'm afraid they're goin' to burn the whole place down and take us with it.

Then I'm fallin'. It's like the room went black and the floor disappeared, rippin' me away to somewhere I don't wanna be. I can tell that I'm spinnin', but I don't know up from down. And then it appears that I'm movin' through clouds. Pinpricks of light begin to appear below me. I'm floatin' high above Moonridge. The town and all of its holiday festivities sprawl beneath me like a miniature model, people like tiny dolls.

But then the image is wrong. The familiar has been stripped away, leavin' behind empty streets and blackened buildings that look like battered corpses. Cut into the landscape is a vast and intricate sigil. It stretches from Skipper Lake at the far western edge to Amethyst Beach nestled in the mountains to the east. At thirteen points along the spiral, pulses of light beat like a second heartbeat. The old mill. The cemetery. The abandoned asylum. The church. All of them burn with the same feverish red then orange light, volatile, and angry.

These are the very points Dex laid out as the Concord hot spots.

I surge forward, drawn toward the old mill. This is where we bound Ravena. Oh my land. Did we make things worse by leavin' her here? Have we poured more power into this point without realizin' it?

I pull back, willin' myself to take in the full spiral once more. I can feel the energy that feeds this structure. Souls, maybe. And I don't know if the spiral is drainin' them or feedin' them.

I feel myself yanked toward the west, toward Skipper Lake. The closer I get, the more familiar the energy becomes. A figure moves at the edge of the lake, blurred, barely there, but then it sharpens into a human-like figure.

A hood is lifted.

Everett.

Calvin's ghostly crush.

His energy is fractured. One part glows soft and steady, but black tendrils twist through it like blood through a vein. The corruption is inside him. He is part of the Concord.

We have to warn Calvin.

Below me, the spiral pulses again. Deeper. Hungrier.

I plunge toward a sickly green point near what must be the falls. The energy thrums with awareness, and I can't pull away. A shadow erupts at the center and locks onto me. One arm begins to stretch upward, limb extendin' to an impossible length, long, boneless fingers curlin' toward me. I try to pull back, but there's nowhere to go.

The fingers latch onto somethin' deep inside me. I gasp. It tugs once, and it pulls the air out of my lungs.

My soul. It's tryin' to rip it free.

Agony tears through my sternum and extends to the tips of

my fingers and toes. This is a desecration. A violation beyond anythin' the human body should have to endure. My mouth opens in a scream, voice risin' in a chorus of agony that echoes through the parlor of my B&B.

"You are the key." The entity's voice echoes in my head. "You are the way. The path between worlds."

Their grip tightens. My soul stretches, pulled in directions it was never meant to bend, warpin' reality with it. Somethin' rips inside me, like fabric.

"Join us. Live forever. Free us all."

A flood of visions crashes into me. The sky on fire. Skipper Lake, full of bodies, screamin' for help. Figures crowd the town square, eyes and mouths wide with horror as winged creatures rip through the sky, snatchin' people off the streets with claws like knives. And at the center of it all stands what's left of me. Blood drips from my arms. I'm no longer Mina Cartwright. I am the gate. The Concord's key.

And I'm smilin'.

"No." The word forms in my mind.

The entity cackles. "One way or another, your soul belongs to us."

It's too strong.

Then, faintly, I hear Vivienne. "I command you to let her go."

I feel warmth on my forehead. Sticky.

"Return!" Vivienne's voice grows louder, and I feel the creature's clutch loosen. "Return to your body, Mina Cartwright. Return now."

The entity's grip shatters with a snap that echoes in my head. I'm dragged backward, wind rushin', screams echoin', away from the spiral, away from the thirteen points, and the terrible vision of blood and death that's bound to come.

The air around me whooshes, then snaps, and everythin' goes silent. My lungs burn as I gasp for air. I collapse against Vivienne, my limbs heavy and useless. The taste of copper floods my mouth, and the tip of my tongue stings.

Fuckin' hell. Did I have another seizure? Did I just make things worse for me?

"Easy," Vivienne whispers, her arms tight around me. "Breathe, Mina. Just breathe."

The parlor is in shambles. Throw pillows lie scattered around us. Candles have burned down to stubs, wax pooled across my hardwood floor.

I attempt to sit up, but my muscles refuse to cooperate. "How long—?"

"Almost an hour." Vivienne adjusts her hold to better support my head.

My throat feels raw. "Did I . . . say things?"

"Many things. In many voices." She smooths my hair back from my damp forehead.

The vision fragments flash behind my eyes. "I saw what they intend to do. And Everett—We have to tell Calvin about—"

She places a finger to my lips. "I know. But you need to rest."

I struggle to sit up. "Did we stop it? The thing . . .?" My voice sounds strange in my own ears. "What's inside me, Vivienne?"

She hesitates, then helps me stand. "I don't know. At least not for sure."

Her face says otherwise. And I know what I saw. What I felt. The entity that tried to rip out my soul was no ordinary spirit.

"Let's get you to bed. I'll clean up the mess before the others get back."

"The thirteen points," I say as she leads me down the hall. "I saw them. And Everett."

"Shh." Vivienne rubs small circles on my back. "Not now. You need rest."

I want to argue, to demand answers, but exhaustion takes over. She helps me into bed, and my eyelids grow impossibly heavy. Did she do somethin' to knock me out?

"Calvin," I manage to whisper. "He needs to know. About

Everett."

"Tomorrow," she promises. "We'll deal with everything tomorrow."

She pulls the covers up to my chin like I'm a child and places a hand on my forehead.

"Sleep," she commands.

And I do.

CHAPTER TWENTY-ONE

Dex

Amber light casts long shadows across the workroom of the Blue Moon Apothecary. No one speaks. Each of us is deep in our research, looking for something we may have missed.

Hazel and La'Tasha huddle around a map of Moonridge embedded beneath the top of the workroom's center table. Coco sits to the side, head in her hand, as Hazel places colored dots at various points. Penny sits nearby in her own reality, ancient books and scrolls piled around her. She's lost in whatever it is she's studying, eyes fixed on the text. She taps the eraser of her pencil against her desk. The rhythm matches the ticking of the clock, counting down the minutes.

"Here, here, here, and here," Hazel says, pointing at various spots on the map. "These are the strongest binding points. Nothing I've tried has been able to weaken them. I have put down five different wards, and they fail within hours. It's so annoying."

La'Tasha picks up a small clay disc bearing a protection sigil etched into its surface. "Have you tried—"

"I have tried everything I can think of," Hazel cuts her off. "The ward at the lake lasted six hours before it cracked. The one at the cemetery barely made it to three." She runs her thumb over the fading sigil. "These are Gran's strongest spells, and these assholes blow right through them."

La'Tasha takes a seat next to me. "Have you called The Regency?"

Hazel sighs and runs a hand across her face. "With everything else I have on my plate? No, Tash. I haven't called them. I figured as Vertus Suprema, it is literally my job to stop evil cults."

"This is bigger than us." La'Tasha taps the table with a finger. The tension between the two of them has been growing all night.

"We've got less than twenty-four hours," Coco adds, glancing at the clock.

"Yeah, thanks. The countdown helps." Hazel begins to pace, and Coco gives La'Tasha a sideways glance.

Across the room, Penny raises her hand and snaps her fingers. "Guys." She clears her throat. "I think I found something."

Hazel moves to her table. I hoist myself up and join them. I peer over Penny's shoulder at a small map inside a book and a wall of text on the tablet next to her.

"I've been comparing old survey maps." She taps the eraser of her pencil against the book on the table. "There's something weird about the library's foundation."

"What do you mean?" Hazel leans closer.

Penny points to a faded diagram. "It's built on a raised foundation with a sealed basement. And look at these symbols carved into the original cornerstone."

She flips to another page showing detailed drawings of arcane symbols. My breath catches.

"It looks similar to a Concord binding sigil," I murmur.

La'Tasha's eyes widen. "Are you saying the library itself is built on a binding point?"

"Kind of," Penny scratches her chin. "There's definitely something underneath it, but the way this looks, it's more like the library sits on top of it to shield it. Like a cage."

"You think there's something under the library?" Hazel studies Penny. "Something the original builders were trying to contain?"

Penny nods. "The records mention a 'sealed chamber' beneath the archives. According to this, it houses 'that which must not be disturbed.'"

The room goes quiet, but the air crackles with energy.

"Maybe this is the secret we've been looking for," La'Tasha says slowly.

Hazel straightens and folds her arms. "It must be important if it's sealed off and hidden."

Studying the map with fresh eyes, I see things we may have missed had Penny not had the idea to look through old permits and other documents that seemed innocuous.

I run a finger over the blueprints. "There's something much bigger at play. I have a feeling someone designed this space as a shield."

Coco shivers, eyes wide. "But a shield for what?"

"For whatever lies beneath the library. There's something down there that the original settlers were trying to keep sealed."

Hazel looks at all of us. "We need to get down there and investigate. Now."

I'm already reaching for my coat. "I'll go. I can sense the binding magic directly, but I could use some magical backup. My powers are still weak."

"I'll come too," Penny says. "I have the keys."

La'Tasha nods decisively. "Count me in."

"While you all are doing that, Coco and I will keep looking for a way to take out some of these bindings," Hazel says. "If we can't stop the ritual entirely, we can at least try to weaken them."

The decision is made.

***

We enter the library through the staff door. La'Tasha's cloaking charm should keep us hidden from any prowling scouts. We descend to the basement, our flashlight beams cutting through air thick with dust. Behind me, Penny sneezes twice, then mutters an apology as if the sound might wake whatever sleeps down here. La'Tasha moves like she's done this countless times, her steps silent on the concrete floor. Mine are not. Each tap of my cane echoes in the cramped space, announcing our presence to the darkness.

"The archives we're looking for should be at the far back." Penny's flashlight beam trembles slightly, casting jittery shadows across faded book spines.

La'Tasha runs a finger along a shelf and grimaces at the thick grime coating her finger. "I can't believe I've never been down here. How far do these archives go?"

"I don't know for sure." Penny pauses at a junction. Shelves run for several feet to our left and right, and there are at least ten more rows ahead of us. "The original building burned in 1912, but this basement is much older. Mrs. Henderson mentioned some sections haven't been touched in decades."

Scanning the walls, I feel for disturbances in the natural flow of energy. Wounded as I am, the wrongness here is unmistakable.

"Am I imagining it, or did the energy shift?" I note as our breath begins to fog.

Penny's fingers spark, tiny blue flashes that illuminate her startled face before fading. "Sorry. Happens when I'm nervous."

"Your magic is just responding to the energy down here," La'Tasha explains gently. "It used to happen to me all the time. Once this is all behind us, I'll teach you how to stop it."

The shelves grow more dense, their contents becoming dustier the farther we go.

Penny stops, her flashlight fixed on the floor ahead. "Look. On the floor. That discoloration."

She points to a section of concrete partially covered by a

tattered rug, its pattern faded to ghosts of what might have been flowers or vines. The most obvious tell is the absence of dust on the floor around the rug. Someone's been down here recently.

La'Tasha kneels and drags the weathered carpet away, revealing a trapdoor, its iron handle blackened with age. Around its edges are symbols drawn in what can only be blood, long dried to the color of rust but still somehow glistening in our flashlight beams.

La'Tasha studies the markings. "Wow. These are old."

"And recently reinforced," I add, noting the variations in color and texture. "Someone has been down here. There's no dust on the floor, and some of this blood seems fresh."

Penny's breath quickens. "What exactly do you think is under there?"

La'Tasha kneels next to the trap door, hands hovering over the ground. "No way."

"What?" Penny asks, kneeling beside her.

La'Tasha's hands begin to tremble. "If I'm reading this correctly, it could be a Crucible Core."

Penny shakes her head. "I don't know what that is."

"Think of it as a magical battery," La'Tasha explains, still studying the sigils. "But a bad one. A really bad one."

"Bad how?"

La'Tasha takes a deep breath. "They're powered by human souls."

"But this one's been corrupted," I say. The malevolence radiating from beneath the trapdoor is strong. Almost toxic. It pulses like a diseased heart. "This one isn't only full of once-humans."

I focus my intent through my cane and coax the scythe to emerge. It slowly transforms in my hands.

"Let me see if I can get the door open so we can get a better look. It may not be safe."

They both scoot back. I trace my blade along the blood sigils. They glow a sickly red, then bubble like boiling blood, the stench of copper and sulfur thick in the air; one by one, each sigil flares and dies. The trapdoor shudders. A deep and mournful groan echoes through the basement as the seal breaks. The door springs open. Stale air rushes up from the opening, carrying the smell of dirt tinged with decay. Penny's flashlight beam reveals a small chamber roughly a foot below, empty except for a stone cube, roughly two feet on each side, bound in bands of black iron.

La'Tasha scoots closer and pushes her glasses up on her nose. "I was right."

Symbols cover every visible surface of the cube. The whole thing pulses with a faint red glow, like the last embers of a burning log.

Penny leans forward, drawn to the cube as if she can't help herself.

"Penny, don't—"

Her fingers brush the surface, and her body goes rigid. A sound escapes her, not quite a scream, but no less horrified. I grab her shoulders and pull her away. She scrambles back, trembling.

La'Tasha rushes to her side. "Are you okay?"

Penny looks between us, shaking her head. "They're trapped. Souls. Thousands of them. They're in so much pain." A tear falls from her eye.

La'Tasha stands and moves to the trapdoor and immediately begins casting a containment spell. "Help me seal it. Temporarily, at least."

I join what little power I am able to muster with hers, and together we trace counter-sigils around the perimeter. It's not enough to completely neutralize it, but enough to contain any possible threat for the time being. The red glow dims slightly. The pulsing slows.

Penny stands, her face ashen. "What are they doing to those souls?"

"This is the work of The Mortician. He gathers them and traps them for exactly this purpose. They use them as fuel. Living energy would be ideal, but trapped souls work especially well if they're bound in suffering. They've added something in there with them to make their suffering even worse."

"What the fuck?" La'Tasha's jaw tightens. "Can we free them?"

"Not without potentially releasing whatever else is in there. There's a reason they put all of these sigils around it. Whatever is in there could be very bad." I test the seal with a tendril of my own energy. It pushes back. "It's aware that we're here."

"What do we do?" La'Tasha asks. "If this is fueling the bindings . . ."

Penny pushes herself upright. "She's right. We need to cut off their power source. If this is what they're using to fuel The Hollowing, we can stop it."

I shake my head. "No. It's too dangerous. We don't know what else is in there. It might unleash something much worse. This could be a setup. For all we know, it could help rather than hinder the ritual. We need to be strategic." I test our magical barrier again, feeling it strain against whatever pushes from within. "And all those lost souls. If we set them free, they won't know where to go."

"Um, hello? Isn't that literally your job?" La'Tasha points out.

"Yes, but Mina is my first priority right now. If we unleash thousands—possibly hundreds of thousands—of unbound souls on top of everything else going on, who knows what could happen."

"I understand," Penny says. "But if we stop the ritual, we could buy Mina more time, and the souls could cause a diversion."

I shake my head. "Too risky." I look down and notice thin cracks appearing in our magical barrier. "We need to go. Now. Something is pushing back. If they send out a scout to investigate . . ."

I don't need to say more. We close the trapdoor and replace the rug, then La'Tasha casts an erasure spell, removing any trace that we were ever here.

***

Filtered moonlight dances across Mina's sleeping form when I enter her bedroom. I rest my cane against the wall and then gently lower myself onto her bed. I place a hand on her back, feeling the slow, steady beat of her heart and her rhythmic breathing beneath my palm.

Hazel and the others are still working, strengthening what protections they can around town. I should be helping them, but I fear there's nothing more we can do. And I needed to see Mina. To know she's okay.

Her eyes open, briefly staring through me before finally focusing on my face.

"Dex?" Her voice is rough and laced with sleep. There's an echo to it that makes me uneasy. She blinks. "What time is it, then?"

"Just past three." I kick off my shoes and swing my legs up onto the bed. "The witches are still working on protections. I wanted to check on you."

Mina scoots closer and lays her head in my lap. I scan her soul. It flickers, unsteady, like a candle fighting the wind.

"Did ya find anythin' new?" she asks, hand rubbing my thigh.

"Yes. At the library. Something called a Crucible Core. It's corrupted. They've been collecting souls. For power."

She nods against me as if all of that made perfect sense. "Of course they have."

"You can feel it, can't you? The pull."

"It's gettin' stronger." She brings herself to sitting and wipes sleep from her eyes. "Like gravity."

"We're still working to stop them. If we can break enough binding points—"

"I've made a decision," she interrupts. She sits up straighter, looking more like her strong and determined self. "I want to go to the festival tomorrow. Just for a while."

I start to protest, but she holds up a palm, stopping me.

"I want my last few hours to be as normal as possible. I want to spend time laughin' with my friends, and then we'll come home well before midnight, and I'm goin' to take my pills and go to sleep." Her voice catches but doesn't break. "I want ya right there with me. I want ya to hold my hand as I go, and then walk with me to the end. Will ya do that?"

The request settles between us.

"Yes." I nod. "But I'm not sure being at the festival is safe."

She places a hand on mine. "I'm goin'."

I swallow and readjust my position on the bed. This is not a battle I'm going to win. "Okay. Whatever will make you happy."

Her expression shifts. She rises to her knees on the bed, bringing her face level with mine.

"What would make me happy is one more night with you."

She kisses me then, soft at first, then with growing urgency. Her fingers move to the buttons of my shirt, clumsy but determined. I should stop her. Should tell her to rest. Should remind her that every moment of intimacy between us breaks rules and changes who I am at my core.

But I don't care about that.

So, I help her. My hands cover hers, steadying them as together we undo each button.

"Are you sure?" I ask, giving her one last chance to reconsider.

Her answer is to pull her t-shirt over her head in a single fluid motion. Moonlight turns her skin to marble, beautiful and pale.

"I'm dyin' tomorrow," she says. "Tonight, I want to live."

Her lips find mine again, and I melt into her. I want this as badly as she does. If this is our last night together, I want to remember every touch, every breath.

Mina pulls me closer, her body pressing against mine. "I love you," she whispers against my lips, words I've heard countless humans speak to each other but never directed at me. Never felt. "I think I've loved ya since ya saved me six years ago."

I don't deserve her love. Don't deserve this moment.

"And I love you," I tell her, the truth of it burning in my chest. "More than I thought possible."

Her smile is radiant. Tears shimmer in her eyes. Our kiss deepens, and for this precious, fleeting moment, death takes a step back, giving us room to exist together, if only for tonight.

CHAPTER TWENTY-TWO

Mina

His lips are like feathers against my neck. Goosebumps start at the top of my arms and find their way down my torso. I arch against him, fingers threaded through his hair, holdin' him close like I might be able to merge with him. Stay with him forever.

"Are you okay?" Dex's breath tickles my collarbone.

I nod, unable to speak. I find my breath. "I'm fine. Really. Please don't stop."

Our mouths collide, hungry and desperate. I run my hand down his chest, across his stomach, and then further down, grippin' the hardness between his legs. He moans, kissin' me deeper. He runs a hand through my hair and lays me back on the bed. He sits up and removes his pants, the length of him poppin' free. It's almost unfair how beautiful he is, and unbelievable that this is even happenin'. That he somehow wants me. Desires me.

He hovers above me, moonlight cuttin' shadows into the planes of his face. His eyes, usually distant and detached, burn with want.

"You're beautiful." His thumb traces my cheekbone.

I want to laugh, but the way he looks at me makes me believe him.

"So are you," I whisper back. I run my hands over his shoulders, down the smooth expanse of his chest. I wrap my legs around his waist, pullin' him closer. Inside of me. We both gasp and sink into the rhythm of the movement, anchorin' me to this world.

"I never thought I could feel this." His voice roughens with emotion.

I put a finger to his lips. "No talkin', love." I lock my heels around his waist and pull him further into me, eyes rollin' back. "We'll talk later."

When he thrusts, I gasp, and it takes me a moment to catch my breath. I'll never have this again, and he knows it, and he's goin' to make it count. For both of us.

We find a rhythm that feels both brand new and familiar, like we were made to move together this way.

His forehead presses against mine, our lips pressed together, mufflin' both our moans.

"Don't hold back." I dig my fingers into his shoulders. "I won't break. I want to feel all of ya."

His eyes flash, and a hungry smile spreads across his face. His movements grow bolder, deeper. I cry out, unfazed by the fact that someone might hear. What does it matter now? Nothin' matters except this moment. Here. Now.

Our bodies move faster, keepin' the release just at the edge, savorin' every moment. Sweat slicks our skin. My heart hammers so hard I wonder if it might give out before tomorrow night. What a way to go that would be.

"Mina," he groans, my name like a prayer on his lips.

My whole body tightens, pleasure buildin' like a wave about to crash. And then it does, washin' over me in pulses that steal my breath, my thoughts, everythin' except the sensation of him inside me, against me.

He keeps goin', bringin' me to climax again and then again and again until I have no energy left. He follows seconds later, buryin' his face in my neck as his body shudders. I hold him through it, my hands strokin' his back, his hair.

For a long moment, we don't move. Don't speak. Just breathe together in the darkness, our bodies still joined. My body drifts on this pleasure high. Only his arms keep me from floatin' away.

Eventually, he shifts to lie beside me, pullin' me against his chest. His heartbeat sounds strong and steady under my ear. Does Death even need a heart? Tonight, it seems he does.

"I should have known," I say, my voice thick with the remnants of pleasure.

"Known what?" His fingers trace lazy patterns on my bare shoulder.

"That Death would be an amazin' lover." I tilt my head to see his face, delighted by the smile that spreads across it. "All that experience watchin' humanity. Ya picked up a few tricks, didn't ya? Dirty voyeur."

I nudge him with my elbow, and his laugh rumbles through his chest and into mine. "I've observed much, yes. But experiencing . . ." He shakes his head slightly. "That's completely different."

I snuggle closer and press a kiss to his chest.

"Did I hurt you?" he asks, noticin' my sudden stillness.

"No." I kiss his chest again. "Just the opposite. For the first time in months, nothin' hurts. Not my head, not my heart. Nothin'. I'm oddly at peace."

The constant pain that's become my unwanted companion has retreated, at least for now. Whether it's the endorphins or somethin' about Dex himself, I don't know. Don't care.

"Will ya get in trouble?" I ask. "For this?"

His arms tighten around me. "Probably. But I crossed that line the moment I saved you six years ago. The last few days just add to my list of transgressions."

"Sorry to be such a bad influence."

I'm not sorry at all.

"The best kind of bad influence," he murmurs as he kisses

the top of my head.

I trace my fingers along his arm. How is it that someone whose job it is to guide souls away from life could make me feel so wonderfully present in my own body?

"Thank you," I whisper.

"For what?"

"For makin' me feel alive one last time. For makin' me feel loved even. It's been a while."

His only response is to hold me tighter, as if he could somehow keep me here through sheer force of will.

I wish he could.

Moonlight sneaks through the gap in my curtains, paintin' streaks across the tangled sheets. I turn in his arms to face him, studyin' his features in the soft light.

His eyes are closed, dark lashes cast shadows on his cheeks. He looks peaceful. Almost normal. Fully human. Did I do this to him?

"I can feel you staring," he murmurs without openin' his eyes.

I trace my finger along his jawline, then continue down his neck, over his shoulder, and across his chest.

"What will happen to ya?" I ask finally. "After . . . ya know."

He knows exactly what I'm askin'. After I die. After he guides me across.

"I don't know." His honesty does nothin' to erase the sorrow in my heart. "I've rarely broken rules in all my time doing this. Funny that most of those rules have been broken in the last few decades, and all center around residents of Moonridge."

"I hate the thought that I could have ruined your future."

He shakes his head and then presses his lips to mine. "Don't. You didn't make me do any of this."

"No regrets, then?" I hold my breath waitin' for his answer.

His hand cups my cheek, thumb brushin' across my skin with such tenderness it makes my chest ache. "Not a single one."

His answer brings unexpected tears to my eyes. I blink

them away quickly. I've done enough cryin' lately. Tonight is for better things.

"Even though I got you stabbed by a Graveborn?"

"Even then." He shifts closer, our foreheads touchin'. "Though I could have done without that particular experience."

His arms tighten around me, and I once again curl against his chest.

"Ya know," I say against his skin, "when I pictured my last days, they never looked like this."

"How did you picture them?"

"Sad. Quiet. I figured I'd be alone in a hospital room somewhere, or maybe here at the B&B with occasional visits from friends who wouldn't know what to say."

"And instead?"

"Instead, I'm naked in bed with the Grim Reaper." I smile as his chest rumbles with another quiet laugh. "Life is full of surprises, isn't it? Even at the end."

We fall silent again. His fingers trace idle patterns on my shoulder, occasionally driftin' down my arm, then back up.

I do the same, memorizin' the planes of his chest, the silky texture of his hair between my fingers. Who knows what memories we carry beyond the veil? I want to take this with me, if I can.

"Do ya remember them all?" I ask. "All the souls you've guided?"

He's quiet for so long I think he might not answer. When he does, his voice is soft with sadness.

"Not all. There have been too many. But some . . ." His eyes meet mine in the darkness. "Some I remember. The ones who thanked me. Welcomed me."

"Which am I?"

His smile is gentle, tinged with a mix of happy and sad, perhaps even a little regret. "I hope you know that you're the only one I've ever loved."

I don't know how to respond, so I kiss him instead, pourin'

everythin' I feel into the pressure of my lips against his.

When we part, I rest my head on his shoulder, my hand over his heart. The steady rhythm under my palm feels like a countdown, markin' the precious hours we have left.

"Can I tell ya somethin'?" I ask. My heart thuds because of what I'm about to admit.

"Anything."

I take a deep breath, searchin' for the courage.

"It's about the day ya saved me," I begin. "About why I was on that bridge."

Once the words are out, it becomes easier, floodgates open. Maybe the darkness makes confession feel safer. Or maybe it's because secrets seem pointless now.

"I was thirty-one when I decided I wanted to die," I begin.

Dex remains still beside me, but I feel his breath hitch.

I take a steadyin' breath and let myself slip back to the darkest years of my life.

"But my life had been shite since I was sixteen. I was an honor student, never in trouble, but I got pregnant when I was sixteen, and apparently that was unforgivable." The old hurt feels distant now, but still vaguely there. "My boyfriend disappeared the second I told him. Refused my calls, transferred schools. His dad was some church elder who couldn't have the family reputation damaged. I don't think I could be more of a Catholic cliché."

I keep myself focused by tracin' absent patterns on Dex's chest.

"My parents gave me two choices. I could keep the baby and leave, or go away, have the baby, and give it up for adoption, and then come back home and spend the rest of my life beggin' forgiveness." My laugh sounds hollow. "I chose to have an abortion instead. Then packed my bags and left."

"How did you survive?" Dex asks softly.

"Stayed with a friend and finished high school. Then this guy Miles swept in like my knight in shinin' armor." My fingers pause their movements. "Except he was no knight and treated his liquor better than he treated me."

I sit up so I'm above him. So I'm less likely to see his reaction. I don't need or want pity.

"He was the first in a parade of men who thought 'I love you' was permission to leave bruises. I got good at makeup, and even better at excuses." I shake my head. "Strange how ya can know somethin' is destroyin' ya but still not leave."

"Not strange," Dex murmurs. "Human. You're not the first and certainly won't be the last."

He's not wrong. I take a deep breath. "Eventually, I met James. He seemed different. Stable job, nice apartment. We got engaged after eight months." My throat tightens slightly. "But he was insecure. Didn't trust me. It started slow, then escalated. He didn't hit, though. Not with his fists anyway. Instead, he aimed for every insecurity I had and used them for target practice."

Dex's hand finds mine.

"I stayed because that's what I did. My best friend Cassie kept tellin' me to leave him, that I deserved better. Turns out she wanted me out of the picture because she was test-drivin' him for herself." The knife twist of betrayal still feels sharp after all these years.

"Mina—"

He sits up, and I shake my head.

"I came home early from a work trip. Found them in our bed . . ." I can still see it if I let myself remember. "I just stood there watchin' for a minute. I couldn't speak. But then it made sense."

Moonlight shifts across our joined hands.

"That's when it hit me. Everyone I'd ever loved had betrayed me. Parents, boyfriends, best friend. Everyone. And the common factor was me." I meet Dex's eyes in the darkness. "My grandmother had died about a month earlier and left me a good chunk of money. Enough to start over somewhere new. But all I could think was—what's the point? I'd just find new people to disappoint me. The problem wasn't them. It was me."

Dex takes my hand and squeezes.

The memory of that day feels both like a lifetime ago and like it was just yesterday. Wind stingin' my face as I stared down at the gray water below. My frozen hands, red and raw, grippin' the metal rail.

"I remember I wore my grandmother's green cardigan. I wanted to take somethin' of hers with me. She was the only one who ever made me feel loved." I trace the outline of Dex's fingers with my own. "And I didn't cry. Isn't that weird? I felt empty. Like I'd already left my body and was just goin' through the motions. I couldn't feel anythin'."

Dex's thumb traces circles on my palm.

"Climbin' over that rail was harder than expected. For a second I thought, 'Wouldn't it be ironic if I accidentally fell while tryin' to jump on purpose?'" My laugh catches slightly.

"I stood there maybe five minutes, starin' down. I think part of me was waitin' for someone to stop me. But no one came." I shrug. "So I took that as a sign, and I let go before I could think about it any longer."

I dab at the tears threatenin' to spill over.

"The thing they don't tell ya about jumpin' is that ya have plenty of time to regret it on the way down. The fall felt like it took forever. Long enough for me to think, 'Wait, I don't want this' and 'It's too late now.'"

My heart pounds at the memory of the gray water beneath me.

"I remember hittin' the water. It felt like concrete. Knocked the breath out of me. Then I was dragged under, and suddenly all I wanted was to live."

Dex's grip on my hand relaxes slightly.

"I fought it. Kicked toward what I thought was the surface, but my clothes felt like they weighed a thousand pounds." I close my eyes, rememberin' the panic, the burnin' pain in my chest. "And then . . . nothin'. Blackness."

The next part is hazy around the edges.

"I think I heard your voice first. I'll never forget ya tellin' me it was goin' to be okay now." I turn to look at him. He has tears in his eyes. "I knew who ya were. And I also remember thinkin' your voice was too kind to belong to Death."

He smiles and waits for me to continue.

"I couldn't see ya clearly at first. You were just this presence in the distance. But I could feel ya reachin' for me." My fingers tighten around his. "And I knew what it all meant, but all I could think was that I wasn't ready. That I'd made a horrible mistake."

I swallow.

"I remember beggin' ya. I don't remember exactly what I said, just that I pleaded for another chance. Promised I'd do better, be better." I shake my head at the memory. "And ya listened. Even though you've probably heard every desperate bargain humans can make."

"You were different," Dex says finally. "Your soul . . . It felt different. I knew it wasn't your time."

"Or maybe ya just broke the rules because ya found me so irresistible."

He doesn't deny it, which tells me enough.

"Next thing I knew, I was coughin' up river water on the bank. Some kayaker had spotted me and called it in." I look down at our joined hands, then tilt my head back and stare at the ceilin'.

"So I took my gran's money and started over. Found Moonridge in some random travel blog about charmin' small towns. The B&B was for sale. It felt like a sign." I smile at the memory. "I built somethin' here. A life. Made a home. Found people who became the family I never really had."

I turn, and my hand finds his face, palm against his cheek.

"It's been an amazin' six years. Thank you," I whisper. "I wish it were longer, but it was enough to discover what a proper life full of people who accept ya actually feels like. Enough to find a place where I belong. Here. In Moonridge. With all these wonderful supernatural weirdos who somehow became my people."

I meet his gaze directly. "And with you. Even if that particular plot twist is straight out of some cosmic joke book."

He pulls me close and rests his chin on my head. I know what he's thinkin'. We're about to face the same choice again, but this time, he won't be able to save me.

"When ya saved me that day," I whisper against his shoulder, "did ya ever imagine we'd end up here?"

"Never." His lips press against my forehead and linger for a beat. "In thousands of years, I never imagined this."

"Do ya regret it?"

He shakes his head. "Not for a second."

I settle against him, my head restin' against his chest, directly over his heart. Its steady rhythm remindin' me that right now he's mine. And I'm his.

CHAPTER TWENTY-THREE

Dex

I catch the toe of my boot on a loose plank at the east end of Mina's porch. My immediate thought is to ask one of the wolves to come and fix it for her, but then I remember that after tonight, it won't matter much.

I tap the end of my cane against the board, forcing the loose nail back into its hole as I gaze out at the slowly setting sun. As much as I'd like to make the day drag on, there's nothing I can do. I can't stop the sun from setting any more than I can stop Mina's fate. Tonight, she will die. And if I don't collect her soul and usher her across in time, she will become the key to the destruction of the human world.

The sun hangs low, painting everything in amber light. The sight is cruelly beautiful considering it's such a dark day. I'm so angry at everything. The turn of events. The Concord. My elders. But most of all with myself because I have failed her in every conceivable way. Hazel and La'Tasha managed to weaken five of the binding spots, but the others remain intact, and if things keep up the way they have, those five could regenerate at least some of their power before midnight. The odds are against us.

The screen door squeaks open, and Mina steps out, wrapped

in a blanket.

"You're broodin' again," she says. Her voice is strong, but her face is gaunt, eyes hollow.

"Not brooding. Planning." I offer an encouraging smile. I won't let her see how worried I am. If I fail tonight . . .

She settles into the porch swing, chains groaning softly beneath her small frame. "Don't lie to me. You're worried about tonight. About me goin' to the festival."

She knows me too well now.

"I don't think I need to remind you just how dangerous it is. The Concord will be watching. In public, surrounded by so many people, we don't know who we can trust which means we can't protect you as effectively."

"I know, but I just need ya to understand how important this is to me." Her green eyes fix on mine. "I'm askin' for life. Just a few more hours of it, surrounded by the people and the town I love."

My argument dies in my throat. How can I deny her this request? After everything she's endured, how can I force her to spend her final hours trapped inside?

But the fear gnaws at me. "If you start to fade in public—"

"Then at least I'll fade doin' somethin' I choose. And you'll be there to take me across." She reaches for my hand, her fingers cool against my skin. "Please, Dex. I need this."

Voices approach from the garden path before I can respond. Hazel leads the small procession, her auburn hair catching the sunset's glow. La'Tasha and Coco follow close behind.

"Reinforcements have arrived," Hazel announces, voice chipper, but the pain in her eyes is evident. She sets her bag on the porch with a thud. "How are you feeling?"

"Like I'm slowly turnin' into a ghost. Other than that, peachy." This draws a sad smile from the trio.

I motion Hazel and La'Tasha to the far end of the porch while Coco stays with Mina. "A word?"

They follow without question.

"She wants to go to the festival tonight." I don't waste time with pleasantries. "I think it's too risky."

Hazel exchanges a glance with La'Tasha. "And you think keeping her here is safer?"

"There are more ghosts in this place than in a graveyard," La'Tasha points out. "And don't forget she was possessed here, and the Concord left one of their binding stones in the garden. I don't think this place is as safe as you think it is."

"At least here I can contain whatever happens. In public, with so many people about and with the Concord watching—"

"The binding points are everywhere, Dex." La'Tasha crosses her arms. "The entire town is their playground now. You think four walls are gonna stop these nasty bitches?"

"We've strengthened the perimeter around the festival grounds," Hazel adds. "Not enough to stop them completely, but enough to buy time if something happens."

"And if she starts to fade? If the Concord tries to take her early?"

"Then we'll fight." Hazel's jaw sets in a stubborn line. "Keeping her locked away won't save her. You know that."

I do know. That's the hell of it. Nothing will save her now.

"She only has a few hours left. Her life is her own to manage now." La'Tasha's voice sharpens. "Let her do this. We don't get to decide for her."

I nod. They're right, but it doesn't make me feel any better. "We have to be diligent. We need to all stick together tonight. Keep her surrounded at all times. No exceptions."

La'Tasha places a hand on my arm. "The fireworks begin at nine o'clock, and they'll last for roughly thirty minutes, and then we'll all slip away and come back here."

"The festivities go until midnight," Hazel says. "The crowd should be big enough that no one will notice we've gone. Hopefully, there will be enough people wandering around that any

Concord watchers will miss us."

Across the porch, Coco sits beside Mina on the swing, their heads bent together in quiet conversation. Coco reaches into one of her bags and pulls out a small pendant on a delicate silver chain. She presents the pendant to Mina, who examines it with curious fingers.

"It's beautiful," Mina says, tracing the intricate pattern etched into the silver disc. "What is it?"

"A tether to help keep you bound to us," Coco says. She places a hand on Mina's knee. "Just a little extra protection tonight."

Coco cups the pendant in her palm, whispers something that no one can hear, then pricks her finger with a small pin. A single drop of blood falls onto the metal, where it sizzles for a moment before disappearing completely. The pendant pulses once with soft blue light.

"And, if you start to fade," Coco explains, fastening the chain around Mina's neck, "it'll pulse to warn you. It can't stop what's happening, but it will alert us and give us time to get you somewhere safe."

Coco wipes a tear from her eye.

Mina touches the pendant, now resting against her breastbone. "Thank you."

"We've agreed on a plan." I settle beside her on the swing. "We'll attend the festival. After the fireworks at nine, we'll all come back here."

"And then?" Her voice is small but steady.

"Then we will be here to support you. Say our goodbyes," Hazel says, tears gathering despite her obvious effort to remain strong. "We will do whatever we can to keep the Concord at bay while you . . ." She can't finish.

"While I die." Mina's hand finds mine. "It's okay to say it, love."

Silence presses down on us.

La'Tasha wipes tears from her face. "Also, we talked and have decided that we're going to keep the B&B open. Between the three of us, we will manage it. We'll hire help. We'll keep the traditions going." She swallows hard and gathers her composure. "I'm just going to need you to give me that famous scone recipe. Okay?"

Mina nods, unable to speak.

"And we're going to rename it," Coco adds, her enthusiasm cutting through the sadness. "Mina's Place. So no one ever forgets."

Mina's grip on my hand tightens. "You guys. It's not your problem to take on. Ya really don't have to—"

"Yes, we do," Hazel interrupts. "This place is special. You made it special. We're not letting that go. It'll be like keeping a piece of you here."

"And maybe you can haunt us," Coco says. "Serious. That would be so cool."

Mina stands, the blanket slipping from her shoulders as she opens her arms. The three witches move as one, enveloping her in a group hug.

I give them their moment and fight back the tears that threaten to spill down my cheeks. Human grief is an emotion I can do without.

"I love you all so much," Mina whispers, her voice thick with tears. "You'll never know how precious ya are to me."

They hold each other for a long moment, until Hazel finally pulls away, wiping at her eyes. "We should go. I still have preparations to finish before tonight. The duties of the fall festival coordinator are never done."

With final hugs and promises to see us at the festival, the witches depart, leaving Mina and me alone on the porch.

Mina turns to me, her face reflecting the day's last light. "I've been tryin' to figure out a way to tell ya' how wonderful ya are. But nothin' seems enough."

"You don't need to thank me," I tell her, brushing a strand of hair from her face. "I'm the one who should be grateful."

"For what? Bringin' ya nothin' but trouble?" Her smile is small and tired.

"For showing me what it means to be human. To feel. To love." The words come easier now. "Even the heartbreak. It's a gift I never expected to receive."

I slip off my long black coat and wrap it around her shoulders. She clutches the lapels, pulling it close.

"It smells like death," she teases weakly.

"No," I reply, my voice unusually soft, "it smells like me."

"Exactly." Her eyes meet mine, filled with a love I've done nothing to deserve. "I love you. I wish we had more time."

I don't tell her that even eternities end too soon when you're with someone you love. Instead, I press my lips to her forehead, holding her close as the first stars appear in the darkening sky.

***

Mina's arm loops through mine as we walk toward the festival, her steps slow but steady. The air around her shimmers slightly, and I'm mildly concerned. This isn't typical of those about to pass, and I can't help but wonder if it's some sort of Concord magic.

Mina points at a woman in punk rock regalia, with a fractured jaw and only one arm, inspecting the candy apple station. There are so many ghosts milling about, and they notice us immediately. Or rather, they notice Mina.

"They're starin'," Mina whispers, her fingers tightening around my arm.

"They sense what's happening to you. You're becoming more like them with each passing hour."

"Great. Just what every girl wants to hear on her last night out." She attempts a laugh that doesn't quite land. "Do I at least look better than the guy with the axe in his head?"

I follow her gaze to a Revolutionary War soldier leaning

against a mailbox, the weapon that killed him still embedded in his skull. I nod. "Much better."

The festival lights grow brighter as we approach, casting the town square in a carnival glow. The band plays a slow, haunting melody from the decorated gazebo, stopping me in my tracks. A funeral march.

Mina looks at me and bursts out laughing. "They're playin' my theme song."

I want to march over and ask them to play something else, but she tugs me in the other direction.

Ghostly heads turn our way. A child skips alongside us for several steps, reaching up as if trying to hold Mina's hand. A businessman with a hole in his chest where his heart should be tips his translucent hat.

"It's like they know me," Mina murmurs.

"They recognize you as the key. You're a potential way back."

"So I'm like a ghost celebrity."

I chuckle. "Something like that."

I buy her a caramel apple and then guide her to the face-painting station, where they transform her pale features with delicate silver and gold stars across her cheeks and forehead.

My attention snags on a figure watching us from a tarot reader's booth. Dahlia stands perfectly still among the chaos, her eyes fixed on Mina. Her gaze meets mine, and for just a moment, I swear her eyes flash crimson. She's in predator mode. All of the wives agreed to help keep watch tonight, and it appears Dahlia is taking her role very seriously.

The gazebo glows from within, lanterns hanging from its ornate roof. The band plays a haunting folk melody about lovers separated by death. Fitting.

"Dance with me?" Mina tugs me toward the small clearing where other couples sway.

"I don't dance."

"Death doesn't dance? That's the saddest thing I've ever

heard." She pulls again, more insistent. "Tonight's the perfect chance for your first. Come on. Just one. For me."

I let her lead me to the dance floor. We move in small circles, bodies swaying together in time with the music. Somehow, she feels lighter in my arms than she did yesterday, as if parts of her are already leaving.

The pendant at her throat pulses once, briefly, with blue light. She doesn't notice, but I do.

"Everyone's lookin' at us," she whispers against my chest.

"Let them look." I pull her closer, breathing in the scent of her hair, her skin. Memorizing her. "We're the best-looking couple here."

She leans back and smiles, her eyes sparkle in the lantern light. For just a moment, she looks fully alive again, fully present. And then she stumbles.

"Are you okay?" I hold her tight.

She rubs her temple. "Headache just hit out of nowhere. I think maybe I should sit. Fireworks should be about to start, no?"

"You're right." Damn it. Time moves too fast. I motion to Hazel that we're going to go find a spot to sit. She nods and taps La'Tasha and Blake, who both turn to look our way.

We make our way to the center of the square. Several families have spread blankets on the grass. Mina and I find a spot beneath an ancient oak, close enough to see both the fireworks and the parade, but far enough away that we can escape easily if we need to. I raise a hand and motion to Hazel, so she knows where we are.

"Thank you," Mina says, leaning her head against my shoulder. "For lettin' me have tonight."

Before I can answer, a sharp whistle cuts through the air. The crowd hushes in anticipation. Then—BOOM! The first firework to announce the beginning of the parade explodes overhead. A burst of red and gold illuminates the entire square, and a toddler next to us screams. People cheer and point upward as more follow, painting the night in brief, brilliant colors.

Mina's face glows with reflected light. The pendant at her throat pulses again, and beneath our feet comes a tremor.

A warning.

The ghosts have all turned to face west, toward Whispering Falls, where the binding point pulses like a beacon.

I tighten my arm around Mina's shoulders and pull her closer as another firework bursts overhead.

CHAPTER TWENTY-FOUR

Mina

The fireworks fade to smoke, leavin' behind the cheers of the crowd and the faint smell of gunpowder. I push back the pain in my skull and force the world back into focus. Everythin' screams wrong. Too bright. Too loud. Festival lights spin around me, and I struggle to stay focused. This is suddenly all too much. Dex's arm tightens around my shoulders, anchorin' me, which is much needed because gravity feels optional.

"You okay?" he whispers, his breath warm against my ear.

No. Not even close to okay. I close my eyes and nod anyway.

Hazel appears next to us, her face painted with tiny gold stars that catch the streetlights. Behind her, Blake scans the crowd with the sharp focus of a predator searchin' for threats.

"There you are," Hazel says. She's tryin' to be casual but lands somewhere between worried and terrified. "How are you feeling?"

La'Tasha, Coco, and Penny appear and form a loose circle around me, chattin' away as if we've accidentally bumped into each other. Like I don't realize they're formin' a protective circle around me.

"You lot are about as subtle as a werewolf at a cat show," I mutter.

Blake's mouth twitches. "I'll have you know, that's offensive to werewolves."

"But accurate," La'Tasha adds with a wink.

Leo and Vivienne appear, and I can't help but smile. They're so different. Leo tall, thin, and casual; Vivienne sleek and chic. Somehow it works. Vivienne reaches out, grabs my hand, and offers a small smile.

Leo leans in and gives me a hug. "Hey, you tough old broad. How are you holding up?"

"Well enough to kick your arse if ya call me old again."

Everyone laughs. Warmth floods my chest and spreads to my fingertips. Despite the threat, this banter, this evening, all feels normal. And that's exactly what I needed tonight.

My vision swirls again, and my head suddenly feels heavy.

"Mina?" Dex's voice cuts through the underwater feelin'. His eyes search mine. "Should we leave?"

"No." My fingers tighten on his arm. The wool of his coat feels like sandpaper against my skin. "I want to stay. I want to see the parade, and then we can go. Okay?"

The world jolts around me like a skippin' record. A child's laugh stretches too long, then snaps back to normal speed. A vendor handin' out samples moves in jerky stop-motion. And oh my land, my vision. Why can't I focus? I feel like I'm tryin' to walk on a waterbed.

I dig my fingers deeper into Dex's arm, afraid I might fall down or float away if I let go.

"We should get something to eat," Hazel suggests. "The food truck with those potato twisters you like is here."

My stomach lurches at the thought of food. "Not hungry."

Blake and Hazel exchange the "Mina's dying, and we don't know what to do" look.

"Maybe just something to drink?" Coco tries. "Hot cider? Tea?"

I shake my head, and instantly regret the movement when

the world tilts sideways. "I'm fine."

"You're not fine," Blake says. "You look like hell warmed over."

"Blake!" La'Tasha hisses.

"What? We're pretending she doesn't?" He gestures at me with a massive hand. "She's practically see-through in this light."

He's not wrong. My skin has taken on a translucent quality, blue veins visible beneath pale skin. I'm like some sort of ink blot test. The pendant pulses against my chest for the third time in as many minutes. Accordin' to Coco it's a warnin', but it's one I'm choosin' to ignore.

"I know you're all worried, but I just want a few more minutes of normal. Okay?"

Dex pulls me closer, his lips brushin' my temple. "Then that's what you'll have."

We continue through the festival, my strange little secret service tryin' their best to act natural. The pendant pulses more frequently now, glowin' just bright enough to be visible through my sweater. Each pulse sends a shock of cold through my chest.

"I think I see Calvin," Hazel says suddenly. She points toward the row of food booths ahead. "At the caramel apple stand."

My vision tunnels strangely so that Calvin seems both very far away and right in front of me at the same time. He waves enthusiastically, a broad smile splittin' his face.

Next to him stands Everett. The pendant flares hot against my skin. A warnin'. Memories of my vision from last night flash through my mind. Everett in a hooded cloak. Everett. Part of the Concord.

Dex's arm tightens around my waist as they approach.

"Hey, guys!" Calvin waves. His cheeks are flushed, eyes bright. "I want you all to meet someone."

Everett stands tall in a 1950s leather jacket, hair slicked back in a perfect ducktail. Unlike the other spirits that float through the festival, he doesn't flicker or fade at the edges. He looks very much human, which makes my stomach burn.

"This is Everett," Calvin says. His eyes sparkle, and his voice lilts when he says Everett's name. He's so far gone that it almost hurts. Someone has to tell him the truth. And since I'm the only one who knows . . .

Everett smiles, but it doesn't look right on his face. He looks worried. "Calvin's told me so much about all of you."

I swear there's an echo to his voice.

Calvin beams, oblivious that he's enamored with a ghost who has ties to the Concord. He stands close enough to Everett that their shoulders touch. "He's visiting for the festival, but I'm hoping I might be able to convince him to stick around."

The naked hope in Calvin's voice drives a spike through my ribs. So much hope. I hate to be the one to kill it.

I open my mouth to tell Calvin about Everett, but the words come out slurred and strange. Time hiccups, and suddenly I'm a few feet to the left of where I started. Dex takes me by the arm and pulls me close.

Why can't I speak?

Penny stands off to the side, her body unnaturally still. Her posture has changed. The usual nervous hunch of her shoulders has been replaced by a rigid confidence. Her eyes dart between Calvin's hopeful face and Everett's crooked smile, her fingers pullin' at the edge of her jacket sleeve.

"What brought you to Moonridge, Everett?" La'Tasha asks.

Can she not tell what he is?

"The festival," Everett answers smoothly. "I always loved it when I was a kid. Decided to visit again this year. Then I met this guy . . ."

Calvin ducks his head, pleasure and embarrassment plastered to his cheeks. "I thought I had imagined him at first, when we collided during the race," he admits. "But then he started showing up every day during my morning runs."

"He can't stay." Penny's voice cuts through the conversation. She steps forward, her usual timidity replaced with focused confidence. Her small fingers form into fists at her sides. "He's one of them. He's dead. And he's a Concord."

Calvin's smile falters. "What are you talking about?"

"The Crucible Core. In the library," Penny continues, her voice trembles, but she's determined. "When I touched it, I saw every soul involved in the Concord's ritual." She takes another step forward and pushes her glasses up on her nose. "Including him. He's not just one of the ghosts fueling the ritual, though. He's a member. He's tied to the Skipper Lake binding point."

Everett takes a step back. He reaches for Calvin's arm, but his hand passes through it. For the first time since he appeared at the race, his perfect solidity wavers, edges blurred. "I don't know what she's talking about." His eyes dart across all our faces.

Before anyone can react, Penny lunges forward and grabs Everett's wrist. Her hand doesn't pass through him like it should with a ghost. Instead, she connects, her fingers closing around translucent skin.

"Penny!" Calvin starts forward, but Blake holds him back with one strong arm.

"Look," Penny commands. She turns Everett's wrist upward. Beneath the cuff of his leather jacket, a mark pulses with sickly green light. A spiral with thirteen points.

Everett yanks his arm back. Panic flashes across his face. His smile grows tight and then falls, eyes wide. "I'm not . . . I didn't . . ."

He turns to face Calvin, hands raised, palms out. "I swear, it's not by choice. I'm bound to them. Please. I need help . . ."

Calvin looks between Everett and Penny, eyebrows pinched. "I don't understand," he says. "What do you mean he's part of the Concord? How?"

Blake steps protectively in front of his brother. "He's been using you to get closer to Mina."

"No!" Everett's form flickers once. "It's not like that. I promise. I never wanted this. I was trapped—am trapped. I'm not willingly one of them." His eyes plead with Calvin. "You have to believe me."

The pendant flares hot against my skin, its blue pulse knockin' against my sternum in a frantic rhythm. A burnin' pain drives through my right eye, straight to the back of my head, and the world tilts sideways.

"Calvin," I begin, but the word comes out stretched and distorted.

The ground beneath us trembles again. People look around, surprised.

"Was that an earthquake? Did you feel that?" I hear someone behind me ask.

And just like that, Everett has disappeared.

Calvin takes a step back, mouth open, expression blank. "Someone needs to explain what just happened," he demands.

Before anyone can answer, the pendant's light explodes outward, and my chest lights up like I'm a TV without a signal. Through the haze and lights, I catch glimpses of my friends' worried, but distorted faces. Their mouths seem to move in slow motion. Beyond them, the first parade float arrives, a massive stag towerin' at its center. Lanterns glow in its wooden chest, pulsin' with the same sickly green light as Everett's mark.

An elongated shadow takes form, weavin' between the stag's antlers. It reaches for me just as my body decides it's had enough. Every muscle locks at once, turnin' me to stone from the inside out. Eyes roll upward. Consciousness separates from my limbs.

Someone's arms wrap around me and gently place me on the ground.

Dex?

"Mina!" His voice reaches me from miles away, though his face hovers inches from mine. "Stay with me!"

The pendant burns against my chest, its blue light so intense it shines through my skin, illuminatin' my veins from the inside. I try to speak, but my jaw is locked tight, teeth grindin' against each other.

Dex shields me from curious onlookers. Hazel's hands move in frantic patterns above my face, her lips formin' words I can't hear over the roarin' in my ears. Penny stands frozen. Blake and Calvin throw worried glances my way while keepin' festival-go-ers at a distance.

"It's just too much stimulation," La'Tasha says to a concerned bystander. "She'll be fine."

I won't be fine. Bony fingers slide into view, and my mind starts to short-circuit. I fight back against whatever claws at the edges of my consciousness. I will not let go of who I am. I'm dyin'. But Dex will take me home, and my friends will protect me.

Your friends are going to die.

The words invade my mind and with them comes an ancient, patient presence, settlin' inside me, drainin' every bit of free will from my limbs.

"The pendant's not working," Coco cries. "It should be stabilizing her, not—"

Yes. Listen to Coco.

"Don't touch it," Dex warns. "It's reacting to whatever's happening inside her."

Inside me. Yes. That's where I am now. Inside. But my mouth no longer obeys my commands. I'm a passenger in my own body, but unable to steer.

The parade drums beat louder, their rhythm matchin' the pulse of the pendant at my sternum. The crowd cheers as the stag float passes, followed by a procession of children with lanterns shaped like spirits. No one notices that my convulsions have stopped. No one sees that my eyes, when they open, are no longer my own.

Another consciousness looks out through them now. I feel its cold curiosity as it uses my vision, scannin' the faces around me. It recognizes Dex immediately. A flutter of ancient fear ripples through it before it returns to calculated patience. *Death can be avoided*, it thinks. *Death can be cheated.* I feel its dismissal of Hazel and the others. *Mere witches, obstacles easily removed.*

"We need to get her out of here," Hazel says, her hand cool against my forehead. "The convergence is too strong."

"The apothecary?" Blake suggests.

"No." Dex's voice is firm. "The B&B. Like we planned. It's time." The last word breaks with emotion.

"Already?" Hazel asks.

"We have to keep her safe and comfortable. We agreed—"

They argue above me. The entity inside me listens. Waitin' for the right moment. I try to move. I will myself to reach for Dex, but the thing inside of me keeps my body still, playin' possum while they debate. The parade continues to move past us. Drums and shouts and the creakin' of floats create a wall of sound that makes communication difficult.

"Fine," Hazel agrees finally. "But we need to move now. Blake, can you—"

The entity seizes its chance. When no one is lookin', my body stands and slips between two vendor booths. Inside my head, I scream. I fight for control of even a finger, anythin'. But I'm locked away, watchin' through my own eyes as my body navigates the crowd like some kind of ninja.

The entity is extremely elegant. My usual clumsy charm has been replaced by somethin' efficient and predatory. It uses gaps in the crowd that I wouldn't have seen, and times its movements to coincide with distractions.

Dex calls my name. The entity forces my head not to turn, my feet to move forward. I reach the edge of the festival grounds in what feels like seconds, the noise and the bright festival lights far behind me. My body turns west, toward the forest that borders town.

Toward Whispering Falls.

In a few short strides, I'm already there. I know this path. I've hiked it dozens of times, but never with this much determination or this much speed.

The entity controls every step, every movement, but still allows me to understand, with growin' horror, exactly what's happenin'. I'm the key. The final piece needed to tear open the veil between worlds.

And I'm bein' delivered right on schedule.

My body glides through the darkened woods. Branches part before me like they're afraid to touch my skin. The forest grows denser as we move away from town. Moonlight filters through the trees in broken patches and illuminates the path I've walked countless times. But tonight, my feet don't follow the well-worn public trail. Instead, they veer off into untouched underbrush, up the mountain toward the sound of fallin' water.

Turn around! I scream inside my head. *Fight!*

The entity responds with amusement. It allows me to twitch my pinky finger, a concession that only highlights how completely it controls every part of me.

Through the trees ahead, blue-white light glimmers off the reflection of Whispering Falls. The tallest waterfall in the county. A 427-foot cascade that tumbles down moss-covered rocks into a pool so clear you can see straight to the bottom. Tourists take selfies here in summer. Teenagers come to skinny dip on hot nights, a respite for those of us who need to get away for a while.

But tonight, the water glows with an unnatural light, each droplet pausin' for a second or two in midair before it crashes down. The mist from the pool doesn't dissipate but hangs, formin' shapes that almost look like faces before dissolvin' into nothin' again.

The entity moves my body up the switchback trails and behind the roarin' veil of the falls. Mist clings to my skin as we break through the last curtain of stone and water, and I find myself at the summit.

A wide clearing opens beside the river that feeds the falls. The water rushes past, silver and fast, before it vanishes over the cliff's edge into the pool far below.

Thirteen hooded figures stand in the grass near the riverbank. Twelve form a perfect circle, and at the center, seated and still, is a figure in red.

My body stops at the edge of the clearing, head tilted. The cloaked figures remain motionless, their faces hidden in shadow beneath heavy hoods. They wear robes of different earthy colors, each one adorned with a different symbol.

A thin keening sound rises from the river that feeds the falls. It sounds almost like a chorus. The mist thickens, swirlin' between the hooded figures. My pendant pulses in response, its rhythm matchin' the horrendous sound that rises from the ground.

"The key arrives," says one of the figures, voice powerful and urgent. "Right on time."

Another figure steps forward, and their hood shifts slightly to reveal their profile.

Everett.

His ghostly face flickers between solid and transparent, and the Concord mark on his wrist pulses bright. But when his eyes meet mine, I sense the same trapped desperation I feel. Control without consent.

The other figures part to create a path to the center of their circle. The ground trembles again, and in the center of the circle, an ancient stone altar erupts from the ground. Carved into its surface is a spiral pattern, each groove stained dark with what can only be blood.

My body is forced forward by whatever, or whomever, controls me. The entity savors this moment, enjoyin' the tension. The anticipation.

It has begun.

The hooded figures begin to chant, closin' in behind me as I'm forced to move toward the altar. Their voices start low, almost subsonic. They vibrate through the ground and up through my bones. The words aren't in any language I recognize, yet somehow, I am able to sense the evil as they call upon whatever it is they intend to pull from the other side.

With each syllable, the pendant pulses harder, its protective blue light now corrupted with threads of sickly green. Coco's magic, meant to bind me to my friends, has been twisted and now anchors somethin' else entirely.

I fight against the thing that controls me, throwin' everythin' I have at it. I manage to raise my left arm. Yes! But then my arm snaps back to my side. This fucker is toyin' with me. It squeezes my consciousness, doin' its best to remove everythin' that makes me who I am. I won't let it.

Stop fighting. Its rocky voice grinds inside my skull. *You were made for this.*

"No," I gasp, and realize with shock that I've managed to speak aloud.

The entity crushes down harder, forcin' me back into silence. We reach the altar, and my body stops before it. The spiral pattern seems to move, the grooves shiftin' slightly when I blink. The blood within flows in a slow, deliberate current.

The chants of the hooded figures grow louder, more urgent. The waterfall's unnatural song rises to match it until the two sounds seem to compete. Above us, clouds scud across the moon's face, momentarily plungin' the ritual space into shadow-thick gloom before silver light breaks through again.

From the far side of the altar, a tall hooded figure steps forward, robes black as wet stone. Pale hands slip from voluminous sleeves, and I can't take my eyes off the long, elegant fingers. They draw a silver blade from the folds of their robe. The blade catches moonlight, reflectin' it in sharp, painful flashes.

"With blood it began," the figure intones, voice deep and resonant. "With blood it shall be completed."

My right hand rises of its own accord, palm up. I fight to lower my arm, but whatever has hold of me is much stronger. The knife hovers above my skin, the tip so sharp it draws a bead of blood the moment it touches me.

"Please," I beg the entity. "Don't do this. Whatever ya are, whatever ya want with me. This can't be what my end is. I'm not the one."

The knife pauses above my palm.

"But you are," the figure before me says. "And there is no other way. You belong to us. And you can either accept that or be bound in resistance. Willing participation will result in a much more pleasant ending."

"I will never become one of you."

The knife descends, slicin' a clean line across my hand. Blood wells immediately, bright red against my pale skin. The entity turns my hand over, coaxin' drops to fall onto the spiral pattern carved into the altar.

Where my blood touches the stone, a blindin' white light begins to roll outward in waves. The spiral begins to turn, slowly at first, then faster. The blood within its grooves flows faster, movin' around the spiral until it spins so fast I can no longer make out the shape.

The thirteen figures sway in perfect unison, their chants reachin' a crescendo as the waterfall's song becomes a scream. The veil rips open like tissue paper.

The Hollowing has begun.

CHAPTER TWENTY-FIVE

Dex

One moment she's beside me, and the next she's gone, dissolved into the churning mass of festival-goers like she was never there at all. My heart pounds as I spin in a useless circle. I scan costumed faces for a flash of red hair. Nothing. The pendant was supposed to keep her tethered, visible. I should be able to track her.

"Mina!" I shout her name, but it's swallowed by the festival noise. Nobody notices the man in black shoving through the crowd. Nobody cares that the world might be ending.

Hazel appears at my side, her face pale. "I can't feel her," she says, voice trembling. "Her energy. It's just gone."

"Not gone." I grip my cane harder, knuckles white. "Taken. The Concord has her. They masked her somehow."

Those bastards have been ten steps ahead of us this entire time.

Blake bulldozes his way toward us, Calvin and Leo on his heels, amber eyes reflecting the festival lights.

Leo sniffs the air and points toward the road leading away from the town center. "We can track her."

Blake heads toward the fountain, and we follow, forcing our

way through the masses toward the edge of the festival grounds. Above us, the stars wink out one by one, clouds gathering out of nowhere to blot out the night sky.

We reach the edge of town, and Blake doesn't waste time removing his clothing. His body twists, bones cracking as they reshape themselves. Fur sprouts along his arms, his face elongating into a muzzle. Calvin and Leo follow suit, their transformations smoother but no less dramatic. Three massive wolves crouch where the men had been.

Blake's wolf form drops his nose to the ground, sniffing intensely before lifting his head and letting out a soft whine. Calvin's darker form nudges his brother. They both turn toward the path that leads to Whispering Falls.

La'Tasha gathers the wolves' clothing and stuffs it in her bag. "Y'all are gonna need this later."

"Who's driving?" Hazel asks. "I don't think we'll all fit in my Jeep."

"We can try squeezing into mine. I'm just over there." La'Tasha presses a button on her key fob, and the headlights of her SUV flash in the dark.

We all move in that direction, but Penny lags behind. "I need to get to the library."

"The library? Now?" Hazel stares at her in disbelief. "Mina is—"

"You don't need me to find her," Penny interrupts. "I just— I have to go."

Before anyone can stop her, she's gone, swallowed by the festival crowd.

Hazel stares in disbelief. "We need her power."

"We'll be fine. We've fought without her before," La'Tasha says. "We need to focus on Mina."

Vivienne arrives, tossing a ring of keys into the air and catching it with a smirk. "I stole these from one of our producers. We can take one of the SUVs we've been traveling in. Lots more room."

Vivienne, the witches, and I pile into the large, black vehicle and follow the wolves' trail. The edge of town rushes by, festival lights fading behind us, swallowed by the dark as we turn onto the winding road that leads toward the falls.

Above, stars flicker like faulty Christmas lights, their rhythm offbeat and uneasy. Clouds slide across the sky, moving against the wind.

Coco clamps her hands over her ears. "Dios mio, I can hear them," she whispers, face pale. "The souls in the binding stones. They're screaming."

I hear them too. A chorus of trapped voices rises like steam from the earth. These are souls that should have crossed long ago. Their pain hums through the air, vibrating straight into my bones.

Vivienne pulls into the campground near the falls, and before the engine cuts off, I'm out of the SUV and moving toward the trailhead, my cane striking the ground with urgency.

The wolves surge ahead, three streaks of fur weaving between trees. The rest of us trail behind them wordlessly, the ascent up the hill more challenging to me than it should be.

"Look at the trees," Coco gasps, pointing.

The forest around us bends, every trunk leaning toward our destination like they're being pushed over by invisible hands.

"The ritual has started. It's reshaping the physical world." My voice is raspy with dread.

Vivienne zips past me and steps out of the shadows ahead. Using her vampire speed. Her perfect makeup is slightly smudged, designer clothes torn from racing through the forest.

The air grows thick as we climb, and the roaring of the falls intensifies, but there's something rolling beneath it. Like chanting.

"Look." La'Tasha points upward, where the clouds have parted momentarily.

The moon hangs wrong in the sky, its usual silver light now

tinged with a yellowish-green haze. Its surface seems to ripple, like something moves beneath it.

"Keep going," I rasp. "We're close."

The trees thin, and the wolves slow and drop into hunting crouches. We follow their lead, keeping just behind the tree line near the clearing at the top of the falls, peering through the last screen of twisted branches. The clearing beyond has transformed into a full-blown Concord ritual site. Thirteen hooded figures stand in formation around a stone altar that wasn't here when I inspected this area a few days ago. And at its center, her red hair shining like a beacon in the unnatural light, is Mina.

Her hand bleeds onto the stone, the spiral pattern beneath it turning counterclockwise. A cone of light shoots upward and disappears into the visibly torn veil between worlds. And through the gap, something moves. Many somethings.

Blake growls, muscles bunching as he prepares to charge. I grab his ruff, holding him back.

"Wait." I hold up a hand, though every part of me wants to rush in and save her. "We need a plan. We can't just charge in," I warn them. "Look."

Ghosts flicker around us. A young man with half his face missing stumbles past, mouth opening soundlessly. A woman in hippie clothing dances alone, limbs jerking unnaturally.

La'Tasha stares in wonder at the translucent forms that fill the forest around us. "The ritual must be pulling them from all over Moonridge."

More disturbing than the ghosts is how time itself seems to warp around us. Patches of daylight shimmer in the darkness as if parts of tomorrow are bleeding into tonight. In one spot, snow falls from nowhere, melting as soon as it touches the ground.

"We don't have the numbers for a frontal assault," Hazel says, already shrugging off her jacket. She kneels on the mossy ground and frantically begins to clear a space. "La'Tasha. Coco. Help me out."

La'Tasha kneels across from her, mirroring the movement. Their hands meet briefly in the center, a spark of energy crackling between them. Then they begin drawing symbols in the dirt. One starts a pattern, the other completes it. Their movements are seamless.

"What are they doing?" I ask.

"Counter-ritual," Coco explains. She pulls crystals from her bag and arranges them in a circle around the other witches. "If we can't reach the center physically, we can try to attack the magic itself to see if we can stop it."

She uncaps a small bottle of water and begins drawing protection symbols that glow faintly as she completes each one.

"Hopefully, these will shield us from being seen," she explains, her voice barely audible over the chanting from the Concord. "But they won't last long."

The werewolves circle our position, creating a perimeter. Blake's massive form leads, his teeth bared as he guards against any threats that might approach.

The symbols spark and then immediately begin to fade.

"Their power is too strong," Hazel whispers. "Try again."

Vivienne stands apart from us, fingers twisting her designer rings. What has her so nervous?

"I want to help, but I don't know what to do," she says when she catches me watching her. "I'm out of practice, and I've not done anything like this before."

I move closer to her, keeping my voice low. "Were you not a witch before you were turned? And your kind has been hunted by the Concord for centuries. Surely you know something about this."

She flinches slightly. "I know, but . . . I've not practiced witchcraft in over a century. I don't know these spells."

Below us, the ritual intensifies. The spiral on the altar spins faster. Mina's head tilts back, mouth open in what might be a scream, though we can't hear it over the ominous chanting and the unnatural roar of the falls.

"They need you. Lend them your power. Just try. For Mina. Please?"

She studies me for a long moment, then kneels beside Hazel and La'Tasha.

"I have an idea." She holds her arm over the sigils that Hazel and La'Tasha have drawn and slices it open with a sharpened nail. Her blood wells up, glowing faintly with its own inner power.

Hazel nods, encouraging her. "Seven drops only," she instructs. "Any more would overwhelm the balance."

Vivienne holds her wrist over the soil, allowing exactly seven drops to fall. Each one hits with a soft hiss. The entire circle pulses once, brightening noticeably.

"It's holding," La'Tasha whispers. She reaches for her bag. "I want to try—"

Hazel stops her. "No. Focus on stabilizing the ground beneath the energy. If we can anchor reality here, maybe the tear won't be able to widen."

La'Tasha hesitates. "I really think—"

"Tash, we don't have time to try new things. Please just do as I say," Hazel hisses.

A shadow passes over La'Tasha's face before she goes to the edge of the circle and places a hand on the ground.

Vivienne and I step back and let them work. The air around our circle shimmers with effort, pushing back against the deep, dark wrongness that emanates from the Concord's ritual space. For a moment, the patches of warped time begin to shrink, and I think their spell might be enough. But then the ritual at the altar shifts. The red-robed figure behind Mina raises both arms, and the chanting shifts to a higher, more urgent pitch. The tear in the veil rips open like a wound under pressure. Wind howls. Mina's body jerks violently. Her back arches. Face contorted in pain.

"It's not enough!" I rise to my feet. "We're out of time. Hold them off. I need to get to her."

Blake and the other wolves stand, ready to charge.

"No. The circle isn't strong enough yet," Hazel wipes a bead of sweat from her forehead.

"Do you need more blood?" Vivienne asks, her fingernail ready to strike.

Hazel holds out a hand, stopping her. "No. We have to give it time to manifest. Spells like this aren't instant. The power has to charge."

La'Tasha watches from the side, arms crossed.

Vivienne steps around Hazel, eyeing the circle. "But look here. What if we—"

"No," Hazel cuts her off. "Just give it time. I know what I'm doing."

"We can't wait any longer." I grip my cane and slam it to the ground. "I'm going in. I have to see if I can save her soul."

"You can't just rush in," Vivienne warns, her eyes fixed on the scene below. "Not in your current state."

"I don't plan to." My cane stretches and darkens as the curved blade of my scythe materializes. "I'm going to meet her somewhere else."

Without waiting for their response, I close my eyes and drop into the space between worlds. Where I might still reach Mina before it's too late.

My consciousness drifts from my body, tethered only by the scythe planted in the earth. The sounds of the falls fade. The Concord's chanting dims. I search for the invisible thread that connects me to Mina's soul, and the space unfolds around me. Memories float past in this in-between space, fragments of memories from those I've guided over centuries.

I focus on finding Mina, pushing aside the distractions. Our connection is weak at first, but the more I search, the stronger it gets.

And then I see her.

She stands ankle-deep in a shimmering, silvery, reflective

substance. Her red hair hangs loose around her shoulders. Her eyes meet mine across the distance, and the worry that sat there earlier evaporates.

"Dex." Her voice echoes toward me. "I thought I'd lost ya."

I cross to her in seconds. "Are you hurt?"

She smiles, but it's tinged with sadness. "No. But I'm afraid. It's gettin' harder to hold on."

Up close, I can see the effort it takes to maintain her sense of self while another presence claws for control of her body. Her form flickers occasionally, edges blurring before solidifying again.

"We're trying to stop the ritual." I reach for her, but for some reason, our hands remain just out of reach, no matter how hard I try. "The witches are working a counter-spell. I'm going to help you—"

"They have me tethered to them, Dex." She looks down at the silver water swirling around her ankles. "I can't get free."

I reach for her again, and an invisible force pushes me back. It's strong. A barrier I somehow can't cross.

"Focus on me. Okay? I won't let them take you. We'll fight."

She shakes her head, her expression calm. Resigned. It terrifies me. "Ya won't be able to help me from here. I need ya to go back and help the others. Weaken the Concord. Break the tether. I have a plan, but ya have to trust me. And ya have to let me go. Promise me."

My chest constricts. "Mina—"

"I won't let them use me to do this." Her voice is strong despite the fear behind her eyes. "It's the only way to break the ritual before it completes."

I nod. She's right. And I hate it.

"I know this isn't the goodbye we had planned, but it's the only way." Her form flickers again. "Tell them to focus on the woman in red. She holds the power. If ya break the tether, it will weaken them. I only need a minute. And when I go, promise you'll be there to catch my soul and take me where I need to go so they can't use me."

"I promise." My voice cracks. "I will."

The water around her ankles rises slightly, now lapping at her calves. The whispers grow louder, more insistent. They don't sound like individual voices anymore but a single hungry chorus.

"I love you, Dex," Mina says, her gaze direct and unwavering. "You'll never know how much."

Pressure builds behind my ribs, and my eyes grow wet. In all my existence, I've never allowed myself to feel enough to warrant tears. But now . . .

The water rises higher, reaching her knees. The hungry whispers grow louder, more insistent. Her form flickers yet again.

I close my eyes, drawing on the last bit of strength I have. "I'll find you. I promise."

Her smile outshines the fear in her expression. "I know ya will."

I reach for her, and this time our hands connect. I pour energy into our connection. It strengthens like a rope pulled taut. Power flows from me to her. Connecting. The water around her legs recedes slightly, and her form solidifies.

"Ya need to go," she whispers, her voice stronger now.

Before I can respond, the space around us shudders violently. Mina's image wavers, then stabilizes one last time.

"It's time," she says.

The space collapses around me, and I'm slammed back into my body with enough force to make my teeth rattle. The hillside around us is filled with flashes of light and screams. Below in the clearing, twelve of the Concord members have collapsed to their knees, clutching their heads in apparent agony. Only the red-robed figure at the center remains standing, their scream of rage cutting through the unnatural howl of the wind.

"What's happening?" I gasp, fingers digging into the earth as I steady myself.

"I don't know," Hazel explains, her hands still weaving

patterns in the air to maintain the circle. "I think we weakened them. They just dropped, like they ran out of power."

The red-robed figure whirls, scanning the hills until their gaze locks onto us. Even at this distance, the heat of that glare is enough to melt a glacier. The familiar magic I sensed rolling off of Hazel when I first arrived is unmistakable now. And stronger.

The anchor is Fiona Thornton.

"They see us," La'Tasha says, her voice clipped with tension.

Fiona lifts both arms. Sleeves fall back, revealing skin etched in glowing sigils. Power churns around her hands, forming undulating cones of blood red light tinged with a slick, oily sheen.

"Brace yourselves!" Vivienne shouts.

The magic hurtles toward us, a dozen small strikes aimed to scatter our group. Hazel and La'Tasha raise a shield in unison. Their power forms an immediate blue wall that absorbs most of the assault. But not all. A bolt slams into the ground near Blake. He's airborne. He hits the ground with a yelp and then rolls down the slope. Another bolt clips Calvin, carving a smoking gouge through his left flank.

But as Fiona turns her attention toward us, the light pouring from the altar dims, and the wild keening goes quiet. Mina jerks. Her head snaps up. She's no longer under their control. She's fighting back. The strength I gave her is working.

She stands and begins to move. She stumbles twice, crawls for a few feet, and then is back on her feet, weaving like someone who's had one too many drinks. She finds her footing and stumbles away from the altar.

Directly toward the cliff's edge overlooking the falls.

"She's moving!" Coco points. Her hand trails blue sparks.

The fallen Concord members stir, some already pushing themselves to their knees. They won't stay down for long. Whatever happened seems to have only temporarily weakened them.

"We need to protect her." My scythe swings in a wide arc, cutting through another magical attack aimed at our position.

Blake shakes himself and charges across the clearing, followed closely by Leo and Calvin, wolf forms blurred as they race toward the Concord members. But Fiona sees them coming. With a vicious gesture, she sends a wave of dark, red energy that catches the wolves mid-leap, throwing them backward like toys.

Hazel's eyes narrow in concentration. "Cover me while I help Mina. She's disoriented. She's going the wrong way."

Except she's not. This was her plan.

Hazel's hands begin a complex series of movements. Sigils burn briefly in the air before shooting toward Mina like golden arrows. The magic wraps around Mina's limbs, threads of light trying to slow her progress toward the cliff. For a moment, it seems to work. She stumbles. Her steps become more labored.

Then she looks up at us and shakes her head. "Stop," she mouths. "Let me go."

I flick my scythe and it severs the golden thread.

"Dex! What are you doing?" Hazel shouts. She sends another bolt of gold energy toward Mina.

It catches her shoulder, but Mina pushes on, the golden threads stretching, then snapping as she forces her way forward.

"It's the only way." My voice is low. "We have to let her go."

She raises one hand toward us in a clear gesture to stop. To stay back.

"No," Hazel whispers as she understands what Mina plans to do. "Mina, don't."

But she's already turning back toward the cliff edge, her movements fluid as she reclaims full control of her body.

"What is she doing?" Coco grabs my arm.

"Ending it," I tell her. "The only way she knows how."

Fiona seems to realize Mina's intent. She abandons her attack on us, turning instead to recapture the escaping key. Magic rockets toward Mina.

Hazel, La'Tasha, and Coco respond immediately, their combined power forming a shield around her that deflects the worst of the attack. Fiona's magic hits the shield and immediately weakens the witches. Coco and Hazel are thrown backward. La'Tasha's the only one left standing, still holding the barrier in place, hands shaking with strain. A trickle of blood trails from her nose.

"We can't hold this long," she grits out, sweat pouring down her face.

Hazel and Coco are immediately on their feet, rejoining their magic.

Below us, the Concord members who had fallen are now mostly upright. They turn their attention to us, adding their power to their leader's. Magic crackles through the air.

Blake, recovered from being thrown, makes another attempt to reach Mina. He's more cautious this time, using the trees for cover as he circles around. Calvin and Leo split off in different directions, creating multiple distractions.

But Mina moves faster now. She breaks into a stumbling run, heading straight for the cliff's edge.

"Mina!" I call her name, the word catching in my throat.

She pauses at the very edge, turning slightly to look back at us. For just a moment, our eyes meet across the distance. She offers a small, sad curve of lips.

Behind her, the red-robed figure howls. They fling one final burst of magic her way, but it's too late.

Mina leaps.

Time fractures.

I want ya to know how much ya mean to me. Ya gave me life right to the end.

Then she's gone. Swallowed by spray and shadow, lost to the roar of water crashing hundreds of feet down.

"No!" The scream tears from Hazel's throat, echoing across the raging river. My knees buckle as something inside me shatters into so many pieces it will be impossible to repair.

The witches' protective circle pulses violently, unable to

contain the surge of energy released by Mina's fall. The sigils carved into the cliffs by the Concord glow blood-red, pulsing like exposed hearts, pulling even more energy.

Are we too late?

Then a change ripples through the air. The tear in the veil above the altar shudders. Edges pull inward. The red-robed figure reaches toward it desperately, trying to hold it open, but whatever connection they had established before has been broken. The key is gone.

I stare at the spot where Mina vanished, body numb and unmoving.

Hazel grabs my arm, her fingers digging in hard enough to bruise. "Dex! The Concord. They're trying to escape! Don't let them get to her."

The hooded figures break apart, fleeing as the ritual unravels. Magic collapses around them. Only Fiona remains, arm outstretched toward the closing tear in the veil, her crimson robe a blood stain on a failed ritual site.

I should go down there. Rip her apart for everything she and the Concord took from me, from us. But I can't move. Can barely breathe.

Mina's gone.

"Dex!" Hazel grabs my shoulders, shaking me hard. "You have to guide her!"

I stab my scythe into the ground and slip into the liminal space, expecting to find the signature of her soul waiting for me.

But the space is empty. She's not there. Nor is there any sign that she's anywhere near. I sit between realms, part of me searching for her soul, the other watching the chaos around me. Are we too late?

"I can't find her. Keep pushing them back." Desperation drowns my words.

Where is she?

The Concord's sigils have begun to flicker. One by one, they glow bright and then sputter, the blood-red glow dissolving into nothing. The tear in the veil shudders violently, edges pulling together like a zipper across the sky. Ghosts that had been drawn to the ritual site freeze mid-movement, then vanish.

The energy surrounding the cliff face doesn't explode outward as I expected. Instead, it collapses inward, imploding with a silent force that makes the air ripple around us. The stone altar begins to crack, hairline fractures spreading across its surface. It begins to crumble, large chunks dropping and hitting the ground with tiny thuds until all that's left is a pile of pulverized stone.

The witches' magic suddenly takes hold, strengthening as the Concord's power fades. The protective circle around us brightens, pushing outward to encompass more ground. La'Tasha and Coco join hands. Their combined power adds to Hazel's, creating a dome of light that shields us from any lingering corruption.

"It's working." La'Tasha's voice comes out hoarse. "The binding points are destabilizing."

Several hooded figures vanish into vapor. Others flee into the forest, swallowed whole by darkness.

Only Fiona remains, still reaching for the sealed tear, as if sheer fury could force it open again.

Then she screams, a sound so raw it makes the trees recoil. Her form twists, collapses inward, and vanishes, leaving behind nothing but charred grass and broken stone.

It's over. The ritual broken.

But where is Mina?

Everyone falls still, the sudden silence deafening after the magical chaos. Bones crack as Blake and the other wolves shift back to human shape. All three of them stand naked and shivering in the sudden cold. La'Tasha reaches into her bag and removes their clothing.

"She did it." Coco's voice comes out small and disbelieving. "She actually did it."

Hazel nods, tears streaming unchecked down her face. The

gold star decorations on her cheeks have smudged, leaving trails like copper across her skin. "She saved us all."

"Did you help her cross, Dex?" La'Tasha asks.

Shame burns through me. "I can't find her."

I should be able to sense her soul. That's my purpose. My power. But there's just emptiness where our connection should be.

"Keep trying," Hazel says, desperation set deep in her voice. "You said you would save her."

"Something's wrong," I say. "The space is empty. She's not there."

"What do we do?" Coco asks.

And to that I have no answer. I collapse to the ground, defeated. I have witnessed every variation of human loss, but I never imagined that it would hurt like this.

She's gone. I failed. The Concord got to her before I could.

"Where's Vivienne?" Leo asks, breaking the silence.

I look around, suddenly alert. He's right. The vampire is nowhere to be seen. She was with us during the battle, but then . . .

Leo walks the perimeter, calling her name.

"Is she injured?" Hazel asks, scanning the forest around us. "Did the Concord hurt her?"

Blake's expression darkens. "Or was she one of them?"

Realization dawns on Hazel's face. "Oh, my God." She sinks to the ground. "That's why they came to town. It wasn't for a simple cast trip. They came here to be a part of the ritual. Vivienne was a member of the Concord."

"No." Leo shakes his head. "There's no way. She adored Mina."

"Or she did a damn good job pretending she did," La'Tasha chimes in.

All those times I trusted Vivienne to be alone with Mina hit me in the face like shrapnel. How had I not sensed it? Of course, it was her. How else would the binding stone have been activated at the B&B right under our noses? She killed us with her kindness. She took advantage of us.

I delivered Mina right to them.

Behind me, I'm distantly aware of Hazel's quiet sobs. For a moment, no one speaks. The silence settles around us, heavy and final.

Then La'Tasha lifts her chin. She wipes her hand across her cheek.

"The ritual's broken," she says softly. "Whatever was coming through . . . isn't anymore. We stopped it."

But we lost Mina.

CHAPTER TWENTY-SIX

Mina

I float in viscous darkness. I can't feel my fingers or toes or the places where my bones should have shattered when I hit the water.

Am I dead then?

Water. I remember water rushing up to meet me, the wind whistlin' past my ears as I fell from the cliff. The memory feels distant, like a scene I watched happen to another person. Did I really jump? Did I choose that action again?

Faces flash behind my eyelids. Dex, his ancient eyes watchin' me. Hazel, her hands weavin' protective magic that couldn't save me from myself. Calvin, Blake, Leo, La'Tasha, and Coco. All of them at the cliff's edge as I ran past.

My name drifts by like a piece of wreckage. I try to grab it, to hold onto that one certain thing, but my hands don't respond.

Do I even have hands anymore?

Did I save Moonridge then?

Light pulses somewhere. Above me? Below?

I try to reach for it, but there's nothin' to move. My body seems to no longer exist. Just a memory. Somethin' I no longer have.

Somethin' tugs at me. Whispers curl around me, words that make no sense yet feel deeply familiar.

"Mina?"

Dex! I have to get to Dex.

Over here. I'm ready. Did I say that out loud?

"Follow the sound of my voice."

No. That's not Dex. It sounds like him, but there's a more ominous echo beneath the voice. Like when I was possessed.

"Move toward me, my darling. I'll save you."

That is definitely not Dex.

But I can't move. I can't see.

Where am I?

Suddenly, I'm surrounded by warmth. Pressure builds around me, and I feel myself bein' tugged toward a bright light.

"Stay with me, Mina. Just a little longer."

Vivienne? How is she here? Her voice sounds different. More frantic. Stripped of its usual polish.

I try to respond, to tell her I need her help findin' Dex.

Vivienne's voice continues, closer now. "I won't let you go. Hold on, hon."

Hands lift me. I know it should hurt. I fell from a cliff. My bones should be broken, my organs ruptured. But I feel nothin'.

"I'm sorry," Vivienne whispers, her voice right against my ear now. "But they don't get to win. And you don't get to leave. Not yet."

Before I can make sense of her words, somethin' sharp pierces my neck. Fire explodes through me and races down my spine. A lightnin' strike that illuminates every nerve endin' I'd forgotten I had. Heat races from the wound and spreads through my chest, my limbs, my head. The comfortable numbness burns away, replaced by agony with texture and sound and color.

My lungs seize. My heart stutters. Stops. The darkness whirls, draggin' me deeper before pushin' me forward toward a strange light. The pain grows stronger. My thoughts grow fuzzy around the edges, harder to hold onto. Maybe this is the real dyin' part. This slow fadin' away of consciousness, of self.

But I don't want to go. Not yet. Dex was supposed to help me. Where is he? He promised he'd help me cross.

A voice cuts through the darkness. Clear and commandin'.

"You're not dead yet, darling. And I'm not letting you go that easily."

The darkness fractures. Cracks appear, jagged lines of light split it apart. The whispers retreat, screamin' as they go.

"That's it. Fight, Mina. Come back."

Sensation rushes back all at once. The cold, wet rock beneath me. The spray of the falls on my face. My eyes snap open. A scream builds in my throat, but doesn't make it past my lips.

Vivienne's face hovers above mine, blood smeared across her chin, her lips. My blood?

"I've got you." Her voice no longer seems to be reachin' from across a canyon, but right here, right next to my ear. "Hold on, hon. I hate to say this, but the worst is yet to come."

A searin' pain grasps the center of my chest and radiates out, a wave of agony that washes away everythin' but the burnin' fire that seems to be spreadin' through my veins.

What the fuck is happenin' to me? This isn't the beautiful, peaceful death that I witnessed with Mrs. Henderson. This is like a hot poker bein' shoved up my arse and out the top of my head, and I want it to stop. Now.

The roar of the falls pounds against my eardrums. Every rock beneath my broken body digs into my skin with perfect, terrible clarity. Vivienne hovers above me, her designer clothes soaked and torn, her perfect makeup streaked with what looks like bloody tears.

"You're back." Her voice cracks. "Thank God."

I try to move and immediately regret it. Somethin's wrong with my left leg, and I can't move my arms. My ribs grind against each other when I breathe.

"Don't move," Vivienne says. She places a gentle hand on my shoulder. "Your body is healing."

Healin'? No. This is hell. Healin' is supposed to be peaceful and restorative. This ain't that.

"I'm sorry," she continues. Fresh blood tears spill down her perfect cheekbones. "I should have asked for permission to do this to you, but it was the only thing I could think to do. I wasn't ready to let you go. None of us were."

My throat works, tryin' to form words past all this bloody pain. "What . . ." It comes out as barely a croak. "What did ya do to me?"

She swallows hard and brushes hair from my face. For the first time since I've known her, Vivienne St. James looks afraid.

"I bit you." Vivienne's fingers trace my neck. The admission hangs between us as another wave of ragin' fire fills my broken body.

"My essence will help you. I promise." She pulls her hand back, blood under her fingernails. "It's healing your broken bones. But it'll also change you. You're not an actual vampire, but you're no longer human either, which means the Concord can't use you. Not like this."

Her eyes flick to the cliff above us. "Your soul is in stasis. It shattered their ritual. I don't know why I didn't think of it sooner. We could have saved all of this from happening."

Her words bounce off my skull. Essence? Stasis?

"Ya bit me?" My voice grows stronger but still sounds strange in my ears.

She nods, but refuses to meet my eyes. "You hit the rocks, and you were dying. Your soul was already starting to separate. I was afraid Dex wouldn't be able to fight them off and get to you in time, so I intervened." Her voice catches. "I had to do something, and it was the only thing I could think of."

Before I can voice any of the dozen questions swirlin' through my mind, a new wave of pain crashes over me. My spine arches off the ground. Muscles seize.

"I'm so sorry. I know this is painful." Vivienne shifts to support my head as my body convulses. "The essence is repairing the physical damage. It won't be pleasant."

No shit. This is worse than not pleasant. I grit my teeth as bones shift inside me, grindin' against each other. My shattered leg straightens with a series of pops. Ribs knit back together beneath my skin, the sensation like hundreds of tiny needles stitchin' me up from the inside.

I cling to conversation, desperate for somethin' to focus on besides my body's reconstruction. "The Concord," I gasp. "Did it work? Did I stop them?"

Vivienne glances around. "I think so. When you died, their ritual paused. When your soul went into stasis, it seems to have completely collapsed."

Another wave of transformation hits. This one centered in my chest. My heart stutters, stops, then restarts with a painful thud. My lungs seize. The sensation of oxygen floodin' back into them is almost as painful as the lack of it.

"Your heart will beat slower now," Vivienne explains, her clinical tone at odds with the concern in her eyes. "You'll breathe less frequently. Food won't satisfy you the same way."

"But I'm alive," I whisper, testin' the word. It doesn't feel quite right anymore.

"Not exactly, but you're here," she says firmly. "That's what matters."

I try to nod, but my neck spasms, another wave of transformation ripplin' through my muscles. This time it reaches my face, my jaw. Teeth shift in my mouth, and my canines lengthen just enough to feel wrong against my tongue.

The pain and sensory overload become too much. I try to scream, but what comes out instead is a sound I never would have thought could come from my body. It's hollow and animal, more growl than human cry.

"Don't fight it," she says. "Let the changes happen. It'll be easier."

I push to my hands and knees, diggin' my fingers into the earth beneath me as another wave of change washes through me.

I push against the earth with my palms, bracin' myself for another wave that doesn't come. I slowly raise my head and open my eyes to a world that seems to have transformed as much as I did. Every tree branch, every star in the sky is crystal clear. The mist from the falls hangs in the air, each droplet containin' its own rainbow. The darkness pulses around me.

I sit up slowly. I test limbs that were shattered minutes ago. My body feels indestructible; the aches and pains I've developed over thirty-seven years of life no longer exist. Even the scar on my knee from fallin' off a swing as a kid has vanished.

"What happens now?" My new voice carries an air of self-assured confidence it never had before.

"It's hard to explain." Vivienne watches me flex my fingers, testin' their new strength. "You're caught between states."

I press my palm against the rough stone beside me. It crumbles slightly under the pressure. "Yes, but between what and what?"

"Human and vampire." She shifts closer to study my face. "But without feeding on my blood, you won't fully turn. You can, if you want, but I'll leave that choice up to you."

I press my hand against my chest waitin' for the beat to come. It's there, but much slower than I'm used to. "And how long can I stay like this?"

Vivienne looks away, her perfect profile sharp against the night sky. "A few months. Maybe a year. It's hard to say. This isn't something we normally do. We typically only share our essence if we intend to fully turn someone."

She stands, brushin' dirt from her ruined designer slacks.

"What happens if I wait too long to decide?"

"The venom in my essence will continue its work, but without fresh vampire blood to complete the transition, your body will start to fight itself. The vampire hunger will grow. The human version will weaken. Eventually . . ."

She doesn't finish, but she doesn't need to. Eventually, I'll die anyway, probably in agony as my body tears itself apart from the inside.

I dig my fingers into the dirt beneath me, needin' to feel somethin' solid and real. I grab handfuls of soil, squeezin' until it crumbles between my fingers.

"So I have a choice."

"Yes," Vivienne confirms. "Which is more than I had."

I look up at her sharply. "You didn't choose to become a vampire?"

A shadow crosses her face. "Few of us did, in my time. It was a different era."

I want to ask more, but another question presses more urgently. "If I do choose to turn, would I be like you? Independent? Or would I be . . ." I struggle to find the right word.

"Bound to me?" Vivienne finishes. "No. You'd be your own vampire. There would be a familial connection between us, but not ownership." Her lips curl slightly. "I've never been interested in keeping pets. But a sister sounds nice. I know forever sounds scary, but it's not so bad."

Forever? It's too big to comprehend. Centuries of watchin' everyone I know grow old and die while I remain unchanged. It almost seems worse than knowin' I'm about to die and leave them all behind.

"And if I choose to let go?" My voice drops to a whisper.

"Then we'll make it peaceful," Vivienne promises. "No pain. Just release. And we'll make sure Dex is there to guide you across like he originally planned."

"I don't want to die." The words break from me like a confession. My voice cracks. A sob builds in my throat.

Vivienne nods solemnly. "I can turn you now . . ."

"No." I hold up a hand and scoot away. "I don't know if I want that either."

Vivienne nods. "Okay, but understand: you can't stay in between forever. This is borrowed time."

No sooner have the words left her mouth than I'm hit with a sharp pain in my abdomen. I double over. My stomach claws at itself, hollow and desperate.

"You need to watch your cravings," Vivienne says as she reaches for her purse. "The vampire essence will make you crave blood. You'll need it to maintain this form, but you can still eat human food. I will warn you, though. There will be moments when the urge to feed on humans hits hard. You have to stay in control."

The word blood makes my stomach lurch with intense hunger, which kind of grosses me out because I've never been a rare meat kind of gal.

She pulls a bag of blood from her purse, and I recoil while my stomach growls. "It's synthetic," she says. "Drink some. It will tide you over for the time being. The others will be down any second, and we can't have you going after one of them."

I tentatively sip the viscous liquid from the bag. The metallic sweetness floods my mouth. And it's good. Damn good. Better than any wine. I gulp it down.

"Easy," Vivienne says. "You don't want to get sick. That's enough for now."

I wipe my mouth, and my ears perk up at the sound of stumblin' footsteps comin' off the hill to our left.

"They're comin'," I say, turnin' toward the path before I even realize what I'm doin'.

I hear them before I see them. My new ears catch their voices from impossibly far away. Seven heartbeats pound at different speeds. Seven sets of lungs work hard. Feet crunch through leaves and twigs as they stumble down the path to the bottom of the falls.

Vivienne rises smoothly to her feet and positions herself slightly in front of me. Protective. I'm not sure if she's protectin' me from them or them from me.

Hazel and La'Tasha appear first, with Coco right behind, the sadness palpable. Blake and Calvin and Leo appear next, eyes on the ground. Then Dex, his shoulders slumped in defeat.

They freeze, a collective gasp suckin' the air from the space around them. Hazel stumbles backward, her hand to her mouth. La'Tasha and Coco look at each other, as if makin' sure they're not seein' things. Blake's jaw drops open while Calvin and Leo look at me like I'm some kind of resurrected mummy. And Dex. Dex stands frozen, his ancient eyes drinkin' in every detail of my transformed features.

The tableau holds for three heartbeats before the werewolves line up between the witches and Vivienne.

"What did you do?" Leo growls. "I thought we could trust you. You're Concord?"

Vivienne laughs. "Concord? No, wolfy. I'm not Concord. I saved her."

I stand, slowly, still wobbly on my feet. I raise a hand and wave to my friends. "Still here. For now."

Hazel takes a tentative step forward. "But you . . . you jumped." She steps even closer. "You're really okay?"

"Aye, pet." Though okay is a weird word to describe how I feel right now.

Glances pass between the rest of the group. Silent questions hang in the air. Then Dex breaks from the others and moves toward me. He stops inches away, his normally composed face raw with emotion. He raises a tremblin' hand and then stops, almost as if he's afraid I'll dissolve if he touches me.

"My God," he whispers. "I thought they took you before I . . ."

I shake my head. "I'm still here, love."

The others approach more cautiously, and form a loose semicircle around us. Blake reaches out, his fingers touchin' my shoulder tentatively. The warmth of his skin feels like a furnace against my cooled body.

"How?" he asks.

"Vivienne," I answer, glancin' toward her. "She . . . interrupted things."

Calvin steps closer, his face a battleground of emotions. "We saw you jump," he says. "No one could have survived that."

"I didn't," I reply simply. "At least, not as I was. And it hurt like hell, let me tell ya."

"Your aura," Coco whispers. "It's weird. It's like Vivienne's. All silvery and wavey."

"So you're in a liminal state?" La'Tasha looks between me and Vivienne. "How?"

Vivienne smiles. "I bit her."

"¡Dios mío! ¿Ahora eres un vampire?!" Coco gasps, her eyes going wide as saucers.

Vivienne laughs. "Not quite. Let's call it vampire essence without full transition."

My enhanced senses drink them in. They're all so alive. So human. So warm.

And I'm . . . not.

I feel both intensely connected to them yet separated by an invisible barrier.

"The Concord scattered when you jumped," Hazel says. She wipes a stray tear from her cheek. "We thought . . ." She can't finish.

"When Dex couldn't find your soul, we thought they'd taken it," Blake completes for her. "We came to recover your . . ."

"My body," I supply when he trails off uncomfortably. "I know. That was the plan."

Dex's face tightens. His hand finally touches mine, his fingers wrappin' between mine.

Leo steps forward, and sweeps Vivienne into his arms. "Thank you," he says, his voice rough with emotion. "For saving her. I'm sorry for doubting you. It's just—"

Vivienne steps back and cuts him off with a kiss. "I'm not one of the Concord," she repeats. "I'm on your side, puppy." Another kiss. "Always have been, always will be."

"How much longer?" Hazel asks. "I mean, can you stay like this forever? Will you eventually become a vampire? What happens exactly?" Her brow furrows with concern as she looks between Vivienne and me.

That's the question, isn't it? The one I'm not quite ready to answer, with its complicated implications and eventual choice. But they deserve the truth, or at least as much of it as I understand myself.

I smile. "Let's not worry about that right now, okay. What matters is that I have time. Longer than I had before. And that's enough for now."

"What are the implications?" Blake asks. "Long-term? Did we stop the Concord for good? Can we, like, go on as normal? Are we rid of them?"

All eyes turn to Dex.

"I'm afraid that's wishful thinking. Vivienne bought us time," he says, carefully choosin' his words. "The Concord's ritual failed tonight, but . . ."

"But they'll try again," Vivienne finishes for him. "They've been working toward this for centuries. They won't just give up."

La'Tasha nods grimly. "And they'll want revenge. Especially on you, Mina."

"They won't have much use for me now, though," I point out. "Accordin' to Vivienne, I don't register as human anymore."

"At what cost, though?" Hazel asks. "I mean, since you're not entirely human, does that mean you're not . . . You're not dying from the tumor anymore?"

I shake my head. "Vivienne said . . ."

"Human diseases can't hurt a vampire. Or a vampire in stasis."

I shudder. A vampire. That's what I am now. Maybe not fully, but it's still too much to wrap my head around.

"So you're cured?" Hope floods Calvin's face.

Vivienne makes a small sound. "It's more complicated than that. The vampire essence has put her in a suspended state. She's not aging, not dying, but she's not fully alive either. It's temporary. Like I said, she can't stay like this forever."

Dex's hand squeezes mine.

"Eventually, she'll need to make a choice. Turn, or die." Vivienne fills them in on everythin' she knows about my current state, and they, like me, are happy to have a little more time while I decide what to do. At least now it's my choice and not some cosmic cult's or some bloody tumor.

While they talk, I walk away from the group, drawn to a quiet pool where the falls settle into clear, dark water. The surface is glass-smooth here, creatin' a natural mirror. I need to see. Need to know what I've become.

I kneel at the edge and lean forward, bracin' myself for a broken and bloodied face. Instead, I find myself. Mostly. My features are sharper somehow. More defined. I've always been pale, but my skin is absolutely luminous now. All that money wasted on skin cream. Who knew all I needed was a couple of fangs to make me absolutely radiant? But the biggest change is in my eyes. Red flecks dance in the green irises, a reminder that I'm somethin' else now.

I touch my face, tracin' the line of my cheekbone that seems more pronounced. My lips are fuller, and when I part them slightly, I can see the subtle elongation of my canines.

Footsteps approach behind me, too light and deliberate to be anyone but Dex. He stops at my side, reflection next to mine. The contrast between us isn't as stark as it used to be, both of us existin' in a space between alive and dead.

For several minutes, we stand and watch our reflections. Words seem inadequate after everythin' that's happened.

Eventually, his arm finds its way around my waist. "I thought

I'd lost you," he says, voice rough. "In all my existence, I've never felt pain like that."

"Ya didn't lose me." I lean closer and melt into him. "I'm right here."

"Yes." His lips find the top of my head. "You are."

"What happens now?" I turn to face him fully. "With you? Us?"

He brushes a strand of hair from my face. "We figure out what your new normal looks like. And we prepare for when the Concord returns, because they will."

"Yes, but . . ." I trail off because I'm afraid to ask. "Will ya have to leave now that I'm not dyin'? At least not yet?"

He sighs. "I don't know. Probably."

I place my head on his chest. We stand together at the water's edge, the falls roarin' behind us, as the sun threatens to rise.

CHAPTER TWENTY-SEVEN

Dex

Mist spirals around my ankles as I kneel in the center of the reckoning chamber. Pockets of blue flames burn on the walls around me, but they do very little to light the space. Shadows and the lack of life swallow everything in this place.

"Reaper Grimm." The Council speaks in unison, their voices layered in harmony. "You have failed in your duty. Again."

I keep my head bowed, not out of respect, but to hide the flash of defiance in my eyes. They don't appreciate anything less than total compliance. They consider it to be too human.

"The soul listed as Mina Cartwright was scheduled to cross." The voice seems to have echoed from the tall shadow to my left. "You were assigned as her guide. Again. Yet you reported back without her."

The figure across from me places the tip of their scythe beneath my chin and guides my head up, forcing me to look at them. "And not only did you not collect her soul, but you left her in a transitional state."

Yet another figure drifts closer. "Explain yourself. And do it well. Your future as a Reaper depends on it."

I scan the circle of hooded figures who line the walls. They never show their true forms here, opting for hoods and ancient theatrics. They expect me to fear for my job. Today, they'll decide whether I am to remain a reaper or be cast out, forced to live as a human. And honestly? I don't care what they decide.

My hands clench behind my back, nails digging into my palms. "Mina Cartwright sacrificed herself to stop the Concord's ritual. She broke their connection to the Hollowing, which in turn—"

"We are aware of everything that transpired. But the fact remains. You failed. She did not cross." The chancellor of Reaper's unmistakable voice cuts through my words like a blade.

After everything Mina endured, they insist on making her success my failure. "It all happened very quickly. As you know, my powers were compromised and . . . I couldn't reach her." The admission still pains me. "Vivienne St. James—the vampire— found her first. And fearing the Concord would reach her before I could, she administered her essence."

The Council stirs, mist patterns churning as they communicate. One of them moves forward, the shadows beneath their hood deepening.

"As we have said multiple times. You failed. Had you not allowed the Graveborn—"

"I did not 'allow' anything." My patience frays. "I was defending myself. How was I to know it had been enhanced?"

"Extended time in the human realm weakens us. You know that, yet you chose to prolong your stay." Another Council member circles closer. "Prolonged human contact makes a Reaper vulnerable. Makes us forget who and what we are."

The truth stings more than I want to admit. "You assigned me this mission," I deflect. "You could have sent me anywhere, yet you sent me to Moonridge."

"To correct a mistake you made years ago," a disembodied voice reminds me.

I take a deep breath and hedge a bet with what I'm about to say. "She wasn't the only reason you sent me. You knew about the Concord, and you knew I was the only Reaper who had the experience to stop them."

"Yes. And you had your assignment, and the night of The Hollowing, you knew your duty was to escort the Cartwright woman—"

"Mina," I breathe deep. "She has a name."

The shadow ignores my outburst and continues. "Why were you unable to reach her?"

"I got caught up in the battle between the witches and the Concord members. I was fully prepared to assist Mina when the time came, but by the time I reached the base of the falls, it was done."

"Your duty was to the soul, not to the living."

My jaw tightens. "No. My duty was to prevent the Hollowing. We all know that. Had we not stopped the ritual, Reapers would no longer have a purpose." I straighten, meeting their collective gaze. "Had they been successful, none of us would be standing here right now."

"Don't celebrate yet." The whisper from my left carries centuries of accusation. "They'll try again. This is temporary."

"But we managed to buy ourselves more time. To prepare. Next time—"

"And you're certain you'll get a next time?"

I bite back a response.

The silence stretches a beat too long, and then another shadow speaks. "You have grown attached to this mortal. Or, half-mortal as it may be."

I clench my teeth and flex my fingers. "Perhaps," I admit.

Silence falls. The mist stills, frozen in mid-swirl. When the leader speaks again, it's tinged with something like guilt.

"We sent our strongest Reaper to complete a task," they say, "We did not account for love."

The word is both accusation and revelation. They knew. They knew Mina was the key to stopping the Concord.

"You engineered this," I point out. "You knew she would need to die to stop the ritual."

"We knew that the Concord was going to try to break the veil, and we knew the woman was the key. Yes. She had to die. And you were to usher her across."

Finally, an admission.

"The Concord's hunger grows," another member says. "For centuries, they have sought to breach the veil, to control death itself. They found their anchor when you failed to collect the Thornton woman decades ago. You could have stopped it then by helping her cross over. You've failed us twice."

"And now what?" Defiance creeps into my voice.

"They'll try again," the leader says. "Their anchor is strong, and her spawn is in Moonridge. This could enhance her power."

"But they don't have a key," I say, "which means we have time to figure out their next step and stop them."

And with any luck, they'll agree and let me stay in Moonridge. With Mina.

"We will deliberate," they announce.

The Council converges, their forms melting into one another like blood on white fabric. I remain kneeling as they confer in that silent, shadowless language of theirs, mist swirling around me like storm clouds deciding where to strike.

Finally, they reform their circle.

"Reaper Grimm, we have reached our judgment," the chancellor announces. "You are to remain stationed in Moonridge."

My shoulders drop as the breath I've been holding escapes in a rush. My fists loosen, fingers tingling with release.

"However." The word hangs like a guillotine blade. "You must return periodically."

There's always a catch. But this is a reasonable one. "How often?"

"The moon's cycle will guide you." One of them glides forward, robes rustling behind them. "Return with each new moon."

"Or?" I suspect I know the answer.

"Or lose your role as a reaper and transform into what you pretend to be." The coldest voice cuts through the chamber. Like being a human is the most detestable thing they can imagine.

"The Cartwright woman remains your responsibility," they continue. "Until she either crosses over naturally or chooses another path."

"Another path? She's in transition," I point out. "If she feeds, she becomes a vampire. If she doesn't—"

"Then she will eventually cross, as all mortals must. Yes, we know. But that choice is hers to make."

One member advances, their form shifting to reveal glimpses of what might be wings, or perhaps ancient, gnarled limbs. "Your presence in Moonridge will draw spirits," they warn.

"I understand."

"Good," they say. "Then you understand that you will not be sent to Moonridge to play house. You will be expected to continue your reaper duties. To guide those who are ready and to enforce the boundaries when necessary."

I bow my head in acceptance. "As I would expect."

The mist begins to thicken, signaling our time is ending.

"One final warning, Reaper Grimm," comes a voice I haven't heard until now. It's familiar, but I can't quite place it. "The Hollowing is paused, not ended. The Concord's hunger grows in the dark. They already seek another key. And the anchor's daughters are now at risk."

"What do you mean?"

Before I get my answer, the chamber crumbles around me, mist unraveling like pulled thread. The last thing I see before being thrust back toward the mortal coil is my own reflection in the swirling vapor.

I wake with a jolt, momentarily confused by the ceiling

above me. The void of the Council chamber has transformed into antique crown molding. Mina's parlor. Her sofa beneath me, my feet dangling awkwardly over the armrest.

I stretch, surprised at how good I feel. I lift my shirt to find that the wound bestowed upon me by the Graveborn has completely healed. The return to the Reaper world restored my abilities.

And now I'm back, their new set of instructions firmly etched into my consciousness. But what was that about the anchor's daughter? Is Hazel in trouble, too?

A clatter from the kitchen breaks my thoughts.

I swing my legs off the sofa, pausing to let a wave of dizziness pass. Reorienting to the human plane always takes me a moment.

I enter the kitchen to find the room has transformed into a witch's workshop. Hazel stands at the counter, grinding herbs while La'Tasha sits cross-legged on the floor, tracing sigils along the baseboards with what appears to be salt mixed with crushed herbs. Coco moves between them, hanging small fabric pouches over each window.

"Good morning, Muerte," Coco says without looking up from her task. She ties a pouch of something that smells like lavender and iron filings over the back door. "Sleep well?"

"As well as can be expected. What day is it?" I ask, easing myself into a kitchen chair.

"Um, it's still Saturday. The day after Halloween. You literally only slept for like an hour," Coco says.

Time is such a strange concept.

"What are you doing?" I ask.

"Patching holes," Hazel replies, not pausing in her grinding. "The Concord's ritual weakened every protective barrier in Moonridge. We're starting here to protect Mina while she recovers."

Thin spots shimmer in my peripheral vision, places where reality wears too thin. La'Tasha mutters under her breath as she works, "Damn Concord punched holes everywhere."

"The Council has agreed to let me stay." I watch their reactions carefully.

Hazel's hands pause before resuming their rhythm. She turns and smiles. "That's great."

"So Death himself is our new neighbor," Coco quips, trying to lighten the mood with a nervous laugh.

"There are conditions," I continue. "I must return to the Reaper realm with each new moon to recharge."

"Or what?" La'Tasha asks, finally turning to face me.

"Or I become permanently human."

That gets their full attention. Coco actually sits down, her eyes wide.

"What does this mean for Moonridge?" La'Tasha asks, standing and brushing salt from her hands. "I mean, are things going to get even weirder around here? Do I need to learn how to be a better ghost hunter? Cuz I admit, my skills are lacking in that area."

"Hopefully not, but it might not hurt," I admit. "My presence will draw spirits. Those who have died in the area, and any wandering ghosts that managed to sneak past a reaper and found their way to town, will be naturally drawn to me. I'll be expected to guide them."

"And Mina?" Hazel asks the question they've all been thinking. "What did they say about her?"

"She remains my responsibility. Until she either crosses naturally or chooses to complete the transformation."

Before anyone can respond, the front door opens, and quick footsteps approach the kitchen.

Penny bursts in, her glasses slightly askew, clutching a messenger bag to her chest. Dark circles shadow her eyes, her clothes rumpled as if she's been wearing them for days.

"I've been looking everywhere for you guys. Did it work?" Her eyes dart between the four of us.

Hazel sets down her pestle and places a hand on her hip. "We managed. What happened to you? Why did you take off like that?"

Penny drops her bag on the chair next to me and removes her jacket. "I went back to the library. I released the Crucible Core."

The witches exchange startled looks.

"By yourself?" Hazel asks.

She nods, eyes stuck on Hazel.

"Girl, what are we going to do with your rogue ass?" La'Tasha asks. "Are you hurt?"

Penny smiles and shakes her head. "I'm okay. I mean, it was intense, but . . . yeah, I'm fine."

"That must be why they all dropped like dead birds," Coco says.

"They dropped?" Penny asks, taking a seat next to me.

"Yes," I say. "Just before Mina was able to get away, they all collapsed. Like someone had cut their puppet strings."

Penny smiles, ignoring Hazel's glare. "So my hunch was right. The Core was the power point for all thirteen binding sites. I thought if I could disrupt it . . ."

"You did," I confirm. "You created the distraction that allowed Mina to regain control. You saved her."

Hazel turns back to her herb grinding and remains silent.

Penny's cheeks flush with pride, then fade quickly. "There's a problem, though. When I released the Core, it didn't just break the Concord's connection. It released every spirit bound to those sites. They're wandering Moonridge now."

Of course they are.

"How many?" I ask.

"Thousands," Penny answers. "Maybe more. Some are just lost souls. Others were trapped for a reason. You were right, Dex. There was a lot more in there than just simple spirits. We may have some cleanup to do."

I feel a tapping at my shoulder, and I turn. I know that feeling. Like someone knocking on the door, asking to be let in. That didn't take long. I stand and reach for my scythe.

"What is it?" Hazel asks, alert to my sudden change.

I point at the window. "A woman. She needs my help crossing over." I move toward the front door.

Morning sunlight casts long shadows across the lawn, and there, beneath the old maple tree, stands the frail figure of a woman, mid-thirties, obviously dead. Blood streams from a gash in her forehead, and she only wears one shoe. She looks up at me with wide, frightened eyes.

"I can't find my children," she says. "Do you know where they are? We were driving to the zoo, and we had a flat tire and then . . ." She holds out a hand like I might be able to fill in the blanks.

My scythe elongates in my hand as I step toward her. "I know. They're waiting for you."

"Where?"

I offer her my hand. "On the other side. I can show you the way."

The woman hesitates, then takes my hand. "We died. Didn't we? That truck. It swerved when I was changing the tire and—"

"Yes." I cut her off. "But you'll be okay."

"Will it hurt?" she asks.

"No," I promise. "It's like falling asleep in one room and waking in another."

I sweep my scythe in a wide arc. The air parts like a curtain, revealing a warm, glowing portal just large enough for her to step through.

"Go on," I encourage her. "They're there."

The woman peers in and smiles. She steps toward the light and passes through. The opening seals behind her, leaving nothing but the last remnants of this morning's fog around the base of the tree.

***

The old floors creak beneath my feet as I make my way back to Mina's room. Soft golden light spills from beneath her door, a warm invitation against the gathering shadows.

I knock softly, twice. A habit I've picked up after spending too much time in this world. Knocking usually isn't something I do.

"Come in." Her voice sounds stronger than I expected. A good sign.

The door swings open, and I find Mina propped against a mountain of pillows, a mug of something steaming cradled between her palms.

"It's dark in here," I say.

"My eyes." She gestures at her face like I'm not sure where her eyes are. "Still very sensitive to light. Vivienne says they'll get better."

I sit next to her and peer at the thick liquid in her mug. "Blood tea?"

She nods. "Never would I have ever thought I'd be drinkin' blood in my tea, but here we are."

"Yes, here we are."

I place a hand on her cheek, suddenly overcome with emotion. This woman has been through so much, yet here she sits, stronger than ever. She was beautiful before, but her skin has taken on an alabaster quality, and her hair seems more vibrant against the cream-colored top she wears. And her eyes. Those have changed the most. Still green, but with an unnatural brightness that reminds me of a cat in the dark.

She kisses my palm. "Ya look like hell."

"I've been there, actually. Not as warm as advertised."

That earns me a small laugh.

"So what's the verdict?" she asks. "Did your bosses fire ya for lettin' me live? Or whatever this is?" She gestures vaguely at herself.

I settle into the chair beside her bed, the wood creaking under my weight. "They're letting me stay in Moonridge. For now. Of course, I am expected to continue my reaper duties. And to watch over you."

"Lucky me. My own personal reaper." She winks.

"More like a guardian. Until you decide your path. I'm still expected to usher you across. If you choose that route, I mean."

She sets the mug down on her nightstand, her hands trembling slightly. Vivienne's brew might be strengthening her, but the transformation is still taking its toll. She leans back against her pillows, eyes fixed on the ceiling.

"What else did they say?"

"I have to return with each new moon to maintain my connection to them. And renew my strength."

"What happens if ya don't?"

"My reaper powers will drain until I become human."

Mina huffs out a laugh. "Well, isn't that somethin'? You have the option to become human, but either way, I have to die." She takes a breath, voice dropping to just above a whisper. "Dyin' terrifies me. But I'm not sure I want to live forever either. Not if that means I keep livin' while everyone I love has to die eventually."

"There's time to decide," I remind her. "It's not a decision that has to be made today."

Mina reaches out, her fingers finding mine. Our hands intertwine on the bedspread.

"I'm just glad we get more time together," she whispers. "However long it is."

My thumb traces circles on her skin. "However long."

Outside her window, another lost soul wanders outside the B&B, seeking guidance that only I can provide. My duty calls, but her fingers tighten around mine, and she pulls me toward her.

The soul can wander for a few more minutes.

CHAPTER TWENTY-EIGHT

Mina

The B&B driveway looks like a tornado hit an overstuffed toy box. Designer luggage and production equipment clutter the drive, and five vampire divas issue contradictory orders to harried crew members. Vivienne commands the center of the storm, tappin' at her phone with blood-red nails. She somehow manages to make standin' and doin' nothin' look fashionable.

"The Louis Vuitton goes in the SUV, not the van." She doesn't look up. A young man with a headset scrambles to redirect a stack of luggage.

I linger on the porch steps, watchin' the chaos with mixed feelings. The Vampire Wives wanted a week of haunted fun. They definitely got what they paid for. Maybe more. Here's hopin' the footage helps rather than hurts my business further. At least their payment will keep the B&B afloat while I figure out what I'm goin' to do if it doesn't.

Caprice sweeps past me, phone held at arm's length as she livestreams her departure.

"And that's a wrap on our Moonridge adventure, besties!" She blows kisses at the camera. "Don't forget to like and subscribe for all the behind-the-scenes tea! I'll be dropping hints about Season Four all week!"

She pauses to air-kiss my cheeks, her floral perfume ticklin' my newly sensitive nose. "This place was, like, so much more exciting than we expected. I'm confident our fans will be obsessed with the footage."

I smile. "Glad someone got what they wanted."

Across the lawn, Dahlia dabs at her eyes with a silk handkerchief. "I simply cannot bear goodbyes. I've really grown fond of this little place."

Her gaze catches mine over the crowd, and she gives me a small smile.

Zara bounds through the front door like an overexcited puppy, her pink hair a beacon as she distributes hugs to everyone, even the bewildered postman who picked the wrong moment to deliver a package. If she's still upset over Mortimer, she hides it well.

"Your aura is so much stronger now," she gushes when she reaches me. She throws her arms around my shoulders and wraps me in a huge hug. "The unalignment has totally realigned!"

Her new-age vampire princess observations still befuddle me. "Thanks?"

She holds me at arm's length, her silvery-blue eyes fixed on mine. "Seriously, the energy currents around you are, like, completely different. So cool."

And then she's off.

Ayana approaches next, her quiet elegance a welcome reprieve from Zara and Caprice's dramatic energy. "Mina, I can't thank you enough for the wonderful time. You took such good care of us."

"The pleasure was all mine." Except for the whole dyin' thing.

"If you decide to stay . . . like this?" She waves a hand up and down. "Let me know. We could use another sane one in the cast." She winks and kisses both of my cheeks. "Bye, gorgeous."

Before I can reply, she's climbin' into the SUV.

Leo lurks near Vivienne, his eyes trackin' her every movement like she's gravity and he's helpless against the pull.

"You promise you'll call?" He's tryin' to sound casual but lands somewhere closer to desperate.

Vivienne's expression softens. Just enough to show she's not as unmoved as she pretends. "I said I'd be in touch when I'm back on the West Coast, didn't I? I have a fashion line launching next week and then hopefully finalizing my divorce. No rest for the vampire divas of the world."

"But you'll call?" Leo presses. "Not just text or whatever?"

She sighs and tucks her phone away to give him her full attention. "Yes, puppy. I'll call." Her perfectly manicured fingers trace his jawline in a touch so intimate I feel like I should look away. "Contrary to popular belief, I do occasionally keep my promises. And I'd love to stay in touch."

Their goodbye stretches, his hands fisted in her coat, her face buried against his neck, until a production assistant clears her throat. When they finally separate, Leo's eyes shine.

"Safe travels," he manages.

"Try not to chase too many stray cats while I'm gone," she replies, genuine affection beneath the snark. She leans in and gives him a quick kiss. "I'll be in touch. I promise."

I turn away, givin' them privacy, only to find Vivienne suddenly beside me. Vampire speed. I still haven't gotten used to it.

"Walk with me." She takes my arm and nods toward the garden path.

The crisp fall air has stripped my herb garden down to bare branches and dried stalks. Only the rosemary soldiers on. We stop near the stone bench, far enough from the chaos of departure to speak privately.

"Do you regret it?" I ask. "Savin' me?"

She shakes her head. "Not at all. I chose to give you time. You deserved that, and you deserve a choice in how things end up for you. What you do with that time and that choice is yours."

She turns to watch Leo awkwardly helpin' the crew load equipment into a van, nearly trippin' over his own feet. "Some humans are worth keeping around."

She presses a business card into my palm. "Another injection of my essence might buy you a little more time." Her fingers close around mine. "I've never tried it before, so no promises. But if things start to go sideways—or if you decide you want to fully turn—please call. I'll come immediately."

The moment breaks as a production assistant calls for Vivienne. Time for departure. Planes to catch and all that. She squeezes my hand once, then glides back toward the controlled chaos of the lot.

I linger in the garden, turnin' her card over in my fingers. It's embossed with just a phone number, no name. Simple, elegant, like everythin' about her.

"She makes it sound so straightforward, doesn't she?"

I startle at Dahlia's voice. She stands just behind me, her blonde hair lit up by the weak November sunlight. I didn't hear her approach. Another vampire trick I haven't mastered.

"The choice between life and death," she continues, movin' closer. "As if either option is truly what it seems."

My skin crawls for some unknown reason. "You would know, I suppose."

Her ice-blue eyes dig into mine. "I've witnessed many transitions over the years. Some successful. Others . . . less so."

She reaches out with cold fingers and brushes a strand of hair from my shoulder. The touch lingers, deliberate. "Choose wisely."

As her hand drops away, her designer scarf shifts, revealin' the edge of somethin' on her collarbone. A mark. Blood-red against her pale skin. A brand of some sort?

My fingers drift to my collarbone. Heat pulses beneath the skin there, like a brand forming from within. Is this a vampire mark? Somethin' we all share? Is mine not completely visible because I haven't fully turned?

Dahlia notices the gesture, and her smile widens. "We'll see each other again, Mina Cartwright."

Before I can respond, Vivienne calls from the driveway. "Dahlia! Your car is waiting."

"Coming, darling!" she calls back, then gives me one last meaningful look before she glides away.

I stand frozen in the garden, one hand still pressed to my collarbone where the phantom heat of an invisible mark burns beneath my palm.

A breeze rustles the bare branches above me and sends a few brittle leaves tumblin' across the lawn. I watch them skitter over the asphalt, remnants of a season slippin' away. I should go inside, but my feet stay planted, like the garden itself is holdin' me still. Like it knows change is comin', and wants me to bear witness.

***

The procession of black SUVs carryin' the Vampire Wives and their team shrinks to pinpricks of red taillights before vanishin' completely around the bend. Their departure leaves the B&B quieter than it's been in weeks. No crew members shoutin' about lost signals, no Ayana hummin' century-old lullabies in the parlor.

The porch swing creaks as I ascend the steps, my body movin' with the new fluid grace that still surprises me. Dex steps outside as he shrugs on his coat.

I lean against his shoulder, our silhouettes mergin' in the early afternoon light. His body feels different now. When I was fully human, he always seemed slightly colder, less grounded. Now we meet in the middle, two beings suspended between worlds.

"Are ya ready to go join the others then?" I ask.

"To celebrate your extended life? Always." He kisses my forehead, light as breath.

We take in the quiet streets, remnants of the festival still present. Storefront windows flash with paper ghosts that flutter in the breeze. They'll all be gone by the time businesses reopen tomorrow, but the real ghosts will continue to lurk. One glides through a trash can and tips his hat as we pass, like a neighbor out for a stroll.

"Morning, ma'am," he says, his voice echoin' slightly. "Fine day to be alive."

Dex and I exchange glances. He doesn't seem to realize he's not among the livin' anymore. And, technically, neither are we.

"I saw him while I was out for my morning walk. He's been trying to direct traffic since dawn," Dex says, glancin' over his shoulder. "Keeps telling cars to slow their horses."

"There're so many of them now."

"The ritual weakened the veil," Dex explains. "And when Penny released the Crucible Core, she freed spirits who were bound to the thirteen points. It's going to take me forever to help them all get to where they're supposed to be."

I clutch his hand. "But not today, right?"

He plants a kiss on my lips. "Not today. They're harmless. For now."

We cross through the park and come upon Penny perched on a bench near the gazebo, scribblin' furiously in a journal.

"Good afternoon, love," I call.

Penny jumps, startled. "Oh! Mina, Dex." She pushes her glasses up with one finger.

"Plannin' to join us for lunch?" I ask.

"I'll swing by in a bit," she says. "I'm documenting the manifestations. I've seen thirty-seven distinct entities in the last twenty-four hours."

I glance down at her cramped handwriting. Each ghost has a timestamp, location, estimated era, and behavioral notes.

"Deceased farmer, corner of Maple and Main, 8:15 AM," I read. "Attemptin' to direct traffic. Temporal disorientation consistent with sudden death trauma. Very detailed, aren't ya?"

"Well, I don't exactly know their names, and they won't talk to me." There's a hint of defensiveness to her tone. "We need to record everything. So we know who the troublemakers are. And be prepared."

"For future ghost invasions?" I raise an eyebrow.

"Future anything," she replies seriously.

Dex pats her on the shoulder. "Great thinking. It could come in handy."

We say goodbye, leavin' her to her ghost documentation.

Ahead, the Blue Moon Apothecary glows with protective magic, windows alight with sigils. The bell above the door jingles as we enter.

"Right on time," Hazel calls. She sits behind the counter, threadin' crystals onto a leather cord. "Been expectin' you."

"Witch intuition?" I lean against the counter and inspect her work.

"Text from Penny." Hazel grins. She holds up the finished charm. "This is for you."

She comes around the counter and ties the small woven bracelet around my wrist. The attached onyx stone rustles against my skin, and I catch whiffs of lavender and sage.

"It won't stop the unraveling," Hazel warns, "but it might slow it."

"Thanks, pet." I examine the bracelet. Subtle magic hums within it. "Every little bit helps."

The bell above the door rings, and Calvin walks in, lookin' beside himself. A small smile plays at his lips when he sees us.

"Mina. Dex." He blinks. "Hi."

"How are you holdin' up, big guy?" I ask. The sadness that surrounds him is palpable.

He shrugs.

"Upset about Everett?"

Calvin stares down at his coffee cup. "Stupid, right? After everything we learned. After what Penny revealed." He shakes his head. "I hate to think that my connection to him somehow put you in danger."

"Stop that, now." I nudge his shoulder. "You're not responsible for ancient cults and their schemes. That's like lovin' the smell of rain then blamin' yourself for a storm that blew in and flooded the town."

He nods. "But I keep thinking. What if he really was fighting the Concord's control? What if he meant it when he said he was trying to fight them?"

"Maybe he was," I say gently. "I guess we'll never know. But don't let that keep ya down."

He nods. "He was just so much fun, you know? I hate to think that he was using me to get closer to you."

"Maybe he'll come back. Some ghosts chose to stay. Maybe he's out there lookin' for ya now."

He shakes his head. "I don't know. I looked for him during my run this morning, and there was no sign of him. I waited at the bench where we would meet for coffee, and he never showed. I think he's gone, gone."

"I'm sorry, pet." I give him a hug.

"Does it get easier?" he asks quietly. "Wanting a person who's not quite here?"

I glance across the room to where Dex sits. "I'll let ya know when I figure it out."

***

After an evenin' of dinner and laughter, Dex and I make our way back down the cobblestone streets of Moonridge. Dusk curls around us in shades of violet, paintin' the distant mountains in silhouette.

"Thank you," I say, wrappin' my arm through his. "For stayin'."

Dex arches a brow. "I wasn't given much choice."

"What would ya have done if they told ya that ya couldn't stay and keep your Reaper title?" I ask.

His mouth curves into that not-quite-smile I've come to treasure. "I think I would've chosen to stay."

My heart is full. This wonderful man—or whatever he is—would give it all up to stay with me. Could I do the same?

We walk in silence. Headlights swing onto Main from Elm, briefly washin' us in their glare. A black SUV—just like the one the Vampire Wives used—glides past. A sudden pain ignites at my collarbone. For a moment, everythin' goes dark.

She walks. She breathes. She dies.

The words echo through my skull, low and ancient.

Then the world snaps back into focus.

"You okay?" Dex asks, concern etched in every line of his face.

"Yeah," I lie. "Phantom pain from the fall."

It's not untrue. It's been less than forty-eight hours, and my body still aches. I swear I can still feel the moment I hit the rocks. Bones shatterin', heart stoppin'.

Above us, the stars begin to emerge. A thrush sings from somewhere in the trees.

A shift. A gentle movement comes from beneath the earth, causin' the cobblestones to tremble under our feet. Dex's grip tightens around mine.

A deep, steady thrum pulses through the ground. A heartbeat.

"What is that?" I whisper, though part of me already knows.

Dex scans the darkness. "Nothing good."

And then it stops. The earth stills. Even the night air holds its breath.

Whatever it was, we'll be ready.

THE REAL VAMPIRE WIVES OF OBSIDIAN HILLS

Episode 11: "Goodbye Moonridge"
FADE IN:
EXT. MOONRIDGE B&B - MORNING
The luxury SUVs are packed and waiting. The VAMPIRE WIVES say one last goodbye to MINA.

MINA: *(hugging each of them)* Thank you all so much for staying. I know the trip didn't go exactly as planned . . .

CAPRICE: *(bouncing slightly)* Are you kidding? This was the most exciting thing that's ever happened to me! Well, besides becoming a vampire. And that one time I accidentally turned into a goat in Cancun.

CUT TO: TALKING HEAD

CAPRICE: *(in the car, emotional)* I learned so much about myself on this trip! Like, I'm definitely not ready for advanced supernatural encounters, but I'm also braver than I thought!

CUT TO: INT. SUV #1 - DRIVING

VIVIENNE: *(looking out the window at the town passing by)* It's strange leaving. I feel like we're abandoning her.

CAPRICE: But she looked so much better this morning! Like, actually healthy instead of that scary pale she was when we first got there.

ZARA: *(thoughtfully)* The spiritual energy around her has definitely shifted. It feels protected now. Stronger.

CUT TO: TALKING HEAD

ZARA: *(to camera)* I don't know what happened in Vivienne's private conversation with Mina yesterday, but something changed. The dark energy that was clinging to her is muted now. Like something is shielding her from it.

CUT TO: INT. SUV #2 - DRIVING

AYANA: *(side-eyeing her)* Dahlia, honey, you've been cryptic this entire trip. Are you ever going to tell us why you really brought us here?

DAHLIA: *(small smile)* Sometimes the best way to help old friends is to surround them with new ones.

CUT TO: TALKING HEAD

AYANA: *(shaking her head, amused)* Three centuries of life, and that woman still manages to speak in riddles. But you know what? I had a blast. Watching ghosts mess with humans never gets old, and I actually like the little innkeeper. She's got balls.

CUT TO: TALKING HEAD - VIVIENNE (PRIVATE)

Vivienne sits alone, more relaxed than we've seen her all season

PRODUCER (O.S.): Vivienne, we need to ask about what happened after the last night of the festival. We saw Mina, and she appeared to have bite marks on her neck.

VIVIENNE: *(calmly)* She did.

PRODUCER (O.S.): You bit her? What are the implications of that?

VIVIENNE: *(leaning forward slightly)* Remember when I said I was going to call in some favors? That was the favor. I got permission from some very powerful people to give Mina some time.

PRODUCER (O.S.): Permission from who? And time for what?

VIVIENNE: Let's just say I cashed in a very old debt.

PRODUCER (O.S.): And the bite?

VIVIENNE: *(matter-of-factly)* Mina was sick, and I gave her more time.

PRODUCER (O.S.): There's a rumor that she was being hunted by some evil cult. What do you know about that?

VIVIENNE: *(staring straight at the camera)* I know nothing about that. As I said. Mina was sick. She had little time left. I extended that time. The bite will keep her alive for a few more months. Until she decides what to do next. Whatever it is, the choice will be hers. Until then, we'll keep her safe.

PRODUCER (O.S.): We?

VIVIENNE: *(smiling softly)* Mina has a lot of people who love her.

PRODUCER (O.S.): And would one of those people be Leo Morales?

VIVIENNE: *(her smile widening)* Among others.

PRODUCER (O.S.): Are you planning to see him again?

VIVIENNE: *(laughing)* Once my divorce from Marcus is finalized, I might just have to make another trip to Moonridge. For the fall foliage, of course.

PRODUCER (O.S.): Of course.

VIVIENNE: *(leaning back)* Besides, someone needs to keep an eye on Mina. The protection I gave her isn't permanent.

PRODUCER (O.S.): So this isn't over?

VIVIENNE: *(shaking her head)* Not even close.

CUT TO: TALKING HEAD - GROUP

All five wives are squeezed into one frame

AYANA: *(raising a champagne flute)* To Moonridge!

CAPRICE: *(clinking glasses)* To my first successful supernatural adventure! And to Mortimer, who died protecting us!

ZARA: *(emotional)* To new friendships and found family!

DAHLIA: *(mysterious as always)* To unfinished business and second chances.

VIVIENNE: *(looking directly at camera)* To Mina Cartwright, who reminded me that some mortals are worth protecting. And to Leo Morales, who better have a good bottle of wine ready for my next visit.

ALL: *(laughing and toasting)* Cheers!

CUT TO: EXT. MOONRIDGE TOWN LIMITS - DAY

The SUVs pass the "Leaving Moonridge - Come Back Soon!" sign

CUT TO: TALKING HEAD

VIVIENNE: *(final confessional, looking serene)* People ask me what it's like being immortal, living for over a century. Most of the time, it's watching everything you care about fade away. But sometimes . . . *(smile)* sometimes you find something worth protecting. Someone worth saving. And occasionally, if you're very lucky, you find someone worth coming back for.

She looks out the window toward the disappearing town

VIVIENNE (CONT'D): Moonridge hasn't seen the last of Vivienne St. James. That's a promise.

ANNOUNCER (V.O.): Next time on The Real Vampire Wives of Obsidian Hills . . .

FADE OUT.

Acknowledgements

If the acknowledgments in this book sound familiar, it's because the same incredible people were involved once again. I owe thanks to all of you for holding my hand through the chaos. Honestly, I think this round might have been even messier than the last.

Ally, Susie, Carter, and "Brick," your editing wisdom, sharp eyes, and design skills are unmatched. This book is cleaner, tighter, and far more readable because of your generous help and occasional tough love. I know I added an extra challenge by choosing (or choosin') to spell in Mina's Scottish accent. I'm still not certain we caught them all, but we did our best! Also, I never would have caught "the door above the bell", or "hand in her head" without your eagle eyes. I'm still laughing about that last one.

To my beta and sensitivity readers: Clay, Corey, Ruth, and Lonnie B. I'm so grateful for your honest, thoughtful, and often hilariously blunt feedback. At least this time we didn't have to figure out who was in whose body or how to explain it clearly. That was a special kind of headache.

To my friends not directly mentioned here (there are many), thank you for letting me disappear for hours and sometimes days without too many questions or interruptions. This is what I was doing when I turned down dinners, canceled plans and left texts unanswered. Your patience with me and my quirks means more than I can say. I often wonder what I did to deserve you all.

And finally, to you, the reader. Thank you for taking a chance on an indie author, and for coming back for book two. I hope you love these weird and wonderful characters as much as I do. Their stories are only just beginning. I know this book was a little darker than the first. Next time, I promise a bit more light, a bit more laughter, and plenty more Moonridge magic, all with just as much chaos. After all, we still have to stop the Concord.

ABOUT THE AUTHOR

Avery Arujo is the pen name of a socially anxious, awkward, and proudly introverted author of the paranormal mystery/romance series *Welcome to Moonridge*. Avery lives in the northern U.S., where the scenery is beautiful, the weather perfect, and the food divine. When not writing, you'll find Avery watching a horror movie or trashy reality TV or reading under a blanket with a cup of coffee, and the world's sweetest dog trying to prove that they are more interesting than any old book.

For more information about the *Welcome to Moonridge* series, or to sign up for the newsletter, visit welcometomoonridge.com.

NEXT IN THE SERIES

Welcome back to Moonridge, where the ghosts are still restless, The Concord 13 wait in the shadows, and time travel has entered the chat.

Calvin Carter is doing his best to keep it together, but that gets tricky when Everett Bradshaw—the ghost he fell for last fall—suddenly breaks free from Skipper Lake and shows up in his house. The good news is, Everett's back, but the bad news is, he's still bound to the Concord, and still very much dead.

But when Calvin uncovers a memory-triggered time portal in the basement of an old shop, a dangerous idea takes hold. Ignoring his brother's warnings, Calvin uses the door to travel to 1958 Moonridge, where Everett is very much alive, and walking straight toward the death that will bind him to the Concord for the next seventy years.

Now Calvin has four days to earn Everett's trust and figure out how to make it back to the present without tipping off the Concord. Or erasing them both from existence for good.

Magic, mystery, and a time-twisted second-chance romance collide to bring Moonridge's magic to a whole new level.

Right Place, Wrong Time *will be available in the spring of 2026.*

For updates, sneak peeks, and early news, visit welcometomoonridge.com and sign up for the newsletter.

Keep reading for a sneak peek of the first chapter of
Right Place, Wrong Time.

CHAPTER ONE

Everett

The caramel apple booth smells exactly like autumn used to when I was alive. Sugar and cinnamon and crisp October air. I breathe it in, trying to commit it to memory alongside everything else about this week.

Calvin laughs at something the vendor says, his whole face lighting up, and the sound hits me square in the chest. I've got maybe three hours left with him. Three hours before I have to walk away from this and help tear the world apart.

"You want one?" Calvin turns to me, that smile I love spreading across his face. The one that makes me thankful I no longer have a working heart, so I can't feel it breaking.

"Sure."

Calvin pays for both, handing me the apple.

I watch him lick caramel off his thumb, and think, *Remember this. It's all you'll have left of him after tonight.*

Because in a few hours, all of this will be over.

Either the Concord succeeds and the world as we know it ends, or they fail, and I get dragged back to Skipper Lake. Either way, I'll never see Calvin again. Either way, what he and I had these last few days ends tonight.

"You okay?" Calvin puts his arm around me and squeezes my shoulder. I'll never get used to being touched again. That's what I've missed the most.

I paste on a smile. "Yeah. Just thinking how lucky I am. To be here. With you."

It's the truest thing I've said all week, and also the biggest lie. Because I'm not lucky. I'm a dead man walking through a borrowed moment, pretending I get to keep this.

God, I want to keep this.

"Come on." Calvin tugs me forward, threading his fingers through mine. "I want you to meet everyone. My brother, my friends. They're going to love you."

My throat goes tight. Family. Tight-knit friend groups. This is what I always longed for.

We weave through the festival crowds, past kids in costumes and teenagers making out behind the fortune teller's tent. The Haunted Halloween Festival is in full swing, everyone having the time of their lives, completely unaware that in a few hours, their entire world will be turned on its head. That somewhere up at Whispering Falls, the Concord is preparing a ritual that'll split the veil between the living and the dead, ending life as all living beings know it.

The binding points are already activated. I did that. Walked through Moonridge, touching each one, lighting them up like candles on a birthday cake, and then kept them activated when the witches tried to extinguish them. All because of something I never asked for, bound to a group I never wanted to join.

I should've said no when Calvin asked me to come tonight. Should've disappeared after our last morning run and spared him this. But I'm selfish and stupid and I wanted one more night. Wanted to pretend, just for a few hours, that I could have this kind of life.

"There they are!" Calvin waves enthusiastically at a group gathered near the game booths. "Blake! Guys!"

My stomach, or what used to be my stomach, drops.

Blake is bigger than Calvin. Definitely more intimidating. Next to him stands a woman with curly auburn hair. She turns and smiles. Hazel. She looks just like her mother, but friendlier. Much less terrifying. But I suppose being the anchor that holds the Concord together is bound to blacken anyone's heart.

The others close in. I recognize La'Tasha, Dex, and Penny from last night—I'd followed them to the library basement and watched them discover the Crucible Core. And there's Mina, the one the Concord intends to exploit tonight. I can see the puppet maker's strings have already activated. She doesn't look well.

"Hey, guys!" Calvin's voice lifts with hope, like he's already decided they're going to accept me. If only. "I want you all to meet someone."

I straighten my leather jacket and paste on my best smile. Friendly. Confident. Because if they even catch a glimpse of how scared I am right now, it could ruin everything.

But maybe that would be for the better. If I tell them—

The Concord bind tightens around my throat. They're always watching. Always in my head. Always—

"This is Everett." Calvin's voice pulls me back.

I offer a small wave. "Calvin's told me so much about all of you." The words come out smooth enough, but I can hear the faint echo underneath. My borrowed humanity is already starting to fade.

Calvin stands close enough that our shoulders touch, and I try not to think about how I'll never feel this again.

"He's visiting for the festival," Calvin continues, "but I'm hoping I might be able to convince him to stay longer. Or at least visit often."

He winks, and the naked hope in his voice might kill me if I weren't already dead.

I want to tell him the truth. That I can't stay. That in a few hours I'll be gone. That I've been lying from the start, even though none of what I feel is a lie. Every moment with him these last few days has been the most alive I've ever felt.

But I can't say any of that. So I just smile and nod and pretend I'm considering his offer.

La'Tasha studies me. "What brought you to Moonridge, Everett?"

"The festival," I answer, keeping my tone even. She's the smart one. The more powerful one. If anyone might catch on to who—what—I am, it would be her. "I always loved it when I was a kid. Decided to visit again this year. Then I met this guy . . ."

Calvin ducks his head. "I thought I'd imagined him at first, when we collided during the race." Like running into me was the best accident of his life instead of the worst thing that could've happened to him.

This is torture. Standing here, pretending to be normal, watching Calvin look at me like I'm someone good. Someone worth introducing to his family.

Blake studies me, shoulders squared, jaw tight. He's already deciding whether I'm good enough for his big brother. Fair enough. If I had a brother, I'd probably do the same. Except Blake doesn't know he should be protecting Calvin from me. From who I'm bound to. From what we're about to do.

Penny hasn't said anything yet. Just stands there, unnaturally still, fingers working at the sleeve of her jacket. But her eyes keep darting between Calvin's face and mine, and there's something in her expression that makes me desperate to leave now.

She knows.

"He can't stay."

The words slice through the conversation like a blade through butter. Penny closes the distance between us, and the nervous, timid girl is gone.

Calvin's smile falters. "What are you talking about?"

And just like that, the fantasy is broken.

"The Crucible Core. In the library." Penny's voice trembles, but she keeps going, keeps destroying everything. "When I touched it, I saw every soul involved in the Concord's ritual." She advances, and I back up instinctively. "Including him. He's not just one of the ghosts fueling the ritual, though. He's a member. He's tied to the Skipper Lake binding point."

The world tilts sideways. Calvin stares at me, eyes wide in confusion and then hurt, and all I want is to sink through the ground and disappear.

Before I can apologize, Penny lunges forward and grabs my wrist.

"Penny!" Calvin starts forward, but Blake holds him back.

"Look." Penny yanks my sleeve up, exposing the Concord's sigil on my wrist, branded into what's left of my soul.

I jerk my arm back, panic flooding through me. "I'm not . . . I didn't . . ."

But I am. And I did. And there's no way to explain that would make this okay.

My human form begins to fade. I reach for Calvin, and he steps away, hurt blooming across his face.

"I need you to listen to me." The Concord's grip tightens around my throat, but I try anyway, reaching for Calvin's arm. My hand passes straight through.

My solidity wavers. The carefully maintained illusion flickers at the edges, and suddenly I'm transforming back into a ghost. Back into the nothing that I truly am.

"I swear, I've been fighting their control." The words tumble out. "I'm different. I'm bound to them, and I don't want to be. I need help . . ."

"I don't understand." The betrayal on Calvin's face almost cracks me open.

"It means he's been using you to get closer to Mina." Blake steps in front of his brother, protective and furious.

"No!" Transparency spreads up my arms. I fight against the fist closing around my throat. I have to get this out. "It's not like that. I didn't want this. I was trapped—am trapped. I'm not willingly one of them. I can help you."

I'm begging now, something I swore I'd never do again after Vince. But this is different.

"Please. You have to believe me."

But Calvin refuses to look at me.

It's over.

The tug starts then. That familiar pull around my middle, the rope yanking me back toward Whispering Falls. The Concord calling me home like the dog I am.

The ground begins to shudder. The crowd reacts, and I turn to Penny, the only one who might understand. The only one who saw the Crucible Core.

"The basement," I force out as my edges dissolve. "The Core. Release it." The words rush out as the pull gets stronger. "Release it, and you stop everything."

It's the only thing I can think of that could sabotage the ritual. And maybe—just maybe—if they release all those trapped souls, I'll be free too.

Then the ground trembles again and the rope yanks hard, and I'm gone.

Ripped away from the festival lights and Calvin's heartbroken face.

Back to the dark.

Back to the Concord.

Read the rest of Calvin & Everett's story now. **Right Place Wrong Time** *is available on Kindle as well as in hardcover and paperback.*